FIGHT FOR FREEDOM

Center Point
Large Print

Also by James J. Griffin and available from
Center Point Large Print:

Death Stalks the Rangers
Death Rides the Rails
Ranger's Revenge
Texas Jeopardy
Blood Ties
Renegade Ranger

**This Large Print Book carries the
Seal of Approval of N.A.V.H.**

FIGHT FOR FREEDOM

A Texas Ranger Jim Blawcyzk Story

JAMES J. GRIFFIN

CENTER POINT LARGE PRINT
THORNDIKE, MAINE

This Center Point Large Print edition
is published in the year 2019 by arrangement with
the author.

The text of this Large Print edition is unabridged.
In other aspects, this book may vary
from the original edition.
Printed in the United States of America
on permanent paper.
Set in 16-point Times New Roman type.

ISBN: 978-1-64358-336-5

The Library of Congress has cataloged this record
under Library of Congress Control Number: 2019943656

Dedicated to all the settlers,
no matter what their race, color,
or creed, who headed West during
the 1800s, into an untamed territory
and uncertain future.

As always, thanks to Texas Ranger Sergeant
Jim Huggins (Retired)
and Karl Rehn and Penny Riggs
of KR Training of Manheim, Texas
for their invaluable assistance.

FOREWORD

Reader Advisory

The words Negro, colored, and in particular nigger are used throughout this book. These words are not intended to be offensive, although they rightfully are by today's standards, but to reflect the standard usage at the time and place when and where the story is set, Texas in the late 1800s. In that period, these words were in common use when referring to people of color, especially in the South, and were usually not meant in the pejorative sense, as they are today. I have chosen not to use today's terms of African-American, or black, in order to maintain the historical integrity of the text and dialogue. During the writing of this book, I consulted with several African-American friends, who all confirmed the language should appear exactly as written.

James J. Griffin, January, 2012

CHAPTER ONE

"Julia, I'm dyin'," Jim Blawcyzk moaned.

"Jim, you're not going to die, at least not yet," his wife responded. "Take my word for it."

"You're not foolin' me one bit," Jim retorted, his voice shaking when yet another chill shot through him.

The big, blonde Texas Ranger lieutenant lay covered by sheets damp with sweat, shivering with cold despite the fever wracking his body. His deep blue eyes were glassy, his cheeks flushed.

"I am dyin', bet a hat on it," he insisted. "Just hope I can hang on long enough to see Charlie again."

Their Texas Ranger son was somewhere along the Rio Grande, on assignment with Company D.

"I give up," Julia said, as she placed a cold cloth on Jim's forehead. "If you don't want to listen to me, there's no point in arguing. Doctor Ginsburg will be here soon. Maybe he'll be able to convince you. In the meantime I've got work to do. If you need me before the doctor arrives, just call me."

"You're gonna leave me here to die all alone?" Jim whined.

"Unless you'd rather I dragged you out to the barn so you can die with Sam and Sizzle by your side, yes," Julia answered, a mischievous sparkle in her eyes. "Now go back to sleep."

Once Julia left, Jim fell into a fitful sleep, dozing until she awakened him an hour later.

"Jim, Doctor Ginsburg is here."

At Julia's side was San Leanna's physician, Doctor Philip Ginsburg. The doctor was in his early forties, with a slender build, dark, wavy hair and bright, deep brown eyes. With his good looks, ready smile, and sense of humor, he was considered the town's most eligible bachelor.

"Jim, Julia tells me you're feeling rather poorly," he said, taking the Ranger's wrist to check his pulse.

"More'n that, Doc," Jim objected. "I'm dyin'."

"Since when are you a physician?" Ginsburg retorted. "Tell you what . . . you stick to Rangerin', and let me do the doctoring. Do we have a deal?"

"I reckon," Jim muttered, clearly not convinced.

"Fine. Now let me check you over more thoroughly."

Ginsburg pulled back the sheets and placed his stethoscope to Jim's chest. After listening to his heart and lungs, he checked the Ranger's temperature. Ginsburg tsked softly after completing his examination.

"What is it, Doc?" Jim demanded. "I am dyin', ain't I?"

"Jim, what'd I just warn you?" Ginsburg answered. "You're unbelievable, do you realize that? You're a man who's taken a beating in how many fistfights is anybody's guess. You've been stabbed, shot by Indian arrows, and had enough bullets taken out of you to sink a small ship. You've even survived being gut-shot, which would normally kill any man. None of that's even fazed you, but now that you're a little bit sick you're convinced you're dying. Trust me, you aren't."

"Doctor, perhaps you should tell me what's wrong with Jim," Julia broke in. "I'm a bit more rational than he is right now. I'm certain it's the fever which has him thinking less than clearly."

"I'm not so sure about that," Ginsburg answered, grinning. "Although you are correct in saying Jim has a very high fever. You said he's also been vomiting, and has diarrhea?"

"That's right. He can't keep anything down. He's also been complaining of aching all over."

"That confirms my suspicions. Jim, you have a bad case of influenza. There's not much to be done for it except ride it out. You just need plenty of rest, and will need to drink as many liquids as possible. Water, or weak tea for the next day or two. After that bland foods, broth and plain bread or toast. Nothing heavier."

11

"Doc, I don't want anything to eat," Jim replied. "Just makes me sicker."

"Not even candy, or apple pie?" Ginsburg questioned.

"Doc, please," Jim groaned.

"Jim Blawcyzk doesn't want to eat, particularly sweets," Ginsburg chuckled. "Never thought I'd see the day. Perhaps my diagnosis is wrong after all. If you're not hungry, Jim, I'd hazard a guess you really are dying."

"You're just joking, aren't you, Doctor?" Julia asked.

"Of course," Ginsburg answered. "I'm merely joshing him. Jim, you only need to follow my instructions. Rest for a few days, take in as many fluids as you can, and eat when your stomach's a bit more settled. In three or four days you should start to feel better. You'll still feel weak and washed out for several days after that, but in ten days or so you'll be good as new."

"See, Jim, I told you you'd be fine," Julia stated. "Are you finally convinced?"

"Not until I'm outta this bed," Jim answered. "Thanks for coming by, Doc, even though you can't do much for me. Reckon I'll just lie here until the angels come for me."

"Believe me, Jim, it'll be a long time before the angels come for you," Ginsburg laughed. "You're too ornery to die, and Heaven sure isn't ready for you. Now, I have to go check on old

Widow Pennypacker. I'll come back to follow up with you in three days. Until then, you just stay in bed."

"I'll see you out, Doctor," Julia offered.

"Thank you."

Once they had reached the front porch, Julia questioned the physician a bit more.

"Doctor, I know you told Jim not to be concerned; however, people do die from influenza. Are you positive Jim will recover?"

"Yes, I am," Ginsburg reassured her. "While it is true that influenza claims lives, it's usually only those who are elderly or infirm, persons who have other health problems, or the very young. Jim is strong and healthy. I have every confidence he'll get through this illness just fine. When I return he'll be feeling much better, you'll see."

"I only wish I could convince him of that," Julia answered.

"Your husband's not the first big, tough man to turn into a baby when he has an illness, and he won't be the last," Ginsburg chuckled, as he climbed into his buggy. "Good-bye, Julia."

"Good-bye, Doctor."

CHAPTER TWO

Four days later, Jim was napping. Although he was feeling somewhat better, as Doctor Ginsburg had promised, and Ginsburg had pronounced him on the way to recovery on his return visit, the big Ranger still wasn't convinced he would survive his bout with influenza.

Julia awakened him with a soft knock on the doorframe.

"Jim, are you awake?" she gently called. "You have company. Captain Storm is here."

"Sure," Jim mumbled. "Tell them to come in."

"Not them, him," Captain Earl Storm laughed. "There's just one of me, unless you're seeing double, Lieutenant. Since you don't drink, that's pretty unlikely."

The captain settled in a chair alongside Jim's bed, while Jim sat up, propped against his pillows.

"Cap'n, good to see you," Jim said. "What brings you by?"

"Heard you weren't feeling well."

"That's not the only reason you came down here from Austin," Jim objected.

"You're right," Storm readily admitted.

"I can see you're about to start a long conversation," Julia interrupted. "Would you like some coffee, Captain?"

"That would be fine, Julia," Storm answered.

"I'll take some too," Jim added.

"Are you certain, Jim?"

"Positive."

"Then I'll make a fresh pot," Julia smiled. Perhaps this visit from his commanding officer was just what Jim needed.

Storm took out his tobacco and papers, rolled a cigarette, and lit it, studying Jim's appearance while he did so. Jim was stripped to the waist, his flesh extremely pale, his face thin and upper torso gaunt. Sweat still beaded his forehead and plastered his thick blonde hair to his scalp. Storm took a long drag on the smoke before he continued.

"Jim, I was about to ask you to take on a special assignment, but how soon do you think you can be back in the saddle?"

"If you need me ready to ride, I can have Sizzle saddled up and ready to go in an hour."

"I need an honest answer, Lieutenant."

"Then I reckon in about a week. That soon enough?"

"That's plenty soon enough," Storm agreed. "I won't need you for two weeks, so that will be more than enough time for you to get back to one hundred percent."

"I should be more'n ready by then, Cap'n. Bet

16

a hat on it. So tell me, what's this special assignment?"

Storm's dark eyes fixed Jim with a steady gaze. He pulled off his Stetson, ran his hand through his dark hair, shoved the hat back in place and rubbed his jaw before responding.

"Jim, how do you feel about colored folk?"

"Colored folk, Cap'n?"

"Yes, colored folk. Negroes."

"Never gave it much thought one way or the other," Jim answered. "I've dealt with 'em before, just like I've dealt with Mexicans and Indians. Far as I'm concerned, they're pretty much like everybody else, most good and some bad. Lot of 'em moved out here after the War and found work as cowboys. Most of those are top hands. Don't forget, we've also had help plenty of times from the U.S. Cavalry out in west Texas, and their buffalo soldiers are some of the bravest, hardest fightin' men I've ever ridden with. I'd ride the river with any one of those colored troopers. Why do you ask?"

"Because I needed to be positive about your feelin's toward them," Storm explained. "There's a bunch of Negroes gonna be arriving by wagon train from Shreveport sometime in the next few weeks. I'll have an exact date later. They're heading to build a settlement northwest of San Angelo. The Rangers have been requested to provide an escort for them until they reach

17

their destination. I'm askin' you to take on that chore."

"Be more than glad to," Jim answered. "However, what's so special about this group? Plenty of Negroes have emigrated to Texas already, and we've never given those special protection."

"Times are changing, and not for the better," Storm explained. "Last couple of colored trains have been attacked by folks who don't want 'em settlin' in Texas. Now, I don't hold much truck with Negroes myself, but I figure they still have the right to try'n make a life for themselves, just like white folks. I don't need to remind you that even though it's been some time since the War was over, feelin's are still raw, and emotions can run high. It's not all that long since Reconstruction ended, and there are still a lot of Yankee carpetbaggers and scalawags who would love to have any excuse to bring Texas under the federal government's control again. You know what that did to us."

"I sure do," Jim nodded. "Last thing we'd need."

Julia stepped into the room.

"Here's your coffee, Captain. Yours too, Jim."

She handed each man a mug.

"Thank you, Julia," Storm said.

"You're welcome. I've got bread to get out of the oven, but if you need more coffee, just call me."

"I'll do that," Storm promised. He took a swallow of his coffee, then continued.

"Jim, another reason we're being asked to provide an escort for this bunch is because the governor received a request directly from Washington. Evidently the *hombre* leadin' the group, a man by the name of Adrian Chatman, worked for the government, and has some influence up there. So you see why it's important these folks reach where they're goin' safely."

"I sure do. Besides, like you mentioned, they have the same rights as every other American."

"Jim, I guess you're the man for this assignment, as I figured. So, you'll accept these orders? You'll be gone more'n a month, plus you'll probably have to spend some time protectin' those folks while they get settled, to make sure no one's gonna bother 'em."

"Just let me know when you'll need me in Louisiana, Cap'n."

"*Bueno*. There's just one more thing. You'll need to take several other men with you. You pick them."

"Several other Rangers just to guard one wagon train?" Jim questioned.

"Like I said, Lieutenant, this is an assignment of extreme importance, to both the governor and the Rangers. I'm not taking any chances. Give me six or seven names."

"All right, Cap'n. Smoky McCue, of course. My boy Charlie, and Ty Tremblay."

"You've got them. Who else?"

"Jim and Dan Huggins. I'll need a second in command. That'll be Jim."

"Fine. One or two more."

"Steve Masters."

"Done."

"And, if you can talk him out of retirement, ol' Bill Dundee."

"Bill Dundee? The cook for your former company? Why him?"

"Two reasons. First, of course, Bill's a Negro. I figure he can help smooth over any problems which might arise, rather'n us Rangers actin' like the overseer givin' orders on some plantation. Second, there probably won't be many of those folks who know how to hunt, or shoot straight. They're gonna need meat. Since Bill's still a crack shot, he'll be able to supply game."

"And also be another gun in case of trouble," Storm noted.

"That's right," Jim confirmed.

"I'll see if I can get him for you," Storm promised.

"Appreciate it, Cap'n."

"Jim, I reckon you'd better get some more rest," Storm said. "You're lookin' mighty peaked."

"I'm feelin' better already, knowin' I've got a job to do," Jim said, smiling.

20

"All the more reason you need that rest," Storm answered. "Plus I've got to get busy sending telegrams all over the state to round up the men you want. I'll stop back in a few days to tell you when to ride for Louisiana. *Adios*, Jim."

"Okay, Cap'n. See you then."

CHAPTER THREE

Ten days later Jim, despite his convictions to the contrary, had just about completely recovered from his illness. Tiring more easily than usual was the only lingering effect, and that was improving every day. Captain Storm had ordered him to report to Headquarters two days hence, so Jim was looking forward to once again being in the saddle. He was in the barn grooming his horses, Sam and Sizzle, when Julia called him.

"Jim, I just finished icing the cake, and I know you want to scrape the bowl and lick the spoon."

"I'll be right there, honey," Jim answered. He gave Sizzle a final swipe of the brush.

"Sorry, pard, but I don't get all that many chances to eat leftover icing," he apologized to the horse. "Charlie used to always beat me to it. I'll be back to turn you out in a bit. Same goes for you, pal," he added, when Sam issued an indignant nicker. "You'll get your peppermints after supper. Now get outside."

After Jim chased the paints into the corral, he put the brush back on its shelf, used his bandanna to wipe sweat from his face, then headed to the house, where a freshly-baked cake was sitting

23

on the sideboard. Julia intercepted him halfway across the kitchen.

"Don't you dare try and sneak a piece of my cake, Jim," she warned. "After you've finished your supper you can have all you want. It'll be ready in about an hour. The icing bowl's on the table. That should hold you until then."

"Not even a little piece, darling?" Jim pleaded.

"Not one crumb," Julia insisted. "You'll spoil your supper if you eat too much cake now. You want to have room for the chicken and dumplings, don't you?"

"You gonna starve me plumb to death. Bet a hat on it," Jim answered.

"I highly doubt that," Julia grinned. "Not with your appetite. Just finish that bowl so I can wash it."

"All right." Jim sighed. He began scraping the bowl.

"Is that icing too sweet?" Julia questioned.

"You're asking me if something's too sweet?" Jim chuckled.

"You're right, I forgot myself for a moment," Julia laughed in reply. "It's useless trying to convince you anything is too sweet. You have the world's biggest sweet tooth, well, perhaps except for Sam."

"Sizzle's no slouch in that department either. For that matter, neither is Charlie," Jim replied.

"I'd hoped Charlie would be home by now,"

Julia responded. "I wanted to spend some time visiting with him before you and he have to ride out. I hope he hasn't run into any trouble."

"Charlie can take care of himself," Jim answered. "He might've just been slowed up by bad weather, or mebbe he was further out in west Texas than Cap'n Storm thought. Don't worry, I'll make sure you have at least one full day with him. Those folks in the wagon train can just wait a day, if need be."

Jim scooped out another spoonful of icing.

"Seems like you made a bit too much," he observed.

"I planned it that way, just for you," Julia replied.

Jim stopped with the spoon halfway to his mouth.

"Someone's comin'. Bet a hat that's Charlie now," he said.

"I don't hear anything," Julia protested.

"Hoofbeats, two horses," Jim answered, putting the bowl back on the table. "Charlie's probably got Ty with him. We'll know shortly."

As Jim predicted, a moment later the front door swung open and Charlie burst in.

"Mom, Dad, I'm home!" he shouted, crossing the room in three strides. He grabbed his mother in a bear hug, lifted her off her feet, and swung her around.

"Charlie, I can't breathe!" Julia gasped.

"Sorry, Mom," Charlie said, releasing her and kissing her on the cheek.

"Howdy, son. Thought you'd be home a day or two earlier," Jim noted.

"Hit some bad storms which slowed us up some," Charlie explained. "Hey, icing!" he exclaimed, when he spotted the bowl.

"That icing's mine. Touch it and I'll gut-shoot you where you stand, Charlie," Jim warned, with a grin.

"You're not even wearin' your gun," Charlie retorted. "You wouldn't stand a chance of pluggin' me."

He gave Jim a playful backhanded slap to the stomach.

"I can get my gun and put two slugs through your middle before you even clear leather," Jim shot back, with a punch of his own to Charlie's belly. Charlie winced at the impact.

"Ow, easy Dad," Charlie yelped.

"Sorry. I didn't think I hit you that hard," Jim apologized.

"It's all right," Charlie answered. "Hey, c'mon outside. I've got somethin' to show you two."

"All right," Jim answered. He and Julia followed their son onto the front porch. Tied to the railing, alongside Charlie's aging paint gelding, Ted, was another horse, a blocky overo paint. Splotches of white stood out starkly against the horse's black coat. The markings on each hip were nearly identical. He had a bald face and a blue left eye.

"What d'ya think, Dad?" Charlie asked.

Jim stepped from the porch and circled the gelding, studying him carefully, while Julia did the same. The horse stood over fifteen hands high and was thickly muscled. He nuzzled Jim's shoulder when Jim stroked his neck.

"He's a nice lookin' horse, Charlie," Jim observed. The horse jerked back when Jim attempted to scratch his ears.

"Sorry, Dad, I forgot to warn you he's a bit fussy about his ears," Charlie apologized. "Some dang fool twitched 'em, and he still doesn't trust anyone handlin' his ears. I've been workin' on that, and he's a lot better'n he was."

"He certainly is a fine animal. Young, too. No more than four years old," Julia said, as she rubbed the horse's nose. She was the manager of their small horse ranch, the JB Bar, and was every bit as much the judge of horseflesh as her husband and son. "Where'd you get him?"

"I bought him off a Mexican feller down in Del Rio," Charlie answered. "The price was right, and since I know Ted's getting too old to be a Ranger's horse, I bought him. I was a bit hesitant because of that glass eye, but after tryin' him out I knew he was a good horse. His name's Splash. I figure I'll use Ted as a pack horse like Dad does with ol' Sam."

"I believe you did well," Julia praised. "I like him a lot."

"Same here, Charlie," Jim agreed. "Far as his blue eye, I've known a lot of horses who had blue eyes, and it don't seem to matter none. A good horse is a good horse, whether he's got brown eyes, blue, or one of each, like Splash there."

"Thanks. I was hopin' you'd both like him," Charlie said.

"Jim, why don't you help Charlie care for his horses?" Julia suggested. "By the time you do that and wash up, supper will be ready."

She glanced at Charlie, a twinkle in her brown eyes.

"You're just like your father, gone for weeks on end, then showing up just in time for supper," she laughed.

"He learned from the best," Jim chuckled.

"That's your opinion," Julia retorted. "Now go settle those horses."

While Julia headed back inside, Jim and Charlie led Ted and Splash to the corral, where Sam and Sizzle were nickering noisily to the new arrivals.

"Might as well turn Splash loose and let 'em get acquainted before we rub them down and feed them," Jim said.

The gear was stripped from Ted, the halter removed from Splash, and both turned out. Sam and Sizzle trotted up to them. With much sniffing of noses, snorting, nickering, and pawing of hooves, they made their acquaintance with the new arrival. Once they were settled, hay was tossed to them, and Jim groomed Ted while Charlie worked on Splash.

"We'll grain yours after supper, same time I feed Sam and Siz, Charlie," Jim said.

"That's fine, Dad," Charlie agreed. "The hay will hold them until then."

Once Charlie's horses were thoroughly rubbed down, father and son headed for the pump and washbench behind the house, where Julia had set out soap, washcloths, and towels. They removed their hats and bandannas, then stripped off their shirts. Once Charlie unbuttoned his shirt, a large bruise which covered most of his belly was revealed, along with a fading bullet scar along his lower left ribs.

"I knew I didn't hit you that hard, Charlie," Jim said. "Where'd you get those?"

"A bunch of smugglers jumped us," Charlie explained. "Had quite a gun battle with 'em. Luckily none of us were badly hurt. I took a bullet along my side, and the bruise is from where I fell on some rocks after I got hit."

"What about the *hombre* who shot you?"

"He's now got an extra bellybutton . . . one that goes clean through to his spine," Charlie answered, with a grim chuckle. "He won't be doin' any more smugglin', or shootin' anyone else."

"That why you're back later'n planned, healin' up?"

"No. Like I said, we hit some bad weather. I stuck with Ty until he got home, then stopped by Jarratt's store to see Mary Jane."

"I should have known," Jim laughed. "You and she decided yet?"

"Just about," Charlie answered. "She's promised me an answer once I get back from this next assignment. Since we'll be gone for quite a spell, Mary Jane says if she can stand bein' alone that long, then she'll know she can stand bein' a Ranger's wife."

"She'll say yes, Charlie. Bet a hat on it," Jim assured him. "Mary Jane's a fine girl, and she loves you as much as you love her. That'll overcome any obstacles in your way."

"I hope you're right, Dad," Charlie answered, shaking his head. "Oh, and please don't tell Mom I got shot."

"I won't," Jim promised. "But she'll figure it out right quick, if she hasn't already. You can't fool a woman about something like that. You'll learn that soon enough once you and Mary Jane are married. Now let's finish cleanin' up. Your Mom'll have our hides if we let supper get cold."

Jim and Charlie went into town early the next morning. Charlie made a last visit with Mary Jane Jarratt while Jim picked up needed supplies at her family's store, including a pack saddle for Ted. Once that was done, they headed home to finish last minute chores. After supper, they cleaned their weapons, then, facing an early start the next morning, headed for bed just after sundown.

Julia and Jim were lying side by side, Julia's head resting on Jim's shoulder while he stroked her long, dark hair. Jim ran a hand lightly over her breasts, then pulled her to him and kissed her.

"Jim, we can't," Julia protested. "Charlie might hear us."

"Charlie's sound asleep," Jim answered. "Besides, this is our last night together for a month or more. The entire population of San Leanna could be in this house and it wouldn't stop me from making love to my wife tonight."

"But Jim . . ."

"Shh. Not another word."

With that, Jim crushed Julia's body to his.

CHAPTER FOUR

Captain Storm was the only occupant of his office when Jim and Charlie, along with Smoky McCue and Ty Tremblay, arrived shortly after sunrise the next morning.

"Mornin', Cap'n. We early?" Jim greeted his commanding officer.

"Yep, as usual, Lieutenant. I figured you and this bunch of fugitives from the Devil's hopyard would be the first ones here. The others should be along shortly. Grab yourselves some coffee in the meantime."

"All right." Jim and the others poured mugs of strong black coffee from the pot Storm always kept simmering on the stove, then settled into the chairs along the wall opposite Storm's desk. Smoky rolled and lit a quirly, as did the captain. They had no sooner touched matches to their smokes when the next arrival appeared, a man none of them recognized. He was young, no more than nineteen or twenty, tall and lanky, with red hair and green eyes. A smattering of freckles dusted his nose and cheeks. The holster on his right hip held a heavy .44 Smith and Wesson revolver.

"Mornin', Captain," he greeted Storm. "Thought I'd be the first one here."

"You didn't have a chance of that, Johnny," Storm chuckled. "There'll be a blizzard in July before anyone gets up earlier'n Jim Blawcyzk. Men, this is Johnny Dexter," he continued. "Johnny, Lieutenant Jim Blawcyzk, his son Charlie, better known as Chip, Sergeant Smoky McCue, and Ty Tremblay."

"Pleased to meet y'all," Dexter drawled. A slight smile played across his lips.

"Johnny's been with the Rangers for little more than a year now," Storm explained. "Most recently he's been with Company C, but a busted ankle laid him up for a spell. He's ready to ride again, and I figured he might come in handy on this assignment."

"Always glad to have an extra man," Jim answered, rising from his seat and shaking Dexter's hand.

"Thanks, Lieutenant," Dexter answered.

"Johnny, get yourself a cup of coffee while we wait for the rest of the men," Storm said.

"Sure enough, Captain."

Dexter filled a mug with the brew, rolled and lit a quirly, then took the chair next to Smoky.

Within twenty minutes, Lieutenant Jim Huggins and his son Dan arrived, followed shortly thereafter by Bill Dundee and finally Steve Masters. Storm waited until everyone was

34

settled with their coffee and cigarettes before beginning.

"Men, first of all I'd like to thank every one of you for taking on this task," he started. "I know it's a bit unusual, asking Rangers to escort a wagon train full of coloreds more'n halfway across Texas."

"Boy howdy, I'd say more than a bit unusual," Steve Masters interrupted. "I'd say danged unusual."

"I reckon you're right, Steve," Storm conceded. "And it's a chore I wouldn't request most of my Rangers to take on. Lieutenant Blawcyzk and I particularly chose all of you as the right men for the job. If any of you feel you can't handle it then speak up right now, and you'll be relieved of this assignment, no questions asked and no hard feelin's."

He paused, waiting for a response, until Dan Huggins finally spoke up.

"Cap'n, if you and the lieutenant picked us special for this job, then I reckon we won't let you down."

"*Bueno*," Storm replied. "I'm not gonna go over all the circumstances why the Rangers have been asked to escort this train. I've already done that with Jim, so he can fill you in on the way to Shreveport. What I am going to emphasize is that you are to protect these folks no matter what, at any price and at all costs."

"In other words, do what the Rangers have always done," Smoky McCue chuckled.

"Pretty much, yes," Storm agreed. "As you're all aware, the last couple of Negro wagon trains tryin' to cross Texas have been attacked. Some folks have been killed, others scared back across the state line. That's not to happen this time. There's already been talk of the federal government comin' back in and runnin' the state again. The man leadin' this bunch has a lot of influence in Washington, and I don't want any attacks on his people to be used as an excuse for the Yankees to reimpose Reconstruction on us. Have I made myself clear?"

"Perfectly, Cap'n," Ty Tremblay answered.

"Fine." Storm opened the top drawer of his desk and removed a thick file. He placed this alongside the boxes of ammunition stacked on the desk.

"You'll be on the trail with those wagons at least three weeks, more likely a month or so. Then you'll be stayin' with those folks until they get settled. Since I figure you'll probably be gone two months or more, I've arranged to have you advanced that much pay."

The captain opened the file and passed several bills to each man. Bill Dundee stopped Storm when he started to hand the former Company D cook his money, a ten dollar bill.

"Hold on there, Cap'n," Dundee said. "I told

you I'd consider takin' on this job, once you explained what it entailed. I didn't promise anythin'."

"You mean you don't want to help the Rangers on this?" Storm questioned, taken slightly aback.

"I didn't say that," Dundee answered. "But this ol' nigger boy's tired of workin' for next to nothin'. I'll take the job, but I want fifty dollars a month, not a dime less."

"Fifty dollars!" Storm exclaimed. "That's twenty dollars more'n a private makes. It's impossible."

"Fifty a month and found, not one penny less," Dundee insisted.

"Bill, I just can't . . ."

"Pay him the fifty, Cap'n," Jim broke in.

"What's that, Lieutenant?"

"You heard me, Captain. Give Bill the fifty a month."

"For a cook?"

"Bill's lots more'n a cook," Jim answered. "He's a cook, scout, hunter, tracker, and a dang good shot, which we'll likely need before this trip is done. He'll also make a fine liaison between us Rangers and the folks we're escortin'. Plus, Bill's got years of experience on the frontier and riding with Company D, and he's a fair hand at doctorin'. He's worth that fifty and then some. Pay him."

"The rest of you feel that way?" Storm questioned.

The other men glanced at Jim, then nodded agreement.

"All right. Bill, you've got that fifty. It'll be ready before you leave."

Storm pulled some more papers out of the file.

"These are your railroad passes. You're booked on the afternoon train from here to Dallas, then you'll connect with the overnight eastbound to Shreveport. You'll meet Adrian Chatman and his party there. Hold on, Lieutenant," he added, when Jim started to protest. "I know you don't particularly like ridin' the train, but it's a lot faster'n travelin' horseback cross-country. Times are changin', and you have to keep up with 'em."

Jim's aversion to nearly all machinery was well-known.

"If it's all the same to you, Cap'n, I'll stick with my horse and saddle as long as possible," he answered. "Besides, Sam's never been happy about bein' on a train ever since that wreck we were in."

"You know it's always about what Jim's horse likes, Cap'n," Jim Huggins chuckled.

"Be that as it may, you'll be taking the train," Storm replied.

"Seems as if it would've been a lot easier for those niggers to use the railroad far as it goes, then finish the journey by wagon, rather than goin' all that way across half the country," Steve Masters observed.

"Mebbe at first glance, but it really wouldn't be," Storm answered. "The train'd be awful expensive for that many folks, and I would imagine most of 'em don't have much money. Don't forget, they'd also have to pay to freight their goods. I'm sure they're like most emigrants, and are bringin' way too much stuff, a lot of it geegaws and junk the womenfolk'll insist they just can't live without, and most of which'll end up tossed out alongside the trail."

"The railroads generally won't let Negroes ride in the passenger cars with white folks anyway," Charlie observed.

"That's a fact, Chip," Storm agreed, then sighed. "Slavery was dead wrong. I've always said that, even though it made me a lot of enemies. But, on the other hand, I dunno if Negroes and whites are meant to live together. Mebbe this Chatman feller has the right idea, settin' up a community for his own kind. There's plenty of room for more folks in Texas, that's for certain."

"Only problem with that theory is that a lot of Anglos don't want Mexicans in Texas, even though the Spanish were here long before us," Jim answered. "Same with the Indians. They were here first, but they've pretty much been driven out of the state. My family and I've faced lots of problems just because we're Polish. Remember how the cowboys from Helena bothered the Polish settlers in Panna Maria, even though

Panna Maria was founded years before Helena? Same thing happened to the Czechs and even some of the Germans. Plenty of whites think they're better'n everyone else, and don't want any other races or nationalities to have anything. Some day that's gonna cause big trouble, bet a hat on it."

"It's already startin' trouble, Lieutenant, which is why you'll be escortin' this wagon train. I just hope there's not more'n you men can handle."

"There won't be, count on that," Jim assured him.

"Good." Storm picked up three sheets of paper and handed them to Jim.

"This is the letter from Adrian Chatman requesting Ranger assistance, and the governor's reply granting his request. The third one is to introduce you and your men to Chatman."

Jim glanced over the papers, folded them, and slid them into his vest pocket.

"They seem in order, Cap'n."

"All right. This ammunition on my desk is for you men, so take as much as you need. Stockin' up on cartridges now will save you from havin' to resupply on the trail later, then askin' the state for reimbursement. Yes, Bill, there's five boxes of .50 caliber shells for your old Sharps."

"Thank you kindly, Cap'n," Dundee said.

"There, I'm finished," Storm concluded. "Are there any questions?"

"Just one more thing, Cap'n."

Jim dug in his shirt pocket and removed a badge, one very similar to the silver star on silver circle many of the Rangers wore. However, the inscription was a bit different.

"Bill, I made this for you. I was holding it until I was certain you'd be comin' with us," he said, passing the badge to Dundee. The old cook squinted while he read the words carved into the Mexican five peso coin.

"Texas Ranger Special Scout," he murmured. "Thanks, Lieutenant."

"You deserve it, Bill," Jim answered. "Besides, I have a feelin' you'll earn it before we're done with this job."

"Bill, I'd suggest you keep that in your pocket until you need it, just like the rest of the men do," Storm cautioned.

"I reckon you're right, Cap'n," Bill answered. He slid the badge into his vest pocket.

Storm glanced at the Regulator clock on the wall.

"You've got a couple of hours to kill before you have to catch your train. That's enough time to head over to the Silver Star for a couple of drinks," he noted. "I'm buyin'."

"If you're buyin', then we're drinkin'," Smoky laughed. "Let's get outta here."

CHAPTER FIVE

"Looks like they're finally pullin' the train up to the loadin' platform," Smoky remarked, watching it roll slowly up to the depot. " 'Bout time."

He took a final puff on his quirly, then tossed the butt to the tracks.

"Seems so," Jim agreed. "Here comes the conductor now."

"I'm sorry, gents," the trainman apologized as he hurried up to the waiting Rangers and their horses. "One of the passenger coaches developed a hot box en route from Fort Worth, so we had to uncouple it. We've been trying to locate another car, but there are none in the yards at the moment. Unfortunately, that means there is only the one car for all the passengers from here to Shreveport. However, there is some good news. Most of the passengers disembarked here in Dallas, so there will be plenty of room for everyone continuing east."

"How soon can we load our horses?" Jim asked.

"We've already put their hay in the car, so once the train stops completely you can board them. You realize we're running late, so it would be appreciated if you get them loaded as quickly as possible."

"We'll do that. *Muchas Gracias*," Jim answered.

Once the train clanked to a halt, a brakeman opened the cattle car door. Except for Sam, who needed much urging before jumping, with a snort of protest, into the car, the horses were loaded without incident, then stripped of saddles, bridles, and packs. After Jim's horses received their peppermints, the mounts fell to munching on hay. The door was secured, and once their gear was stowed away in the box car preceding the cattle car, the Rangers hurried to the train's sole coach. The conductor stopped Bill Dundee at the bottom of the steps.

"I'm sorry, but coloreds aren't allowed to travel in the passenger coaches. You'll have to find a place in one of the freight cars, or perhaps ride with the horses," he stated.

"What was that?" Bill said.

"Railroad rules don't allow Negroes to ride with white folks," the conductor reiterated.

"Bill, let me handle this," Jim ordered.

"There's nothing to handle, sir," the conductor answered.

"There sure isn't, bet a hat on it," Jim retorted. "We're Texas Rangers, all of us, including Bill. He rides with us."

"I'm sorry, Ranger . . ."

"Lieutenant Blawcyzk. That's BLUH-zhick," Jim answered.

"I'm sorry, Lieutenant. I just assumed this

44

man was hired as a hostler to help with your horses. I've never heard of a buffalo Ranger. Nonetheless, he still can't ride in the coach. No darkies can."

Jim's blue eyes glittered like chips of ice as he struggled to control his rising anger. He grabbed the conductor by his shirtfront and lifted him into the air, then hung him by his suspenders from the hook on the express car used to grab mailbags when a train rolled through a town without stopping.

"Mister, either Bill rides with us, or you'll ride like that all the way to Shreveport," he growled. "Which is it gonna be?"

"You men stay outta this," Smoky ordered, when several trainmen hustled up.

"But . . . I'll lose my job," the conductor sputtered.

"You let me worry about that," Jim answered. "I'll make sure you don't. You've got ten seconds to decide."

"All right, you win, Lieutenant," the conductor conceded. "Please let me down so we can get rolling."

"That's more like it," Jim said. "Guess you'll ride inside after all."

Once freed, the conductor shouted his "All Aboard!" while Jim and his men hurried into the coach. Moments later, with the banging of couplers and hissing of steam, the train rolled out of the station. It cleared the yards at nine-forty five, slightly more than an hour late.

Once the train chuffed away from the city, the Rangers quickly settled down. Johnny, Charlie, Dan, and Ty began playing a game of five card stud, while Steve, Smoky, and Jim Huggins engaged in quiet conversation. Jim Blawcyzk and Bill Dundee stretched out their legs and tilted their Stetsons over their faces. Bill soon dozed off, while Jim silently said his evening prayers. Once he was finished, Jim also attempted to sleep, but his restless mind would not allow it.

I know I've always said I'd never quit the Rangers, but maybe it's time I hung up my guns. Lord knows it ain't gettin' any easier traipsing all over the country on the back of a horse. Me, Jim Huggins, and Smoky've been Rangerin' a long time, and we're dang lucky none of us have been killed . . . yet. It's probably time to let the youngsters take over. Look at Charlie and his buddies. They're faster, stronger, and smarter than we've ever been. Bet a hat they'll use their brains a lot more'n their fists and guns to track down the bad guys. I miss Julia more and more every time I leave her, too. Yet here I am again, on a train headin' out to escort a wagon train full of coloreds across better'n half the state. Not that it bothers me they're not white folks. Heck, I've always said people should be able to live wherever they want, and Texas has more'n

46

enough room for settlers. It's bein' gone two months or more that's stickin' in my craw. It'd be real easy to toss my saddle on the fence, pull off my boots, and spend the rest of my nights sittin' in my rockin' chair on the front porch. Wouldn't have to eat my own cookin' any more, either.

Jim ruefully chuckled, then sighed.

You're not foolin' anyone, least of all yourself. You have the same fight with yourself every time you head out, but soon as you're home a few days, the itch to be on the trail takes over. You'll never quit the Rangers, and you know it. Now, get some shut-eye.

He pulled his Stetson lower over his face and slowly drifted off to sleep.

Some time later, Jim awakened when the train jolted to a stop. The lamps had been turned low, and almost everyone was asleep.

"What're we stoppin' for?" he asked the conductor, who had risen from his seat and was heading for the car's rear platform.

"Water stop. We won't be more than a few minutes," the trainman answered.

"Will I have enough time to check our horses?"

"You should. The whistle'll give you warning when we're ready to roll again."

"Jim, you don't need to check the horses," Steve sleepily muttered. "They're fine."

"Steve, you should know by now Jim's always

47

gonna check the horses every chance he gets," Smoky answered, yawning. "Nothing you or anyone else says will change his mind."

"Lieutenant, if it's all right, I'll join you," Johnny offered. "I reckon there's a wheel or two on this train needs waterin'."

"Sure, that's fine, long as you forget the lieutenant nonsense and call me Jim. Let's go."

They headed for the cattle car. Once they reached it, they paused alongside to relieve themselves, or, as Johnny called it, "water the wheels." That chore completed, they opened the car door and climbed inside.

"You like ridin' the train, Blue?" Johnny asked his blue roan quarter horse, with a pat to his nose. The horse whickered a soft response.

"How you boys doin'?" Jim asked his paints. Sizzle nuzzled his shoulder, while the usually fearless Sam whinnied nervously, then buried his muzzle in Jim's belly. The horse had never completely gotten over being trapped in that train wreck.

"I know, you don't like this," Jim sympathized. "But you'll have a lot of ground to cover over the next few weeks, so try'n take advantage of it. You'll be off this train by mornin'."

He slipped both horses a peppermint, then stopped when movement along the tracks caught his eye.

"Johnny," he hissed. "Quiet."

48

"What is it, Jim?" Johnny whispered in return.

"Take a look out there, near the coach. What d'ya see?"

"Appears to be some men boarding the train," the young Ranger answered. "Wait a minute . . ."

"That's right. Looks like they're up to no good. I'd bet my hat on it," Jim confirmed. The men he had spotted were furtively approaching the passenger coach. In the dim light it was hard to be certain, but their hats appeared to be pulled low, and bandannas covered their faces.

"How many are there?" Johnny asked.

"Seems to be four," Jim answered. "I'd also imagine there are at least a couple more up in the locomotive, holdin' guns on the crew."

"Well, if they're tryin' to rob this train, I'd say they just made the biggest mistake since buttermilk," Johnny answered. "How do you want to handle this?"

"We'll jump out the other side of this car," Jim explained. "You head for the engine, I'll take the coach. I'd guess they'll have a man standin' guard at each end while the other two rob the passengers. I'll surprise 'em and grab one of the guards. If the others try'n shoot, with luck I'll drill 'em before they can make a move. Same goes for you, don't take any chances. If you can get the drop on your men, fine, if not, shoot 'em and worry about what happens afterwards."

"What about Sergeant McCue and the other

men? You think they might try'n stop them?"

"I doubt it. They were still half-asleep, so most likely they were caught settin'. Plus, they're not gonna risk any of the other passengers gettin' hurt, especially since there's a few women and kids in there. It's gonna be up to us. You ready?"

"I sure am," Johnny replied, a big grin crossing his face. "What're we waitin' for? Let's go."

"Take off your spurs first," Jim ordered. "I don't want their jinglin' to give us away."

"All right."

Once Johnny's spurs were removed, the two men slid from the cattle car, pulled their guns from their holsters and edged their way alongside the train, sticking to the shadows cast by the cars in the dim moonlight. When they reached the coach Jim halted just before the rear door, while Johnny continued to the front of the train. Once the young Ranger had reached the tender, he waved his pistol, indicating he was ready. Jim nodded in return, then climbed into the coach, slamming open the door. As Jim had guessed, there was a lookout at each end of the car, while two others were relieving the passengers of their belongings. The conductor was huddled on the aisle floor.

Jim wrapped his arm around the nearest lookout's throat.

"Texas Rangers!" he shouted. "Drop those guns

50

and get your hands in the air! One false move and I'll plug you!"

The guard on the far end of the car started to thumb back the hammer of his pistol. Before he could pull the trigger, Jim shot him through the stomach. The man doubled up and collapsed to his face. Just as he hit the floor, gunfire erupted from the locomotive.

One of the other robbers whirled to face Jim, bringing up his gun. Jim put a bullet in his chest, slamming him backwards to fall atop his downed companion. The third outlaw dropped his gun and raised his hands high.

"Don't shoot, Ranger!" he pleaded.

"All right, just stand hitched," Jim ordered. He jabbed his gun barrel deeper into the last man's spine.

"What about you?"

"I'm givin' up, Ranger. Don't hanker for a bullet in my back."

The fight was over before the other Rangers could even leap from their seats. The rest of the passengers sat in stunned disbelief at the sudden turn of events. From the front of the train now came only silence.

"Smoky, I sent Johnny to the engine, figurin' these renegades would have men jump the crew. Take Ty and see what's happened up there. Rest of you help me with these *hombres*."

Charlie was now covering the first robber, while

Jim Huggins was already kneeling alongside the men Jim had shot.

"You won't need any help with these two. One's dead, and the other doesn't have long."

"I didn't want to kill 'em, but they didn't give me any choice. Had to stop them before they hurt any of the passengers," Jim answered. "My handcuffs are with our gear. Dan, would you mind getting them for me?"

"Not at all," Dan answered.

"Get mine also, Dan," his father requested. "We'll need two sets."

"Sure, Dad. I'll get a couple more, in case Johnny's got a prisoner or two."

"Bring some rope, too," Jim added. "I'll want to hog-tie these men."

"I'm gonna check on Smoky and Ty," Bill said. "Sure hope nothing's gone wrong up there."

"Go ahead, Bill," Jim answered.

Jim nudged his man with his pistol.

"You and your pardner get on the floor in that corner. Conductor, where's the next station?"

"Longview's the next stop," the trainman replied.

"Good. We'll leave these *hombres* and the bodies with the sheriff there."

"We're already running late," the conductor objected. "I can't hold this train for you."

"Can't help that," Jim answered. "Far as holdin'

this train, you don't have a choice. We won't be all that long."

The front door opened and two men, one clutching a bullet shattered shoulder, the other with his hands over his head, entered, with Johnny close behind, his gun trained on them. He glanced at the bodies.

"See you've got everything under control here, Lieutenant," he said.

"Seems like you have too," Jim answered. "Where's Smoky and the others?"

"Helpin' patch up the engineer. One of these ranahans pistol-whipped him. He'll be fine, and is waitin' on word whether to start this train rollin' again."

"Soon as we get these men tied up and the bodies moved to a box car, we can get movin'," Jim answered. "Steve, you mind lettin' the engineer know that? Tell him it'll be about twenty minutes. Stay with him until we get rollin' again. Send Bill and the others back. I'll need him to check the wounded man."

"Sure," Steve agreed. "It'll probably take a bit more time'n that anyway to get goin'. I don't imagine the crew had a chance to fill the water tank before they were jumped."

Within a few moments, Dan had returned with the handcuffs and rope. Shortly after that Smoky, Ty and Bill also returned. The surviving outlaws were cuffed and their ankles tied, then settled onto the floor at the rear of the car.

"Ranger, I'm gonna bleed to death," the wounded robber complained.

"I'll check his shoulder, Jim," Bill said. He pulled open the man's shirt to study the wound.

"You'll live to spend a long stretch in Huntsville," Bill assured the prisoner. "For now I'm just gonna bandage that hole to stop the bleedin'."

One of the other men glared at Jim.

"Just our luck we'd pick a train filled with Rangers to rob," he complained. "Never even got to rifle the express car."

"You wouldn't have gotten much," the conductor told him. "We're not hauling any valuables on this run."

"You mean there's no gold in the safe?" the robber exclaimed.

"No gold? Heck, there's not even a hundred dollars in the safe," the conductor chuckled.

"Didn't you fellers realize there's not much profit in robbin' trains anymore?" Smoky pointed out. "Why, even Sam Bass only got a few hundred dollars from his last robberies, before he got killed in Round Rock."

The robber cursed him roundly.

"Just keep shut," Jim ordered. "Unless you also want me to gag you."

Once the bodies were removed and the outlaws secured, the train resumed its eastward journey.

Jim and Bill had barely settled in their seats when the conductor stopped at their side.

"Ranger," he said, looking straight at Bill. "I reckon I owe you an apology for actin' like I did back in Dallas. You and your partners saved our bacon tonight, that's for certain. If it hadn't been for you Rangers, who knows what might've happened."

"I appreciate that," Bill answered. "And don't trouble yourself about it."

"Nonetheless, I'm grateful," the conductor reiterated. "Anytime you need to take a train, just tell 'em Dave Jackson says you've got free passage anywhere you want to go."

CHAPTER SIX

Just after eight the next morning, the much-delayed train pulled into Shreveport. Jim and his men had now pinned their badges to their vests, so they would be easy to recognize. Waiting on the platform for the Rangers was a man matching the description in the letter Captain Storm had given Jim. He walked up to them as soon as they disembarked.

"Lieutenant Blawcyzk?"

"I'm Lieutenant Blawcyzk. You must be Adrian Chatman."

"That's right," Chatman confirmed, taking Jim's hand in a firm grip. Chatman was tall, a couple of inches taller than the six foot plus Blawcyzk, huskily built, barrel-chested and with broad shoulders. His hair was close-cropped, and his dark eyes peered from behind a pair of pince-nez spectacles. A ready smile crossed his pleasant-featured face.

"How was your trip?" he continued.

"Not too bad, considerin'," Jim answered. "Let's get the introductions out of the way. These are Lieutenant Jim Huggins and Sergeant Smoky McCue. The others are Rangers Steve Masters, Johnny Dexter, Ty Tremblay, Jim's son Dan, and my son Charlie, who everyone but me calls Chip. Finally, we have special scout Bill Dundee. We're not very formal in the Rangers, so all of us go by our given names."

"That's fine. So do I. I'm pleased to meet y'all," Chatman answered, nodding to the others, who returned his greeting.

"As soon as we retrieve our horses, we'll be ready to move out," Jim continued. "Where's your wagons?"

"A little west of town, about three miles from here," Chatman answered. "The local authorities wouldn't let us stay within the city limits. They didn't want a bunch of colored folks hangin' around, so I didn't dare bring anyone else with me to meet you. My horse is tied out front."

"Don't plenty of colored people already live around here?" Ty questioned.

"Sure do, but those are their own coloreds, not transients," Adrian explained. "I think the good people of Shreveport are afraid we'll decide to settle down here permanently rather than move on. Truthfully, the sooner we're shut of Louisiana, the happier we'll be. We just want to get out of the South and over to west Texas."

"You might not find things all that much better in some parts of Texas," Jim warned him.

"We're all willing to take our chances," Adrian answered. "Can't do any worse than we already have. Some of us have tried sharecropping, others have attempted to start farms or businesses, but the people in power everywhere in the South are doin' everything they can to make sure poor folks don't get the opportunities to move ahead, and I mean poor coloreds and whites alike. No, there's nothing left in the South for us. Moving to Texas and starting our own community is our best hope."

He paused and smiled.

"I'm sorry for getting on my soapbox. Didn't mean to speechify at you."

"That's okay," Jim assured him. "Besides, everyone of us feels the same way about Texas. It's the finest place in the world to set down roots. It's a long way to San Angelo, so we'll have plenty of time to talk on the trail. We'll get our horses now, then meet you in front of the station. It'll take us a little time to saddle up and get the pack horses loaded, but we'll be quick as we can."

"That's fine," Adrian answered. "I'll be ready when you are."

The Rangers' horses were quickly unloaded and saddled, the pack rigs secured on Sam and Ted's backs. Once everything was set, the lawmen mounted up and rode around the dilapidated depot to the bustling main street. Chatman was waiting there, mounted on a dapple gray gelding. His saddle was a well-worn McClellan, most likely a U.S. Cavalry discard. Several white men were eyeing him suspiciously. One challenged him just as the Rangers rode up.

"Nigger," he called out, "I don't believe you own that horse. No shiftless darky would have enough money to buy a fine animal like that. You must've stolen it. I'm sending for the law."

He pulled a battered old Colt Dragoon pistol from his belt and started to point it at Adrian. Before he could finish, Jim had already pulled his Peacemaker from its holster and leveled it at the man's stomach.

"You might want to put that gun away, right now, unless you'd prefer I blow a hole clean through you," he ordered.

The gunman halted with his pistol still pointed downward, not daring to finish his draw under the glare of Jim's glittering blue eyes and that unwavering Colt pointed at his middle.

"Just who are you to tell me what to do?" he demanded.

"Texas Rangers. We're here to guarantee this man and his party safe passage to west Texas," Jim answered.

"Texas Rangers? In case you hadn't noticed, Mister, you're in Louisiana. You Rangers don't have no authority in this state."

"Perhaps we don't, but Mister Sam Colt does," Jim retorted, thumbing back the hammer of his revolver. "You want to argue with him?"

The gunman hesitated, then slid his gun back behind his belt.

"No, I reckon not," he grudgingly conceded. "But you and that nigger better watch your backs until you're out of Louisiana."

"Thanks for the warning, but I reckon we don't need it," Jim answered. "You or any of your friends try and bushwhack us and you'll find out you bit off way more than you can chew. I'd suggest you just forget all about us, because you'll live a lot longer if you do. Bet a hat on it. Smoky, you and the rest of the men take Adrian and get outta here. I'll be along in a few minutes. Just gonna make sure none of these men try'n follow us."

"Sure thing, Lieutenant," Smoky answered. "Adrian, get in between us."

Bunched around Adrian, Smoky and the other Rangers trotted away from the station. Jim kept the gunman and his friends covered until his men were just out of sight.

"Just remember what I said," he warned, backing Sizzle, then turning and riding away, Sam following. He waited to holster his gun until he was certain of not being trailed.

At Sizzle's ground-covering lope, it only took Jim a few moments to catch up with the others.

"I don't think you made us any friends back there, Jim," Smoky chuckled. As always, he had a cigarette dangling from his lips.

"I wasn't tryin' to make any," Jim answered. "Adrian, you doin' all right?"

"I'm fine, Jim," the big man responded. "I appreciate you gettin' me out of that scrape back there, though."

"*Por nada*," Jim said. "By the way, do you carry a gun?"

"Living in Washington, I never felt the need. In addition, a Negro carrying a revolver is just begging for trouble. So, to answer your question, no. I do have a shotgun in my wagon, but that's mainly for hunting and protection from varmints."

"You might want to consider buying a handgun, for protection from two-legged varmints like those back there," Jim advised. "If you need pointers in how to shoot, one of us'll be happy to help you."

"I'll consider it, and appreciate the advice," Adrian answered.

"How much farther to where you're camped?" Charlie asked.

"Little more than half-a-mile now. Soon as we get there, I reckon you'll want to say something to everyone."

"Not quite yet," Jim answered. "If we get rollin' right away, we can cross the state line before dark. I'll feel a lot better once we're back in Texas, where these badges we're wearin' have some authority. Unless you have any objections,

Adrian, we'll wait until tonight to meet with your people."

"None at all. As I've already said, the sooner we're in Texas, the better."

"How many settlers are in your bunch?" Dan asked.

"We've got one hundred and thirty three souls, plus all their worldly possessions, crammed into sixteen wagons. The oldest one is Shirley Bell, who's eighty six. The youngest is two year old Bobby Mann, plus there's three women who are expecting. It's my job to get them all safely to their new home."

"And ours to make sure that you do just that," Jim Huggins replied.

"Hold on a second," Smoky broke in. "Looks like a rider comin' this way, fairly hard."

The dust cloud he'd observed soon materialized into a dark-skinned man on a galloping coal black horse.

"That's Jep!" Adrian exclaimed. "He was supposed to stay with the wagons until I returned. Sure hope this doesn't mean trouble."

"Reckon we'll know in a minute," Bill said.

A moment later, the rider reached the Rangers and pulled his horse to a stop.

"Sure glad to see you, Adrian," he began.

"Why? Is anything wrong?" Adrian responded.

"Not a thing, leastwise there wasn't when I left. Your folks were gettin' worried that something had happened to you back in town, so I finally had to give in and come searchin' for you, that's all. Where the devil have you been?"

"The Rangers' train was late, that was the only problem," Adrian explained. "Couldn't very well leave without them, could I?"

"No, I reckon not," the rider conceded.

"Guess I should introduce you," Adrian continued, "Rangers, this is Jep . . ."

"Hawthorne," Jim concluded. "Jep, what in blue blazes are you doin' here in Louisiana? Last time I saw you, you were up along the Red. That was what, two, three years ago. Then I heard you'd drifted up to Montana or Dakota territory."

"Jim Blawcyzk, you ol' curly wolf!" Jep exclaimed. "You heard right, but one of those winters up north was more'n enough for me. Nearly froze my backside off. Soon as the snow melted enough so the trails were passable, I hightailed it right back here for Texas."

Hawthorne was a large man, half black and half Cherokee. His features showed his heritage, his hair jet black and wavy, his dark eyes set off by high cheekbones and a prominent nose. He was dressed in buckskins, with moccasins on his feet. A faded old United States cavalry campaign hat, with an eagle feather stuck in its band, was pulled down low over his face. A huge chaw of tobacco bulged out his left cheek.

"You know Jep?" Adrian asked.

"Known him for years," Jim answered. "We've gotten into and out of a few scrapes together."

"Boy howdy, that's for certain," Jep agreed.

"That's good news, then," Adrian said. "I hired Jep as a scout for our train. I guess you'n he'll get along just fine."

"Either that or they'll kill each other," Smoky chuckled. "But hirin' Jep's the smartest move you could've made, Adrian. If any man can get your folks through to San Angelo, come Hell or high water, it's Jep."

"I appreciate that, Smoky," Jep answered. "See you haven't changed much either, except you've put on some weight."

His gaze settled on Charlie.

"Jim, don't tell me that's your boy."

"Sure is," Jim answered. "He's ridin' with the Rangers now."

"Well, I'll be jiggered! Last time I saw you, Charlie, you were knee-high to a grasshopper. You've sure filled out, boy. Pity you look just like your old man, though."

"You're just jealous because we're both a lot better lookin' than you'll ever be, Jep," Jim laughed.

"This is all well and good, but shouldn't we get a move on, Lieutenant?" Johnny asked.

"Who's this young whippersnapper?" Jep asked.

"Johnny Dexter. You know Bill Dundee, of

course. Rest of the boys are Lieutenant Jim Huggins and his son Dan, Ty Tremblay, and Steve Masters."

"Now that the pleasantries are out of the way, that red-headed young'n's right," Jep said. "They'll be worried plumb to death until Adrian shows up. Let's go, Mack!"

He turned his horse and put him into a lope, the Rangers strung out behind.

CHAPTER SEVEN

As Jim had hoped, nightfall found them a few miles inside Texas. They had made slightly better progress than he had expected, mostly because once the wagons had gotten under way, Jep Hawthorne kept them rolling at a steady pace. The Rangers were amazed at how well Jep kept things under control, especially considering the condition of some of the equipment. There were two heavy Studebaker freight wagons and a couple of Conestogas in decent shape, but the rest of them had seen far better days. Two of the wagons were pulled by pairs of horses, one by a team of oxen, and the rest by mules. There were also a few saddle horses and some spare mules, as well as three milk cows, the last following reluctantly, tied to backs of wagons. As was the case with nearly all wagon trains, except for the drivers, the elderly, and the very young or ill, most of the emigrants walked alongside their conveyances, sparing the teams.

Jim had requested to talk to the group once the animals had been cared for, and before supper was started. He was just about finished grooming his horses when Adrian approached, accompanied by another man and two women.

"Jim, before you make your speech, I'd like you to meet my mom and dad, Frances and Dwain, and my sister, Sheryl."

"I'm pleased to meet y'all," Jim said, shaking Dwain's hand, then touching two fingers to the brim of his Stetson in greeting to the ladies.

Like his son, Dwain was a big man, with deeply-chiseled features. Frances was a buxom woman, slightly on the short side. She had a pretty face, set off by a ready smile and framed by shoulder-length ebony hair. Sheryl was also a handsome woman, slim and nicely figured.

"It's we who are grateful to you and your Rangers," Frances said. "After all, you needn't have answered our request."

"I'm not so sure about that, ma'am," Jim replied. "It's pretty hard to say no to Captain Storm, let alone the governor of Texas."

"No matter, your assistance is appreciated," Frances reiterated. "We all feel much better having you along."

"Mom, I hate to cut this short, but you'll have plenty of time to talk later," Adrian broke in. "Jim, everyone'll be ready for you in a few minutes."

"I'm just about done here," Jim answered, giving Sam a final swipe of the currycomb, then slipping him and Sizzle their peppermints. "I'll get the rest of the boys together and see you in five minutes."

"We'll be waiting."

The other Rangers had tied their horses to a picket line, while Sam and Sizzle, who would not stray far from Jim, were turned loose. Jim rounded up his men and they headed to where the settlers were gathered around a huge live oak. Once they had fallen quiet, Jim began to speak.

"Folks, don't worry. I'm not much for long speeches, and I'm certain you're all as hungry as I am, so I won't take much of your time. For those who haven't gotten our names, I'm Lieutenant Jim Blawcyzk. That's pronounced 'BLUH-zhick.' It's a mouthful, so just call me Jim. These are Sergeant Smoky McCue and Lieutenant Jim Huggins, along with Rangers Dan Huggins, Jim's son, and my son Charlie, better known as Chip. Then we have Steve Masters, Ty Tremblay, Johnny Dexter, and special scout Bill Dundee. We'll be accompanying you all the way to your destination.

"Now, Texas isn't the wilderness it was just a few short years ago, especially here in the eastern part of the state. However, that doesn't mean there won't be a lot of hard travelin' ahead. You've still got a month or so to where you're headed, and the farther west we get the drier and more rugged the land will become. There'll be some stretches so flat and with so few landmarks you'll swear we're just goin' in circles, bet a hat on it. Water will also become scarce, so you can't be wastin' any. There'll be treacherous river crossings and quicksand, poisonous plants, and cactus spines that'll puncture your hide and fester if you don't pull 'em out right quick. You'll also need to keep an eye out for rattlesnakes, the occasional wolf, mebbe even a mountain lion that's drifted out of its territory. Probably the nastiest critters we might come across are the wild boars. You sure don't want to tangle with one of those. They've got a wicked temper, and tusks that can tear you to shreds.

"You've undoubtedly heard there could be trouble from two-legged renegades. That might happen. Now, as far as you folks bein' colored, that'll be less of a problem once we get past the Brazos or thereabouts. There weren't any plantations in west Texas, and few slaves. There's also a lot fewer people, and plenty of room for everyone. Out there men, and women, have to depend on each other without overly worryin' about their skin color. I ain't sayin' you won't run into folks who don't like Negroes. I've run into plenty of people who don't care for Polish like me. Same goes for Czechs, Mexicans, you name them. It's just that there won't be as many. You're more likely to have problems from outlaws, or mebbe ranchers who don't want any more settlers, period. That's why we're ridin' with you, and will be stayin' with you for a while until you're settled.

"I want to make it clear that Adrian and Jep are in complete charge of this train . . . until trouble starts. However, if it does, then every one of you'll need to do exactly what we say, without hesitation, and without question. Handlin' trouble is us Rangers' job, not yours. That job'll be a lot easier if you follow our orders.

"Just one more thing before I'm finished. Please stay away from my horse Sam, the palomino and white one. He's a one-man animal. Sam was whipped half to death by his previous owner, so he doesn't trust anyone but me. He'll take a chunk out of your hide if you get too close."

"Whipped half to death. Just like was done to a lot of slaves by overseers on plantations," came a voice from the crowd.

Jim flushed.

"I reckon you're right. There's no call to treat an animal like that, and even less to treat a human being that way."

Jim paused and sighed.

"And I've said enough. I'm sure lots of you will have questions, so just look one of us up durin' supper, and we'll be glad to answer 'em. Adrian, you have anything to add?"

"Not a word for now, Jim . . . except let's get supper started."

Supper was a routine affair, consisting of bacon, beans, and, in place of the usual biscuits, corn

71

pone. The Rangers had separated so each could take his meal with some of the travelers, getting to know each other better. Adrian had asked Jim, along with Smoky McCue and Jim Huggins, to join him, Jep, and some others who were considered leaders of the group. These included Fletcher Harris, who had been taught basic book-keeping as a trusted servant on a large Alabama plantation; Devon Jones, a preacher from Maryland, and Sam Tatum, who had learned medicine from his master, a physician who tended to the well-to-do of Natchez, Mississippi, a town which had largely escaped the ravages of the War. The physician, a kindly man, had granted Sam his freedom shortly after the War began. Even now, Sam still carried his manumission papers, years after the Emancipation Proclamation. Also with them was Adrian's grandfather, Lawrence Young.

"Jim," Adrian questioned, "did you mean what you said, that we might not be bothered all that much just for bein' colored once we reach west Texas, or were you tryin' to softsoap us?"

"I can't give you any guarantees, Adrian," Jim answered. "However, I can tell you a lot of Texans, most of them from the west part of the state, didn't want to leave the Union, and voted against secession. Quite a few refused to fight for the Confederate Army. Some of 'em even got lynched for their beliefs. You're also headed for an area where there aren't many other folks, which means anyone wantin' to hassle you would have to go out of their way to do so."

"Which there are more than enough people willing to do," Lawrence said, shaking his grizzled head.

"You're correct," Jim agreed. "But there aren't as many of those in west Texas. That said, unfortunately there will always be someone who doesn't like someone's skin color, or language, or religion, and so on. Bet a hat on it. Whites, Mexicans, and Indians have been fightin' in these parts forever, it seems like. Dunno when it'll end, if ever. Heck, I can't even guarantee some of my own men don't care for colored folks."

"Jim, we all know plenty of Rangers don't like Mexicans, Negroes, and especially Indians, but I don't think that applies to any of the men ridin' with us," Smoky objected.

"Smoky's right, but even if it did, they'd do their job," Jim Huggins added. "Mister Young, I'd say you have no worries on that account."

"Lieutenant, I appreciate the respect, but please, call me Lawrence. Everyone always has."

"All right," Huggins smiled.

"Seems like we've got company comin'," Jep noted. "Over thataway. Wonder what they want?"

Approaching the group were several boys of various ages.

"I can imagine, but we'll let them tell us," Jim chuckled.

73

The boys hesitated once they grew near.

"C'mon and join us," Jim invited. "It's all right."

"Are you sure?" asked the apparent leader, a skinny youngster of about thirteen.

"I'm certain," Jim assured him. "I'll need your names, though. In case you didn't catch mine earlier, it's Lieutenant Jim Blawcyzk."

"Sure, Lieutenant Blaw . . ."

"Whoa . . . just call me Ranger Jim. That'll save you from sprainin' your tongue," Jim laughed.

"All right. I'm Tom McGraw, and these are my younger brothers, Isaiah and Nathaniel."

"Which is which?"

Isaiah and Nathaniel were identical twins, about eight.

"I'm Nathaniel," the nearest piped up.

"The others are Dave Crenshaw, Gator Crown, and Joey Stark," Tom concluded.

"And who's that in the back?"

"Her? That's Daisy Cutler. She's just a girl who likes taggin' along."

"I'm not just a girl," Daisy protested. "I can fish and do all sorts of stuff as good as any of you boys."

"Pleased to meet you boys . . . and you, Daisy. What can we do for you?" Jim asked.

"You're really cowboys?" Gator questioned.

"Sometimes," Jim answered, "but mainly we're lawmen, who try'n keep the bad guys in line."

"Can you teach us to shoot?" Joey asked. "That way we could help you if any outlaws try and rob our folks."

"Mebbe someday, after we get where we're goin'. Anything else?"

"We were wonderin', are we gonna be attacked by any wild Indians?" Isaiah asked.

"It's not very likely," Jim answered. "There haven't been any Indians in these parts for years. Besides, not all Indians are wild. Plenty of them, like the Tonkawas, were friendly to the whites who first came to Texas."

"You mean we're not gonna get scalped?" Isaiah insisted. He sounded disappointed.

"Not hardly," Jim chuckled.

"You boys just might, if you don't stop botherin' these men. You better get back to your folks, and get ready for bed," Devon Jones warned, with a twinkle in his eyes. "Same goes for you, Daisy. A young lady shouldn't be out and about this time of night."

"They're not botherin' me," Jim assured him. "However, Reverend Jones is right, it's time for bed. There is one more thing before you leave, however."

"What's that, Ranger Jim?" Daisy asked.

"I need you to help me eat some of these."

Jim dug in his hip pocket for some of the peppermints he always carried for his horses. He passed those to the children.

"What are these?" Tom asked.

"You sayin' you've never had peppermints?" Jim replied.

"No, none of us have."

"Well, you're in for a treat. They're candy, and they're real good. Just pop them in your mouth and you'll see."

The youngsters eyed the sweets dubiously, until Joey, the youngest, slid his candy between his lips. He broke into a broad smile.

"Ranger Jim's right. These are real good. Thanks, Ranger."

"You're welcome. Long as it's all right with your folks, I'll let you have some, regular. But right now it's time for all of you to skedaddle. We'll be rollin' soon as it's light enough to see."

"Rest of you say thanks to the Ranger, and good night to everyone," Jones ordered.

"All right, Reverend," Tom agreed. He and the others made their thanks and goodnights, then headed back to their respective wagons.

"Right nice bunch of kids," Smoky observed.

"There's a whole passel more of 'em where those came from. This train is loaded with young'ns," Jep answered.

"They sure are nice kids," Jim Huggins agreed. "Now I think we should all take Jim's advice and turn in."

"Sounds reasonable," Lawrence said. "We'll see y'all in the mornin'."

• • •

Jim rolled out his blankets at the edge of camp, near where Sam and Sizzle were grazing. As much as he liked company, especially since he spent so much solitary time on the trail, some evenings he only wanted to be alone with his thoughts. This was one of those.

So far, so good, he thought. *We got out of Louisiana without any real trouble. These folks hirin' Jep Hawthorne as their guide is a real break too. If anyone can get them where they're goin', it's Jep. They also seem pretty well organized, considerin'. Wish they had a few more spare animals, and a lot of their equipment's in pretty bad shape, but that can't be helped. With luck it'll hold together until we get past San Angelo. 'Course, with over four hundred miles ahead of us, anything's liable to happen. We'll just have to deal with things as they come.*

Jim began to say his evening prayers, until he was interrupted by a sweet voice drifting over the assembled wagons.

"Sometimes I feel like a motherless child,
"Sometimes I feel like a motherless child,
"Sometimes I feel like a motherless child,
　　"A long ways from home,
　　"A long ways from home,
　　　　"True believer

"A long ways from home,
"A long ways from home."

That sure is a lovely voice, he thought. *I like the song, too.*

He propped himself on one elbow to better hear the singer's low melody as the mournful tune continued.

"Sometimes I feel like I'm almos' gone,
"Sometimes I feel like I'm almos' gone,
"Sometimes I feel like I'm almos' gone,
"Way up in de heab'nly land,
"Way up in de heab'nly land,
"True believer
"Way up in de heab'nly land,
"Way up in de heab'nly land.
"Sometimes I feel like a motherless child,
"Sometimes I feel like a motherless child,
"Sometimes I feel like a motherless child,
"A long ways from home
"There's praying everywhere."

A single tear trickled from the rugged Ranger lieutenant's eye. He drifted off to sleep with the song still echoing through his head.

After the meeting broke up, Adrian walked through the camp to make his final check and say goodnight to everyone. That done, he spread

78

his blankets and lay down beneath his wagon. His mother and father were apparently already asleep, for no lantern light glowed through the canvas cover, and he could hear his father's gentle snores.

He lay gazing at the bottom of the wagon bed for quite some time.

Perhaps I will be able to pull this off after all.

Adrian had been beset by misgivings almost from the moment he had decided to uproot himself from Washington, ask his family to leave their homes, and organize a group of freemen and ex-slaves to start a new community in Texas. Doubts expressed by friends and acquaintances only added to his uncertainty.

I wasn't sure if I should even try to start a new town. Nearly changed my mind more than once. Too many obstacles to overcome, you won't be wanted no matter where you go, you've got a good life right here. Why give up everything you have to head west?

The objections had grown even stronger once Adrian had announced his intended destination, west Texas.

"Why Texas, of all places? Are you crazy? If you must go through with this fool notion, at least settle in someplace more civilized. Why not Kansas or Iowa, or maybe Oregon? Somewhere other Negro towns have already been established. Anywhere but a former slave state like Texas."

Didn't matter that I'd been hearin' for years that everything is bigger and better in Texas, or that there were plenty of wide open spaces for anyone with enough gumption to spread out and make something of himself in Texas. All that counted was Texas had been a slave state. Well, with any luck I'll prove them all wrong. So far we're off to a good start. Besides, I've been fascinated for a long time by the stories I've heard about Texas, the ranches, the cattle drives, the cowboys. If I'm wrong, and this dream of mine turns out to be a bust, at least it'll be my dream, no one else's. And no one's gonna take that away from me without a fight.

Adrian hadn't even been sure he should ask for help from the Texas Rangers. Negroes seeking protection from a southern state's law organization was unheard of since Reconstruction ended. Well, since Texas was as much a western as southern state, Adrian had taken the chance, not expecting a reply. Much to his surprise, the governor had agreed to his request. Now here he and his party were, in Texas, with Ranger protection. That had already proved invaluable back in Shreveport.

I figured the governor would send a few broken-down Rangers, men well past their prime. Instead, these seem like real fine lawmen he sent. Lieutenant Blawcyzk and his kid, real friendly, but both seem like they'll brook no nonsense.

Almost look more like brothers, with that blond hair and blue eyes. Same for Lieutenant Huggins and his boy, both have the same brown hair, although the lieutenant's is turnin' gray, and the same eyes. Smoky McCue. I can see where he got his name, with that black hair frosted at the tips. I've only known him a few hours, and I can already tell he's real fond of that thin moustache, too. Not to mention his cigarettes.

Ty Tremblay. That's one tall, skinny kid. Funny color of hazel eyes, but they match his brown hair. He seems like a steady customer, not quite like the redhead, Johnny Dexter. I'd guess Dexter's a good hand with a gun, but he's awfully cocky. Ty's more like a younger Steve Masters, except Steve's shorter and has brown eyes.

Bill Dundee. Now there's a surprise. Never would have expected to find a colored man ridin' with the Rangers, even if it is only as a scout. I'd hazard Bill's well past the downhill side of fifty, if he's a day. Sure seems like a reliable hand, though, and Smoky tells me he's a dead shot with his rifle. Lieutenant Blawcyzk seems to set some store by Bill, too.

Adrian grimly chuckled to himself.

You've got to keep in mind you really don't know any of these men. After all, they are white Texans, except for Dundee. Sure, they appear to be trustworthy, but appearances don't mean much. If trouble starts, they just might turn their backs and ride away. And who'd question their actions? No one, that's who. Nobody'd take the word of a bunch of Negroes against the word of the Texas Rangers.

He sighed deeply.

No use worryin' until the time comes. Who knows, maybe we won't have any trouble, although I wouldn't bet a hat on it, as the lieutenant says. I'd better just get some sleep.

Adrian smiled when the words of *Sometimes I Feel Like a Motherless Child* came softly to his ears.

"Christine's singing always makes a body feel comforted," he whispered. "Maybe I'm concerned over nothing."

CHAPTER EIGHT

By the time the sun was just appearing on the eastern horizon the next day, the animals had been fed, breakfast eaten, and gear stowed in preparation for the day's travel. Jim found Jep helping another of the emigrants hitching his mules.

"Mornin', Jep."

"Mornin', Jim. I don't believe you got to meet Bull Mason last night."

"No, don't believe I did," Jim answered, offering his hand. Mason took it grudgingly, eyeing the Ranger with hostility, if not downright hatred.

"Like I told Adrian and I told Jep, we don't need any Rangers helpin' us," he grumbled. "No one else neither, for that matter."

Mason was a big man, slightly shorter than Jim, but broad and powerfully built. His fists were almost as large as Jim's head, his arms thick and muscular. Extremely dark eyes glowered from under thick brows. Despite being in his early thirties, Jim would guess, Mason's head was entirely bald.

"I don't reckon you do," Jim answered, with a friendly chuckle, "but some of these others probably do, especially the women and kids. Can't hurt to have us along."

"Bull, I warned you once already, if you don't care to abide by our rules, you're free to pull out anytime you want," Jep added. "You care to do that right now?"

"No, I reckon I don't," Mason answered, turning his attention back to his team.

"Don't mind Bull, Jim," Jep said. "He's just a stubborn cuss . . . kinda like you that way."

"It's all right," Jim answered. "I came over to let you know we're ready to ride, and to see if we could help out anywhere?"

"No, don't believe so," Jep replied. "There's only a couple more teams to hitch up, then we'll be ready to roll."

"Ranger, there's some extra room in my wagon. Why don't you put your supplies in with mine, and let your pack horses take it easy?" Mason offered. "It's gonna be a long trip, so it wouldn't be a bad idea to spare your pack animals until they're really needed."

"You mean that, Bull? I thought you didn't care for me," Jim answered.

"Never said I didn't like you, just that I didn't need your help."

"Bull's also real fond of horses and mules. He treats them real good, so he's worried more about Sam and Ted than you, Jim," Jep added.

"In that case, you're a man after my own

heart, and I accept, Bull. *Muchas Gracias*."

"It's nothing, Ranger."

"Jim, soon as you quit palaverin' and get your stuff loaded, we can get goin'," Jep ordered.

"All right, I'll have that done in a few minutes, Jep. Which route are you planning on? The main road to Dallas and Fort Worth, then cuttin' southwest?"

"Nope. I figure on headin' cross-country soon as we get past Tyler. We'll cross the Trinity, then if need be rest for a day or two and re-supply at Corsicana. The roads are rougher, but it's a more direct route. Once we leave Corsicana, we'll head for Waco and take the suspension bridge across the Brazos. The toll's a mite costly, but it's a lot safer than usin' one of the ferries downstream or tryin' to ford the river."

"There's a lot fewer towns along the way, and far less people to count on for help," Jim pointed out.

"Exactly," Jep answered. "With this group, I figure the fewer folks we run across, the less likely we are to have trouble, if you get my drift."

"I reckon you're right," Jim admitted. "Well, since you say everyone's all set, I'm gonna head back and mount up. Oh, by the way, who was that singin' last night? She sure had a pretty voice."

"The lady? That's Christine Fletcher, and you're right, she certainly can sing. She and her husband Joe were house servants in Virginia.

They've got the eighth wagon in line. I'll introduce you to them tonight."

"I'll appreciate that, Jep," Jim answered. "See you on the trail."

With unusually cool weather and relatively good roads, the day's travel had been easy. Jep had called a halt an hour before sunset, taking advantage of a glade of live oaks surrounding a small, shallow pond.

"We made it a good distance today, Jep, a bit more'n twenty miles," Jim observed. "If we can keep this pace up, we might shave a few days off the trip."

He, along with Charlie and Smoky, were having supper with the guide, along with Adrian and his parents, and two of his aunts, Debbie Youngsnead and Ruthenia Washington.

"That'd be nice, but highly unlikely," Jep responded. "Not with river crossings ahead of us, and the land gettin' dryer and rougher once we start west from Waco. More renegades out that way too."

"Do you really expect trouble from outlaws, Mr. Hawthorne?" Debbie asked.

"You never can tell, ma'am."

"Don't worry about outlaws, Debbie," Ruthenia tried to reassure her. "Don't forget, we bought pistols before we left in case of trouble. Rangers, we sleep with those pistols under our pillows, and keep them hidden in our petticoats during the day. If any man tries to molest us, he'll be in for a very unpleasant surprise."

"Spoken like a true Texas woman, Miz Washington," Smoky chuckled. "You'll fit right in out here."

"Smoky's right, but I still wish so many of you folks weren't walkin'," Charlie said. "We all feel pretty guilty letting you walk while we're ridin'."

"Don't trouble yourself about that, Chip," Adrian answered. "Most of us have never sat a horse, but quite a few have spent time working in the fields, so we're used to walking. Besides, since you Rangers' job is to keep watch for trouble, you need to be on horseback. It wouldn't do much good havin' old folks and kids in the saddle if a group of raiders comes down on us."

"I reckon you're right, Adrian. Still sticks in my craw, though. Unlike this soup your ma made, which is real good."

Charlie tipped the last contents of his bowl into his mouth.

"Thank you," Frances said. "I did the best I could with some sweet potatoes and turnips I had. I would have liked to put more in the soup, but we're conserving supplies. We need to stretch them as much as possible."

"No need to apologize," Charlie answered. "Besides, it's still better'n my dad's bacon and beans."

"Considerin' your dad's cookin', that's not much of a compliment, Chip," Smoky laughed.

"I never noticed you turnin' 'em down, Smoke," Jim retorted.

"A starving man won't ever refuse a meal, no matter how bad," Smoky shot back.

"All right, let's change the subject," Jim ordered. "Adrian, speaking of riding, I've been meanin' to tell you that's a real nice horse you've got."

Jim had been admiring Adrian's dapple gray gelding. The horse was well built, and seemed to have plenty of stamina.

"You mean Shadow? Yes, he's a good animal, even if he is getting on a bit in years," Adrian answered. "He was a Union cavalry mount. In fact, he was at Appomattox when Lee surrendered. Beggin' your pardon, Jim," he hastened to add. "I didn't mean to rub salt in old wounds."

"There's no apology needed," Jim assured him. "Even though I was still a youngster, I was one of those Texans I mentioned who thought seceding was a real bad idea. Although I was just a kid, I did spend the last year of the War as a Ranger on the frontier, attemptin' to keep Comanches and white renegades at bay. When most of the men went off to fight for the Confederacy, the Indians started raidin' more, tryin' to get back land they'd lost. Toss in deserters from the Army, mix in plenty of white and Mexican desperadoes, and you had a genuine recipe for trouble. Texas was a real wild and dangerous place back then. Still is in some parts."

"Not where we're headed, I hope," Dwain said.

"It could be," Jim answered. "I'm not gonna try and paint a pretty picture for you. There's still not much law in west Texas, except what a man makes for himself."

"We hope to change a little of that," Adrian said. "We want to establish a real community."

"As long as you've brought that up, how do you folks plan on makin' a go of it?" Jim asked.

"We've got people who can do all sorts of different jobs," Adrian explained. "Fletcher and his family are going to open a store. Sam will be the town physician, obviously, and Devon will have his church. We've got carpenters, a blacksmith, even a saddle maker. We'll build a school and send for a teacher as soon as we can. Until then the young'ns will be taught at home. The only advantage to the Negro of being kept in slavery was some of us did learn trades. Unfortunately, that was a small minority. Most of the people on this train were field hands, so we'll have mainly farmers. One thing we're going to attempt is raising peanuts. That's a good cash crop."

Jim shook his head.

"I dunno. You're settling on some mighty dry

land. It's more suited to ranching than farming."

"You've struck on my son's secret," Frances said, smiling. "It's always been his dream to be a cowboy and have his own ranch."

"Mom's right," Adrian admitted. "Once we're established in Freedom, I plan to purchase cattle for my land, and start a herd. I've even got a brand picked out, the Rafter AC. It's already registered with the state."

"Well, you could do worse," Jim answered. "I'm sure you're aware that a lot of colored men have come to Texas and learned cowboyin'. Most of them are top hands, and can hire on at any ranch they choose."

"You mentioned Freedom, Adrian," Smoky said. "Never heard of it. Whereabouts is that?"

"Freedom's going to be the name of our new town," Adrian explained. "Our land's about eighteen miles northwest of San Angelo, along the North Concho River. So you see, it's not as dry as you think."

"It's not as wet as you think, either," Jim noted. "The North Concho's not very big, and quite often it dries to a trickle or less. Dunno how much you'll be able to depend on it for irrigation, if that's your plan."

"Boys, I can see this discussion is about to go on all night, but it's time we hit the hay," Jep broke in. "Sunup comes early."

"Tell us something we don't know, Jep," Jim

laughed. "But I guess you're right. Folks, we'll say our good nights, and see you in the morning."

After leaving Adrian and his family, Smoky and Charlie headed for their blankets, while Jim, as always, went to check on his horses one last time before turning in. He found Sam and Sizzle peacefully grazing. They whickered a greeting when they spied their rider, and trotted up to him, nuzzling his hip pocket for a peppermint.

"Of course I've got your candy," Jim said, giving each paint a treat. He scratched their ears while they worked on the sweets, then patted their necks while they nuzzled his chest. Suddenly, both mounts lifted their heads, pricked up their ears, and snorted. Jim whirled, pulling his gun from its holster.

"Don't shoot, Ranger Jim!" came a young voice from the gathering dusk. "It's only me and Nathaniel."

"Isaiah?" Jim echoed, sliding his gun back. "What're you two doin' out here? And never slip up on a man like that. It could get you shot."

"We're sorry," Nathaniel said. "We just wanted to see your horses. They sure are pretty."

"Thanks," Jim answered. "Tell you what. It's late, and just like people, horses need their rest. How about you visit with them tomorrow? Besides, I'd bet a hat you're also looking for peppermints. I just happen to have some right here."

"You're right. We were hopin' you'd give us a candy," Isaiah admitted.

"Just one each," Jim admonished. "Plus one to take back to your brother."

He reached into his pocket to get the candies. Just as he did, a mournful howling shattered the still night.

"Indians!" both boys shouted as one. They jumped into Jim's arms and knocked the startled Ranger flat on his back.

"They're gonna scalp us!" Nathaniel cried.

"Those aren't Indians, they're just coyotes," Jim gasped. "Let me up so I can breathe, will ya?"

He pushed the boys aside and sat up.

"Coyotes?" Isaiah repeated. "What are coyotes?"

"Kind of wild dogs. They look like a wolf, only they're smaller, and nowhere near as dangerous," Jim explained. "They're mostly scavengers, just like buzzards, and mainly eat dead animals, or else they hunt stuff like rabbits and mice. They generally don't bother people."

Both boys shivered when the coyotes howled again.

"They sure sound awful scary," Nathaniel half-whispered.

"Nah, they just like howlin' at the moon," Jim answered. "They're a bit early tonight, since it's just risin', but they'll probably keep up that racket most of the night. They won't come near the wagons, since they don't like the scent of humans, plus the fire will keep 'em at a distance. Tell you what, though, why don't I walk you two back to your wagon?"

"We'd feel a lot better if'n you did, Ranger," Nathaniel said.

"Good. Besides, your folks'll be gettin' worried. I'd imagine you didn't tell them where you were goin'."

"No, we didn't," Isaiah admitted. "They told us not to bother you Rangers."

"You're not botherin' me at all," Jim said, adding with a chuckle, "if you were, I'd be the first one to give you a swat on the behind and tell you to skedaddle."

"He means it too, Nathaniel," Isaiah said. "So let's go."

"You don't have to tell me twice. Not with those coyotes howlin'," Nathaniel said, shuddering just a bit when the pack started yelping yet again. "C'mon, Ranger Jim, I'm ready to go home."

The next two days were uneventful, the wagon train making slow, steady progress. The only excitement had come when Joey Stark spotted a strange animal and called to Steve Masters, who was riding just behind the Starks' wagon, for help.

"What's wrong?" Steve asked.

"That critter," Joey said, pointing ahead. "What is it?"

"That? That's an armadillo," Steve answered.

"It surely is a strange creature," Joey's mother, Penelope, noted.

"Will it attack us or our mules?" Joey's older sister, Mary, asked.

"No, he won't bother you," Steve assured them. "He's got long claws, but only uses them to dig up ants, termites, or other bugs. An armadillo doesn't need to worry much about other critters eatin' him with that armor he's got. He'll just mosey out of the way if he decides we're getting too close."

"He still scares me," Joey said. "Ma, can't I ride in the wagon for a while?"

"Don't be silly," his mother answered. "Besides, the baby's asleep. I don't want you wakin' him."

"Don't be such a sissy, Joey," Mary scolded. "And ma's right. You don't want to be wakin' up Moses."

"I'm not a sissy," Joey retorted, struggling to keep from crying.

"I'll tell you what, Joey. You can ride with me for a spell, and help keep an eye out for other critters. You never know, we might see a razorback hog, or mebbe even a fox or deer."

Steve leaned over in the saddle and lifted

the six year old to the back of Shenandoah, his chestnut gelding.

"You comfortable, son?" he asked, once the boy was settled in front of him.

"I sure am, Ranger Steve . . . and I'm riding a horse! *Yay!*"

Penelope looked over from her perch on the wagon bench and smiled.

"Steve, I'm truly grateful to you for all your help. That goes for all of you Rangers."

Since discovering that Penelope Stark was a young widow with three small children, one of the Rangers had been sticking close to her at all times.

"Heck, no need to thank us, ma'am," Steve answered. "We're happy to oblige. Besides, you and your youngsters are real fine folks."

Steve blushed slightly, hoping the attractive Negress didn't notice. He'd taken this assignment reluctantly, not particularly caring for the Negro race. Steve had been taught from childhood that colored folks were lazy, shiftless good-for-nothing's, and the ones he'd met in the course of his Ranger career had only reinforced that conviction. However, over the past few days, he'd grudgingly come to realize his preconceived notions were wrong. The people on this train were as hard-working and decent as any whites, more so than quite a few of those. He'd particularly come to admire Penelope Stark. It took an awful lot of gumption for a widow woman with three kids, one still an infant, to strike out for a strange land.

"Ranger Steve, there's another armadillo!" Joey exclaimed. "Two or three more, too."

"Well, Joey, let's scatter those critters," Steve answered. He put Shenandoah into a lope.

That night, just after supper, Jim was visiting with two of Adrian's uncles, Kyle Young and Lawrence Young, Junior, and Lawrence's wife, Lashay.

"What do you folks think of Texas so far?" he asked.

"There's plenty of room for a man to spread out that's for certain," Lawrence said.

"From what I understand, we haven't even seen the wide open prairie yet," Kyle added.

"That's right," Jim agreed. "One section, the *Llano Estacado*, is so flat and has so few land-marks you could wander for days without realizin' you were lost. The Spanish *padres* marked their way with stakes so they could keep track of direction. That's how the Staked Plain got its name."

"It seems to me the land is mighty dry," Lashay observed.

"It can be," Jim agreed. "But there can also rainstorms so heavy you can't see your horse's ears in front of you, and blue northers so fierce they drop a foot of snow in a day. Then again, there are lots of days like this one, weather so nice it makes a body glad to be alive."

"Looks like someone wants you, Jim," Kyle said. "Right over there."

Nathaniel and Isaiah were standing quietly near a scrub cedar.

"Did you boys want me?" Jim asked.

"Well, yeah, sort of," Isaiah answered.

"What my brother is tryin' to say is, do you have any more peppermints?" Nathaniel continued.

"I think I can dig up a couple," Jim laughed, reaching in his hip pocket and removing several candies. "If I run out, though, you're gonna have to explain to my horses why they're not getting any more treats."

"We won't take too many, and thanks," Nathaniel answered. He took the candies, then he and his brother scampered away.

"How about you folks? Would you care for a peppermint?" Jim asked the Youngs.

"I believe we might, thank you," Lashay replied.

Jim passed around more candies. He and the Youngs spent the next hour in conversation, until Steve Masters rode up. Joey Stark was still perched on the saddle in front of him.

"Howdy, Steve. See you've got a friend," Jim called.

"Sure do. Joey's gonna make a fine wrangler. We came by to let you know things are quiet. You still want to set a guard tonight?"

"Yeah, I do," Jim confirmed. "Check with Jim Huggins. He'll assign the watch."

"All right."

Steve paused, then chuckled.

"Jim, looks like you've got some *compadres* too. And you sure ain't gonna believe your own eyes."

"What d'ya mean?"

"Look over yonder."

Approaching were Nathaniel and Isaiah, mounted double on Sam, Jim's vicious-tempered, one man horse. The big paint plodded docilely along as both barefooted boys nudged his ribs with their heels.

"Nathaniel! Isaiah! What in blue blazes are you two doin' with my horse?" Jim exclaimed. "Didn't I tell you to stay away from Sam, no matter what?"

"But he likes us, Ranger Jim," Isaiah answered. "We were eating peppermints, gave him one, and then since he seemed so nice, we climbed on his back. We're sorry, but we wanted to ride him, so bad."

Sam stopped in front of Jim and, as was his habit, buried his muzzle in the Ranger's belly, causing Jim to grunt. Jim rubbed the gelding's nose.

"Sam, thanks for not hurtin' these kids," he murmured, and gave him another peppermint.

"Boys," he continued. "Takin' a man's horse without permission is a real serious thing out west. A man depends on his horse for his very life, which is why horse thieves can be hung, since stealing a man's horse is practically the same as killing him."

"Ranger Jim, we didn't know. Besides, we weren't stealin' Sam. We only wanted to ride him around the camp," Nathaniel explained.

"I know that," Jim answered. "What's more important is you disobeyed my orders to stay away from Sam, since he can be a killer. He only lets me or my son Charlie handle him. Well, I guess I should say usually only lets me or Charlie handle him, since you boys and Sam seem to be gettin' along just fine."

"You mean this is the horse you didn't want us to go near?" Nathaniel answered. "We thought it was the other one."

"You thought I meant Sizzle? Not hardly. Sizzle loves everybody. He wouldn't hurt anybody," Jim explained.

"But you said don't go near the pal . . . palo . . . heck, what was it?" Isaiah answered.

"The palomino and white. That's Sam. This horse."

"We took the wrong horse, Nathaniel," Isaiah stated, chagrined. "But Ranger Jim, we didn't know what palomino meant. We thought your reddish colored horse was the palomino."

"I'm sorry, boys," Jim said, recognizing his mistake. He should have realized that some, if not most, of the emigrants would have little knowledge of horses, and would not know a palomino from a sorrel.

"I should have made myself plainer. A goldish or yellowish horse is a palomino, while a reddish or coppery one is a sorrel. But as long as Sam didn't hurt you, there's no real harm done. However, if you take anyone's horse again without asking, I'll swat your bottoms so hard you won't be able to set a horse for a month. All right?"

"All right," Nathaniel agreed.

"Then everything's forgotten. Now, you can ride Sam while I take you back to your wagon. It's time for bed. I'm ready to turn in too. Kyle, Lawrence, Miz Lashay, thank you for the coffee. I'll see you in the morning."

"Good night, Ranger. Same to you, Nathaniel and Isaiah," Lashay smiled.

"G'night, Miz Young, and both Mister Youngs," Isaiah replied.

It didn't take long for the rest of the children to discover Nathaniel and Isaiah had ridden Sam. By the next morning, they were all begging to ride one of the Rangers' horses. Since Sam and Ted were no longer carrying gear, Jim and Charlie allowed them to be put to work as babysitters, although Sam, true to his cantankerous nature, would only let the McGraw twins on his back. Even their older brother Tom couldn't approach the ill-tempered paint. That left only Ted, and with so many kids clamoring to ride, Adrian's great aunt, Ida Freeman, worked out a schedule. The smaller children rode double on the gentle gelding's bare back, while the bigger kids took their turn riding solo.

Late in the afternoon two days later, Jep left his usual position at the front of the wagons and rode back to Jim, reining Mack alongside Sizzle.

"Jim, I don't like the looks of that sky," he said, pointing toward the northwest.

"I don't either," Jim agreed. "I think we're in for a real whopper of a storm. In fact, I'd . . ."

"Bet your hat on it," Jep concluded, grinning.

The day had dawned exceptionally hot and humid, even for this part of Texas, and for the past several hours there had been no breeze at all to stir the oppressive air. The wagons had made little progress, the teams pulling them plodding along, sweat soaking their hides. Several of the women, and even a few of the men, who usually walked had been forced to give in to the conditions, climb into one of the wagons, and ride. Now, however, thick dark clouds were boiling up on the horizon, jagged lightning streaks already slicing through them.

The distant rumble of thunder rolled across the prairie.

"I have a feelin' this one's gonna be a real frog-strangler," Jep continued. "We'd better pass warnin' along the train, and start lookin' for a place to hunker down and ride this thing out. We could even be in for a twister."

"Not much luck of finding a spot to take shelter," Jim answered. "And I sure hate the thought of being stuck out here in the open."

"I seem to recollect a place a half-mile or so from here where there's a kind of dip in the land," Jep replied. "Might be our best bet, in fact our only one."

"If we get a cloudburst, will it flood?" Jim asked. "We sure can't chance gettin' caught in a gullywasher."

"Should be all right, since it's a broad section, and any water will spread out and stay shallow. Once we reach it we can turn the wagons along a bank, without goin' all the way to the bottom."

Just then Daisy Cutler, who was taking her turn on Ted along with Bonita BonSecoeur, walked the horse up to the pair.

"Ranger Jim, I sure want to thank you for letting us ride your horse," she said.

"You need to thank Charlie, not me," Jim answered. "Ted's his horse."

"You mean Ranger Chip?" Bonita asked.

"That's right, but that will have to wait," Jim

said. "There's a big storm brewing, so I need you to jump down off Ted and go back to your own wagons. We're going to have to find shelter right quick. Are the McGraw twins still riding Sam?"

"The last we saw them they were," Daisy answered. "That was a while ago, though."

"They were lollygagging behind the last wagon," Bonita added.

Another clap of thunder, much louder, announced the storm was quickly approaching.

"Jim, we've got to get these wagons movin' fast right now!" Jep urged. "I'm gonnna have Adrian stop the train so everyone can jump into a wagon, then get the teams runnin'. We're just about out of time."

"Trouble brewing?" Flavius Mannion asked, when his wagon rolled up next to the lieutenant and scout.

"Sure is," Jim answered. "A monster of a storm. Flavius, can you pull your wagon out of line and keep an eye on Daisy and Bonita until their folks reach you?"

"I certainly can," Mannion agreed. "They'll be safe with me for a few minutes."

"All right. Girls, you wait right here with Mister Mannion until your folks drive up. Turn Ted loose, he'll stick close by. Jep, you go ahead and have Adrian call a halt. I'll round up the other men and spread word for everyone to get into a wagon. Soon's that's done, I'll have Bill let you know, then you can head for that hollow fast as these teams can move. Let's just pray we beat that storm."

"What about you?" Jep asked.

"I've got to try and locate Nathaniel and Isaiah!"

With that, Jim whirled Sizzle to gallop away. A vivid bolt of lightning rent the clouds over their heads, and the first huge, cold drops of rain spattered the dusty earth.

The storm broke in its full fury just as the first wagons began their descent into the meager shelter of the shallow depression. Jep ordered the wagon drivers to turn off the trail to the right, hoping the slight upslope would provide enough of a windbreak to keep the wind from overturning any of the rigs, and would also bring them sufficiently lower than their surroundings to protect against lightning strikes. Before half the train had made the hollow, the wind increased in fury, while the rain became a blinding downpour. The sky turned dark as late dusk, the inky blackness shattered whenever lightning tore through the clouds.

Smoky McCue, slicker-covered, hat pulled low and held in place by its chinstrap, raced up to Jep and slid his steeldust gelding, Soot, to a halt.

"It'll be a miracle if we don't lose some of these wagons," he screamed to be heard over the howling wind. "Wind's gonna topple a few for sure."

"Mebbe not," Jep shouted back. "There's only five left to go. Ride on back there and hurry 'em up, will ya? Looks like Fletcher's mules are givin' him trouble."

"Sure thing."

Smoky headed Soot back to the Harrises' wagon, spun his horse, grabbed the off mule's harness, and spurred Soot. The gelding dragged the recalcitrant mule along, its mate forced to keep pace or be jolted off its feet. A moment later, the Harrises' wagon turned into the hollow, the rest soon following.

"Nothing to do now but ride it out," Jep told Smoky, once all the wagons were stopped. "Might want to get off your horse and under a rig."

Before Smoky could respond, Charlie Blawcyzk rode up, accompanied by Ty Tremblay.

"Smoky, Jep, either of you seen my dad?" he asked.

"Last I knew he was tryin' to locate the McGraw twins," Jep answered. "They were ridin' Sam somewhere behind the wagons."

"I've gotta find him," Charlie shouted, starting to turn Splash. Smoky grabbed Splash's reins.

"You can't find anything in this storm," he said. "You'll only get lost yourself, or mebbe get crushed by your horse if he slips and goes down. Your dad can take care of himself."

"What about those kids?" Charlie protested.

"They're probably already safe with your dad," Jep replied.

"Jep's right, and you know Sam won't let anything happen to him or his rider," Smoky added. "Best thing you can do is just wait here until this storm blows over. Once it does, your dad'll come riding up, wonderin' what the fuss was about."

"Smoky and Jep are right. The lieutenant knows what he's doin'," Ty said. "He'll be fine, you'll see. So will Isaiah and Nathaniel."

"Reckon you're right."

Reluctantly, Charlie gave in. He huddled miserably in his saddle while the rain beat down.

For the next forty minutes, the storm raged, pounding the wagon train with its full fury. The wind increased to a deafening roar, buffeting the wagons, the rain practically a solid wall. A torrent of water began coursing through the hollow. Men and women eyed the rising waters with trepidation, even as they struggled to hold the terrified mules, horses, and oxen from breaking away.

"Sounds like a twister comin'!" Smoky called to Jep, when the wind began shrieking with the voices of a thousand demons.

"If it is, you'd better pray to God it swerves off before it reaches us," Jep called back. Both men, along with Charlie and Ty, were hunkered alongside the Chatmans' wagon, hanging onto their horses' reins for dear life.

"We gonna make it through this?" Adrian screamed, from where he and his father were holding their team.

"I dunno," Jep shouted. "All we can do is hang on."

The tempest roared even louder, sounding like a freight train bearing down on the wagons. Just when Smoky was convinced the wind would carry the wagons off, it suddenly switched direction, and rapidly died down. Within fifteen minutes, the skies began to clear, the deafening thunder now merely muttering in the distance. Slowly, men, women, and children emerged from their wagons.

"Everyone seems to be safe," Smoky noted. "I'll ride back and make sure."

"I'll go with you, then start lookin' for my dad," Charlie said.

"There's no need, Chip. Look."

Smoky pointed toward the rear of the column of wagons, to where Jim, holding Sizzle to a shuffling walk, was leading Sam, with a thoroughly drenched Isaiah and Nathaniel still perched on the paint's back. Jim stopped at the McGraws' wagon, where Ivy and Terrence, the boys' parents, and older brother Tom anxiously waited.

"Nathaniel! Isaiah! Praise the Lord you're safe!" Ivy shouted.

"Safe until I get my hands on them," Terrence rumbled. "Where did you get off to? What were you thinking, disappearin' and scarin' your mother half to death like that?"

"You're in big trouble now," Tom smirked.

"Hush, Thomas!" Ivy ordered. "Nathaniel, Isaiah, your father is right. Now get off that horse, and don't plan on riding him again anytime soon. You're also going to get your britches swatted."

"Aw, Ma," Nathaniel protested. "We were just lookin' for Indians followin' us."

"Yeah, or outlaws," Isaiah answered. "Can't have them sneakin' up on us."

"Like I've told you boys, bet a hat there aren't any Indians or outlaws in these parts," Jim said.

"You mean we're never gonna get to see any shootin'?" Isaiah whined.

"You'd better hope not," Jim chuckled.

"You two get inside the wagon, and leave the Rangers worry about Indians and outlaws," Terrence ordered. "Lieutenant, I thank you for finding my boys and bringing them back safe."

"No thanks necessary," Jim answered. "Besides, they weren't hard to find. Sam won't stray far from me, so he was waitin' right behind the last wagon. Only problem was the rain came down so hard no one could see more'n a hundred feet. Once it stopped, I spotted your boys right quick."

"Nevertheless, we're grateful," Ivy answered.

"I'd better check on the others," Jim stated.

"I'll be back to check on the boys later. Try not to be too hard on 'em. They remind me of myself when I was their age."

"All right," Terrence agreed.

Jim turned Sizzle and headed to where Smoky and the others waited, next to the Chatman wagon.

"See you found those two all right," Adrian said.

"Yeah, I knew Sam wouldn't go off with 'em," Jim answered. "Now we'd best find out about the rest."

"Everyone, look!" Frances cried, pointing to the eastern sky. There, not one, but two brilliant rainbows arced across the heavens. Everyone stopped what they were doing to gaze at the beautiful sight.

"Wow! That's really something!" Dwain exclaimed.

"I believe the Lord is telling us we're welcome in this land," Frances replied.

"I'm certain He is," Jim agreed, adding under his breath, "however, it's not the Lord I'm worried about."

"Mebbe He is, but we've still got a long way to go," Jep reminded her. "So let's see what damage has been done."

Miraculously, the only storm damage was some torn canvas on two of the wagons. The hollow drained almost as rapidly as it had filled, so within an hour Jep had the wagons moving again. They made camp shortly before sunset. Just before supper, Devon Jones proposed a brief prayer service of thanksgiving for their deliverance from the storm.

"You and your Rangers will join us, won't they, Lieutenant?" he asked Jim. "I trust you're men of faith."

"I reckon we will, Reverend," Jim answered. "Long as you remember to call me Jim, that is. Far as being men of faith, I can't speak for all my men, but Charlie and I sure are. Born and raised Catholic, and still try to get to Mass every Sunday. 'Course, bein' on the trail so much sometimes makes that impossible."

"I had a feeling your faith in God is strong. I haven't heard you curse or take a drink of liquor . . . Jim," Jones replied. "Nor your son."

"I have to confess I like a good beer," Charlie admitted, "but I do try to follow the Commandments."

"And I purely enjoy playin' poker," Jim added.

"What about you, Lieutenant Huggins?" Jones questioned.

"Southern Fried Baptist, both me and Dan," Huggins chuckled.

"Same here," Steve Masters said.

"Far as me, I'm a Methodist," Smoky declared.

"Yeah, there's a Methodist to his madness," Jim laughed. "Oof!"

He grunted when Smoky shot a hard back-handed slap to his stomach.

"Don't mind Jim, Reverend. He's just been out in the hot Texas sun for way too many years. It's addled his brain," McCue stated.

"How about you, Ty?"

"I believe in the Bible and Our Lord Jesus Christ as Saviour," the young Ranger declared.

"Bill?"

"I believe in God too, but I find him more in the outdoors than any church," Dundee explained.

"Johnny, I haven't heard you say anything," Jones continued.

"I'm sorry, Reverend, and I mean no disrespect to any of you, but I don't believe in any of that. Far as I'm concerned life is what it is right here and now, not some paradise waiting on the other side of the Great Divide. That doesn't mean I won't come to your service. I'll do that to please you and the lieutenant here."

"The only One you need to please is God, Johnny," Jones softly replied. "And you will be welcome at the service, even in your dis-belief."

"We'll be there," Jim assured him.

"Fine. Plan on seven thirty."

As Reverend Jones had promised, the service was brief. After some prayers of thanksgiving and a short sermon, the preacher asked Christine

Fletcher, accompanied by her husband Joe on a battered guitar, to conclude the service with a hymn.

Christine stood on a wagon seat, overlooking the gathering. She was a buxom woman in her early fifties, who wore her hair piled high on her head and gathered at the nape of her neck. Joe, about the same age and balding, sat at her feet. Jep Hamilton, harmonica at the ready, stood next to the wagon tongue.

"I believe all of you know this song, except perhaps for some of our Ranger friends," she began. "So please help me, especially on the refrain. Now, all join in with *Go Tell It on the Mountain*."

Jep blew the first notes on his harmonica, while Joe strummed the opening chord on his guitar. Then, Christine lifted her sweet voice into the evening air.

"Go, tell it on the mountain,
"Over the hills and everywhere
"Go, tell it on the mountain,
"That Jesus Christ is born.
"While shepherds kept their watching,
"O'er silent flocks by night,
"Behold, throughout the heavens
"There shone a holy light."

"Everyone put your hands together and sing . . ."

"Go, tell it on the mountain,
"Over the hills and everywhere
"Go, tell it on the mountain,
"That Jesus Christ is born.
"The shepherds feared and trembled,
"When lo! Above the earth
"Rang out the angels' chorus
"That hailed our Saviour's birth.
"Go, tell it on the mountain,
"Over the hills and everywhere
"Go, tell it on the mountain
"That Jesus Christ is born.
"Down in a lowly manger,
"The humble Christ was born
"And God sent us salvation
"That blessed Christmas morn.
"Go, tell it on the mountain
"Over the hills and everywhere
"Go, tell it on the mountain
"That Jesus Christ is born." [1]

---

1 While today *Go Tell It on the Mountain* is considered a Christmas carol, it is in fact a traditional Negro spiritual, and was originally sung throughout the year, not just at Christmas time.

CHAPTER NINE

Two days later the wagons were crossing a slow-moving creek, without incident . . . until Charlie's new gelding decided without warning to roll in the water, dumping his rider and thoroughly soaking him. Charlie grabbed the paint's reins once both regained their feet and dragged him from the creek, threatening his horse with various and severe repercussions. Raucous laughter arose from the creek bank.

"Hey Chip, why you takin' a bath?" Dan called. "It's not Saturday."

"It ain't, but I'm sure glad he did," Ty answered. "He was smellin' worse'n a three day-dead polecat."

"Don't insult the polecats, Ty," Bill said. "They smell like a rose compared to Chip."

"Charlie, I thought you named that horse Splash for his splashes of white," Jim said, laughing. "Didn't realize you named him 'cause he likes to splash in the water. You wanna do that once more?"

"He pulls that again he'll be stayin' in the water, permanently," Charlie threatened, at which point Splash placed his nose to Charlie's chest and pushed hard, shoving him backwards into the creek yet again.

Charlie stumbled from the creek, muttering. He stalked up to his horse, who promptly put his head over Charlie's shoulder and sighed happily.

"Splash you, aw, doggone it, I can't stay mad at you, boy," Charlie said, scratching the gelding's ears. Splash was finally letting his ears be handled without fuss.

Jep Hawthorne rode up.

"Are all you Rangers gonna take a bath, Jim, or are we gonna keep movin'?"

"No, only Charlie," Jim answered. "We'll be right along."

Once the crossing was completed, as usual the Rangers strung out alongside the wagons. Jim and Smoky were alongside the Fletchers' wagon. Jim was whistling softly as they rode along.

"Jim, I couldn't hear you singing with us during the prayer meeting," Christine chided him. "You know when you sing you pray twice. Are you shy about singing?"

"Christine, be real grateful Jim didn't sing," Smoky answered, chuckling. "You know how the Lord gives each of us different talents and abilities? Well, He sure didn't give Jim here any musical skill. Jim's voice can peel paint off a barn. In fact, one time about seven or eight years ago we were surrounded by a bunch of

Comanches. There were Apaches, Kiowas, and Sioux mixed in. Even a couple of Osage. There must've been more'n a hundred of them, mebbe two hundred. We were out of ammunition, those Indians were closin' in, and things sure looked bleak. I figured we were goners for certain. Then all of a sudden, Jim starts into singin'. Next thing you know all those Comanch' turned tail and ran like the devil hisself was after 'em. Hearing Jim's voice, I'm sure they were convinced he was. No, Jim saved our lives, but my ears still hurt just recollectin' that day."

"Smoky, stop lyin' to these folks," Jim protested. "You know darn well there've never been any Sioux in Texas."

"All right, I exaggerated a trifle," Smoky admitted.

"Christine, Joe, we'll be by again a bit later," Jim said. "Gonna head back and check the other wagons."

The day grew excessively hot and humid, even for Texas, heat rising in shimmering waves from the parched earth. Progress was slow due to the heat, both man and beast wilting under the extreme temperatures. By the time Jep called a halt for the night, with only five miles made that day, everyone's tempers were frayed. When Jep spat a stream of tobacco juice into the dust alongside eighty-six year old Shirley Bell's wagon, some

117

of it splattered on her mules' hooves. The widow stalked up to him and slapped his cheek hard.

"Mister Hawthorne!" she exclaimed. "I've put up with your nasty tobacco chewing because you're our guide, but I will not tolerate your spitting that awful stuff on my animals!"

"Please, Shirley, I'm positive Jep didn't mean to hit your mules," Kyle Young, another of Adrian's uncles, tried to soothe the angry woman. "It was just an accident."

"If he does it again I just might 'accidentally' take his gun and put a bullet right between his eyes," Shirley retorted.

By the time the animals were cared for and everyone gathered for supper, nerves were still on edge. Bill and Jep had been unsuccessful at hunting any game for the past several days, so instead of fresh meat supper was once again bacon, beans, and corn pone.

Hearing the grumbling as the meal was dished out, Jim made an announcement.

"Listen, everyone, I'm as tired of bacon and beans as all of you. I've been saving this surprise for the right time, and I believe this is it. Tomorrow for breakfast, I'll make my famous stick-to-your-ribs flapjacks. I guarantee you'll enjoy 'em."

"Not your hotcakes, Jim," Smoky protested. "The animals have enough weight to haul, without addin' more from your lead sinker hotcakes.

Besides, we've got several stream crossings ahead. You fill these folks with your hotcakes and they'll sink, or get stuck so deep in the mud they'll never get out, sure as shootin'."

"Smoke, I'm sick and tired of your bellyachin' about my cookin'," Jim snapped.

"Not as sick and tired as I am of eatin' your cookin'," Smoky shot back.

"That's it, McCue. You want a bellyache, I'll give you a real bellyache . . . a lead one!"

Jim grabbed for the Colt on his left hip. Smoky drew and shot a split second before Jim brought his gun level. Jim screamed in pain, clutched his chest, and pitched backwards.

"You . . . you shot my dad!" Charlie shouted, yanking his own gun. Smoky whirled to face him. Charlie aimed just above the sergeant's belt buckle and fired. Smoky grunted, clawed at his belly, jackknifed, and crumpled.

Powdersmoke hung heavy in the thick, humid air, while the stunned onlookers stared at the two men lying sprawled in the dirt, one motionless, the other with hands clamped to his middle as he writhed in agony. Charlie stalked up to Smoky, gun still at the ready.

Smoky looked up at him and groaned.

"You might've put a bullet in my belly, Chip, but even with a .45 slug in it, my gut still don't hurt as bad as when it's full of your father's hotcakes."

"Then I reckon I should put you out of your misery."

Charlie aimed his six-gun at Smoky's chest.

"Don't do it, Charlie. He ain't worth the powder to blow him away. Bet a hat on it."

Everyone turned in disbelief to see Jim pushing himself to his feet, laughing.

"You mean you're not shot, Lieutenant?" Dwain Chatman asked.

"Nah," Jim answered, sliding his gun back in its holster. "The kids, particularly Isaiah and Nathaniel, have been pesterin' us about seein' a bit of shootin', so we figured we'd oblige 'em. Just been waitin' for the right time. With everyone so cranky, this seemed like it."

"We thought it'd break the tension some," Smoky added, dusting himself off and pulling out the makings. "So we loaded our guns with blanks and put on a little show for y'all."

"Or more likely scare us half to death," Frances stated. "However, I guess there's no real harm done."

"How about it, boys?" Jim called to the McGraw twins. "Was that enough gunplay for you?"

"It sure was, Ranger Jim," Isaiah answered. "Can you show us how to shoot like that?"

"Mebbe when you're a bit older you can learn," Jim answered.

"I'd bet Ranger Steve can shoot faster'n anybody, even the other Rangers," Joey shouted, from where he stood alongside Steve Masters. "Ain't that right?"

"I'd rather not find out," Steve chuckled. "The lieutenant's awful good with a six-gun."

"Enough talk about guns. Get back to your supper, all of you kids. You need to finish before it storms," Ivy McGraw ordered. She glanced at the sky, where distant lightning flickered on the northern horizon.

"No need to worry about rain tonight, Mrs. McGraw," Jep assured her. "That's only heat lightning. Any storm that far off'll dry up before it reaches here. Tell you what, if it'll make you feel better, after supper we'll sing a mite. I'll teach y'all *The Old Chisholm Trail.*"

"That sounds like a fine idea," Christine agreed. "I'd love to learn a cowboy song or two."

"It'd be a real accomplishment just to learn all the verses to *Chisholm Trail*," Jep chuckled. "There's supposed to be more'n a hunnert of them. Story goes only one cowpoke managed to learn 'em all, and when he tried to sing the entire song in a saloon one night he was gunned down before he got halfway through. But we can sing fifteen or so before we turn in."

Once supper was done, most of the emigrants gathered around Jep, who held his harmonica.

"You're all gonna sing the chorus after each verse," he ordered. "It goes like this: '*Come a*

121

ty yi yippee yippee yay, yippee yay, come a ty yi yippee yippee yay.' Now I'll play it once to give you the tune, then we'll start. Every time we reach the chorus, I'll point at you. I'm even gonna let Jim sing."

He spat a stream of tobacco juice into the dust.

"Ready?"

Jep placed his harmonica to his lips, and softly blew the notes.

"All right, here goes."

"Come along boys, and listen to my tale, gonna tell you my troubles on the ol' Chisholm Trail."

"All of you."

"Come a ty yi yippee yippee yay, yippee yay, come a ty yi yippee yippee yay."

The singing lasted until nearly midnight, Christine and Joe Fletcher joining Jep in leading the song. Everyone slept peacefully that night, caressed by a cool northerly breeze, which finally broke the day's heat.

The opinions of Jim's breakfast were split just about evenly, half in favor of his notoriously heavy flapjacks, half complaining their stomachs would never be the same. One thing all agreed on: those flapjacks were certainly filling. No one was eager for dinner, so noon came and went with only a brief stop to water the animals and give them a breather. The northerly breeze had persisted, freshening as the day progressed, so with the cooler weather they had been making good progress.

Jim was riding alongside Adrian Chatman, a few wagons back from the head of the train, when Isaiah and Nathaniel came trotting up to them on Sam, followed closely by their brother, Tom, and Gator Crown on Ted.

"Ranger Jim!" Tom called excitedly.

"Yeah, Tom. What seems to be the trouble?"

"Indians! Over yonder!"

"I've told you boys before, there aren't any Indians left in these parts. You've been readin' too many dime novels."

"Me and Isaiah can't hardly read at all, yet," Nathaniel protested. "And there are so Indians. Look over there. Smoke signals!"

Nathaniel pointed to a column of thick black smoke staining the northern horizon. It grew rapidly in size, coiling and writhing like an angry snake.

"Boys, that's not an Indian smoke signal," Jim stated. "I need you to do something for me. Ride back and find Lieutenant Huggins and send him up here. I believe he was with Bull Mason. Also, if you see Scout Dundee, please tell him I need to talk with him, right away. Then get back to your folks. Turn Sam and Ted loose, they'll stick with the other horses. No lollygaggin' now."

"Then those are Indians gettin' ready to attack us," Gator insisted.

123

"No, like I said, there's no Indians, but I need Lieutenant Huggins right away. Do as I asked and get him for me."

"We're on our way, Ranger," Isaiah answered. He turned Sam and sent him back along the column of wagons.

"What is that, Jim? A fire?" Adrian asked as soon as the boys were out of earshot.

"It sure is, a prairie fire. A big one. With this wind gettin' stonger, it's liable to be right on top of us before long."

"Do you have any idea what started it?"

"Probably dry lightning from those thunderstorms last night."

"Dry lightning?"

"Yep. This time of year, quite often thunderstorms will produce a lot of lightning and wind, but little if any rain. A lightning bolt'll hit the ground and set dry grass or brush afire. Add in no rain and a lot of wind and you get a wildfire that can last for weeks and travel for miles, chewin' up everything in its path."

"Is there anyplace we can take shelter?"

"That's why I sent for Jim and Bill. They know this part of Texas a lot better'n I do. If there's anywhere we can hole up and wait out this fire, they'll know it."

A moment later Jim Huggins rode up, with Bill at his heels.

"Jim, some of the boys said you needed us right

away. Somethin' about Indians," Huggins said.

"No Indians, but a lot more trouble than a whole passel of Comanch'," Jim answered. "Take a look over there."

Huggins cursed softly when he spotted the billowing smoke.

"That thing's movin' like a runaway locomotive on a downhill grade. We ain't got much time."

"Tryin' to make the Trinity's our best bet," Bill suggested. "It's only a few miles from here."

"You're right, but it'll be real close. Even if we make the river there's no guarantee that blaze won't jump it," Huggins replied.

"Is the Trinity deep enough to roll the wagons into and mebbe wet 'em down?" Jim asked.

"It is in a lot of spots," Huggins answered. "There's some fairly high banks that might help too. Also a couple of small lakes that might work."

"Sure wish I could tell whether that fire's on both sides of the river, or just this one," Bill said.

"That won't really matter if we can't reach the river in time," Adrian answered.

"Adrian, the fire won't be our only worry if we do have to stay in the Trinity all that long," Huggins replied.

"What do you mean?"

"The Trinity's chock full of gators and water moccasins. Even the alligator gars can be nasty," Huggins explained.

"Still, it sounds like the river is our only option."

"You're right, so let's get these wagons rollin'," Huggins ordered.

Swiftly, everyone was gotten into wagons or on horseback, then the teams whipped into a run. The ominous cloud of smoke seemed to grow with each passing minute. By the time the wagons neared the Trinity, the acrid odor of burning brush could be detected, and the smoke's base glowed orange from the flames.

"We gonna cross the river, or hunker down in it?" Jim asked when they neared its banks.

"Lookin' at the size of that blaze, we'd better find a wide and deep section and hope to God it protects us," Huggins answered. "That thing's big enough to jump the river, easy. The Trinity coils back and forth like a sidewinder, so our best bet is to find a stretch parallel to the direction the wind's blowin'. That way, with any luck the fire'll go past without getting too close to the river. The brush along the banks won't be quite as dry, so that should slow it some too."

The livestock, terrified by the approaching flames, needed no encouragement to plunge into the turbid waters of the Trinity. Huggins had the teams turned upstream, to where the banks were a bit higher than in most spots. At that location, the river was nearly a hundred yards wide, and the water was deep enough to reach over most of the animals' shoulders.

"Everyone who can, get into the water," he ordered. "Blindfold your livestock so they can't see the flames. Wet the blindfolds first. Also wet a rag or bandanna and cover their noses. That'll cut the smell of smoke and make 'em less likely to panic. Once that's done, cover your own faces. Then get more wet rags or buckets and start splashin' water on your wagons. Get them as soaked down as you can. Keep an eye on the kids and old folks. Make sure they stay under canvas, but if a wagon catches fire be certain someone is there to grab 'em when they jump. We don't want anyone drownin'."

Drivers jumped from their seats into the almost neck-deep water, covering their animals' heads and gripping their harnesses tightly, while speaking soothingly to them. The same was done with the saddle horses. Men and women frantically tossed water onto the canvas covers. Even the older children and some of the elderly travelers helped, reaching with buckets from their shelter in the wagons to scoop water from the river and wet down the inside of the canvas.

The searing heat of the approaching fire could now be felt, despite the protection of the water. Horses whinnied in fear, mules brayed and oxen lowed in terror. Soft prayers could be heard, along with curses from some of the men. Ashes, along with burning embers, began falling from the sky, threatening to set the wagons ablaze.

"Jim, it looks like it's burnin' on both sides of the river," Smoky shouted to Huggins from where he stood in the middle of the Trinity, holding tightly to his steeldust, Soot, who trembled with fear. Somehow, despite being in water up to his chest, Smoky had still managed to roll and light a quirly, which dangled from the corner of his mouth.

"It is," Huggins confirmed, "but I'm hopin' not for long. The river takes a wide loop and circles back on itself just above here. The land in between is mighty boggy. The northwest wind pushin' the fire along should also force it away from the far bank. If we have any luck at all, when the fire hits the bend it'll be pushed back away from the other side of the river, and whatever flames do manage to make it that far should burn themselves out in that swampland. All we can do is hunker down and hope for the best."

"And pray," Charlie added from where he stood between Ted and Splash.

Within fifteen minutes, the prairie fire was on top of the wagons, crackling flames leaping some fifteen to twenty feet in the air. The air grew so thick with smoke and ash that breathing became nearly impossible. All along the column of wagons, men, women, and children fought their individual battles against the flames, slapping wet rags or dashing buckets of water on any embers that landed in a wagon or on a canvas top.

Occasionally an animal screamed in pain when a hot ember landed on its neck, scorching its hide.

For what seemed an eternity, but was in fact less than thirty minutes, the emigrants and Rangers remained in the shelter of the Trinity, while the fire raged around them. Then, almost as quickly as it had arrived, the blaze was gone, pushed past by the furious wind. Its only remnants were a few smoldering patches and some acrid smoke still hugging the riverbanks.

"Looks like we've survived the worst of it," Jim Huggins announced.

"We were real fortunate, too," Bill added. "Just like you said, seems the fire got blown away from the west side of the river."

"Let's get out of this water, then we can check on everyone and take stock of the damage," Huggins ordered. "Adrian . . ."

"Over here, Lieutenant."

"We'll camp right here tonight. No point in tryin' to go any further. Everyone's too worn out."

"All right," Adrian agreed.

"I'll start the wagons rollin'," Jep said.

Soon, most of the wagons were out of the Trinity, with the exception of two which had sunk into the muddy bottom. The drivers' urging the mule teams to pull harder had no results.

"Dunno how we'll get this wagon unstuck," Miles Freeman muttered in frustration.

"Just get in front of your mules, Miles, and pull when I holler," Bull Mason ordered. "Adrian and I'll have you and Darcy Conway's rig out of here in no time."

"All right," Freeman shrugged. He jumped from his seat and stood in front of his team.

"Now, Miles!" Mason shouted. While Miles pulled hard on the mules' reins, Mason and Adrian, muscles bulging under their shirts, lifted the back of the wagon and shoved hard. Wheels creaking, the rig rolled about two feet.

"Again!" Mason shouted. This time, the wagon rolled nearly four feet.

"Again!"

After six attempts, Freeman's wagon finally pulled free of the muck, and rolled onto dry land.

"Now let's take care of Darcy," Mason said.

Five minutes later, the last of the wagons was on solid ground.

"Sure would hate to get Bull angry with me," Ty observed. "One punch from him'd tear a man's head off."

"All right, let's see what needs to be done," Jim ordered. "We don't have a lot of daylight left."

"There's no rush, Jim," Jep answered. "We're gonna stay here a couple of days and lick our wounds. There's at least one wagon with a cracked axle, another with a busted wheel, a few more damaged, and quite a bit of our supplies got ruined by soakin' in the river. We can't go anywhere until those wagons are fixed. Tomorrow, someone'll need to head over to Corsicana and buy more supplies."

A woman's cry of pain came from one of the wagons.

"That's Ellie Nolan," Mason exclaimed.

Willie Mae Madden, another of Adrian's aunts, hurried up to the group.

"Mr. Hawthorne, you aren't planning on moving anytime soon, are you?" she questioned.

"No, Miz Madden. We're going to rest a spell."

"That's good, because all of this jouncing hasn't done Ellie any good. She's going to have her baby, right now!"

CHAPTER TEN

At ten o'clock that night, Joshua and Ellie Nolan became the proud parents of a girl, their first-born. The baby was named Lacey, after Ellie's late grandmother. Reverend Jones baptized the infant with water from the Trinity, the same river which had most likely just saved all their lives.

Now, well before dawn the next day, Adrian and Bull were preparing to head for Corsicana. Jim Blawcyzk and Ty Tremblay would accompany them. The Rangers were already mounted, Jim on Sizzle, his big sorrel paint, and Ty on Bandit, his palomino quarter-mustang cross, waiting for Bull to finish readying his team.

"You *hombres* about ready to head out?" Jim asked. "It's a bit more than twenty miles to Corsicana, so even settin' a good pace it'll take us at least five hours. I'd like to get there by eleven so we can conduct our business, rest the horses and mules a bit, then turn around and get back here before dark."

"Just finishin' up," Bull answered. He gave a final tug on the harness to make sure it was secure, then climbed into the wagon seat along-side Adrian. He slapped the reins on his mules' rumps.

"Hup, Beauregard, Jezebel . . . get on up there!"

With snorts of protest, the mules broke into a shuffling walk.

Jim's old paint Sam whinnied to him when they passed the rope corral.

"You just stay there and rest a spell, pardner," Jim called back. "I'm not gonna be long. Nathan and Isaiah'll be by later to visit you, I'm sure. And I'll bring back more peppermints for you."

The trip to Corsicana was uneventful, although a bit slower than Jim had hoped. It was close to eleven-thirty by the time the entourage rolled down the main street, passersby staring at the unusual group, two Negroes and two Texas Rangers. They stopped to water the animals from a trough in the town plaza, then continued another block, where Bull pulled his team to a halt in front of McInroe's Mercantile.

"Sure feels good to get down and stretch," Adrian said, after jumping from the seat.

"Ty, you and Bull wait out here while Adrian and me get the supplies," Jim ordered, once he and Ty had dismounted and looped their horses' reins over the rail. "Keep a close watch. First sign of any trouble come get me."

"You expectin' trouble, Jim?" Ty asked.

"Always am, bet a hat on it. That's how a Ranger stays alive, you know that. Besides, some of these folks don't look all that friendly. Adrian, let's go."

A gray-haired, rather plump woman in her late fifties stood behind the counter. She smiled broadly when Jim stepped through the door, the smile quickly fading when she saw Adrian following. The look in her eyes became a mixture of fear and hatred.

"Elroy!" She called. "Elroy, get out here right now. There's a nigger in the store."

"What?" came a muffled voice from the back room. A moment later a balding, heavyset man about the same age as the woman shoved aside the curtain covering the doorway and joined her.

"What's that you said, Matilda?"

"See! A nigger!" The woman repeated, pointing at Adrian. "Do something, Elroy."

"What're you doin' in my store, boy?" the shopkeeper demanded.

"I'm here to purchase supplies. I'm leading a wagon train to west Texas, and we lost some of our staples when we had to outrun a brush fire and ride it out sitting in the Trinity. Some of our wagons got busted up pretty good too, so we're stuck by the river until we get them repaired."

"Looks like that fire done caught up to you, dark as you are, boy."

The shopkeeper laughed at his crude joke, then continued.

"Get out of this store before I take my shotgun to you."

"Adrian, let me handle this," Jim offered.

"And just who might you be?" the shopkeeper demanded.

"Texas Ranger Lieutenant Jim Blawcyzk. Some of us Rangers are escorting Mr. Chatman's party. Now, all we want to do is purchase the goods we need, then we'll be on our way."

"Never thought I'd see the day, Rangers protectin' niggers," the shopkeeper muttered. "Listen, Ranger, it wouldn't make no nevermind to me if Jesus Christ Himself was escorting that bunch of darkies. I don't take colored money."

"Adrian, give me some of your funds," Jim requested.

"Sure, Jim."

Adrian reached inside his shirt and removed several banknotes. Jim did the same, taking five yellowbacks from his vest pocket. Jim placed the bills on the counter.

"See here, Elroy. All this money looks the same to me. Mine's the same color as Mister Chatman's."

"Your money wasn't sittin' in no stinkin' nigger's pocket," the shopkeeper sneered. "So just pick up those bills and get on outta here. Go down the street to Solomon's place. I'm sure he'll be more than happy to do business with you. Those Jews ain't particular who they take money from, long as they can get their grubby hands on it. They'll take over the entire country if we let 'em."

"That's funny," Jim said, picking up the bills. "I've heard the same thing said about Negroes, too, that they're gonna take over the country. Hasn't happened yet. C'mon, Adrian, let's go. No use arguin' with a man dense as a rock, bet a hat on it. You'll just run out of breath."

"That's right, get out of here, both of you. Allowin' a filthy nigger to traipse right in here, leering at me and ready to violate a decent white woman the first chance he gets," Matilda cried, almost hysterically.

Adrian turned to face the woman. He bent at the waist in an exaggerated bow.

"Beggin' your pardon, Miz Matilda, ma'am, but I ain't about to go violatin' y'all," he stated, in an overblown Mississippi drawl. "I'se mighty particular about the white women I violate, yes'm, Miz Matilda, I sure is. They all gotta be pretty young things, nice'n tender with gentle eyes and real soft voices. Gotta have slim figures, too. Nice little pieces of fluff. Those are the kind I go around violatin', Miz Matilda . . . and Lordy, you ain't qualified, surely you ain't."

"Why you uppity son of a . . . ," the shopkeeper began, reaching for his shotgun. He stopped short when he found himself staring into the barrel of Jim's leveled Colt.

137

"I wouldn't try that if I were you, Mister," he warned. The Ranger was struggling to contain his laughter so he could hold the gun steady.

"Adrian, get on outside," he ordered.

"Yassar, Massa Ranger Jim, right away, Massa."

As soon as Adrian was through the door, Jim followed him, backing out and keeping the shop-keeper pinned with his Colt. Once outside, Jim burst into uncontrollable laughter.

"What the devil happened in there?" Bull demanded.

"We'll tell you on the way to the next store," Jim answered. "Suffice it to say Adrian gave me the best laugh I've had in a month of Sundays. Adrian, you sure put that harridan in her place."

"I probably shouldn't have," Adrian said. "Liable to stir up trouble, but I couldn't help myself."

"I wouldn't worry about it," Jim answered. "Besides, I'd bet my hat it's been a long time since that dried-up old prune's been violated by anyone . . . includin' her husband."

"There's a woman in there needs violatin'?" Bull said. "I'd be willin' to take on that chore."

"Trust me, Bull, if you met Miz Matilda, you'd swear off women for the rest of your natural-born days," Adrian replied. "Meantime, we'd best try our luck at the next place."

• • •

Solomon's General Store was located two blocks from McInroe's. The owner, Hyman Solomon, greeted Jim and Adrian warmly.

"I'm sorry you ran into trouble at McInroe's," he sympathized. "Sorry, but not at all surprised. While we Jews have been part of the community here in Corsicana for quite a few years now[2], there are still people hereabouts who don't like us bein' around. Try not to judge the entire town by a person like Elroy McInroe."

"We won't," Jim assured him.

"Fine, fine. Now, let me fill your order, then since it's almost noon you'll have dinner with us. It won't be fancy, but it will be filling. My Sophie makes the best *kugel* and potato *latkes* in the entire state."

"We don't want to put you out," Jim protested.

"We sure don't, and besides, do you want it known you broke bread with a colored man?" Adrian questioned.

"Pshaw. Who cares what the *meshugennehs* think? Let their tongues wag. Those that already hate us still will, and those that don't won't change their minds just because we had a Negro to dinner," Hyman scoffed. "Plus, Sophie would

---

2 Corsicana has been home to a large group of Jewish residents almost from the town's earliest days. In 1898 a large, distinctive onion-domed synagogue, Temple Beth-El, was erected. This historic structure still stands today.

139

tan my hide if she knew we had guests and I didn't invite them to dinner. So, enough with the arguments already. You'll buy the things you need, we'll load your wagon, then we'll eat."

As Hyman had assured them, the meal was indeed delicious, and filling. Despite Sophie's protestations they hadn't eaten nearly enough, the men were stuffed to the gills. Sophie insisted on sending the leftovers along with them.

Jim was half expecting trouble when they rode back past McInroe's. However, there was no sign of the shopkeeper or his wife, only two customers entering the store. He had no way of knowing McInroe was across the street in the Corsicana Cantina, where from behind the grimy windows he pointed them out to a group of hard-eyed riders.

"Dunno why we have to ride so far to intercept those niggers," Bud Ellison complained. "Seems like we should be able to jump 'em just a few miles out of town."

"You only worry about what to do when we catch up to 'em, and let me do the thinkin' for this outfit," Wes Caldicott answered.

Caldicott and his gang were trailing Adrian and his companions at a safe distance, making certain they would be far enough behind not to be discovered. Caldicott was a young man,

140

in his early twenties. While all ten riders were certified hardcases, Caldicott was the undisputed leader of the bunch, despite his relative youth. He was tall and lean, with dark hair and eyes. He was dressed in his usual outfit of a checked shirt, jeans, and a battered brown hat, with a red bandanna looped around his neck. The Smith and Wesson .44 revolver he favored had seen plenty of action. His horse was a light gray Appaloosa cross, with darker chest and random black spots over its body.

Ellison continued his complaining. He pushed back his Stetson to wipe sweat from his brow, revealing pale blue eyes and a shock of sandy hair.

"Still don't make sense to me, waitin' until they're almost at the Trinity to bushwhack that bunch."

"Bud, let me try to get this through your thick skull," Caldicott answered. "Then if you've still got questions, a bullet in your teeth'll put a stop to 'em right quick. First, McInroe couldn't tell us exactly where along the river those wagons are holed up. We need to follow that wagon until we're close enough to figure out where the others are at. Second, McInroe said the nigger who came into his store had a wad of bills big enough to choke a horse, which means it stands to reason there's got to be even more money on the rest of those coloreds. We don't want to chance killin' a couple men and takin' only what they've got when we have the opportunity to get much bigger game. McInroe said his wife doesn't want us ambushin' those men too close to town, either. We sure don't want to cross Matilda. We've done pretty well workin' for her, lettin' her set up travelers and freighters for us to rob. Who'd ever suspect an old woman storekeeper of being the brains behind this outfit?"

Caldicott paused to take a drag on his cigarette.

"Thirdly, and most important, there are two Texas Rangers protectin' those niggers. Why Rangers would be protectin' niggers I have no idea, but the fact remains they are. We have no clue how many other Rangers might be back with the wagons, so we need to be mighty careful, and make sure we catch them by surprise. I don't need to tell you tanglin' with the Rangers is an awfully ticklish proposition."

"Wes is right, Bud," Joe Sheely agreed. "Besides, McInroe told us Matilda said to make certain we're far enough from town so no one'd connect us to Corsicana, just in case anyone stumbles across the bodies before the buzzards and coyotes take care of 'em."

"With any luck we won't have to count on the scavengers," Caldicott answered. "If those niggers are camped alongside the river, we'll just toss their corpses in the Trinity and let them float away."

"All right, you're talkin' smart," Ellison finally

conceded. "You have any idea where we're gonna ambush that wagon?"

"Yep. Assuming they stick to the main road, we'll circle around 'em about two miles before the Trinity, where the road dips into a ravine. There's a grove of live oaks just off the trail which'll make perfect cover. Those *hombres* won't know what hit them."

"We'll be back with the others soon," Bull Mason noted, as his wagon topped a small rise, the mules slowing when they reached the summit. He started to slap the reins on their rumps to pick up the pace.

"Hold on a minute, Bull," Jim ordered.

"Somethin' wrong, Jim?"

Mason pulled his team to a halt.

"Mebbe. I dunno. I don't like the looks of that arroyo ahead."

"What do you mean?"

"I'm not certain. It's just a hunch, but something just doesn't seem right."

"I don't see anything amiss, Jim," Ty answered.

"I don't either," Jim agreed. "There's nothing I can put my finger on. Still, I've got a gut feelin' trouble's waiting for us down there. I'd bet my hat on it."

"I'm not gonna argue with your gut, that's for certain," Ty replied. "It's been right too many times before."

"What should we do, Jim?" Adrian asked.

"No way around that spot, so we're gonna head through that arroyo on the dead run, that's what," Jim explained. "If anyone is down there waitin' to drygulch us, they're expecting we'll be at a walk, especially with your wagon loaded down. That'll make us real easy targets. Let's not give 'em that chance. I'm guessin' if anyone is waitin' to jump us, they're hidden in that grove of live oaks. Bull, keep your mules at a walk until just before we reach those trees, then kick 'em into a run."

"All right, Jim."

Bull flicked the reins, putting his team into a slow walk, holding them back on the downslope. Once they reached the bottom, their speed increased slightly.

"Now, Bull. Go!" Jim ordered.

"Hyaah! Get up there, Beauregard, Jezebel!"

Mason slapped the reins hard on his mules' rumps, sending the startled animals leaping forward. Jim and Ty kicked their horses into a hard gallop, one on each side of the wagon.

Wes Caldicott watched in disbelief as the wagon thundered through the draw. With Bull keeping his team at a run, he had them alongside the grove of oaks before the outlaws could even react.

"Those Rangers must've sensed somethin'," Caldicott yelled, with an oath, when their quarry raced past.

"How, Wes?" Ellison asked. "There's no way they could've spotted us."

"I dunno, but they figured it out," Caldicott replied. "Well, they ain't gonna get away from us. After 'em."

Caldicott pulled his bandanna over his face, yanked his Smith and Wesson from its holster, and spurred his Appaloosa out of the trees, his men strung out behind. Caldicott aimed his gun at Jim's broad back and fired, but missed when his horse stumbled, the bullet ripping the air over the Ranger's head. The other outlaws followed suit, sending a fusillade of lead after the fleeing men.

"Knew there was something wrong," Jim shouted. "Bull, get those mules movin' faster."

He unshipped his Winchester, turned Sizzle, halted the gelding, and took aim at one of the raiders. He pulled the trigger, and his target was knocked out of the saddle with Jim's bullet in his chest. Jim whirled his horse around and tore after Bull and the others.

Ty had pulled out his six-gun and was turned in the saddle, firing back at their pursuers.

"Ty, you stick with Bull and Adrian. Keep goin' until you reach the others," Jim ordered. "They're only about a mile or so from here. Warn 'em there's trouble comin'."

"We'll never be able to outrun them," Ty protested. "Not with that heavy load. Bull's mules are worn out."

"I'm gonna pull up at the top of the draw to try'n slow 'em up a bit," Jim answered. "No matter what happens, don't stop until you reach the camp. Get movin'!"

Jim pounded Sizzle to the peak of the slope, then turned, stopped the horse, and fired once again, another robber spilled to the ground by his accurate shooting. Before Jim could dismount and take cover, a bullet tore into him, spinning him from his horse's back.

"We got one of 'em," Caldicott shouted in triumph. "Now let's get the rest."

Johnny Dexter glanced up at the sound of pounding hooves and gunfire. He spotted Bull Mason's wagon and Ty Tremblay, their pursuers close behind, as they raced around the bend to where the wagons were camped.

"Rangers! Trouble!" Dexter shouted, grabbing his Colt from its holster. The other Rangers had also heard the gunshots, and were already taking cover and readying their guns.

Johnny's first snap shot took the hat from one of the outlaws' heads. Several shots from the rest of the men slowed the raiders long enough for Bull to reach the dubious shelter of the wagons, parked haphazardly along the riverbank. The boggy ground had not provided enough solid land to form the wagons in a circle. Ty Tremblay jumped from his still running horse in a rolling dive, then scrambled under one of the wagons. Bull pulled his team to a halt, he and Adrian taking cover under the rig.

Another volley of shots from the Rangers sent the outlaws swerving for the shelter of the brush, except for one. That man was targeted by Bill Dundee, who was deadly accurate with his ancient Sharps single-shot buffalo gun. Bill put the Sharps' huge .50 caliber slug through the man's chest, punching an exit wound in his back as large as a fist, and slamming him hard to the dirt.

"Ty! What the devil's happened?" Smoky McCue shouted. "Where's Jim?"

"Dunno, Smoke. These bushwhackers were waitin' on us a mile or so back. Would've gotten us all, too, except Jim sensed something was wrong. He ordered us to get here fast as we could while he hung back to slow 'em up. Can't say what's happened to him."

"If my dad's not on their backs, they must've got him," Charlie cried, starting to come to his feet. "I'm goin' after him."

Smoky put a restraining hand on Charlie's shoulder and pulled him back down.

"You're not goin' anywhere, Chip," he ordered. "You'd be cut down before you got a hundred yards. Soon's we fight off these sidewinders, we'll go find Jim."

Jep sidled up to Smoky and settled alongside him. Further down the line of wagons, Jim and Dan Huggins were dug in, waiting for the outlaws' next move. Steve Masters and Johnny Dexter were hunkered down in a patch of scrub, while Bill Dundee had repositioned himself into Preacher Jones's wagon bed, well-protected by the thick oak sides.

"You think they'll try and wait us out, or try and rush us, Smoky?" Jep asked.

"I'd imagine they'll try and pick off a few of us, then, if that doesn't work, they'll rush us," Smoky replied. "They must realize we've got plenty of food and water, so we can outlast 'em. Doubt they'll wait much longer, since it'll be dark soon. Adrian . . ."

"Yeah, Smoky?"

"Make sure everyone's under cover, especially the women and kids. Have any man who has a gun and can use it be ready for when those *hombres* rush us. Be careful yourself, too. You don't want to catch a bullet in the back."

"No, I reckon I don't," Adrian agreed, grimly chuckling. "Dunno how much good my men'll be tryin' to hold off those raiders. The ones who can shoot have only hunted game, not men."

"As long as they can send bullets in those outlaws' direction, that'll be good enough," Smoky answered. "It'll give 'em a little more to worry about."

"All right," Adrian agreed. "C'mon, Bull, let's take care of business."

● ● ●

For the next forty-five minutes, the outlaws kept up a steady fusillade from the brush and bogs, the Rangers, Jep, and some of the emigrants returning their fire. With both sides dug in, none of the scores of bullets found a target. Finally, the raiders' guns fell silent.

"Either they're givin' up, or they're getting ready to rush us," Jep noted.

"Or they've figured out a way to get around behind us," Charlie said.

"I doubt that," Smoky disagreed. "Too many bogs and too much quicksand. They'll be chargin' us any minute now. All this brush'll give 'em some cover and make 'em hard targets to hit. We've got to stop 'em before they reach these wagons. If they get in among us, they'll have a good chance to pick us off, then finish off the women and kids. We can't let that happen."

Perspiration rolled down the lawmen's faces and soaked their shirts while they awaited the outlaws' charge. Tension mounted until, with a Rebel yell, the raiders burst from cover at a dead run, riding low over their horses' necks, zigzagging the mounts to keep from being easy targets.

"Here they come!" Jim Huggins shouted. He leveled his Winchester and fired, his bullet catching one of the outlaws in the shoulder and knocking him from his saddle. Bud Ellison slumped over his horse's neck and rode out of the fray when Ty put a bullet through his stomach.

Three more of the raiders were cut down, two by bullets, the third when his horse was shot from under him. That man landed head-first, breaking his neck when the horse went down.

Joe Sheely and Wes Caldicott managed to elude the rain of bullets and reach the wagons. A bullet from Caldicott's gun ended the life of Abraham Martin, a widower with three teenaged children. Before Caldicott could find another target, Bull Mason leapt from his wagon and dragged the outlaw leader off his Appaloosa. Caldicott landed on his back. Bull grabbed the renegade's shirt-front and pulled him to his feet. He drove a powerful punch into Caldicott's belly, a blow so ferocious Caldicott vomited blood as he doubled over. Bull next landed a punch to the point of Caldicott's jaw, the impact snapping his neck. Caldicott's eyes glazed and he dropped, head twisted at an awkward angle.

A bullet from Joe Sheely grazed Mason's neck, staggering him. Bill Dundee reversed his empty Sharps when Sheely galloped by, slamming the heavy rifle's butt across Sheely's middle. The impact knocked Sheely from his saddle to lay sprawled on the ground, moaning with the pain of several broken ribs.

Silence descended over the wagon camp, a gentle breeze rapidly dissipating the clouds of powdersmoke.

"I'm goin' to find my dad," Charlie declared, as he reloaded his pistol. "I've gotta find him before dark, bet a hat on it, and there ain't much daylight left. Rest of you can finish up here."

"All right, Chip," Jim Huggins agreed. "Ty, you go with him. Since you were the last one with the lieutenant, you'll have the best idea where to find him. Both of you be careful, just in case these renegades left a couple of men holding back."

Charlie retrieved his horse, threw the blanket and saddle on Splash's back, slid the bridle over the gelding's head, and swung into the saddle.

"C'mon, Ty, let's go."

"Shouldn't be too much further, Chip," Ty tried to assure his worried friend. "The arroyo where they ambushed us isn't far off. I'm sure we'll find your dad's just fine. As he'd say, I'd bet my hat on it."

"I sure hope you're right, Ty," Charlie answered, the anxiety in his voice clear. "The sun's just about down, and if we don't find him before dark . . ."

Charlie's voice trailed off. He pulled Splash to a halt, then stood in his stirrups to scan the horizon.

"Up ahead, Ty! It's Sizzle!" he shouted. "He's gotta be with Dad." He put Splash into a gallop.

As Charlie had said, a moment later they rode up to where Jim lay on his back in a large patch of prickly pear and cholla. A red stain spread over the downed Ranger's shirtfront. Sizzle was standing patient vigil over his rider, occasionally dropping his head to nuzzle Jim's face, then paw at his ribs. He looked up and whinnied at Charlie's and Ted's approach.

Charlie slid Splash to a stop alongside his father and leapt from the saddle.

"It's all right, Siz, we'll take care of him," Charlie told the paint, as he knelt at Jim's side.

"Dad!" he called, cradling Jim's head.

"Is he alive?" Ty asked.

"He's still breathin', but I can't tell how bad he's hit," Charlie answered. He opened Jim's shirt to reveal an oozing bullet hole just under his right shoulder.

"Least it appears the bullet didn't hit a lung."

Ty removed the canteen from his saddlehorn, dismounted, unscrewed the canteen's cap, and passed the vessel to Charlie.

"Try givin' him a little water," he suggested.

Charlie held the canteen to Jim's lips and dribbled a bit of water into his mouth. Jim sputtered, then choked. His eyes opened.

"Charlie. What're you tryin' to do, drown me?"

He attempted to push himself up, but fell back.

"Take it easy, Dad," Charlie ordered. "We'll get you help quick as possible."

"I'm all right, just took a bullet," Jim insisted.

"Listen to Chip, Lieutenant," Ty urged. "You're bleedin' pretty heavy."

Ty removed the bandanna from his neck and passed it to Charlie, who placed it over Jim's wound. Charlie then took his own neckerchief and used that to tie the bandage in place.

"That's the best we can do until we're back at the wagons, Dad," Charlie said.

"The wagons. Did . . . those . . . ?"

"No," Charlie answered before Jim could finish. "We fought 'em off."

"Good . . . good," Jim murmured.

"Chip, let's get him on his feet," Ty said. "Lieutenant, can you ride?"

"Bet a hat on it," Jim answered.

"We'll see," Charlie replied.

Jim was pulled to his feet and helped over to his horse. When he attempted to mount, dizziness overcame him, and he slumped against Sizzle's side.

"Dad, you'd best ride with me," Charlie said.

"Reckon you're right, Charlie," Jim gasped.

Charlie and Ty lifted Jim to Splash's back. The rugged Ranger let out a scream of agony when he hit the saddle.

"Your shoulder hurt that bad?" Charlie questioned.

"Not my shoulder, my butt," Jim replied. "Feels like a thousand needles are stuck in it."

"Mebbe not sewin' needles, but it probably sure

153

is full of cactus needles. We pulled you out of a big clump of prickly pear, Jim," Ty explained.

Despite the dire situation, he and Charlie couldn't help but chuckle at Jim's predicament.

"Don't worry, Dad. I'm sure Sam Tatum can take care of those, along with diggin' the bullet out of you," Charlie assured him, as he pulled himself onto Splash, settling in front of his father. Once Ty was also mounted and Jim had his arms wrapped around Charlie's waist, leaning against his son's back, the horses were turned back toward the Trinity, their pace held to a fast, steady walk.

CHAPTER ELEVEN

"Dad, looks like they found Jim," Dan Huggins called to his father, when he spied Ty and Charlie approaching the camp. "Appears he's been hurt."

"Go tell Sam Tatum he's got another patient coming," Jim Huggins replied. "I'll let the others know."

"Right away," Dan agreed.

Jim had once again slipped into unconsciousness, so Charlie and Ty rode straight for Tatum's wagon. By the time they reached it, the medical man, along with Dan, was already waiting. Ty immediately swung out of his saddle.

"Bring him right inside," Sam ordered.

"Soon as we get him off this horse," Charlie answered. "Dan, give Ty a hand gettin' my dad off my horse and carryin' him into Sam's rig, will you?"

"Sure thing, Chip. How bad's he hurt?"

"Took a bullet in his shoulder, and has some other, uh, injuries," Charlie explained.

Ty and Dan lifted Jim from Splash and carried him into Tatum's wagon, Charlie following.

"Put him on that cot over there," Sam ordered, indicating one of the two beds in his wagon. The other was occupied by Joe Sheely, whose ribs were tightly bound. He was in a deep sleep, brought on by the effects of the laudanum Sam had given him.

Jim was placed on the cot, and Sam knelt alongside him. By the time he had removed the wounded lieutenant's gunbelt and shirt, the rest of the Rangers had reached his wagon. Smoky McCue and Jim Huggins pushed their way inside.

"How is he, Sam?" Smoky questioned.

"Can't say for sure yet, but I believe he'll survive, long as I can find the bullet and dig it out," Sam explained.

Jim's eyes flickered open.

"Don't worry about me. I'm all right. What happened here?"

"We fought off those renegades," Smoky answered. "Killed all but three of 'em, and one of those won't last 'til morning. He took a bullet through his stomach. Other two are prisoners. One of 'em's right across from you, the other's under guard in Bull Mason's wagon."

"What about our folks?"

"We lost one man, Abraham Martin," Smoky said. "Bull Mason got grazed by a bullet, and Jep got clipped by another. Only other casualty was Joe Fletcher, who twisted an ankle divin' for cover."

"Lieutenant, you might think you're all right, but that's your opinion, and it's dead wrong," Sam broke in. "You're still losing blood, and that bullet has to come out. Let me get to work. After you rest, then you can continue this conversation. I've got one question before I start, however."

"What's that, Sam?" Jim replied.

"You don't mind an ol' nigger workin' on you? Lots of white folks wouldn't let a colored man touch 'em."

"Don't matter to me if you're purple with pink dots and green stripes, long as you can get the bullet out of me," Jim answered.

"I'll do my best," Sam promised.

Sam knotted a cloth and shoved it in Jim's mouth, for the Ranger to bite down on against the pain while Sam probed for the bullet.

"Chip, you might want to hold down your dad while I work on him," Sam suggested.

"Sure, Sam."

Charlie took up a position at the head of the bunk and placed his hands on Jim's shoulders, while Sam prepared his equipment. He liberally poured whiskey over Jim's shoulder and upper chest, dousing the bullet hole. That done, he placed his medical tools in a shallow pan, poured more whiskey over those, and waited a few minutes for them to sterilize. Finally, he lifted a probe and thin-bladed knife from the pan.

"Are you ready, Lieutenant?"

Jim nodded.

Sam had a deft touch with scalpel and probe, more skilled than many actual physicians. It only took him a few moments to locate the bullet and slide it out of Jim's shoulder. A few minutes more and the bullet hole was plugged, dressed, and bandaged.

"You're all set, Jim," Sam said, taping the final piece of bandage in place. "What you need now is rest. I can give you something to help with that."

"No laudanum," Jim ordered.

"I wasn't planning on it, although I do use it, as the prisoner over there can attest," Sam answered. "One thing we coloreds learned, out of necessity, was how to use wild herbs and plants for medication. In addition, we were taught plenty of home remedies by our parents and grandparents, who brought many of them over from Africa. I can brew up a tea which will dull the pain and help you sleep, without the mind-numbing effects of laudanum."

"That would be all right, I guess," Jim reluctantly agreed.

"Hold on a minute, Sam. You're not finished quite yet," Charlie objected.

"Charlie, not another word," Jim warned.

"What do you mean, Chip?" Sam questioned.

"Charlie . . ." Jim repeated.

"Sorry, Dad, but this has to be done. Sam, we pulled my dad out of a big clump of prickly pear and cholla. His backside is full of cactus spines, so many he could hardly sit my horse to ride back here. Those needles have to come out, or else they'll work their way in even deeper."

"Which means they'll fester," Sam concluded. "Your son's right, Jim. I'll need to remove those spines."

"You're not touchin' my *dupa*," Jim insisted.

Sam sighed. "Lieutenant, would you like your tombstone to read 'Here lies Texas Ranger James J. Blawcyzk, who died from an infection of his rump'? Because that's what will happen if you don't let me pull out those spines. I'm certain you've had to have cactus needles removed more than once in your career."

"But not from back there," Jim answered.

"Sam, let me handle this. No point arguin' all night," Smoky offered. "Listen, Jim, you gonna let Sam do what needs to be done, or do I have to take my gun barrel to your head and knock you out cold?"

"Reckon I couldn't stop you, lyin' here like this," Jim muttered.

"That's right," Smoky answered.

"So you're givin' me no choice."

"It's not me or any of your partners who aren't giving you a choice, Jim," Sam said. "It's those cactus needles. If they don't come out, the odds are you will develop an infection, which will most likely lead to blood poisoning and kill you."

"You win, Sam," Jim conceded.

"Now you're making sense," Sam replied.

"Chip, would you mind giving me a hand getting your dad's boots and pants off?"

"Not at all," Charlie grinned. "It'll give me a chance to get even for all the times he tanned my backside when I was a kid."

"You're still not too big for me to do it again. Keep that in mind, Charlie," Jim retorted.

Charlie pulled off Jim's boots, then unbuttoned his jeans and slid them off, followed by his woolen drawers.

"Help him roll onto his stomach, Chip," Sam requested.

"Glad to, Sam."

Charlie slid his hands under Jim's side and flipped him onto his belly.

"Chip seems to be enjoying his dad's predicament a bit too much, Ty," Dan noted.

"He sure does," Ty agreed, chuckling. "Wouldn't want to be in his boots once the lieutenant's up and around again."

Sam gave a low whistle, then tsk'd softly once he saw the number of cactus spines sticking from Jim's buttocks, backs of his thighs, and lower back.

"This will take quite some time, Jim," he stated. "It's also going to be quite a delicate procedure."

"Why?"

"Because you have so many needles in your rump it resembles a porcupine," Jim Huggins broke in, laughing.

160

"You sure got stuck, pardner, no 'butts' about it," Smoky added.

"Laugh now, all of you, but I'll have the last one, bet a hat on it," Jim gritted. "Don't y'all have something better to do than hang around here?"

"Not a thing, pardner," Smoky answered, still laughing. "Supper's not quite ready, so we can't eat yet. It's just about full dark, so there's not much to do until morning."

"Well, find something!" Jim snapped. "How about tryin' to locate those two men I shot? Here, you're only in Sam's way."

"They're not in my way at all," Sam disagreed.

"See, Sam says we're not botherin' him. Besides, you'd think a man'd be grateful to have his *compadres* with him in his time of need, wouldn't you, Lieutenant?" Ty asked Jim Huggins.

"Some men are just plain ungrateful, that's all, Ty," Huggins replied. To Jim he continued, "It's too late to search for those men tonight. That'll have to wait until sunup."

"If you're all about finished joking around, I'd like to get to work," Sam said.

"All right, we're done," Smoky chuckled.

"Jim, those spines in your backside aren't the only thing I'm worried about," Sam noted. "There's also a few needles which managed to lodge themselves in your lower belly and, um, privates. That's going to be the delicate part of this procedure, removing those."

"Removing the lieutenant's privates?" Dan deadpanned, one eyebrow raised.

"Not his privates, the cactus needles," Sam answered, trying to keep from laughing, but failing miserably.

"Glad y'all are finding this so hilarious," Jim grumbled.

"Chip, could you hold the lantern a little closer?" Sam requested. "I need more light before I get started. It's a shame my wife can't be here to assist, but Dahlia's with Ellie Nolan, helping with the baby."

"Sure, Sam."

Charlie lifted the lantern from its hook and held it closer to his father.

"There's no chance in the world I'd ever let your wife see me like this, Sam. I'd die first, bet a hat on that," Jim said.

"Which would probably happen," Sam answered. "I'm going to start."

Sam doused a pair of pliers and a set of tweezers with whiskey, then began by yanking at one of the larger spines sticking out of Jim's backside. Jim grimaced and jerked slightly when the spine was removed.

"The more you keep still, the faster this will go," Sam warned him. "As many spines are stuck in your hide, it's going to take long enough as it is. Jumping around will only prolong the agony."

Sam pulled the next spine, Jim yelping in pain when this one tore his skin as it was removed. Smoky winced in sympathy with his long-time riding pard.

"Y'know, I believe Jim's correct," he noted. "There's no point in any of us staying here watching, except for Chip. Supper must be ready by now. Besides, I could use some fresh air."

"Smoke, you're right," Jim Huggins agreed. "The others must be wonderin' how Jim's doin', so we'll let them know. Jim, we'll be back later to check on you."

"He'll most likely be sleeping, but stop by if you wish," Sam said.

"If you're goin', get goin'," Jim growled.

"All right, we get the point," Huggins replied, "or rather, I guess you did, Jim . . . lots of 'em."

Still laughing, he ducked out of the wagon, the others following.

It took Sam the better part of an hour to remove all the spines from Jim's buttocks and lower back. Once that was done, he had to clean off the blood which trickled from each wound, then coat the holes with salve and, lastly, tape clean bandages in place. Then, Jim was rolled onto his back so Sam could complete the delicate task of removing the remaining spines from Jim's belly and groin. Again, the wounds were coated with

163

salve, and finally, the sheets were pulled up to Jim's waist.

Sam straightened up, arched his back to relieve the cramped muscles, then poured water into a basin to wash his hands.

"I'm sorry that took so long, and that it hurt as much as I'm certain it did, Jim. I tried to be as careful as possible."

"It was more embarrassing than painful," Jim answered.

"I wouldn't doubt that for a minute," Sam agreed. "I'm also afraid to say it will be better if you don't try'n pull your britches on for a while, two or three days anyway. They'll just irritate the injuries. In addition, you won't be sitting a horse for a spell."

"I'll be up and around by tomorrow, bet a hat on it," Jim retorted.

"I'll take that bet," Sam answered. "I've been admiring your Stetson since we first met . . . and this will be a wager I can't lose."

"Dad, you'd better listen to Sam," Charlie urged. "A few days' rest won't hurt you . . . and you'll heal quicker if you take it easy for a spell."

"Speaking of rest, Jim, I'll brew that tea now," Sam said. "Chip, I don't need you any longer, if you'd like to get supper. If it's not too much trouble, could you bring some back for me? I'd like to keep watch over both my patients for tonight. Usually my wife would take a turn doing that, but she'll be with Ellie and her baby all night."

"It's no trouble at all. I'll see you in a bit," Charlie answered. "I'll want to spend the night with my dad anyway, so I can sit watch for a spell."

"I'd appreciate that. Take your time eating. Bolting food isn't good for a person's digestion," Sam cautioned.

Once Charlie left, Sam built a small fire outside of his wagon, boiled a pot of water, then mixed in several types of dried herbs and leaves, allowing the concoction to steep for several minutes. He poured the brew into a thick mug, straining it through a piece of muslin.

"Jim, I know this smells awful, but it really doesn't taste all that bad. It will dull some of the pain and also help you sleep," he noted, then passed the steaming mug to the Ranger. Jim wrinkled his nose at the odor.

"You're certain?" he questioned.

"Absolutely," Sam answered.

"All right."

Jim took a tentative sip, grinned slightly, then downed the rest of the tea in two large gulps.

"You were right, Sam. It didn't taste bad at all."

"I told you," Sam answered. "Now roll over on your stomach and lie down. I don't want you placing any pressure on your backside tonight, and you'll be sleeping shortly."

"All right." Jim shifted onto his belly, then Sam pulled the sheets up to his neck.

"Anything else you need at the moment?" Sam asked.

"Don't think so," Jim answered.

"Fine. Jim, as long as we're both here with no one else around, there's something I've been meaning to ask you."

"What is it?" Jim asked, with a yawn. The tea Sam had prescribed was already taking effect.

"Why are the Texas Rangers helping a bunch of colored folk? Not that we don't appreciate it, but it's kind of unexpected, to say the least."

"A couple of reasons, Sam," Jim explained. "First, we were asked to by the governor. Second, we Rangers don't like seein' innocent folks attacked for any reason, as has happened to more'n one group of Negro emigrants lately."

"What you say may be true, but it would have been quite simple for you and your men to merely ride away when those men attacked us. Then they could have wiped us out easily, while you would have been able to claim you Rangers were caught by surprise and overwhelmed by twenty, thirty, or even more outlaws. Heck, you could even have joined them. No one would have been able to question your account, or prove there were far fewer ambushers than you stated, especially considering the only victims would have been a bunch of coloreds."

"You don't know the Rangers very well," Jim answered, again yawning. "When we're given a job to do, we do it. In addition, those drygulchers didn't just attack your people, they also ambushed us. That makes it personal. No one bushwhacks a Ranger and gets away with it."

"Still . . ." Sam insisted.

"Nothing more to say," Jim said. "Except this. Sure, lots of people aren't happy to see Negroes movin' into Texas. However, most of those same people don't like havin' Mexicans, Irish, Chinese, Polish, Germans, and so on around either. You get my drift?"

"I guess so," Sam admitted.

"Good. Besides, there's one more thing. I like you folks, and I believe most, if not all, of my men do also. There may be one or two who don't, but if there are they'll keep their feelin's to themselves, and do the job they've been ordered to do. Bet a hat on it. Does than answer your question?"

"It does, Jim. It surely does," Sam answered.

"Good. Now I'm gonna get some shut-eye."

Jim started to murmur his evening prayers, but Sam's tea took effect before he was halfway done. Within five minutes, Jim was softly snoring.

By an hour after sunrise the next morning, Johnny Dexter and Bill Dundee returned with the bodies of the two men Jim had shot. They stopped at Sam's wagon to check on Jim and let him know the men had been found, dead.

"You won't be questioning either one of them," Bill informed the lieutenant. "Looks like they died real quick. You drilled both of 'em plumb center."

"Reckon they got what was comin' to 'em," Johnny added. "How about you, Jim? How you feelin'?"

"Like a man who's been shot," Jim answered.

"Men, I hate to interrupt, but I have to clean out the lieutenant's wounds and change the dressings," Sam said. "If it's not too much to ask, could you come back a bit later?"

"Sure," Bill agreed. "Jim, we'll see you after breakfast."

"I understand Abraham Martin will be buried before the morning meal," Sam said. "I'll allow Jim to attend if he feels up to it."

"Sam, neither you nor anyone else could keep me away. Bet a hat on it," Jim replied.

"Fine. Bill, Johnny, we'll meet you there."

Bud Ellison succumbed to his wounds sometime during the night. He and the other dead outlaws were buried in a common grave. Prayers were said over them by Devon Jones, with the Rangers, Jep Hawthorne, and a few men from the train as witnesses. That chore completed, it was time for the services for Abraham Martin.

Abraham's final resting place had been dug beneath a large cottonwood tree, on a knoll overlooking the Trinity. His three children, seventeen year old Peter, fifteen year old Josie, and fourteen year old Stuart stood alongside the grave, quietly sobbing as their father's canvas-wrapped body was committed to the earth.

"Lord," Devon Jones prayed, "Abraham Lorenzo Martin was a good man, whose only real loves on this Earth were his dearly departed wife, Tregertha, and his three children who stand before You today. His one reason for making the arduous journey to a new land in Texas was to provide a better life for those children. While, in Your Divine Will, Lord, You did not see fit for Abraham to reach his destination, all of us gathered here before You will be certain to help Abraham's children achieve his dream of owning a farm of their own in Texas. Amen."

"Amen!" echoed the men, women, and children gathered around the grave.

"Lo, though Abraham walks through the valley of darkness, Lord, we are certain You will bring him to the light, to rest in Your bosom, and be refreshed by still waters, such as those beside which we leave his earthly body today. Amen."

"Amen!"

"Abraham, be not afraid. God the Father, Our Lord and Saviour Jesus Christ, and the Holy

Ghost, will go before you always. Come, follow Them, and They will give you rest. Amen."

"Amen!"

Devon picked up some clods of earth and tossed them onto Abraham's body.

"Ashes to ashes, dust to dust. Lord, we send Abraham's soul to You. May he rest in Your heavenly light forever. Amen."

"Amen!"

"Peter, Josie, Stuart . . ."

Abraham's children took more dirt, sifting it through their fingers and sprinkling it on their father's body. As they did, and several of the men began shoveling dirt into the grave, Christine Fletcher's voice drifted over the congregation.

"Swing low, sweet chariot
"Comin' for to carry me home,
"Swing low, sweet chariot,
"Comin' for to carry me home."

"I looked over Jordan, and what did I see
"Comin' for to carry me home.
"A band of angels coming after me,
"Comin' for to carry me home."

"Swing low, sweet chariot
"Comin' for to carry me home,
"Swing low, sweet chariot,
"Comin' for to carry me home."

"Sometimes I'm up, and sometimes I'm down,
"Comin' for to carry me home
"But still my soul feels heavenly bound,
"Comin' for to carry me home."

"Swing low, sweet chariot
"Comin' for to carry me home,
"Swing low, sweet chariot,
"Comin' for to carry me home."

"The brightest day that I can say,
"Comin' for to carry me home.
"When Jesus washed my sins away,
"Comin' for to carry me home."

"Swing low, sweet chariot,
"Comin' for to carry me home,
"Swing low, sweet chariot,
"Comin' for to carry me home."

"If I get there before you do,
"Comin' for to carry me home."
"I'll cut a hole to pull you through,
"Comin' for to carry me home."

"Swing low, sweet chariot,
"Comin' for to carry me home,
"Swing low, sweet chariot,
"Comin' for to carry me home."

"If you get there before I do,
"Comin' for to carry me home,
"Tell all my friends I'm comin' too,
"Comin' for to carry me home."
"Swing low, sweet chariot,
"Comin' for to carry me home,
"Swing low, sweet chariot,
"Comin' for to carry me home."

CHAPTER TWELVE

The rest of that day was spent repairing damaged wagons, replacing shoes which a few of the mules had lost, and sorting through supplies to salvage whatever had not been ruined by soaking in the Trinity.

Jim spent an uncomfortable day, the effects of Sam's tea wearing off after only about three hours. Across from him, Joe Sheely was still in a laudanum-induced sleep, occasionally groaning or muttering something unintelligible.

Just past noon, Sam cleaned Jim's wounds and changed his bandages, but, despite his entreaties, Jim had refused any more tea, insisting he wanted to remain awake. At that, Sam decided he could not chance the Ranger reopening his shoulder wound, so he bound Jim's arm in a sling to prevent excess movement. Between the oven-like heat under the wagon's canvas cover, the pain of his wounds, and now almost unbearable itching where Sam had removed the cactus spines, Jim was ready to leave his cot, Sam's orders or no. The only thing keeping him in that stuffy wagon was the fact Sam had hidden his clothes.

At suppertime, Jep Hawthorne stuck his head under the flap.

"You up for some company, Jim?" he asked.

"I reckon," Jim answered, with a shrug.

"Good."

Jep stepped into the wagon, followed by Steve Masters and young Joey Stark. The youngster had attached himself to the Ranger after the armadillo incident, and they were now practically inseparable.

"Jim, wish I could have gotten here earlier, but I was guardin' the prisoner we took," Steve apologized. "How you doin'?"

"That's all right, Steve," Jim answered. "Far as how I'm doin', I'm about ready to crawl out of my skin, my *dupa's* itchin' so bad . . . and I can't scratch it."

"What's your *dupa*, Ranger Jim?" Joey asked.

"It's his backside," Steve answered. "When he got plugged, Ranger Jim landed in some of that cactus he warned y'all against."

Joey giggled, then quieted.

"Sorry, Ranger Jim. I didn't mean to laugh at you."

"That's all right, Joey," Jim assured the boy. "It is pretty funny what happened. Even I have to admit that."

Jep uncovered a tin plate and placed it on Jim's lap, along with a knife and fork. He also put a mug of coffee alongside the bed.

"Bill had some good luck huntin'," Jep

explained. "We have fresh meat tonight, and the boys knew you'd want some."

Jim eyed the contents of the plate skeptically. Besides beans and collard greens, there was a slab of meat he didn't recognize.

"Don't look like any meat I've ever seen, Jep," he objected. "What in blue blazes is it?"

"It's alligator," Joey piped up, before Jep could answer.

"Alligator?" Jim echoed.

"Yeah, alligator," Jep confirmed. "Bill shot a big bull 'gator in one of those sloughs along the Trinity. Skinned him out and got plenty of meat. Go ahead, give it a try."

"Yeah, try it, Jim," Steve urged.

In his long Ranger career, which often took him where game was scarce, Jim had learned to eat the meat of almost any critter, when necessary to survive. However, he had never before sampled alligator.

"You sure it's all right?" he asked.

"Sure is, Jim. 'Gator can be mighty tasty."

Hesitantly, Jim cut off a piece of meat, speared it with the fork, and shoved it in his mouth. It took some effort to chew the tough meat.

"Well, Jim?" Steve asked. "Tastes like . . ."

" 'Gator," Jep interrupted.

"That's right, it tastes just like 'gator," Jim laughed.

• • •

When the wagons resumed their journey two days later, Jim had reluctantly given in to Sam's orders, and his still-tender backside and shoulder. Instead of riding Sizzle as was his preference, Jim remained confined to his bunk in Sam's wagon. When Sam suggested he would be riding inside for several days, Jim told him in no uncertain terms that he would be back in the saddle before they reached Corsicana. In addition to Joe Sheely, now awake but still uncommunicative, merely glaring at the Ranger now and then, a space had been made for the other wounded outlaw, Frank Daniels. Daniels's right arm, like Jim's, was bound in a sling. His shoulder wound, Sam had declared, was slightly more serious than the Ranger's, but not crippling. As long as infection didn't set in, the outlaw should fully recover.

Jim gave a soft yelp when the wagon jounced over a deep rut. Joe Sheely burst into laughter.

"Frank, the Ranger there had a whole mess of cactus spines taken out of his butt. Funny to watch the 'doctor' checking him. Couldn't have happened to a nicer feller."

The wagon dipped into a chuckhole, and Sheely chuckled again when Jim grimaced with pain. This time Sheely's laugh was cut short when the wagon jerked out of the hole, sending pain stabbing through his ribs.

"You'd think that nigger would be able to miss

at least one pothole," Sheely muttered, with a curse.

"You'd think *you'd* had been able to hit at least one nigger with a bullet," Daniels retorted. "Or mebbe a Ranger," he added, with a glance in Jim's direction. "At least I managed to nail this one."

"Fat lotta good that'll do you," Sheely shot back. "Least if you'd killed him you might've gotten away with it. Now you're lookin' at a long stretch in Huntsville. Shootin' a Ranger's pretty much frowned upon. Quickest way to a cell."

"Or a rope," Jim added. "Since one of you sidewinders killed a man, you'll both likely be hanged. Add in you shootin' a Ranger, Daniels, plus bushwhackin' a troop of Rangers, and like your pardner says, you'll be swingin' from a rope before the month is up."

"That just ain't so, Ranger," Sheely answered. "There ain't no way possible you can prove it was me or Frank who shot that nigger."

"Don't have to," Jim replied. "Both of you were takin' part in a crime where a man was killed. That makes you accessories to murder, which is as much a hangin' offense as if you shot the man yourself. All that needs to be proved is you were part of the bunch which attacked this wagon train, and there are plenty of witnesses to that effect."

Jim left unsaid what he, and undoubtedly

the others, were well aware of . . . that no jury of white men in Texas would convict another white man for the murder of a Negro. However, attacking the Texas Rangers was another story. He'd let the men stew awhile and see what developed.

They rode in silence for the next forty minutes, the only sound uttered by any of the three an occasional grunt when the wagon jounced over a particularly rough stretch of ground. From the corner of his eye, Jim observed the prisoners, noticing that Frank Daniels seemed to be studying him. Finally, Daniels spoke up.

"Ranger, you really think we might hang?"

"I'd bet my hat on it," Jim replied. "And I really like this hat."

"How about if I had some information you might could use?"

"That'd depend on what kind of information you mean."

"If I spill my guts, you figure you can manage to keep my neck out of a noose?"

"That'll be up to the judge and jury, but if you've got something worthwhile, I'll put in a good word for you. Might help, might not. That's all I can promise."

"Lemme think on that awhile."

Daniels fell back into silent thought.

Despite the jouncing and attendant pain, Jim did manage to doze off for a spell, until he became aware of Daniels calling him once again.

"Ranger, you awake?"

"Reckon I am now," Jim yawned.

"I've been givin' what you said some hard thought. I'm willin' to pass along some information if you'll put in a good word with the judge for me. I don't much hanker to hang."

"Daniels, don't tell this lawman a thing, I'm warnin' you," Joe Sheely spoke up from his bunk.

"Why should I keep my mouth shut?" Daniels retorted. "I've got nothing to lose. Mebbe you're willin' to hang, but I sure ain't if I can avoid it."

"Ranger," he continued, "Wes Caldicott wasn't the real leader of our outfit."

"Wes Caldicott? Can't say as I recognize the name," Jim mused.

"Daniels, I'm warnin' you" Sheely threatened.

"I'm not worried," Daniels replied. "Nothin' you can do to me now."

"Sheely, let him talk, or I'll gag you myself. Don't think this shot-up shoulder'll stop me. Bet a hat on that," Jim added.

"Thanks, Ranger," Daniels said. "I'm not surprised you didn't hear of Wes or the rest of us, since we pretty well stuck to these parts, and were mighty careful to make sure we only robbed strangers or travelers, so that we most likely wouldn't be recognized. Plus, we always were tipped off who to hit."

"Who tipped you off?"

179

"Elroy McInroe."

"McInroe? The *hombre* who owns the general store back in Corsicana?"

"That's him, only he wasn't the brains behind the outfit either. His wife, Matilda, was."

"That nasty, mean, foul-tempered old woman?"

"That's right. Whenever a traveler, wagon train, or freighter who appears to have money or a valuable cargo comes into Corsicana, they usually stop at the McInroe's store, since it's the biggest in town. Matilda can almost always worm enough information out of them to see if they're worth robbin'. Once they leave town, she'll have Elroy get in touch with Wes . . . or I reckon I should say did, since Wes is dead. That big buck snapped his neck like it was a toothpick."

"And once you committed a robbery the spoils would be brought back to the store for the McInroes to dispose of."

"That's right. We'd cache the stuff for a couple of weeks, then bring it in a few pieces at a time, mostly durin' the middle of the night. A few days later, we'd get our cut. It was a pretty profitable arrangement. That enough for you to put in a good word for me?"

"It might be," Jim answered. "However, I need more proof. Right now it's just your story against the word of the McInroes. I don't need to tell you folks'll believe them, not some highwayman."

"All the proof you need is in the storeroom

180

back of McInroe's," Daniels explained. "We hit three freighters a couple of weeks back, and most of the goods are still waitin' to be moved. So, we got a deal?"

"I'll have to get a warrant and search the place," Jim answered. "If you're givin' it to me straight, I'll see what I can do. That's all I can promise."

"That's better'n nothin', Ranger. Thanks."

CHAPTER THIRTEEN

As Jim had promised, despite his still-healing wounds he rode Sizzle into Corsicana. He ordered the wagons to go into camp three miles outside town, while he, Smoky McCue, Steve Masters, and Johnny Dexter took the prisoners into town. The other Rangers would remain with the train.

"Dunno how the townsfolk will react when the McInroes are arrested," he stated. "Corsicana was a big slave-holdin' town before the War. No sense in havin' y'all too near if trouble starts."

By the time the Rangers and their handcuffed prisoners reached the brick, solidly built Navarro County Courthouse, they had attracted a large number of curious onlookers.

"Steve, you and Johnny stay here and keep an eye on things, while Smoke and I bring these two inside," Jim ordered, as they reined up opposite the courthouse, in front of a building marked "Navarro County Sheriff's Office." A smaller sign next to the door read "Robert Meader, Sheriff."

"Sure thing, Lieutenant," Steve agreed.

They dismounted, Steve and Johnny taking up positions on the sidewalk, while Jim and Smoky headed inside with their prisoners.

The only occupant of the office was seated at a desk in the far back corner. He looked up with a disinterested glance when the door opened, but jumped to his feet when he spied the Rangers' silver star on silver circle badges pinned to their shirtfronts, and the handcuffed men they led.

"Rangers! Sure didn't expect to see any of you around these parts," he exclaimed. "I'm Sheriff Bob Meader. Looks like you have a couple of prisoners you need me to take off your hands."

Meader was tall and lean, with thinning sandy hair and eyes of a peculiar gray/green shade, not quite hazel. The corners of his lips crinkled in an easy smile as he greeted the new arrivals.

"Sure do, Sheriff," Jim answered. "I'm Lieutenant Jim Blawcyzk, and this is Sergeant Smoky McCue. Soon as we get these two locked up we need another favor from you."

"Another favor?" Meader repeated. "Be happy to oblige if I can. Meantime, follow me."

He took a ring of keys from a peg, and opened a heavy oak door which led to a short hallway. At the end of the corridor was a bank of cells, several of which held prisoners. Meader opened one of the empty cells and beckoned to Sheely and Daniels.

"Inside," he ordered.

"I need to see a doc," Sheely complained. "My ribs still hurt somethin' awful."

"You won't be worried about your ribs once

your neck gets stretched," Smoky retorted. "Just get in that cell."

"These boys up for murder?" Meader asked.

"Among other things," Jim replied. "Sheely, you'll see the doc after we take care of our other business."

Sheely muttered a curse at the Ranger, but stepped into the cell and settled on one of the bunks. Daniels did likewise.

"You're too late for dinner, and supper won't be brought until five, so you might as well make yourselves comfortable," Meader told them, as he locked the door. "C'mon, Rangers, let's take care of the paperwork."

"Have a seat," he ordered, once they were back in the office. "Coffee on the stove if you want some."

"Appreciate that, Sheriff," Jim answered.

"Heck, the name's Bob," Meader replied, as he took mugs from a shelf and passed one to each of the Rangers. "How'd you pronounce yours again?"

"It's BLUH-zhick. Easier to just call me Jim."

"Boy howdy, it sure is," Meader agreed. "Reckon that means I can call you Smoky, Sergeant."

"Reckon it does," Smoky grinned.

Once they were settled, all three with cups of coffee, Smoky with the usual quirly dangling from his lips, Meader opened a desk drawer and pulled out two forms.

"All right now, what's those prisoners' names, and the charges?"

"Joseph Sheely and Frank Daniels," Jim answered. "Charges are assault on peace officers, assault, attempted robbery, attempted murder, and accessory to murder."

"That's some list," Meader noted, as he started to fill out the forms. "Joseph Sheely and Frank Daniels, you say?"

"That's right, Sheely and Daniels."

"That's Sheely . . . S-h-e-e-l-y?"

"Yep."

"And Daniels?"

"Correct. Daniels."

"All right then."

For the next few minutes, Jim and Smoky waited, drinking their coffee while the sheriff completed his paperwork. Finally, Meader pushed back his chair.

"That's done. Now, you said you had another request, Jim?"

"That's right. I need a couple of warrants. A search warrant, and two arrest warrants."

"Shouldn't be a problem. Judge Warner is probably in his office. Who's the warrants for?"

"Elroy and Matilda McInroe. Search warrant's for their store and warehouse. Charges for now are receiving stolen goods, and conspiracy to commit larceny and robbery. Once we search their premises there may be more."

"The McInroes?" Meader echoed.

"Yeah, the McInroes. Frank Daniels will swear they've been arranging robberies of travelers through these parts for quite some time," Jim explained. "In fact, I've got his signed and sworn deposition in my shirt pocket, just waitin' for the judge to examine."

"You mean Elroy and Matilda?" Meader repeated.

"That's what I said, Sheriff," Jim answered, his patience starting to wear thin.

"I know, I know. Just wanted to make sure," Meader said, shaking his head. "Wish I could say I'm surprised, but frankly, I'm not. I've kinda suspected the McInroes were up to no good for quite some time now, but haven't been able to get anything on them."

"What makes you say that?" Smoky questioned.

"Nothin' specific, just a gut feelin', plus little things I couldn't quite put my finger on. Frank and Matilda have always seemed to have more goods in their shop than were delivered. Also appears like they've got more money than a fair to middlin' sized general store could bring in. Matilda's always dressed real fancy, too."

"Bob, there's quite a crowd outside, wonderin' about those prisoners," Jim said. "Couple more Rangers out there too. We'd better see the judge before word gets around. Could make the

McInroes suspicious. You sure he's in his office?"

"I can find out right quick. Just need to ring him up," the sheriff answered.

"Ring him up?"

"That's right. We've got some of those new-fangled telephones here in Corsicana. There's one right over in the corner. Give me a minute and I'll know for certain if Judge Warner is in."

"I'd like to see that," Smoky said.

"Make that the both of us," Jim answered. "Can't believe you've already got telephones. We've been supposed to be getting phones for Ranger Headquarters for quite some time, but the legislature still hasn't approved the funds."

"You're more'n welcome to see mine," Meader answered.

Jim and Smoky followed the sheriff to the phone hanging on the wall. Meader picked up the earpiece, put it close to his ear, turned the crank, and waited. A moment later he spoke into the mouthpiece.

"Mabel, Sheriff Meader here."

"I know that, Sheriff," a female voice crackled. "I keep telling you I know your ring, and the location of your phone from the switchboard. Now, who did you want me to reach?"

"Judge Warner."

"Judge Warner. I'll ring him now."

"It'll only be a minute," Meader assured the Rangers, while they waited. Sure enough, shortly

Mabel's voice crackled through the earpiece once again.

"Sheriff, I have Judge Warner for you. Go ahead, please."

"Thanks, Mabel."

"Judge?" Meader continued.

"I'm here, Sheriff. What can I do for you?"

"There's a pair of Texas Rangers in my office who need some warrants issued. Can I bring them over?"

"Certainly, Sheriff. I'll see you momentarily."

"Thanks, Judge. Be right over."

Meader replaced the mouthpiece in its cradle. He grabbed his hat, settled it on his head, then buckled his gunbelt around his waist, adjusting the holster on his left hip.

"Let's go see the judge."

Judge Howard "Blue" Warner was a man of few words, his attitude businesslike and right to the point. He was a heavy man, with gray hair he kept combed precisely in place, a neatly trimmed beard, and penetrating brown eyes. He'd earned his nickname as one of the only three people in Corsicana who had voted against secession from the Union at the start of the War Between the States. Despite that, his reputation for complete impartiality and utter fairness kept him on the bench after the conflict and through Reconstruction. The judge favored fine wines

189

and expensive cigars. Smoky readily accepted his offer of one of the cheroots. He had the cigar barely halfway smoked before Warner had listened to Jim's statement, examined the deposition of Frank Daniels, and signed warrants for the arrests of Elroy and Matilda McInroe.

"Never would've guessed they'd be running an operation like this, Lieutenant, but from what you've presented, there certainly is more than enough evidence to arrest the McInroes," Warner stated. "Here's your warrants."

"Thanks, Judge. I appreciate it," Jim answered. "Smoke, Bob, let's get over to the McInroe store."

The crowd outside the sheriff's office, bored with waiting, had mostly dissipated by the time Jim, Smoky, and the sheriff emerged from Judge Warner's office and summoned Steve and Johnny to join them. Only a few remaining stragglers followed when the Rangers and sheriff retrieved their horses and rode the three blocks to the McInroe's establishment. With not a word from any of the lawmen, the curious onlookers could only speculate as to why several Texas Rangers would be interested in a small town general store. Their interest was further piqued when the lawmen drew their guns before entering the store. As at the sheriff's office, Steve and Johnny remained outside to keep watch on the bystanders.

Both Elroy and Matilda were behind the counter

when the Rangers and sheriff stepped inside. McInroe glanced away from the customer he was serving, giving a start when he spotted three leveled six-guns pointing in his direction.

"Sheriff Meader, what's the meaning of this?" he demanded.

"Just take it easy, Elroy. We don't want any trouble," Meader advised. "The Rangers here have warrants for your arrest, as well as Matilda's."

"What? That's not possible!" McInroe spluttered. "Wait a minute! I recognize you, Ranger," he continued, spotting Jim. "You were here a few days ago."

"That's right, he was with that nigger," Matilda stated. "We didn't do anything wrong, except order the colored man out of our place. Then this Ranger took up for him."

"That's not why we're here," Meader answered. "The warrants are for receiving stolen goods and conspiracy to commit robbery, assault, and accessory to murder. There's also a search warrant for these premises. They're legitimate, signed by Judge Warner."

"That's preposterous!" McInroe exclaimed. "Who would dare make such unfounded accusations against my wife and myself?"

"One of your hired guns," Jim softly replied. "He'll testify he was part of a gang recruited by you to rob travelers and freighters in this area."

"That's ridiculous," McInroe protested.

"Is it?" Jim answered. "Your gang tried to rob the wagons we're escorting to west Texas. Their ambush didn't work, and except for two of 'em they're all dead. One of those two has already given a written deposition implicating you and your wife."

"You have no proof!" Matilda declared.

"We will once we search your storeroom," Jim said. "Your man gave a pretty thorough description of goods taken from a group of freighters you had robbed a few weeks back. Those items, along with his testimony, should be enough evidence to send both of you to prison for a good, long time. Bet a hat on it."

"Sheriff . . ." McInroe began.

"Nothin' I can do, Elroy," Meader replied. "You can talk to your lawyer once you're locked up. Mebbe he'll be able to convince Judge Warner to allow you and Matilda to post bail, I dunno. But we've wasted enough time here. Are you going to come along quietly, or will we have to 'cuff you? I'd rather not do that."

"I reckon you're giving us no choice," McInroe answered. "We'll come along peacefully. But mark my words, we won't be in your jail long, Sheriff. You can also be certain once this is all straightened out we'll have your badge."

"That's enough talk," Jim said. "Get movin', right now."

"We'll have your badge, too, Ranger," Matilda retorted.

"I wouldn't bet your fancy feathered hat on that, lady," Jim replied. "Let's go."

The diminished crowd again grew rapidly once it was realized the McInroes were on their way to the county lockup. By the time the prisoners were secure in their cells, more than fifty citizens had gathered outside the sheriff's office.

"Think that mob outside'll give you any trouble, Bob?" Jim asked Meader.

"I doubt it. They're more curious than anything. They'll disperse once ordered to," Meader answered. "I'll send for a couple of my deputies, just in case."

"Good. Smoke, you and Steve stay here and help Bob search the McInroe store. Give him a hand with that crowd if need be."

"Okay, Jim," Smoky answered.

"Johnny, you and I'll head back to the wagons and tell Jep it's okay to start rollin' again. We've been delayed too long already."

"Sure, Jim." Johnny lifted the gun from his holster. "You sure you wouldn't rather have me stay here in case there's trouble, though?"

"I'm sure," Jim answered. "Smoke, we'll be back in a couple of hours, three at the most."

"We'll be here waitin'," Smoky assured him.

When Jim and Johnny emerged from the office,

quite a few of the crowd shouted questions at them.

"I'm sorry, but I can't give out any information," Jim answered. "Sheriff Meader will make a statement at the appropriate time."

He and Johnny untied their horses, mounted, and trotted away, the crowd still yelling after them.

The wagons were about a half-mile out of Corsicana when Jim Huggins spotted an approaching rider. He and his son Dan were taking their turn with Jep Hawthorne and Adrian Chatman at the head of the train.

"Someone comin', Jep. Better stop 'til we see what he's up to."

"You think he means trouble?" Adrian asked.

"Dunno. That *hombre*'s really pushin' his horse," Huggins observed. "Dan, better let Jim know."

"Sure thing, Dad. I'll bring him right up."

While Jep ordered a halt, Dan turned his horse to ride back along the column of wagons. He found Jim about halfway back, where he was riding alongside a wagon occupied by yet two more of Adrian's aunts, Carrie Mae Watley and Ruthell Allen. The two women were describing their plans for the home they would be building in Freedom.

"Miz Ruthell, Miz Carrie Mae, I hate to

interrupt, but we need Lieutenant Blawcyzk up front for a few minutes," Dan said, tipping his hat slightly to the ladies.

"Mercy me! There's not more trouble, is there?" Ruthell exclaimed.

"No ma'am, we don't believe so, but someone is coming. We'd like the lieutenant to speak with him," Dan explained.

"Thank goodness," Carrie Mae said. "I believe I've had all the excitement a body can stand over the past few days."

"I've gotta agree with you there, ma'am," Dan answered. "The lieutenant won't be long, I promise."

"Be back quick as I can," Jim agreed. "C'mon, Siz, let's go."

He put the gelding into a trot.

When Jim and Dan reached the lead wagon, the rider had just arrived. He pulled his lathered dun to a halt, and raised his right hand in greeting. A deputy's badge was pinned to his cowhide vest, and a bloody streak marked his left shirtsleeve.

"Howdy! I'm Deputy Harry Carter from Corsicana," he called out. "Which one of you's Lieutenant Blawcyzk?"

"That'd be me, Deputy," Jim answered. "What can I do for you?"

"There's tall trouble back in town," Carter answered. "Sheriff Meader sent me to warn you, and to say he needs help fast as possible."

"What's goin' on?"

"Bunch of the McInroe's friends are stirrin' up trouble. They've got the sheriff and your pardners pinned down in the jail, along with Fred Murphey, another deputy. They're tryin' to break Elroy and Matilda out. Also say if this wagon train attempts to go through town they'll stop it."

"You weren't at the jail with the others, Deputy?"

"I was, but I got lucky. I was usin' the privy out back when the mob showed up. Bob shouted out one of the cell windows, warnin' me they were comin' and to make a run for it. Real fortunate my horse was still saddled and hitched behind the courthouse, rather'n bein' in his stall at the livery stable. Even then, I nearly didn't make it. Got creased by a bullet just when I climbed into the saddle. Guess the man who tried to drill me wasn't that good a shot."

"Good thing he wasn't," Jim agreed. By now the other Rangers, always alert for trouble, had also reached the front of the train.

"There any way we can skirt town and avoid this problem?" Ty asked.

"Not without takin' a fifty or sixty mile detour," Carter replied. "The bridge along the old road's been washed out for months. You could try cuttin' cross-country, but it'd be pretty tough on your rigs."

"We can't do that anyway," Jim pointed out.

196

"Sure couldn't leave your boss and our pardners facin' that mob on their own."

"I know that, Lieutenant," Ty responded, a trace of exasperation in his voice. "Just wanted to find a way to keep these folks out of harm's way, if possible. After all, we are supposed to be protectin' them, not causin' more difficulties for 'em."

"Ty, I believe I can speak for all of us when I say we appreciate your concern," Adrian answered. "However, we colored folks have been surviving by avoidin' trouble for so long now it's almost second nature. High time we changed that. So, Lieutenant Blawcyzk, any way we can help we sure will. After all, if it hadn't been for us you Rangers wouldn't even be here in the first place."

"I'll keep that in mind, Adrian, however, we've faced down plenty of mobs before. We should be able to handle this one without too much trouble. Deputy, how many men do you think are gonna try and storm the jail?" Jim asked.

"Probably sixty or seventy at the most. Just about everyone in Corsicana's mainly law-abiding citizens, and don't hold no truck with troublemakers. Only thing that might stir a few more folks up is this region was a major slave-holdin' area in the past, so Negroes are still looked down on by a lot of people around here."

The deputy nodded at Adrian and Jep.

"No offense meant."

"None taken," Adrian assured him.

"Seventy lawbreakers, and nine Rangers, if you count me. Those odds seem about right," Bill Dundee noted, lifting his huge Sharps from its scabbard. "How you want to handle this, Jim?"

"We'll all go into town, and stop three blocks before the jail," Jim answered. "Then, I'll go ahead and try and talk some sense into that mob, along with you Bill, Charlie, and Ty. You too, Deputy. Jim, you, Dan, and Johnny remain with the wagons until we see what develops."

"You certain you should have the wagons come into town, Lieutenant?" Johnny questioned. "Seems like they'd be trapped if trouble starts."

"Any trouble won't get that far, bet a hat on it," Jim declared, his eyes glittering like chips of blue ice.

"Are you positive?" Johnny insisted.

"If my dad says there won't be any trouble for the wagons, then there won't be," Charlie answered, his eyes reflecting the same grim determination as his father's.

"The odds are you won't get anywhere just talkin' to that mob, Jim," Dan observed.

"I know," Jim agreed. "That's why I want Bill with me. A .50 caliber slug or two from his Sharps, partin' the hair of a few *hombres*, is liable to cool 'em off right quick. Bet a hat on it."

"What if it doesn't?" Johnny asked.

"That'll force me to use another option."

"What's that?" Johnny pressed.

"You'll see," Jim replied.

"It won't be pretty, Johnny, I'll tell you that," Jim Huggins added. "I've seen Jim use it before."

"Enough palaverin'. Jep, Adrian, get everyone who's not mounted into a wagon. Let's get movin'," Jim ordered.

"We'd better hope your deputy got through and help's on the way, Bob," Smoky said, as he loosed another shotgun blast over the heads of the mob. "Dunno how much longer we can hold out."

He ducked when yet another bullet shattered one of the few remaining panes of glass and ricocheted off the back wall.

"You've sure got that right," the sheriff agreed. "So far no one's gotten hurt, but that can't last much longer. We'll have to start aimin' lower pretty soon."

"Which will really get that mob howlin' for blood," Deputy Fred Murphey added. "If Harry did get through, how long do you figure before your pardner arrives, Ranger?"

"Jim won't waste any time. If he's comin', it won't be long now."

"Looks like it's still a standoff, Dad," Charlie noted, when they reached town a short while later. Shouts and curses from the mob, directed at the defenders of the jail, rose on the thick, humid air, along with traces of powdersmoke.

"Let's change that," Jim answered. He and his chosen men pulled their rifles from their scabbards and put their horses into a trot. The enraged crowd, absorbed with the lawmen they had trapped in the jail, never noticed the Rangers, even when they pulled their horses to a halt less than two hundred feet away.

"Time to get their attention. Now, Bill," Jim ordered.

Bill nodded, leveled his rifle, and fired. The deep-throated roar of the heavy Sharps, and the sound of its heavy .50 caliber slug whistling just over their heads, turned the mob's concentration away from the jail and to the new threat, six grim lawmen sitting well-trained, unmoving horses, rifles leveled. Bill had already slid another round into his single-shot buffalo gun.

Jim edged Sizzle forward. The silver star on silver circle badge pinned to his vest glittered in the sun, leaving no doubt as to his identity.

"Which one of you is the leader of this bunch?" he demanded.

One of the men separated himself from the crowd, scowling. He held a new Winchester carbine, which he wisely kept lowered.

"I reckon that'd be me."

"You got a name?"

"Mike Dowling. Man just behind me is Ben Talley. We speak for all these folks."

"All right, Mister Dowling, you have exactly one minute to break up this mob and go home, peacefully."

"And if we don't?"

"Then we'll break it up for you, which means quite a few folks get hurt, probably some killed. Not to mention arrests made. And you'd be the first on to take lead, Dowling. I'd make sure of that."

"Ranger, you've got guts, I'll give you that," Dowling answered. "I'd say the odds are on our side, though. We've got you way outnumbered, and we're not leavin' here until Elroy and Matilda McInroe are turned loose."

Dowling glanced at the wagons in the distance.

"We also have no intentions of lettin' a whole passel of niggers come into town. You can just have them turn those wagons around right now."

Jim shifted just slightly in his saddle.

"The McInroes are stayin' right where they belong, in a cell. They've been arrested on several serious charges, not the least of which is accessory to murder."

"The McInroes have done a lot for this town," someone shouted from the midst of the mob. "They ain't gonna stay in jail just because some stinkin' coloreds claim they was robbed."

"It wasn't just these people they're accused

of robbin'," Jim replied. "There were plenty of others. The McInroes will have their day in court, but no mob is gonna bust 'em out of jail. Bet a hat on it."

Jim paused, then continued.

"Far as this wagon train, they're just passin' through. Through town is the quickest way, so that's what they'll be doin' . . . unless you'd rather have them settle down right here, instead of continuing on their way to west Texas. This seems like a nice place for new settlers."

"Ranger, you've got a big mouth, and like I said, it seems to me you're in no position to be givin' orders. We ain't budgin', and those wagons aren't goin' another ten feet further," Dowling snarled.

"All right," Jim shrugged. He turned Sizzle, signaling the others to do the same.

A ragged cheer went up from the mob at the Rangers' apparent retreat.

Jim gave a shrill whistle as he approached the wagons. Sam trotted up to him. Jim dismounted and began stripping his gear from Sizzle, transferring it onto Sam. He tightened the cinches, then climbed onto Sam's back.

"They didn't listen?" Jim Huggins asked.

"Did you expect them to?"

"Not really, Jim."

"Good. You know what's next."

"Sure do, but you'd better explain it to the others."

"Reckon you're right. Jep, Adrian, we're gonna charge that bunch. I'll be in the lead, the rest of my men close behind. Stay about a hundred yards behind us. Soon as we break a hole through that crowd, you head on through, at a run. Don't stop until you're clean out of town. We'll catch up to you soon as we finish up."

"What if someone gets in our way?" Adrian asked.

"Then you run 'em down." Jep answered. "Right, Jim?"

"Right."

Once again, Jim had Bill fire a shot just over the mob. Then, giving the Rebel yell, he dug his heels into Sam's ribs, sending the paint rocketing forward, the horse ignoring his bad leg in the excitement of the moment. The rest of the lawmen formed their horses into a wedge, close on Sam's heels.

Sam slammed into the mob, wicked yellow teeth tearing, steel-shod hooves slashing. Mike Dowling attempted to aim his gun to put a bullet into Jim Blawcyzk's chest, but before he could bring the weapon level Sam clamped onto his throat, crushing Dowling's larynx and ripping open his jugular. Blood spurted from the severed vein, staining Sam's muzzle crimson. The big horse galloped on, his shoulders bowling over several men, to be trampled in his headlong dash. Guns firing and screaming the Rebel yell, the other Rangers and Deputy Carter followed Sam's lead, their horses plowing into the now-panicked crowd. Men scrambled in terror, trying to avoid that phalanx of charging horseflesh and determined lawmen.

"Now, Adrian!" Jep yelled, seeing an opening through the mob. He put his horse into a gallop, the wagons strung out behind. Before the crowd could even think of reorganizing, the wagons were upon them, and thundering through.

"Knew Jim'd handle things," Smoky shouted triumphantly from inside the jail, observing the mob scatter. "Let's give him a hand."

He, Steve, Sheriff Meader, and Deputy Murphey headed outside. As soon as Meader stepped through the door, Ben Talley, who had managed to dive out of the way and roll against the boardwalk just before Sam reached the mob, took a snap shot at the sheriff. Meader's mouth opened in an "O" of shock and pain when Talley's bullet caught him in the belly. His knees buckled, and he half-turned as he toppled, fingers tightening on the triggers of the shotgun he held, close-bunched shot from both barrels driving splinters from the wooden sidewalk. Meader fell onto his side, stretched out across the doorway. Before Talley could fire again, four bullets from Ranger guns slammed into him, ripping through vital organs and killing him instantly. The impact rolled Talley several times before his bullet-riddled body lay face-up and unmoving.

The mob was completely routed, many of its members lying in the street with broken bones and ripped flesh, the others gone from sight, having run for their lives. The lawmen quickly took charge of the area.

"Dang!" Johnny Dexter exclaimed to no one in particular, taking in the carnage. "Reckon Lieutenant Blawcyzk meant what he said. This sure wasn't pretty."

Steve knelt beside the downed sheriff.

"He's still alive," he said. "Dunno for how long."

"Let's get him inside, then we'd better find a doctor quick," Smoky ordered.

"I'll handle that," Murphey answered. "Doc Stout's probably already on his way, so I'll have someone bring him straight here."

"All right," Smoky answered. He and Steve picked up Meader under his shoulders and by his ankles to carry him inside the jail and place him on a bunk in one of the cells. Smoky opened the sheriff's shirt to examine his wound. He shook his head when he saw the oozing bullet hole.

"Don't look good, Steve. He's bleedin' pretty heavy."

"No, it sure doesn't," Masters agreed. "Better hope that doctor gets here fast."

Smoky took a sheet from another bunk, tore it in squares, and placed several of those over

Meader's belly in an attempt to staunch the bleeding. The rags soon were soaked through with blood. The door opened, but to his disappointment it was Jim Blawcyzk who entered, not the physician. With him was Deputy Murphey.

"Heard the sheriff took a bullet. How bad is it, Smoke?" he asked.

"Pretty bad," Smoky answered. "He's belly-shot. You seen a doctor anywhere? Deputy there sent someone to find one."

"Not yet," Jim replied. "Few men outside need one too."

"Everything under control out there?" Steve questioned.

"Yep. No worries there," Jim replied.

The door opened again, to reveal Sam Tatum, who carried his medical bag.

"Sam, what in blue blazes are you doin' here?" Jim demanded. "Thought I told Jep and Adrian to make sure no one stopped until well out of town."

"I turned back. Figured there'd be hurt folks needin' help," Sam explained. "Looks like I was right. Lieutenant Huggins told me the sheriff was wounded, so I hurried right here."

"You're not a minute too soon," Smoky said. "Bob's in a bad way."

"Where is he?"

"Right back there, in a cell," Steve indicated.

"Wait a minute," Deputy Murphey protested.

"You can't allow a colored man to work on a white. Besides, is this man even a doctor?"

"Deputy, this man took a bullet out of my shoulder, and he did a better job than most physicians would," Jim answered. "Far as a colored man working on a white one, do you really think it matters when the white man's life is at stake?"

"I've treated an awful lot of bullet and knife wounds in my time, Deputy," Sam added. "However, if you'd prefer to wait for a white man, then I can't fight you."

"Sam, there's no time to waste," Jim answered. "Deputy, let this man get to work. If you try and stop him, I'll toss you in a cell myself."

"You really think he can save Bob's life?" Murphey shook his head doubtfully.

"Can't make any promises, but he's your boss's best shot."

"Jim . . ." Smoky winced.

"Sorry, Smoke." Jim apologized for the unintended pun.

"Ranger, I'll trust you," Murphey decided. "Mister, I'd appreciate you doin' everything you can to save Bob's life. He's a mighty fine man."

"I'll do my best, I assure you of that," Sam promised. "I'll need some help. Start boilin' water, and if there's a bottle of whiskey anywhere around here I can use it. A couple of bowls and a shallow pan, also."

"I'll take care of them," Murphey answered.

By the time Sam was alongside Meader's bunk, the sheriff had regained consciousness. He looked at Sam through pain-glazed eyes. Sweat beaded on his forehead.

"Who the devil are you?" he asked.

"I'm the man who's gonna try and keep you from meetin' him, at least right away," Sam answered. "Name's Sam Tatum. Let me take a look at you."

Sam pulled the rags off Meader's abdomen to examine the wound. He tsked softly, shaking his head.

"Don't bother wastin' your time on me," Meader gasped. "I know I'm done for. Gut-shot. Just a matter of how long it takes, and how painful."

"Don't be givin' up so quick," Sam retorted. "Yeah, you're gut-shot, but not shot in the guts, at least I don't believe so."

"You're talkin' loco," Meader protested. "Either I'm gut-shot or I'm not. And from the way my belly hurts, I'd bet a hundred dollars I took a slug right through my guts."

"I'll take that bet," Sam answered, as he wiped blood away from the bullet hole. "You did take a bullet through your gut, but from what I can determine looking at where it hit and the angle I think it took, it missed your guts, or more properly your intestines, entirely. I'll know more once I locate the slug and, hopefully, get it out. If

208

it didn't perforate any intestines or a kidney, then you do have a chance of surviving, as long as the bleeding stops, and you don't develop blood poisoning. It will take several days before we can be certain. Right now, the most important thing is removing that bullet from your abdomen. As soon as your deputy brings that whiskey and hot water, I'll get to work."

A few moments later, Murphey entered the cell, carrying the supplies Sam had requested.

"Pour some of the whiskey in that pan," Sam ordered.

"Sure."

Murphey filled the pan almost brim-full with the liquor. Sam took a knife, scalpel, forceps, and probe and placed these in the pan.

"I'm gonna need two of you to hold him down while I dig for the bullet," Sam requested.

"Steve'n I'll handle that," Smoky offered.

"Fine." Sam picked up the bottle of whiskey.

"Sheriff, this is gonna hurt something fierce," he warned.

"I'd reckon." Meader attempted a rueful grin, which came out as more of a grimace.

Sam doused the bullet hole with whiskey. Meader screamed, his body jerking when the fiery liquor hit the open wound.

"Sorry, but that had to be done," Sam apologized. "Now I know it will be difficult, but you need to keep as motionless as possible while I probe for the bullet. I don't need to tell you what will happen if I make a slip."

"We'll keep him down, Sam," Steve said.

"Good."

Sam removed the scalpel from the pan and sliced open the skin above and below the bullet hole, slightly enlarging Meader's wound. That done, he gently inserted the instrument into the bullet hole. Carefully, he slid the probe deeper into Meader's belly.

"I know this hurts like the dickens, but I'm being as gentle as I can, Sheriff."

Without warning, the office door slammed open and another man burst into the jail, hurrying to where Meader lay. He was of average height, and stout, with a long dark beard and thick eyebrows. A medical bag was in his right hand.

"What's going on here? Who is this man?" he demanded, his brown eyes blazing with fury.

"Reckon I might ask you the same question," Jim answered.

"I'm Doctor Hiram Stout. I would have been here sooner, but had to stop to treat two other badly wounded men. Now let me at my patient."

"I'm sorry, Doctor, but I can't do that," Sam said, from where he was working on the sheriff. "I've already got this probe several inches into his abdomen. I can't remove it now."

"But . . ."

"But nothing," Sam answered. "I could use some assistance, however. If you wouldn't mind, could you pass me an instrument when I request it?"

Stout began to protest yet again, but something in Sam's calm voice and quiet, confident manner held his tongue. Instead, he stood at Sam's side.

"I sure hope you know what you're doing," he said.

"My master was a prominent physician in Natchez," Sam explained, as he continued probing for the bullet. "He taught me a lot about practicing medicine. Later, during the War, I treated an awful lot of soldiers, most of them young boys with terrible wounds. Arms and legs torn off by shrapnel, brains blown out by Minie balls or bellies sliced open by sabers. Horrible sights I'll never forget, sights that still bring nightmares. I believe I can save this man, as long as the bullet didn't perforate an intestine. We'll know shortly."

Stout watched Sam work with grudging admiration. The Negro had a deft touch, and dexterous fingers more sensitive than most surgeons Stout had worked alongside.

A moment later, Sam felt the probe strike something solid.

"There. I've found the bullet. Sheriff, just a few more minutes."

Meader grunted something unintelligible.

"Doctor Stout, would you hand me the forceps?"

"Certainly."

Stout removed the forceps from the pan and handed them to Sam. Moving extremely carefully, Sam slid the forceps into Meader's abdomen, following the probe, until they clamped around the bullet.

"Got it," Sam said. Slowly, he removed the forceps, then the probe. He held the bullet for Meader to see.

"There's your lead, Sheriff. Doctor Stout, would you like to close the wound, or would you prefer that I do so?"

"You're doing a fine job so far," Stout answered. "Far be it from me to say I could do better."

"Thank you."

Sam doused the wound with more whiskey, stitched it shut, then dressed and bandaged it.

"Doctor Stout, I don't have any laudanum with me. Would you have some to administer?"

"I certainly would," Stout answered. He opened his bag to remove a brown bottle and a tablespoon.

"Wait, Doc," Meader said. "Mister Tatum, how about it? Am I gonna pull through?"

"I can't say for certain, as I'm sure Doctor Stout will attest; however, I am almost positive the bullet missed your intestines, but struck your liver and diaphragm. If that's the case, then blood poisoning will be the biggest worry, and your biggest challenge. Offhand, I'd say your chances of survival are better than fifty-fifty, which are much better odds than I'd have given when I walked in here."

"And getting as much sleep as possible will increase your chances, Bob, so let me give you this laudanum," Stout added. He gave the sheriff two spoonfuls of the medication.

"I'll check on you in a couple of hours, and spend the night here," he told Meader. "You'll sleep at least until I return."

"Thanks, Doc. Thanks, Mister Tatum," Meader answered, already beginning to drift off.

"Mister Tatum," Stout said. "I must admit you are far more competent than many actual physicians I have known. Your touch while searching for the bullet in Sheriff Meader was simply amazing. Would you consider remaining here in Corsicana? I could use a good assistant, and I assure you the salary would be more than fair."

"The name's Sam, Doctor."

"All right, Sam . . . as long as you call me Hiram. Now, will you think about my offer?"

"Hiram, I appreciate it, I really do. However, I have to remain with my friends. I'm sure no one's had the chance to tell you yet that we're on our way to west Texas to start a new community. Here in Corsicana, I know there's at least one fine doctor, you. In Freedom, our new town, there will be no physicians. So you see, while I'm extremely grateful for your generous offer, I must, regretfully, decline. I trust you understand."

"As much as I hate to be turned down, I certainly do understand your reasons, and wish you all the best. Meanwhile, if you can give me a couple of hours or so, there are still quite a few men who need treatment for their injuries, including several with broken bones. Would you mind giving me a hand?"

"Not at all, as long as those men don't mind being treated by a Negro," Sam answered.

"Those that object will be left for last, that's all," Stout answered. "Once the pain gets to be too much their objections will dry up and blow away like tumbleweeds in a strong wind."

"Then let's get to work," Sam grinned.

CHAPTER FOURTEEN

The Rangers remained in Corsicana just long enough to arrest several men Smoky, Steve, and Deputies Murphey and Carter identified as ringleaders of the mob, and to allow Sam enough time to assist Doctor Stout in treating the injured. As it turned out, that was also sufficient time for Elroy and Matilda McInroe to turn on each other. Discouraged by the failed attempt to break them out of jail, they started accusing each other of being the one who had really arranged for the robberies and killings. It was with grim satisfaction, knowing both would either hang or receive long prison terms, that the Rangers departed, once again escorting the Chatman wagon train on its westward journey. Before leaving, Jim had extracted a promise from Doctor Stout that either he or one of the county deputies would send a telegram to San Angelo, advising of Sheriff Meader's progress in his recovery.

The next several days were mercifully uneventful, the weather unusually pleasant, even benign, with warm, rather than excessively hot and humid, days and cool nights. The travelers encountered only a few minor difficulties, and made camp just outside Waco late one afternoon.

"Waco's the last big town we'll see until we reach San Angelo, so tomorrow morning we'll stop for supplies before headin' on," Jep ordered. "Make sure you have a list of all the essentials you'll need, because goods'll be hard to come by from here on out. Just keep in mind we don't want to overload the wagons. Water'll be scarce, so we can't make it any harder on the animals than we have to. No finery, fripperies, or pretty gewgaws. Only absolute necessities."

After everyone had settled and supper was eaten, Charlie and Ty, along with Dan and Johnny, approached Jim and Smoky as they were grooming their horses.

"Dad, if it's all right with you, we'd like to head into town and have a little fun," Charlie requested. "We haven't had a break since we left Austin, and this'll be our last opportunity to kick up our heels until we reach San Angelo."

"I dunno," Jim answered. "Can't chance havin' any of you getting into trouble."

"We won't start any scrapes, Lieutenant," Dan promised. "We just want to have a couple of beers, mebbe dance with a lady or two, and play some cards."

"I'll go along with 'em to keep 'em in line if that'll help, Jim," Steve Masters offered, from where he was checking his horse's hooves.

"Yeah, but who's gonna keep you in line, Steve?" Smoky laughed.

"I'm still not sure it's a good idea," Blawcyzk said. "Jim, what do you think?"

"I say let the kids go," Lieutenant Huggins replied. "You forgotten what it was like to be young, Jim?"

"No, I haven't, which is the main reason I'm not sure allowin' these boys to go into town is the wise thing to do."

"Dad, you mean you weren't always the perfect–don't get out of line–never raise a ruckus *hombre* I've forever thought you were?" Charlie asked.

"Chip, I could tell you stories about your dad in his younger days that would make your hair stand on end," Smoky grinned.

"You do and I'll gut-shoot you where you stand, McCue," Jim growled. "Particularly since any you'd tell would be downright lies. All right," he continued to Charlie, "I guess you can go. Can't deny a break from all this might do you some good. Don't get back too late, though."

"I'll make sure they're home before midnight, Pop," Steve said.

"Doesn't have to be that early, but all of you had best be ready to ride by sunup," Jim answered.

"They don't need to be up with the sun," Bill Dundee stated. "Since we have to wait until the stores open, we won't be rollin' out until about eight tomorrow mornin'. So just go, enjoy yourselves, and get back whenever you want. In fact,

Jep and I are plannin' on doing just that. There's a couple saloons in the Negro quarter I'd like to visit again. With any luck, there's a certain lady I recollect who'll still be workin' at one of 'em. I'd sure like to renew her acquaintance."

"Didn't know you were in charge of this outfit now, Bill," Jim protested.

"I'm not, but I also know you'd order these boys back by nine o'clock, given your druthers."

"You're right at that," Jim agreed, with a chuckle. "All right, what're y'all standin' around waitin' for? If you're headed to town, git!"

"Yessir, Lieutenant," Ty answered. "Let's ride, boys! We're goin' to town!" he whooped.

Even a bustling cow, cotton, and railroad town like Waco stood up and took notice at the unheard of sight of a long wagon train of Negroes, escorted by a group of Texas Rangers, rolling into town. Passersby stopped and stared as the train made its way through the busy streets, then pulled up when it reached the block-long Waco Cattlemen's and Farmer's Mercantile.

"We'll go in a few at a time, so as not to over-crowd the store," Jep ordered.

"Are you certain they won't refuse us service, or cause us any other problems?" Frances asked.

"Yeah, Jep. Are you certain? After all, we don't want a repeat of what happened in Corsicana," Dwain added.

"No, they sure won't," Jep assured them. "As long as your money is good, Bailey Dailey, the owner of this place, will be more'n glad to see you. I've done business with him many times."

"Bailey Dailey?" Adrian chuckled.

"Oh yeah, nearly forgot. As long as your money's good and you don't make fun of his name, *then* Bailey'll be more'n glad to see you. Just remember what I told all of you last night, no unnecessary purchases. Essential goods only."

"You needn't worry about that," Adrian assured him. "We have to stretch every dollar as far as we can. I want to make sure we arrive in San Angelo with enough cash reserves to tide us over for several months, if necessary."

The sun was high in the sky by the time everyone finished their shopping and the wagons were rolling once again. They moved steadily through town until they reached the suspension bridge over the Brazos River. The imposing structure, the longest single-span suspension bridge in the world at the time it was erected, had been designed and built by the renowned Roebling firm, which would later design and construct the Brooklyn Bridge in New York City, connecting the borough of Brooklyn to Manhattan Island. In the late morning sun, the bridge's twin double towers, constructed of three million locally-produced bricks, loomed against the clear blue sky.

"Lord A'mighty, are we gonna cross that thing?" "T" Daniels, another of Adrian's uncles, asked in disbelief as he gazed at the structure.

"We sure are," Jep confirmed. "It's a lot faster'n safer than takin' the ferry, or swimming the river. We could head upstream to a crossin' at a shallow ford, but that'd take us miles out of our way, and still be dangerous. This bridge is the smartest option."

"Those bits of thread don't hardly seem as if they could hold that thing up in the air like that," Daniels protested, referring to the cables strung from the towers which supported the bridge deck.

"Those aren't bits of thread, they're thick steel cables," Jim answered. "I've crossed this bridge many times. Lots of cattle have been driven across it too, and a good-sized herd all bunched together weighs a lot more'n this outfit. We'll be perfectly safe."

"I reckon I've got no choice but to take both your words for it," Daniels replied, doubtfully. "But if that thing collapses and I drown, I'll make sure'n come back to haunt y'all."

"If the bridge goes down there won't be none of us around to haunt," Jep retorted. "But that ain't gonna happen. Jim, let's go talk to the bridge keeper and pay the tolls."

He spurred his coal-black gelding, Mack, into a slow jog, Jim on Sizzle alongside. It only took a moment to reach the bridge keeper's gatehouse.

The keeper was already waiting for them, gazing past to the gathered wagons and stock.

"Mornin', gents. You folks figurin' on crossin' the river here?" he asked.

"Sure are," Jep answered.

"Ranger, are you with this man's outfit?" the keeper next questioned Jim.

"Yep, I am. There's nine of us Rangers all together."

"All right. There's no toll for you lawmen, of course, nor your mounts. Far as the wagons and the rest, toll's five cents a head for the livestock, two bits for each wagon, and a penny for anyone walkin'. One of you got a count for me?"

"Sure do, and I've got the money all ready," Jep asked.

"You won't object if I double-check as your people cross, will you?" the keeper asked.

"Already figured you would," Jep chuckled. He handed the keeper a sack of bills and coins.

"Here's the toll. I'll wait until everyone's across so we can settle any discrepancy."

"Discrepancy?"

"Difference."

"Oh, difference. Why didn't you just say so? All right, bring your wagons across."

After the keeper opened the heavy gate which prevented travelers from crossing without paying the toll, Jep waved the wagons forward. With Adrian's in the lead, they headed onto the bridge.

Humans and livestock reacted in various manners as they stepped onto the bridge's wooden deck, some tentatively, others confidently. A few of the mules balked at the deck rumbling hollowly under their feet and vibrating under their weight, but were convinced by shouts and whips to keep moving. Some of the emigrants prayed for their safety in making the crossing, while others gazed in amazement at the magnificent structure easing their passage, high above the murky Brazos.[3]

When Joe Fletcher eased his mules onto the bridge, Christine, seated alongside him, broke into song.

"The Gospel train's a-comin'
"I hear it just at hand
"I hear the car wheels rumblin'
"And rollin' through the land."

The others started joining in when Christine reached the refrain.

"Get on board little children
"Get on board little children
"Get on board little children
"There's room for many more."

---

3 The Waco Suspension Bridge still stands today, serving pedestrian and bicycle traffic crossing the Brazos River.

"I hear the train a-comin'
"She's comin' round the curve
"She's loosened all her steam and brakes
"And strainin' every nerve."

"Get on board little children
"Get on board little children
"Get on board little children
"There's room for many more."

"The fare is cheap and all can go
"The rich and poor are there
"No second class aboard this train
"No difference in the fare.

"Get on board little children
"Get on board little children
"Get on board little children
"There's room for many more."

Singing joyously in glorious song, the emigrants crossed the Brazos, rejoicing in the realization they had finally reached the beginnings of west Texas, and their goal was within reach.

CHAPTER FIFTEEN

Once Waco had been left behind, the following days stretched on in seemingly endless drudgery, while the wagons made their slow journey across the increasingly parched land. As Jep had warned, water did become more scarce, even the few rivers they crossed running low at this time of year, often little more than puddle-interspersed mud flats and quicksand, rather than flowing bodies of sweet water. He finally pulled Adrian and Jim Blawcyzk aside during a mid-afternoon rest stop, which was intended to allow the weary animals a break more than anything else.

"Wanted to speak with you both while we had the chance without any of the others overhearin' us," he explained.

"Something the matter, Jep?" Adrian asked.

"Not quite yet, but there may well be soon," Jep answered. "Jim, you probably know what I'm about to say, but since Adrian's still a tenderfoot, all right, one tough tenderfoot," he interjected, when Adrian began to protest, "but a tenderfoot nonetheless, I'm certain he doesn't understand what we're up against."

"If we've got a problem, quit beatin' around

the bush. Tell me what it is," Adrian answered. "You're right, I have no idea what it could be. We haven't had any trouble since leaving Corsicana, and I was hoping there wouldn't be any more, unlikely as I realize that is."

"It's water," Jep answered. "We're startin' to run low, and if we don't find more soon we're gonna have to go on half-rations. Few days after that we'll have to cut the rations in half again. That'll be tough on a lot of your folks, especially the oldsters and young'ns."

"Not to mention the livestock," Jim added.

"I thought we still had plenty left," Adrian objected.

"Might seem like it, but there's nowhere near what we need remaining in the barrels. I'd hoped to get fresh water when we crossed Pecan Bayou, but even you could see what little water was flowin' wasn't fit to drink, son."

"We'll be reaching the Colorado in a couple of days, Jep. Should be plenty of water then," Jim said.

"Should be, but we can't count on it, dry as it's been," Jep replied. "I've never seen the Pecan dried up like it is. Sure, we hit those storms back in east Texas, but I'd wager it hasn't rained out this way for a couple of months, mebbe longer."

"I wouldn't bet my hat against it," Jim answered.

"So what do we do?" Adrian asked.

"For now, just let the menfolk know, quiet-like, to start savin' as much water as they can," Jep explained. "We won't cut back rations for the women, kids, and stock for another day or two. With luck, either it'll rain, or we'll find a waterhole somewhere. Jim, if you don't have any objections, I'd like to ask Dundee to scout ahead and see if he can locate one. He's good at finding water, no matter how parched things are. You know that."

"You want Bill, you've got him," Jim answered.

"Good, then that's settled. Let's get rollin' again. Adrian, you pass the word to the men."

"Will do," Adrian agreed, a worried look crossing his countenance.

"Don't worry, Adrian," Jim assured him. "We'll be just fine."

While the wagons rolled slowly along, those walking alongside trudging through the dust under the blazing hot Texas sun, Bill Dundee put Spook, his dark blue roan, into a steady trot. Before half an hour had passed he was well ahead of the others.

Bill stopped at one patch of greenery, hoping to find a small spring or waterhole. However, he was sorely disappointed to find only a patch of mud, its surface already cracked and drying. He dismounted and unstrapped a small shovel from his saddle, only to be more frustrated when his digging came up with no water, just more muck. His thirsty horse nosed the moist earth and whickered his displeasure.

"I'm sorry, boy. I know you're thirsty. So am I," Bill comforted the gelding. He took his canteen from the saddlehorn, opened it, and poured half the contents into his hat. He placed that in front of Spook's nose, allowing him a short drink. Bill then took two swallows of water for himself.

"Let's push on, Spook," he urged as he swung back into the saddle. "There's gotta be water out here somewhere."

He heeled the horse back into a walk.

Bill had gone another three miles when he spotted dust on the distant horizon.

"Looks like we ain't the only ones out here, Spook," he remarked to his horse. "Better hope that ain't some renegade Comanches who jumped the reservation. Doubt it, though. From the size of that dust cloud I'd hazard it's only one rider, and no Comanch' worth his salt would make that much sign. Mebbe with some luck this fella knows where there's water."

Nonetheless, being cautious from years on the frontier, Bill loosened the old Navy Colt he wore in the battered holster on his right hip before kicking his horse into a slow jogtrot. His single-shot Sharps wouldn't do much good if he got into a running gunfight with the approaching rider.

The dust cloud soon materialized into another

lone horseman, a dust-beaten cowboy who was mounted on a splendid sorrel gelding. When he spied Bill and reined the horse to a halt, the spirited animal pranced a bit before stopping, neck arched proudly. The gelding's coat, even under its coating of dust, shone like a newly-minted copper penny.

"Howdy, Mister," the cowpoke called out. "What brings you way out here all on your lonesome?"

"Howdy yourself," Bill replied. "Far as bein' out here on my own, that ain't exactly true. Name's Bill . . . Bill Dundee. I'm helpin' scout for a wagon train passin' through, headed for west of San Angelo."

"My handle's Derek . . . Derek Frahm," the cowboy answered, with a friendly grin. He was tall and lanky, with closed-cropped brown hair and steady eyes. His gear and clothing, unlike his horse, were plain and serviceable, and well-worn. The only thing fancy about him was the bright yellow silk bandanna looped around his neck.

"Pleased to make your acquaintance, Bill," he continued. "Don't see any dust from your wagons, though. Exactly how far back are they?"

"I'm not certain," Bill admitted. "I'm scoutin' out ahead, lookin' for water. We're runnin' low, and most of the streams and waterholes are dried up. I'm kinda hopin' you can tell me where to find some."

"Water? That's not a problem at all," Frahm answered. "My ranch is less than a mile from here. I've got a good, deep well. You're welcome to all the water you need." Frahm glanced up at the lowering sun. "In fact, why don't you and your people plan on spendin' the night at my place? It's gettin' late, so you can't travel much farther today anyway."

"That's right kind of you, Derek," Bill replied. "But there's more'n a hundred people following me, including a bunch of Texas Rangers. In fact, I'm a special scout for the Rangers."

He dug in his pocket to show Frahm the badge Jim had carved.

"All the more reason to stay then. My wife'll be pleased for the company. We don't see many folks way out here. I'll slaughter a steer, and we'll make a celebration of it. Reckon you haven't seen much fresh meat for quite a spell."

"Not as much as we'd like, no. Game's been kinda scarce," Bill admitted.

"Then it's settled. I'll ride with you back to the wagons, then lead you folks to my spread."

"Should give you a word of warnin' first, Derek," Bill said. "Except for the Rangers, the folks are all Negroes, like me."

"Don't matter none to me," Frahm replied. "Folks is folks, and company's company."

"Then we'll accept your invitation," Bill replied.

● ● ●

The Frahm ranch, the Circle D+S+F, was located in a hollow about three-quarters of a mile off the main road. In contrast to its brown, dusty, sun-baked surroundings, the place was highlighted by several species of trees, including cottonwoods, live oaks, and even a few far out of place maples, as well as several acres of lush grass. There was even a large vegetable garden. Two windmills spun in the stiff breeze, pumping water into stock tanks. The buildings themselves were sturdily built of cedar logs and shakes. Curtains at the windows and flowerboxes on the windowsills, filled with colorful blooms, added a feminine touch.

On the ranch house's porch stood a woman watching the approaching wagons, flanked by two young boys.

"That's not a mirage I'm seein', is it, Derek?" Jep asked as they neared the ranch.

"Nope, it sure ain't. That's my spread, and it's for sure-enough real," Frahm answered. He raised his dusty black Stetson over his head, waved it in a circle, and whooped. The woman on the porch waved in return.

"Sam! Company's comin'!" he cried, kicking his horse into a lope.

A short while later, with the wagons still rolling into the ranch yard, Frahm was introducing his family to the train's leaders.

"Sam, this is Lieutenant Jim Blawcyzk of the Texas Rangers, and his son Chip. Man next to them is Bill Dundee, a special scout for the Rangers. You'll meet the rest of their pardners shortly. Then we have Adrian Chatman, leader of the group, along with Jep Hawthorne, who's bossin' the train. Men, my wife Samantha, and my boys Austin and Colin."

"Pleased to meet you all," Samantha said, smiling brightly. She was a buxom woman, a bit on the short side, with long, straight dark hair and deep brown eyes. Austin was the older of the two boys, about six years old, with brown hair, while Colin, about four, was a towhead. Both boys were staring in amazement at the column of wagons, people, and livestock coming into the yard.

"Sam, these folks have been travelin' a long way, and still have quite a distance to go," Frahm explained. "They're short on water, so I told 'em they could fill up their barrels here. Also told 'em I'd slaughter and roast a steer, so we could have a real celebration, then they could rest here for the night. Figured you wouldn't mind, and would be grateful for the company."

"We really don't want to impose, ma'am," Adrian said.

"Pish-tosh," Samantha answered. "It's no imposition at all. We have plenty of water and food, and will be happy to provide what you need. Besides, as my husband said, I'm certainly glad for the company. We can go weeks out here, sometimes even a month or more, without seeing another soul. We won't have another word about imposing. This will give me a chance to gossip with some of the womenfolk."

"And don't bother arguing with my wife," Derek added, laughing. "I haven't won one with her yet, so I doubt you'd have any better luck. C'mon, I'll show you where to park your wagons and bed down your stock, then we'll start gettin' supper goin'."

By now, after weeks on the trail, the travelers were veterans at setting up and breaking down camp, so it seemed no time at all before the wagons were in place and the livestock settled for the night. While the steer, spitted over a fire, roasted, the women worked on the accompaniments. Samantha broke into her larder, and the women from the train dipped into their supplies. Soon, bread, corn pone, pies, and cakes were baking in the kitchen stove and in Dutch ovens outside, while vegetables from the Frahms' garden were supplemented by sweet potatoes and turnips from the wagons.

"Mercy sakes, everything smells delicious," Frances Watley exclaimed.

"Sure hopes it tastes as good as it smells," Allen Young, another of Adrian's uncles exclaimed, as he snatched a piece of corn pone.

"If you don't get out of this kitchen you won't

ever find out, as you won't get another bite," Frances warned him.

"Brother, I guess she sure told you," Louis Young, another uncle, laughed. "We'd best get outta here. Mebbe they need some help turnin' that steer."

"I know when I'm not welcome. Let's go," Allen snorted.

"You're welcome in my kitchen anytime, as long as you're not underfoot, like right now," Samantha answered. "So get along. Supper won't get done any faster by you two hangin' around and getting in our way. Shoo!"

"Yes'm," Louis answered, with a grin. "Don't mind Allen. He just can't reason when it comes to his stomach. I'll get him out of your way."

While supper was readied, some of the men took the opportunity to relax, while others worked on mending harness and checking wagons. Colin and Austin, excited at meeting other children, made fast friends with several of the youngsters from the wagons who were near their age.

"Want to see something?" Austin asked Joey Stark. He and Joey were standing alongside the corral which held Austin's and Colin's pinto ponies.

"Sure," Joey agreed.

"Look at this."

Austin pulled a slingshot from his back pocket and handed it to the other boy.

"What is it?" Joey asked.

"It's a slingshot," Austin answered. "Give it back to me and I'll show you how it works."

"All right." Joey handed the weapon back to his newfound friend.

"Watch that fencepost," Austin ordered. He picked up a pebble from the ground, settled it into the slingshot's pouch, pulled the pouch back and let the rock fly. It struck solidly in the center of the post.

"Wow! Mind if I try that?" Joey asked.

"Sure, go ahead," Austin agreed.

After several attempts, Joey did manage to make a hit on the post.

"I did it, Austin!" he exclaimed.

"Told you that you'd get the hang of it," Austin answered. He started to say more, but was interrupted by the ringing of the triangle hanging from the porch roof.

"Shucks, that means supper's ready, so we don't have more time for you to practice," Austin complained. "Mebbe after we eat we can work on this again."

"Sure thing," Joey answered. "But right now I'm starvin'."

"Reckon I am too," Austin agreed. "Race you to the house."

"Derek, how'd you find a place like this, with plenty of water in the middle of such dry country?" Jim questioned, as they were eating supper.

"Pure dumb luck," Frahm replied. "We were planning on settlin' further west, but our wagon horses busted loose one night, while we were camped not far from here. By the time I caught up to 'em, they were right in this spot, grazin'. I realized they must have scented water, and that's what made them bust loose. The horses found only a tiny spring, but I figured with this much greenery around here there must be a good source of water. Took a chance, started diggin' around, and before you know it I hit plenty of water. Came bubblin' out of the ground like a fountain. Must be an underground stream that comes close to the surface here, near as I can figure. So, Sam and I staked our claim and homesteaded right here."

"I don't remember that, Dad," Colin spoke up, from where he sat in his father's lap.

"Of course you don't," Derek chuckled, tousling the boy's hair. "You weren't even born then. Neither was your brother, for that matter. You two came along later."

"Well, you sure lucked into a pretty spot," Jim noted. "I'm surprised no one else has homesteaded around here."

"We've got the only reliable water source," Derek explained. "A few folks have tried, but weren't able to ride out the dry months."

"What about the big ranchers?" Smoky asked. "Seems to me they'd like to get at this place, if as you say it's the only dependable water for miles."

"That was my thinking too," Derek answered, "But they haven't bothered us. I guess it's because while there's enough water for our needs, there's really not sufficient supply for more'n a few cows, and we have an agreement to give their stock access to my water if a drought gets too bad. Plus we've been here long enough no one questions our ownership of the land. We get along fine with the cattlemen. In fact, I run my cows with theirs. Even though I've got the only dependable year-round water source for miles, there are enough smaller waterholes and creeks, a few of which rarely dry up, scattered around this territory to support cattle, long as you don't mind ridin' a big range. Besides, if anyone did bother us, I could change their mind right quick."

Frahm patted the Remington revolver he wore on his right hip.

"Sam's a pretty good shot with a rifle, too," he added.

"Well, it sure is a nice spread you've got," Smoky agreed.

"Our little piece of Paradise right here on earth," Derek agreed.

After supper was finished and the dishes cleaned and put away, the emigrants and the Frahms spent an hour singing, then, before retiring, Devon Jones led a brief prayer service. It was close to midnight before everyone was finally settled in their beds or blankets, all soon sleeping peacefully under the star-studded Texas sky.

CHAPTER SIXTEEN

"Ranger Jim, do you really have to leave today? Can't you stay awhile longer?" Austin pleaded, as early the next morning Jim was saddling Sizzle. He and his brother had taken an instant liking to the Ranger lieutenant, whose ruthless determination to mete out justice to lawbreakers belied his true easy-going nature, especially when dealing with kids.

"Yeah, Ranger Jim, can't you stay, please?" Colin begged.

"Wish I could, but we've really got to be on our way," Jim answered. "Tell you what, though. I can't promise for certain, but if my pards and I ride through here on our way back, we'll be sure and stop in . . . that's if it's all right with your folks."

"It certainly is," Derek called from the end of the corral, where he was grooming his sorrel. "Boys, you have to stop pestering the Ranger now. He needs to be on his way."

"They're not botherin' me," Jim said. "Besides, in a few years I figure they'll make real fine Texas Rangers. Bet a hat on it."

"You mean that, Ranger Jim?" Colin exclaimed.

"Wouldn't have said it if I didn't," Jim answered.

An hour later, their water barrels filled with sweet water from the Frahms' well, and supplies supplemented with peas, green beans, and carrots from the Frahms' garden, the emigrants resumed their westward trek once again, minus one member. Roy Delacroix decided to remain at the Frahms' as a hired hand, with aspirations of becoming a cowboy. Something about Delacroix had convinced Derek the young man would make a fine cowpuncher, a man to ride the river with. Derek assured Roy that, under his tutelage and with hard work, he would quickly become a top hand.

After leaving the Circle D+S+F, the travelers settled into their routine once again, the days stretching on as the wagons made ten, twelve, or occasionally, on a good day, fifteen miles across the prairie. By now, they were paralleling the Colorado River, so even though the river was running far below normal, water was no longer the concern it had been. The only excitement during the past several days had been caused by young Joey Stark. Steve Masters had made a rudimentary slingshot for the youngster, who had been begging for one ever since playing with Austin's. Despite the Ranger having to use strips of rawhide rather than rubber for the weapon, the branch he had chosen still was supple enough so Joey could fling a rock quite some distance. When old Shirley Bell bent over to retrieve a pot, Joey had struck her square on the bottom with a good-sized pebble, an act which earned him a sound paddling. After a couple of days, however, the incident had been forgotten. The slingshot was returned to Joey, and Steve, one evening, showed the boy how to skip rocks across the surface of the slow-moving Colorado.

Three days later, Steve was grooming Shenandoah when Penelope Stark rushed up to him.

"Ranger Steve, Joey's missing!" she cried.

"What's that, Miz Stark? What's wrong?"

"Joey's missing. I can't find him anywhere. He's not at our wagon, and not with Nathaniel or Isaiah, either. None of the other boys have seen him."

"All right, Miz Stark, try and stay calm. Take a deep breath," Steve advised, picking his saddle and blanket from the ground and tossing them on his gelding's back. "I'll find Joey. He can't have gotten far. Try and think. Where did you see him last?"

"He was in our wagon, watching the baby for me while I fetched some water. Usually I'd have either Joey or his sister do that, but I wanted to visit with Ellie Nolan and her baby. I did that, then got the water. When I returned, Joey asked about supper. I told him it would be ready as soon as I got the baby to sleep, so he said he'd find something to do. That's the last I saw of him."

"And you don't know which way he went?"

"No, I surely don't. You have to find him, Ranger."

"Don't worry, I will. A boy Joey's age will leave plenty of sign. I'll have him back here in two shakes."

Steve slid the bridle over Shenandoah's head and slipped the bit into his mouth, then swung into the saddle.

"Miz Stark, why don't you start supper while you're waitin'?" he suggested. "It'll help keep you from worryin', and I'd reckon Joey'll be good and hungry once I bring him back."

"All right," Penelope half-heartedly agreed. "And thank you, Ranger."

"That's what I'm here for," Steve answered, turning Shenandoah and heading for the edge of camp.

Steve, like most of the Rangers, was an expert tracker, and it didn't take long for the experienced lawman to find Joey's trail. The youngster's bare feet had scuffed up the sand at the bottom of a shallow arroyo. The boy had also snapped off a branch or two from the brush as he evidently explored the ravine.

"C'mon, Shenandoah, let's get him," Steve

urged, kicking the horse into a slow lope. They had gone another two hundred yards and were rounding a bend when Steve pulled the gelding to a halt, horrified at the sight of Joey, standing less than six feet from a rattlesnake poised to strike. The boy stood transfixed, watching the snake coil and rattle. He gripped his slingshot tightly. Evidently he had tried to hit the poisonous reptile with a rock from the sling and missed. Now that snake was ready to sink its fangs into the boy's leg.

"Don't move, Joey!" Steve shouted. "Don't even breathe."

He lifted his Colt from its holster, aimed carefully, and fired, cursing when his first shot missed and ricocheted away. Quickly, Steve triggered again, this bullet taking the rattler's head clean off. Steve leapt from his horse.

"Joey, are you all right?" he exclaimed.

"Yeah, I . . . ," Joey began to answer, stopping short at the sudden snapping and crackling of dry branches, accompanied by high-pitched squeals. "Ranger Steve!"

Several wild boars, evidently angered by the gunshots, perhaps one struck by Steve's errant bullet, burst out of the brush, charging directly at the helpless boy. Steve had already leveled his gun before Joey's cry, and now fired the four remaining bullets in its chamber at the crazed hogs, dropping two of them. The rest kept coming, even more enraged by the additional shots. Steve turned for his horse, hoping to grab Joey and outrun the crazed hogs, only to find that Shenandoah, scared out of his wits by the squealing pack, had run off. He cursed the loss of his gelding, the sole chance of escape.

Steve raced the gap between himself and Joey, tackling the youngster in a long dive, the Ranger huddling over Joey in a desperate attempt to save the boy's life by shielding him with his own body. The lead boar lowered its head and slammed into Steve's side, its long, razor-sharp tusks ripping open flesh and muscle over the Ranger's ribs like a scalpel. The impact flipped Steve onto his back, still gripping Joey. The other hogs converged, tusks ripping into the Ranger and boy in their maddened, killing frenzy.

Jim Blawcyzk and the rest of the Rangers were hunkered around a fire, for the first time in a long time relaxing completely . . . or at least as completely as Texas Rangers on duty ever did. There had been no sign of any real trouble since leaving Corsicana, even the weather cooperating with a string of refreshingly cool days, a soft northerly breeze keeping the usual oppressive heat and humidity at bay. They'd not even seen any other riders or freighters the past few days. Better yet, they could finally sense the end of the journey approaching, despite the many miles still remaining to San Angelo. So, before taking their turns at watch for the night, they were enjoying final cups of coffee and, for those who smoked, cigarettes.

Sam and Sizzle wandered up to Jim, nickering, then nuzzling his shoulder as they begged for treats. Unlike the rest of the mounts, confined in a rope corral or tied to a picket line, Jim's paints were always allowed to roam free. They would never stray far from him.

"Better give those horses some peppermints, Dad, or you'll never get any peace tonight," Charlie advised. "Bet a hat on it."

Since joining the Rangers, Charlie had picked up his father's favorite expression.

"I reckon," Jim agreed, pushing himself to his feet and digging in his hip pocket for some candies. He gave one to each horse, then his head jerked up at the sound of two gunshots, with four more following in quick succession.

"Trouble!" he exclaimed. "Doesn't sound like it's too far out of camp. Reckon we'd best see what it is. C'mon, Siz."

He headed for the rope corral to retrieve his gear, with Sizzle and Sam at his side, the other Rangers following. Jep and Adrian were already waiting when they reached the horses.

"Trouble, Jim?" Adrian asked.

"Dunno for certain, but I wouldn't bet a hat against it," Jim answered, lifting his saddle and blanket from the ground and tossing them on Sizzle's back. "We'll check it out."

"Horse comin' fast," Bill stated. His keen ears had picked up the sound of rapid hoofbeats. A moment later, a terrified Shenadoah galloped into the camp.

"That's Steve's horse!" Smoky exclaimed. "Thought Steve was just visitin' the Starks."

"He was, last I saw him," Jep confirmed.

Quickly, the Rangers readied their horses and climbed into their saddles. A grim-faced Jim Blawcyzk ordered them forward at a gallop.

The tracks left by Shenandoah in his frenzied flight were plain enough to follow. It only took the Rangers a few minutes to reach the arroyo, where, cautious of ambush, Jim slowed to a walk. They rode into the ravine, a moment later coming upon Steve and Joey.

"Lord, no!" Jim exclaimed, seeing the bloodied remains of his fellow Ranger and the youngster. Behind him, he could hear gasps of shock as the other men took in the carnage, each one nauseated at the grisly scene. Charlie, Ty, and Dan dropped from their saddles, sickened to their stomachs, and vomited, while Johnny Dexter slumped over his horse's neck, trying to hold down the bile rising in his throat.

Steve had been disemboweled by the hogs' sharp tusks and slashing teeth, most of his face torn away, so much so he was barely recognizable.

246

His arms were still clamped protectively around Joey, whose stomach had also been ripped open. One of the boy's arms was practically torn off, his right ear missing. Blood covered the ground, soaking into the sand.

Jim Huggins pointed at the two dead hogs.

"Looks like Steve tangled with those things," he observed. "I'd reckon they came after Joey. Steve did his best to save the boy, but just couldn't. Unusual for that many hogs to be runnin' in a pack. Must've been a bunch of juvenile males, I'd figure."

"Snake involved too," Smoky added, pointing out the headless rattler. "Appears as if Steve got it before the hogs."

"Don't really matter none, does it?" Bill said. "One of us has got to break the news to Miz Stark, plus we've got to give Steve and Joey proper burials, and right quick."

"You're right, Bill," Jim answered. "Charlie, you and Ty ride back with me. Get a couple of tarps to wrap the bodies and carry 'em back to camp. I'll round up Adrian and Preacher Jones, tell them what's happened, then inform Miz Stark. Rest of you stay here until Charlie and Ty return."

"I purely don't envy you that task, Jim," Johnny choked out.

"Thanks, son," Jim answered. "When you get back to camp, whatever you do, make sure no one sees those bodies. Wrap them real tight, and keep 'em covered. That's a gruesome sight no one should ever have to see."

After locating Adrian and Devon Jones, Jim allowed them a couple of minutes to compose themselves. The preacher, after a brief prayer, removed a jug from his wagon.

"Lord knows I ain't a drinkin' man, but at a time like this a swallow helps me steel myself," he explained. He and Adrian both took long pulls from the jug. Then, before heading for the Stark wagon, they found Frances, Ellie Nolan, and Christine Fletcher. The women would help to comfort Penelope.

Penelope was pacing alongside her wagon, her daughter Mary huddled underneath, holding Moses, her infant brother. At the approach of the three men, Penelope cried out, alarmed.

"Preacher Jones, what's happened to Joey? What's happened to my boy? Something awful has happened. Oh please, Preacher, tell me my boy's all right."

Jones took the widow's hand, holding it gently.

"Penelope, I wish I could say that Joey is just fine, but he's not. There's no easy way to say this, but he and Ranger Masters have gone home to the Lord. I'm sorry, Penelope."

"No!" Penelope dropped to her knees with an anguished wail, sobbing piteously. Behind her, Mary sniffled, tears rolling down her cheeks.

Frances took the baby from Mary, then Christine hugged the girl tightly.

Ellie knelt alongside her friend, trying in vain to assuage her grief.

"Penelope, I don't have the words to say," she began. "There really aren't any I can find, except we're all here for you."

"What, what happened?" Penelope asked.

"Near as we can tell, Joey must've stumbled on a pack of wild hogs," Jim explained. "Steve tried to save him, but couldn't. Joey wasn't alone when he died. His friend was with him."

"My boy, where is he? I want to see my boy," Penelope cried.

"The other Rangers are bringing him back right now," Adrian answered. "He'll be here soon."

"I want to see him," Penelope reiterated.

"Miz Stark, I surely don't want to say this, but you can't," Jim answered. "Those hogs, well, they didn't, um, they . . . You'll want to just remember Joey the way he was, always laughin' and funnin', full of vinegar."

"I want to see my son," Penelope insisted. "Why don't you want me to see him? Why?"

Jim swallowed hard before answering, tears rolling down the cheeks of the rugged, hardened Ranger lieutenant. He hated what he would have to say next, but knew it was the only way he could keep the devastated mother from demanding to see her son's body.

"Miz Stark, I just can't let you. Joey and Steve were pretty well torn up by those hogs. Their bodies are really mutilated, and you can't hardly recognize their faces. Trust me, it's better that you don't see them."

"Listen to the lieutenant, Penelope," Preacher Jones urged. "He's right, hard as it is to say. Just think of Joey as he was, and now of his soul glowing brightly in the presence of the Lord."

Penelope's only response was a wracking sob.

"Preacher, I've got to meet the men," Jim said. "They'll be back soon. Once they are I'll send for you. We'll need to have the burial as quickly as we can."

"I know," the preacher replied. "We'll remain here with Penelope until then."

Once the bodies were returned to camp and the graves dug, everyone gathered for the brief service for Ranger Steven Masters and young Joey Stark. Penelope's grief had settled into a stunned acceptance. She stood, eyes lifeless, next to her son's final resting place.

"Friends," Devon Jones began, "none of us can know the ways of the Lord. We know not His plans for us. All we do know is He intends for each and every one of us to be with Him in Paradise, at the time He sets. While none of us, in our profound sorrow, can understand why God chose

250

this day to call Joey Stark and Steven Masters home to Him, we can find some measure of comfort from our sorrow in the secure knowledge that Joey and Steven are most assuredly with Him. Like someday, too, as we will share in the joy of being with our Lord and Saviour, they are indeed already sharing the joy of being in His presence. While Steven and Joey did not know each other for long, they did become friends in the short time of their acquaintance, and it is fitting that they travel together to Paradise. It is the sure knowledge that, when the Lord is ready, we will be reunited with Joey and Steven in His presence, which will overcome our present sorrow. Indeed, we will mourn, as is proper and right, but we will also, with time, realize that our beloved Joey and friend Steven are in a far better place, away from the travails of this world. Amen."

"Amen."

"Ashes to ashes, dust to dust. We commit the earthly bodies of Joey Stark and Steven Masters to the dirt from which they came, Lord, and their eternal souls to You. Amen."

"Amen."

The preacher picked up a handful of dirt and tossed it onto the canvas-wrapped bodies. While the graves were filled, Christine Fletcher's voice floated through the still air, as she sang a particularly melancholy rendition of *Nobody Knows the Trouble I've Seen*.

"Nobody knows the trouble I've seen,
"Nobody knows my sorrow.
"Nobody knows the trouble I've seen,
"Glory Hallelujah!"

"Sometimes I'se up, sometimes I'se down,
"Oh, yes, Lord.
"Sometimes I'se almost onto the ground,
"Oh, yes, Lord.
"Although you see me goin' 'long so,
"Oh, yes, Lord.
"I have my trials here below,
"Oh, yes, Lord.
"If you get there before I do,
"Oh, yes, Lord.
"Tell all-a my friends I'se comin' too.
"Oh, yes, Lord."

"Nobody knows the trouble I've seen,
"Nobody knows but Jesus.
"Nobody knows the trouble I've seen,
"Glory Hallelujah!"

CHAPTER SEVENTEEN

Jep Hawthorne ordered the column of wagons to a halt. He pointed to a collection of distant buildings scattered on the western horizon.

"Adrian, there it is. That's San Angelo just ahead. We'll be rollin' into town in little more'n an hour or so. You did it, Mister Chatman. You got your people to their new home."

"I couldn't have done it without your help, Jep," Adrian replied. "You and a lot of others. And I didn't quite get everyone home."

His joy at finally reaching his destination was tempered with sadness at the memories of Abraham Martin, young Joey Stark, and Texas Ranger Steve Masters, who now lay in lonesome graves on the prairie.

"Nonetheless, it was your idea, and you who did all the work, organizing, raising money, buying the land, and so on," Jep answered. "You should be proud of yourself, son. Now, before we hit town, you'd better come up with a plan to keep things in hand."

"Already have," Adrian explained. "There's a livery stable, Montgomery's, at the edge of town which has several good-sized corrals where we can keep the animals. I've already made arrangements for that, and for us to camp on an empty lot just next to the stable. We'll stop there, I'll head into town to finalize the paperwork for the land, make the last payment, and pick up the deed. Once that's finished I'll turn everyone loose to get some shoppin' done. Meantime, I've arranged to purchase building supplies at a place called Tomlinson's, so I'll place the order, and later take a couple of the men to pick those up. We'll spend the night here, then first thing tomorrow head for Freedom."

"Not every store's gonna welcome a bunch of coloreds," Jep noted.

"I'm aware of that, but those that don't will be losin' out on an awful lot of money," Adrian answered. "Been a long time since Waco, and even back there no one bought a lot of stuff, since we didn't want to haul excess goods another couple hundred miles. Most everyone's ready to spend some cash, especially the womenfolk."

"I can't say as I blame 'em," Jep chuckled. "I don't require much, but even I'm ready to pick up a few more supplies, and mebbe do a bit of drinkin'. By the way, speaking of cash, I'd advise you to be careful with that money you'll be taking to the land office. Plenty of men would kill to get their hands on that much *dinero*."

"Don't worry about that," Adrian answered. "I've already asked Jim Blawcyzk for one of his Rangers to accompany me. He's taken on that chore himself, so anyone foolish enough to try and rob me will have to get past him first, which is no easy task, I'm certain."

"Boy howdy, you can say that again," Jep agreed. "Well, let's get rollin'."

"Adrian, I know you're anxious to get to the land office, and I don't blame you, but I need to check in at the sheriff's office first, then stop at the Western Union. There hasn't been the chance to send any messages to Headquarters since Waco, so I need to get that done. It'll only take a few minutes. You stick by my side until I'm finished. Don't want you out of my sight with that cash you're carryin'. I'm kinda surprised you didn't have a bank draft drawn," Jim said, after they left the others at their chosen camp site, and rode into town. Quite a few of the passersby stared at the unusual pair, a Negro and a Texas Ranger, whose badge glittered brightly on his vest.

"I thought of it, but didn't want any delay while the draft was presented and paid. Cash talks loudest, and quickest," Adrian explained.

"You can bet your hat on that," Jim agreed, laughing. "There's the sheriff's office, just ahead."

They reined their horses to a halt, dismounted, and looped their reins over the hitchrail. Jim slipped Sizzle a peppermint, then they headed inside the office. The man behind the nearest desk looked up at their approach.

"Ranger! I'm Sheriff Cecil Franklin. What brings you to San Angelo? Got a prisoner you need held?" he asked, eyeing Adrian.

"Name's Jim Blawcyzk, Lieutenant Jim Blawcyzk to be precise, and no, not exactly, Sheriff," Jim answered. "This here's Adrian Chatman. He's leadin' a bunch of folks who are gonna establish a new town about fifteen miles northwest of here."

"Oh, yeah, I've heard something about that," Franklin replied. "Didn't realize it was gonna be a colored town, though. We don't have all that many coloreds in Tom Green County. There is one fairly well known nigger, a preacher man named James Walker, who moved here from Kentucky. In fact, until recently, he was the only Protestant minister in all of the county. Rest of the sky-pilots are mostly Catholic priests. Sorry for jumpin' to conclusions and assuming you were a prisoner, Mr. Chatman. It's just that whenever a Ranger comes into town with another man, he's usually bringin' in some outlaw."

"Apology accepted, Sheriff," Adrian answered.

"Adrian's wagons are just at the edge of town," Jim continued. "I only wanted to advise you we were in town. There's several more Rangers with me, asked to escort the train at the Governor's request. Adrian and I will be stopping at the Western Union and a couple other places,

256

including the land office. Once we've concluded our business, the rest of his folks plan on doin' some shoppin'.""

"We're staying overnight, then heading out first thing in the morning," Adrian added.

"Well, y'all have a good stay," Franklin answered. "Just don't stir up any trouble."

"Not planning on it," Adrian assured him. "We're too close to our destination for that. Besides, most of the folks with me are married men and women and their children. Also got a couple widowers, and one eighty-six year old widow. Hardly the trouble-makin' type."

"Glad to hear it," Franklin said.

The Western Union office was diagonally across the street from the sheriff's office, so Jim and Adrian headed there next.

"Mornin', gents," the young clerk on duty greeted them, pushing back the green eyeshade from his forehead. "What can I do for you?"

"I need to send a telegram to Ranger Headquarters in Austin," Jim answered.

"Figured as such, looking at the badge you're wearin'," the clerk responded. "You wouldn't be a Lieutenant Blawcyzk?" he asked, mangling Jim's surname.

"That's BLUH-zhick," Jim chuckled, "and yes, I sure would be. Why? You got a message for me?"

"Sure do, around here somewhere," the clerk

replied, turning to a wall of pigeonholes and rummaging through them. "Ah, here it is."

He handed Jim a yellow flimsy. Jim quickly scanned its contents, then smiled.

"What is it, Jim? Good news?" Adrian asked.

"Sure is. Sheriff Meader back in Corsicana's gonna pull through. His doc expects a complete recovery."

"That is good news," Adrian agreed. "Meader seems like a fine man."

"Ranger, you wanted to send a wire?" the clerk urged.

"Sure do." Jim scribbled out a message on the requisite form and handed it to the clerk.

"Captain Storm Ranger Headquarters Austin Stop Reached San Angelo Stop Steve Masters killed in accident Stop No other incidents Stop JB"[4]

"This'll go right out," the clerk assured him, after scanning the message.

"*Muchas gracias.*" Jim paid the fee, and the clerk hunched over his key, clicking out the message.

"Captain Storm won't wonder what happened to Steve?" Adrian asked as they left the office.

"He will, but I'll write up a full report and mail it to him in the next few days," Jim answered, as they headed for their horses. They remounted,

---

4 *"Stop"* was used to end a phrase in a telegram as punctuation was an extra charge.

and following the directions Adrian had, headed several blocks south, to the Tom Green and Coke County Land Brokers. Once again, the horses were tied, Sizzle given a peppermint, and the two men entered the solidly-built, two story brick structure. A prim young woman, glasses perched on her nose, greeted them.

"Good day, gentlemen. How may I help you?"

"I'm here to see Asa Miller," Adrian answered.

"Certainly. May I tell him who is calling?"

"Adrian Chatman."

"Is he expecting you, Mr. Chatman? Mr. Miller is a very busy man, and seldom sees anyone without an appointment. I don't recall him mentioning anyone by your name."

"He is expecting me; however, I did not know for certain when I would arrive here in San Angelo," Adrian explained.

"Fine. I'll check and see if he is available."

The woman rose and disappeared down a corridor.

"Not the friendliest, is she?" Jim questioned.

"I'd prefer to think of her as being efficient," Adrian answered.

A moment later, the woman returned, accompanied by a heavyset, balding man in his mid-fifties. A gold watch chain was draped across his rather large paunch.

"Mister Chatman," he stated, extending his

hand to Jim. "Miss Phelps just told me you were here. I'm pleased to meet you. Did you have a pleasant journey?"

"Um, I'm afraid you're mistaken," Jim said. "I'm Ranger Lieutenant James J. Blawcyzk." He indicated Adrian. "This is Mr. Chatman."

"You're Mr. Chatman?" the land broker sputtered, flushing. "But, I was expecting . . . I mean, you're not quite what I'd pictured," he concluded, recovering somewhat from his initial discomfiture.

"You mean you weren't expecting a colored man," Adrian replied.

"I have to say yes, that's correct. Mister Burleson never told me you were a Negro."

"Really was no need to, was there?" Adrian asked.

"I guess . . . well, no," Miller answered. "It's just that . . ."

"Mr. Miller, I hate to rush you, but I have a lot of things to get done," Adrian continued. "I'd like to pay you the balance due and pick up the deed to my property."

"Deed? Oh, the deed." Miller echoed.

"Is there a problem?" Adrian asked, sensing the man's hesitation.

"Well, I mean, that is, the title, may be . . ."

"Mr. Miller," Jim broke in. "I'm assuming you have an agreement to sell Mr. Chatman a parcel of land, and that he has already advanced you quite a sum of money as down payment. Would I be correct?"

"Yes. Yes, Lieutenant."

"Now, Mr. Chatman has the cash to pay off the balance, and is prepared to do so immediately. In exchange, you will produce a signed deed for the property you have agreed to sell him. I've been a lawman for a good many years, sir, and trust me, I'm very good at reading people. Right now I'm reading you, and you don't want to sell a colored man any land, am I right?"

"That, that's not it at all," Miller harrumphed.

"Oh, but I think it is, Miller," Jim snapped, his voice growing hard and his eyes glittering like chips of blue ice. "Now, you're going to get the deed to Mr. Chatman's property, he is going to give you the balance promised, and you will sign the deed over to him. If you don't, I'll place you under arrest for fraud, and for appropriating funds under false pretenses. You'll be facing a long prison sentence, bet a hat on it. Do I make myself clear?"

"Yes, I believe you do, perfectly clear." Miller gulped hard. Sweat was now glistening on his brow. "Miss Phelps, would you bring the Chatman file to my office? I'll also need you to witness the transaction and the signatures."

"Certainly, Mr. Miller," his secretary answered.

"Gentlemen, if you'll follow me to my office, we can conclude our business. Right this way."

Miller led them to a large, oak-paneled office, where they settled into brown leather chairs. Pointedly, he didn't offer drinks from the decanter of whiskey on the sideboard, nor cigars from the humidor on his desk, although he poured a tumbler full of whiskey and lit up a cigar for himself.

Once Miss Phelps arrived with the necessary papers, the transaction was concluded in just a few moments, it being plain the faster Adrian and Jim were out of Miller's office the happier he would be. The moment the money had been paid, the deed signed and in Adrian's shirt pocket, the land broker brusquely dismissed them.

"I don't mean to be rude, but I have other appointments, and I am already behind schedule. Good day, gentlemen."

"Good day to you, sir, and thank you," Adrian replied.

"*Adios*," Jim added. "One more thing, Miller. You're to get that deed over to the county land office and have it recorded today. I'll be checking to make sure that you do. If it's not, there's a law on the books about tampering with official county and state documents."

"I'll have that done before the day is out," Miller answered. "Now, if you'll excuse me . . ." He turned away, picked up a file from his desk, and opened it.

Once they were outside, Jim said, "Adrian, I

didn't realize you'd bought land sight unseen. You took an awful chance there, pardner."

"Not really," Adrian disagreed. "I knew it would be highly unlikely anyone would want to sell land in this area for a colored settlement. So, I had a white friend of mine from Washington, Solomon Burleson, come down here, acting as my agent, to find suitable land and arrange the purchase. Solomon's a native Texan, was aware of my requirements, and had legal authority to act in my stead. I knew I could trust him implicitly, so I wasn't concerned at all."

"Remind me never to get in a poker game with you, Mr. Chatman," Jim chuckled. "I'd most likely lose my shirt."

"You sure would," Adrian answered. "Along with your trousers, boots, socks, hat, and probably your underwear."

"Brr. That could get a mite chilly in January," Jim chuckled, shuddering as if cold. "Where to now?"

"Tomlinson's store, to arrange delivery of the supplies I ordered," Adrian answered. "It's a few blocks from here, if my information is correct."

After a short ride, they were reining up in front of a rambling building with "Tomlinson's Lumber, Hardware, and Building Supplies" emblazoned across the front. A yard to the rear was bustling with workers loading and unloading wagons, as well as several freight cars shunted onto a siding. When Adrian and Jim entered the establishment, they were in a large showroom, well-organized, its counters stacked with merchandise. There were several clerks waiting on lines of customers. It took a few minutes until one of the clerks was free, and came over to wait on them.

"Howdy, gentlemen. Welcome to Tomlinson's. How may I be of assistance?"

"I'm Adrian Chatman. I have a special order placed with Mr. Tomlinson," Adrian answered. "Is he available?"

"That's him in the back corner," the clerk answered. "I'll take you to him."

"Mr. Tomlinson," the clerk called as they neared him. "Gentleman here is asking for you. Says his name is Adrian Chatman."

"Mr. Chatman, a pleasure. I'm Hezekiah Tomlinson," he said, shaking Adrian's hand. "How was your journey? Not too difficult, I hope?"

Tomlinson was tall and slim, in his late forties, with wavy gray hair and gray eyes. His accent was from somewhere back East, probably New Jersey. The merchant didn't seem bothered one bit to have a Negro in his store.

"We had some trouble, including losing three people, but that's not unexpected for a trip like ours," Adrian answered. "In fact, we probably had fewer problems than most wagon trains, thanks to this man and his partners. This is Texas Ranger Lieutenant Jim Blawcyzk."

"Again, a pleasure, Lieutenant," Tomlinson said, shaking Jim's hand.

"Easier to just call me Jim."

"All right," Tomlinson answered, then continued to Adrian, "Mr. Chatman, I am sorry for your losses, even though they are to be expected during an arduous undertaking such as yours."

"Thank you, sir."

"Please, Hezekiah."

"Certainly. Hezekiah. And I'm Adrian. Now, about the supplies I ordered. How soon will you be able to deliver them?"

Tomlinson hesitated. He looked embarrassed.

"Adrian, I don't know how to explain this. I won't be able to deliver your goods, at least not all that you ordered, for the foreseeable future."

"What do you mean?" Adrian responded, his voice tight with controlled anger. "I'm depending on those supplies to build our new town. We've come a long way, and my people can't live in covered wagons forever. They need roofs over their heads, so they can finally get settled and begin rebuilding their lives." He took a deep breath, then continued. "I hope you're not refusing to sell me those supplies because of the color of my skin."

"No, no, that's not it at all," Tomlinson hastened

to assure him. "I don't care about the color of a man's skin, only the color of his money. It's just that my major lumber supplier had a disastrous fire at their main warehouse, and I haven't been able to find a new source of building materials. I will be able to provide you a portion of what you'll require; however, I do need to ration my goods so I'll have at least some for all of my regular customers. I'll refund whatever money is left from that which you advanced me when you placed the order. I hope you understand, and that will be satisfactory."

Adrian sighed. "I reckon I don't have much choice, and I appreciate your supplying what you can. However, this still presents quite a dilemma. The order I had placed was for the bare minimum needed to get started building Freedom."

"We should be able to find more supplies somewhere else," Jim said. "San Angelo's a good-sized town."

"That's right, Ranger," Tomlinson agreed. "In fact, I have an idea, much as I hate to send my customers to the competition. There's a new store that opened recently, Thompson and Manley's. They're located about ten blocks east of here, at Chadbourne and Oakes. Since they haven't had a chance to establish much of a clientele, I'm certain they'll be able to provide you with most, if not all, of what you'll need. In the meantime, why don't we step into my office? We can settle our business, and arrange to have your goods delivered as expeditiously as possible."

"I guess I can't ask for more than that," Adrian conceded. "You're certainly being fair, Hezekiah."

"That's how I've built the business I have, treating the customer right," Tomlinson answered.

Once Adrian had finalized his arrangements with Tomlinson, he and Jim headed for Thompson and Manley's General Mercantile, Building Supply, and Hardware Emporium. The firm was in a brand new building which took up almost an entire city block. Unlike Tomlinson's, however, there were few customers inside, and only two sales clerks. One of these, a woman in her late thirties, short and slim, with long brown hair, peered at them through a pair of spectacles when they entered.

"Good afternoon. I'm Kim Thompson. How may I help you?"

"You must be one of the Thompsons in Thompson and Manley," Jim answered. "My friend here is in need of quite a few building supplies, as well as a good amount of lumber."

"We can certainly provide that," Kim answered. "As far as the name, I'm the only Thompson in Thompson and Manley. One of the founding partners."

"I stand corrected," Jim answered. "I'm

Jim Blawcyzk, Texas Ranger. This is Adrian Chatman."

"Pleased to meet you both," Kim said. "Let me call Dan in, since it appears you'll be placing a large order."

She stepped over to a device which consisted of an enclosed box, on which were several buttons. She pressed one of these, and a blue light appeared over it.

"Dan will be in shortly," she stated.

"You mean just by pushing that button he'll know you want him?" Jim asked.

"That's right. This machine is my own invention. I'm hoping to have it patented shortly," Kim explained.

"How does it work?" Adrian asked.

"It's rather complicated, but basically there's a battery inside the box, and those wires running from it go to various locations in the store and yard. There are lights and buttons at each location. The lights are color-coded, so, for example, the blue light, along with a chime, will tell Dan I need him in the showroom. A red light would indicate someone is needed in the office, green at the railroad siding, and so on."

"That's pretty amazing," Adrian said.

"I'd bet my hat Captain Storm would love to have one of those at Headquarters," Jim added. He turned when the back door opened.

"Here's Dan now," Kim said.

"You needed me, Kim?" he called. Manley was slightly above average in height, somewhat thin, with thick, silvery hair.

"Yes, Dan. This is Mr. Chatman and Ranger Blawcyzk. Mr. Chatman needs to place a large order for lumber and supplies."

"Well, we can certainly use the business," Manley noted. "How did you hear of our firm, Mr. Chatman?"

"Hezekiah Tomlinson. I had placed an order with him quite some time back, but he was unable to fill it completely. I've purchased a sizeable tract of land a few miles northwest of here, to start a new settlement. I've got a wagon train with the first residents camped at the edge of town, next to Montgomery's Livery."

"Ah, yes, the fire at Moran's warehouse." Manley nodded. "That has put a crimp in Tomlinson's business. Kim, we'll have to let him know we appreciate his referring customers to us."

"Yes," Kim agreed. "In the meantime, let's go to the office and get to work on Mr. Chatman's order. I'm certain he's anxious to place it so he can be on his way."

"One question first," Adrian said. "How soon will you be able to deliver the goods? We should be ready for them the day after tomorrow, or one day later at the most."

"We'll have them delivered when and where you require them," Manley assured him.

"Fine, then you have my business," Adrian answered.

Once the necessary supplies were tallied up and paid for, Kim placed the order sheet in an enclosed tube, which hung from a set of cables threaded through a series of pulleys running up the wall, then the length of the ceiling. The cable ran through a flap-covered opening in the the back wall of the room. Kim released a lever, and the tube shot along one of the cables and disappeared through the opening.

"What in blue blazes?" Jim exclaimed.

"That's another invention of mine and Dan's," Kim answered. "It saves a lot of time and steps."

"That's one length of cable you're looking at, which is mounted to a pair of spring-loaded flywheels at each end," Manley explained. "Once the flywheel is released, the cable is also released. The trickiest part was figuring out a way to have both flywheels released at the same time by one lever when the system is put into use. You'll note the cable runs in both directions. It pulls the tube along to another station in our stockroom, where our warehouseman will retrieve it and read the order. There's another lever at that end, so once he receives the order he'll send an acknowledgement back. In just a few minutes you'll have confirmation that everything you've ordered is in stock and will be delivered as requested. Meanwhile, may I suggest we have a cup of coffee while waiting?"

"Sounds good to me," Jim said.

"Same here," said Adrian.

"Good." Manley took the pot from a corner stove and poured four mugs of the brew. A few moments later, the cable hummed, and the tube reappeared. Kim opened it and took out the slip of paper inside.

"We have everything you need, and it will be delivered to you on Thursday. Is that satisfactory, Mr. Chatman?"

"It is, as long as you call me Adrian. If this order works out, you'll be receiving quite a bit more business from me."

"Then we can look forward to a mutually profitable relationship, Adrian," Manley said. "Before you leave, is there anything else you'll need?"

"Not at the moment. We really need to get back to the wagons," Adrian answered. "We've already been gone far longer than I'd planned."

"We understand," Kim said. "So we'll say good-bye and thank you for now, and see you on Thursday."

"On Thursday."

CHAPTER EIGHTEEN

With all the residents of the new town pitching in, putting together and erecting buildings in the same manner as a communal barn raising, Freedom rose rapidly on the almost table-flat site Adrian had purchased. The land's only variation in contour was at its closest proximity to the North Concho, where it had a gentle roll, broken in places by an occasional shallow arroyo. After only two weeks, the township had been platted, lots staked out, the main street and plaza marked off, and the principal buildings raised. That done, work was about to begin on individual homes and smaller shops. The weather had cooperated, so construction proceeded at a pace faster than even the most optimistic had anticipated. In addition, none of the trouble Captain Storm had expected materialized. Except for a few curious cowboys stopping by to observe the activity, the newcomers had been unmolested. Adrian had attempted to entice Jep Hawthorne to settle in Freedom, but his entreaties had fallen on deaf ears. Five days after leading Adrian and his party to their destination, the scout rode off.

"I've got to keep movin'," Jep had explained. "Can't stand when civilization starts crowdin' in on me, and that's what you're doin' here, pardner, civilizin' this place. No, it's time for me to mosey on. I'll more'n likely stop by again some day, but right now I need to head for Wyoming Territory. Haven't been up that way for quite a spell, and I'd like to get there before the snow flies."

Now, Adrian was taking a break from his chores, standing in the middle of what would be the town plaza, looking around in satisfaction. Jim Blawcyzk was with him, the Ranger lieutenant still vigilant despite the peacefulness of the past two weeks.

"The town is coming along, isn't it, Jim?" Adrian asked.

"Sure is," Jim agreed. "You picked a fine spot, or I guess I should say your agent did. This location's got plenty of water from the North Concho, which seldom runs completely dry, and more decent land for farmin' than I'd imagined. Still, quite a bit of it is more suited to cattle ranchin'."

"Which is what quite a few of us, includin' myself, plan on doin', Jim."

"I just hope none of the big ranchers already settled here object to sharin' the range with your beef, Adrian," Jim cautioned.

"There's plenty of land for everyone," Adrian responded. "As long as we don't cut off anyone from their water rights, which we have no intention of doing, we should be fine. It'll also help that quite a few ranchers already have colored cowboys on their payrolls."

"It's true slavery was never as prevalent here in west Texas as back east, but there's still plenty of folks who don't care for Negroes," Jim pointed out.

"The same could be said for any city in the North or East, also," Adrian said. "Sure, lots of whites wanted slavery abolished, but God forbid any of those freed slaves settle in those same whites' back yards. That's why so many of us are heading west and starting our own communities."

"I see your point," Jim answered. "Meantime, wonder what's up over yonder. Sure hope it ain't trouble."

Several of the Rangers had been out on patrol. Now, they were riding into town at a lope. A moment later, they reined up alongside Jim and Adrian.

"Anything wrong, Smoke?" Jim asked.

"Not a thing. Quiet as a tomb out there," Smoky answered.

"Dad, gotta ask you something," Charlie spoke up.

"What is it, Charlie?"

"Since it's Friday night, and things have been so peaceable around here, me'n Ty, and Johnny and Dan, were wonderin' if we could ride into San Angelo, spend a couple of nights there, and have some fun."

"I dunno," Jim answered, thumbing back his Stetson and scratching his head. "Sure would hate to see things stirred up."

"Aw, c'mon, Lieutenant," Ty pleaded. "We've been out here for weeks now, and we're hankerin' for some excitement. We're all just about ready to go plumb loco."

"We sure are," Dan added.

"What d'ya think, Smoke?" Jim asked the sergeant.

"I say let 'em go and enjoy themselves," Smoky answered. "Young'n's have got to blow off some steam, or they'll go plumb loco and get into all sorts of ruckuses. You forgotten what it's like to be young, Jim?"

"No, I sure haven't, and that's what worries me," Jim answered.

"We can take care of ourselves, Jim," Johnny assured him.

"I know that, but I don't want to see you get into a situation where you have to," Jim answered. "However, I guess if you're all dead set on goin', it'll be all right. Go ahead, have a good time, but be back here on Sunday afternoon. And stay out of trouble."

"We sure will, Dad. And thanks."

Charlie lifted his hat and circled it over his head, putting his heels to Splash's flanks with a whoop.

"Yeehaw! We're goin' to town," he shouted.

Their horses at a dead run, the four young Rangers headed for San Angelo.

"Where do you think we should head first?" Dan asked, as two hours later they reached the outskirts of San Angelo.

"Dunno. Let's just keep ridin' until we find someplace that catches our eye," Ty answered.

"That's as good a plan as any," Charlie agreed.

Several blocks later, Johnny pulled his horse to a stop.

"Whoa, boys. There's a likely-lookin' place," he said, pointing to an ornate, two-story brick structure. A number of scantily-clad women lounged on the front porch, while others were perched in the open second-floor windows, seated on the windowsills and displaying long, shapely legs. A sign ran across the entire width of the building, proclaiming it to be "Lady Victoria's Saloon, Gambling Emporium, and Opera House" in bold, three-foot high red letters.

"Those . . . those dresses ain't decent," Ty stammered.

"Mebbe not, but those gals sure are pretty," Dan answered. He eased his horse back into a slow walk.

Several of the women beckoned to the Rangers when they approached.

"C'mon in, boys, and we'll show you a real fine time," one of them promised.

"I reckon we will, and I reckon you sure can, honey," Johnny replied. "Soon as we put up our horses we'll be there, and holdin' you to that promise."

"You won't be disappointed," she assured him. "Plenty of space along the hitchrail in the side alley for your broncs. You hurry up now, hear?"

The horses were given a quick drink from a trough out front, then tied, their cinches loosened.

"Let's not keep those ladies waitin'," Johnny urged. With the redhead in the lead, the quartet of young lawmen trooped inside.

"Welcome to Lady Victoria's," a woman just inside the door called. "I'm Victoria Norman, the lady in Lady Victoria's. What's your pleasure, gents?"

Victoria Norman was a bit on the short side, with a round, pretty face and an ample figure, her yellow satin dress cut to emphasize its curves. Her dark brown eyes sparkled with life, and her wide smile seemed to light up the room. Unlike most women, who wore their hair piled high in the style of the day, her dark hair was combed straight, falling gracefully to her shoulders. Two other women were with her.

"Reckon some drinks for now, then mebbe a game of cards or two," Charlie answered.

"Don't forget, we also want to make the acquaintance of some of those fine-lookin' women Lady Victoria has here," Johnny added.

"That might be arranged, but not quite like you think, cowboy," Victoria answered. "And before any getting acquaintances happen, how about some names to go with those handsome faces?"

"I'd be Johnny Dexter," the redhead answered. "My pards are Charlie Blawcyzk, better known as Chip, he's the blond one. Others are Ty Tremblay and Dan Huggins. We're all Texas Rangers."

"Ooh, Rangers." Victoria gave a slight shudder. "I reckon we're safe tonight, ladies."

"I would imagine so," one of the other women agreed.

"As long as we have your names, let me introduce you to these two young lovelies," Victoria continued. "May I present Amanda Cruz and Krishia Rivera?"

"Pleased to meet you, cowboys, or should I say Rangers? I'm Krishia," the shorter of the two said. Her Spanish heritage was clear in her dark hair and eyes, and deeply tanned skin. A slightly upturned nose somehow complemented the beauty of her face, and the black dress she wore showed off her slim figure to perfection.

"And I'm Amanda," the other announced. Like Krishia, her Spanish heritage was plain, with her dark hair, which she wore tied in a bun, and wide brown eyes. However, her skin was somewhat lighter, indicating the blood of other ancestors, possibly northern European, mixed in. She was slightly fuller-figured, and clad in a dress of pure white. What caught the Rangers' eyes, however, were the stockings that she wore. They had peacock feathers painted on them in vivid, lifelike colors, the feathers winding their way sinuously up Amanda's perfectly-formed calves and thighs.

"Those are the prettiest stockings I've ever seen," Johnny gasped.

"You like them, really?" Amanda said, lifting her left leg until it was parallel to the floor, then still higher, until she held it just under Johnny's nose. "I painted them myself."

Johnny gulped, hard, seeming to choke on his words.

"I sure do," he finally got out. "And not just the stockings, either."

"Amanda and Krishia are my two lead dancers," Victoria explained. "They'll be putting on a show a bit later. You'll stay to see that, of course."

"Of course we will," Charlie answered.

"What about meeting some of the other ladies?" Dan questioned. "They sure seemed fine."

"If you mean what I think you mean, I hate to disillusion you, Ranger," Victoria replied. "My place is strictly a saloon, gambling house, and theater. If you want the other kind of 'entertainment' then I suggest you head for Miss Hattie's Parlor House, two blocks south."

"That's not what I meant," Dan answered. "Just

wanted to have a pretty lady by my side, mebbe buy her a drink or have a dance."

"Speak for yourself, Dan," Johnny objected.

"It doesn't matter either way, since my girls aren't allowed to drink, or dance with the customers," Victoria answered.

"But, what about all those gals outside?" Ty protested.

"They are out there to entice customers," Victoria answered. "And it worked, didn't it? Y'all came in."

"I reckon it did," Ty admitted.

"Don't sound so disappointed," Victoria said. "I've got the best drinks in town, and the most honest games in San Angelo. Plus, I guarantee you'll enjoy the show. That leg Amanda showed you is just a sample of what you'll see. Lady Victoria promises a good time, and Lady Victoria always keeps her promises. So, what do you say?"

"I say, show us to the bar," Charlie shouted. "C'mon, boys!"

Lady Victoria's was set up a bit differently from most saloons. It did have the usual long, mirror-backed bar, along with the expected games of chance. However, at the far end of the room was a curtained stage, with quite a number of tables arranged in front of it. Instead of escorting the Rangers to the bar, Victoria made certain to seat them at one of the front row center tables.

"The first drinks are on the house, boys," she assured them. "If you want to gamble while waiting for the show, I can send over one of my housemen so you can play cards right here. Now, what're y'all havin'?"

"Beer," Charlie requested.

"Same here," Ty answered.

"Whiskey for me," Johnny said.

"Make that two," Dan added.

"All right." Victoria beckoned to a tall, willowy, auburn-haired woman waiting near the bar.

"Gentlemen, this is Louisa. She'll be taking your orders for the evening. Louisa, two beers and two whiskeys, on the house. After that, whatever are the gentlemen's wishes, you take care of them."

"With pleasure," Louisa smiled, revealing dazzling white teeth. "I'll be back with your drinks shortly. I hope you'll enjoy the evening."

"I'm certain we will," Johnny answered.

The Rangers spent the next two hours drinking and playing poker, awaiting what everyone assured them would be a spectacular performance. The Lady Victoria gradually filled to capacity, so by now, thirty minutes before show time, men were standing three deep in the back, and the air was thick with tobacco smoke. The atmosphere grew more tense with anticipation at each tick of the clock. As the moment approached for the elaborately-embroidered, green velvet curtain to rise, whistles, catcalls, and shouts filled the air. The noise dropped to an expectant hush when Victoria slipped from behind the curtain, taking up a position on the left side of the stage. She was now dressed in a spangled gold silk gown, a huge, feathered hat of the same hue on her head. She held a feathered fan in front of her face, which she slowly lowered.

"Patience, boys, patience," she purred. "Those of you who have been here previously know my shows are worth the wait. Those of you who haven't, well, you're in for a real special evening."

She turned to the right and pointed the fan toward the curtain.

"Now, without further ado, Lady Victoria's presents Krishia Rivera and Amanda Cruz in their spectacular Parisian Revue!"

The curtain rose, to reveal an eight piece orchestra at the rear of the stage. The players immediately commenced a soft, French tune, the music gradually becoming louder and faster. Then, one dancer appeared from each of the wings, followed quickly by another, then still more, until there was a row of dancers across the entire width of the stage, the troupe consisting of the same women who had been lounging on the porch and in the windows earlier. All were dressed in identical outfits of long, ruffled, flowing skirts which reached to their ankles, low-cut red, white, and blue blouses, and scarlet-dyed feathers in their hair, which was intertwined with scarlet ribbons.

"Gentlemen," they intoned in unison, "we are pleased to introduce to you that devilish duo, the scandalous twosome of San Angelo, Krishia and Amanda!"

With high-pitched whoops, the two featured performers, dressed in silver-sequined outfits of the same cut as the others, emerged from the wings, cartwheeled to the center of the stage, and gave a high kick. Immediately, the orchestra burst into a can-can, using the music which was most associated with that dance, the *Infernal Galop* from Jacques Offenbach's operetta, *Orpheus in the Underworld*.

The audience gave a collective gasp of surprise when the dancers lifted their skirts to reveal layers of petticoats and black silk stockings, then roared appreciatively when they performed a series of high kicks and provocative leg movements in time to the music, their whoops and squeals complementing the bawdy dance. The shouts became louder as the dancers went through their routine of impossibly high kicks, cartwheels, and splits, all the while holding their voluminous skirts high to reveal those shapely, black-stockinged legs. When the number concluded with the women all landing a synchronized split at the front of the stage, the men went wild, their shouts of approval roaring to a crescendo which shook the building to its eaves. It was nearly five minutes before the audience settled enough so the show could continue.

Forty-five minutes later, the show concluded with an encore of the same can-can. This time, to thunderous applause, the dancers took their bows, Krishia and Amanda being called back to the stage six times by the appreciative audience. Without warning, a cowboy rushed from the audience, grabbed Amanda, and kissed her roughly.

"Get away from me, you!" Amanda protested, slapping him across the face. Instead, the cowboy pulled her closer.

"Oh, you wanna play rough, do you, honey?" he growled.

Johnny Dexter leapt from his seat, grabbed the offending cowpuncher by the shoulder, and spun him around.

"The lady said she didn't want you pawin' her, Mister," he said. "So just leave her alone and go back to your friends."

"I only want to have some fun with this good-lookin' female," the clearly intoxicated cowboy answered. "And just who do you think you are, orderin' me around?"

"I'm a Texas Ranger, that's who. Now if you don't settle down and leave the lady alone, I'll have you tossed in jail," Johnny answered.

"A Texas Ranger? Oh, now I recognize you. You're one of the Rangers who rode into town with that bunch of niggers awhile back. Well, let me tell you somethin', Mister Ranger, us Rouses don't much care for niggers, and we don't cotton to anyone telling us what to do, especially two-bit tin stars. That means nobody orders Pete Rouse around, least of all a penny-ante lawman. My daddy's the biggest rancher in these parts, and he won't take it kindly, your tryin' to tell me what I can and can't do. In fact, we were plannin' on runnin' those niggers off soon as you Rangers left, but now I'm figurin' we won't wait that long."

"Shut your fool mouth, Pete," one of his partners called.

"Don't try'n quiet me, Mark," the cowboy answered. "In fact, mebbe I'll just take care of this Ranger right now."

With that, Rouse swung at Johnny's chin. Johnny easily ducked the punch, and sank his own fist into Rouse's belly. The cowboy folded into a left to his chin which staggered him.

Instantly, Rouse's companions charged the stage, only to be met before they could reach it by the other Rangers. Charlie caught the first man in line with a punch to his nose, then someone slammed a hard blow to Charlie's kidneys. Ty returned that man's punch with one of his own to the jaw, while Dan dropped another with a vicious left to the gut. Now, most of the women fled the stage as a full-fledged brawl erupted inside the Lady Victoria. Fists flew, while tables and chairs were thrown, or smashed over combatants' heads or backs. One man was tossed over the bar, to land hard on his back. He lay there, stunned, blood dripping from a gash on his forehead. Several others lay unconscious, or were trying to crawl away from the carnage.

One cowboy attempted to pull his pistol and level it at Johnny's back.

"Oh, no you don't, Mister. That's not fair!" Amanda screamed. She drove a kick to the man's groin. He screamed, grabbed his crotch, and dropped to his knees in agony. Krishia then smashed a half-empty whiskey bottle over his head, toppling him to his face.

The blast of a double-barreled shotgun roared through the room, its ominous roar almost immediately stopping the fight. Victoria, along with three of her bartenders, stood there, all of them gripping sawed-off Greeners.

"Stop it, all of you, and get out of here!" she ordered. "The next shots won't be over your heads." Her expression and the tone in her voice left no doubt she meant exactly what she said. If anyone defied her order, there would certainly be more bloodshed this night. Men began slowly filing out of the bar, those that could. The rest lay where they had fallen, some groaning, others, out cold, completely oblivious to their surroundings.

"I'm sorry, Victoria," Johnny attempted to apologize. "I just couldn't let that *hombre* man-handle your gal like that."

"Don't trouble yourself about it, Ranger. If you hadn't stepped in, someone else would have. This wasn't the first brawl to break out in my place, and it sure won't be the last. We'll have everything cleaned up and be back in business by tomorrow night. Come see us then, if you're still in town."

"We will be, and I reckon we'll take you up on that invitation," Johnny answered. "Figure we'd best leave now." He and his partners trooped out of the saloon.

The Rangers were halfway across the street when a shout came from behind them.

"Ranger!" Pete Rouse screamed in fury. "I ain't done with you, Ranger. Turn around and go for your gun."

Johnny and his companions attempted to ignore the challenge, not changing their pace as they kept walking.

"Ranger, either face me or I'll drill you right in your back, you no good son of a . . ."

Johnny's hand was a blur as he whirled, pulled his gun from its holster, thumbed back the hammer, and fired in one smooth motion. Pete Rouse gasped when the Ranger's bullet struck him in the upper abdomen, just below his breastbone. He staggered back two steps.

"Ranger. You . . . you killed me," Rouse stammered, then collapsed onto his back, his right hand still gripping his gun.

Rouse's companions started to go for their guns, only to stop, realizing the other Rangers had already pulled their guns, and they were staring down the deadly barrels of the lawmen's forty-fives.

"Matthew," Rouse called to his older brother, who stood next to him, "I'm killed. That Ranger killed me. Never expected . . ." His voice trailed off.

"Ranger," Matt Rouse snarled at Johnny, "there's nothin' I can do right now, with you and your pards holdin' guns on me, but you're a dead man. I'll get you, or one of my brothers will, or my dad will have you hunted down like a dog. But you ain't gonna get away with killin' my little brother."

"Anytime you're ready, Mister," Johnny challenged.

"Take it easy, Johnny," Charlie tried to calm him. "We don't want any more trouble. There's been enough already."

"Chip, if this *hombre's* askin' for trouble, I sure ain't gonna back down from it," Johnny answered.

Before Charlie could respond, any potential

for more violence was nipped in the bud by the arrival of three town marshals, as well as Sheriff Franklin and two of his deputies. Each man held a rifle leveled at the combatants.

"All of you, put up those guns, right now. I'll blast the first man who makes a wrong move to Kingdom Come!" the sheriff ordered. "Now, exactly what happened here?"

Guns were slid back into holsters, hands carefully edged away from the weapons.

"Man lyin' there accosted one of the dancers from Lady Victoria's," Charlie explained. "My pardner there tried to stop him, and a fight broke out. We left, but that *hombre* followed us, and told my pardner if he didn't draw he'd shoot him in the back. We tried to walk away, but he wouldn't have none of it. Johnny had to shoot him. It was self-defense."

"What's your name, son?"

"Chip Blawcyzk. And it's not son, it's Texas Ranger Chip Blawcyzk. My pardners are Rangers Johnny Dexter, Dan Huggins, and Ty Tremblay."

"You're all Rangers? Reckon you're ridin' with Lieutenant Blawcyzk, and you must be kin to him."

"That's right, Sheriff, we are," Dan confirmed. "And Chip's the lieutenant's son."

"Anyone else here see what happened?" the sheriff questioned.

"It's like the Ranger claims, Sheriff," Victoria

answered. "I saw the whole thing from my porch. If he hadn't shot Pete Rouse, then he would have been murdered in cold blood, shot in the back."

"That ain't exactly right, Sheriff," Matt Rouse objected. "My little brother never had a chance."

"It's exactly right, Sheriff," Krishia spoke up. "That man tried to have his way with Amanda, and the Ranger there stopped him. It's a good thing he did, too."

"Yeah, otherwise I would have had to punch that no-good snake in the head," Amanda added. "I would have, too."

"Knowin' you, Miss Cruz, I have no doubt about that," the sheriff chuckled. "Ranger, it appears you're in the clear, but things are a mite different than in the old days. We're gonna have to hold a coroner's inquest, so I'll need to ask you to stay in town for a couple of days. I'll have it scheduled for Monday morning, early as I can."

He took a quick look at Pete Rouse's body.

"You say Pete had already started to draw before you, Ranger?"

"I didn't, but yeah, that's a fact, Sheriff," Johnny confirmed. "I knew he was gonna pull his gun and shoot me in the back, so I had no choice but to get him first. His gun was already out when I plugged him."

Franklin gave a low whistle.

"Whew! That's some shootin'. You nailed him

dead center, even though it appears he already had the drop on you. Still doesn't change anything. You'll have to remain here until Monday. I'll need the rest of you back here as witnesses, also."

"All right, Sheriff," Johnny reluctantly agreed. "We were gonna get a room at the San Angelo House, so you'll find me there if you need me."

"That'll be okay, as long as you agree not to leave the hotel," Franklin responded. "Take your meals there, but don't leave the building except to use the privy."

"Is that an order, Sheriff?" Johnny asked.

"Let's just say I'd greatly appreciate you stayin' put . . . and can make life real difficult for you if you don't," Franklin answered.

"I wouldn't plan on needin' that room for long, Ranger," Matt Rouse snarled. "Only thing you've gotta worry about is whether I plug you in your belly or your back. I ain't particular which."

"Matt, that's enough out of you. You and your brothers take Pete's body down to Shaughnessy's, then head for home. You have anything to say, you can say it at the inquest come Monday."

"Sheriff, I . . ."

"I mean it, Matt!" Franklin snapped. "Take your outfit and leave, right now. Get movin'."

"We'd better leave, Matt," Jody Rouse, another brother, said. "We'll let Dad decide how and when to handle this Ranger and his pards."

"All right," Matt reluctantly agreed. "After Pete's buried we'll settle things. Let's go."

Pete's body was picked up and carried to where the Rouses' horses waited, then tied belly-down over his saddle. Franklin and his men kept an alert watch on them until they rode out of sight.

"Johnny, one of us will have to ride back to Freedom and let the lieutenant know what happened," Ty noted, once the Rouses were gone.

"I reckon that falls to me," Charlie answered. "You and Dan stay here and keep an eye on Johnny."

"There's no need for that," Johnny protested.

"It'll be better that way," Charlie answered.

"Sorry, Ranger, but I'm gonna ask you and your pardners to leave San Angelo," the sheriff said. "The Rouses have a lot of friends in this town. Feelin's are gonna run high, so it'd be better if none of you are around until things settle down."

"All the more reason for us to stay," Ty answered. "Besides, you can't order us out of town, Sheriff. Any Ranger's authority supersedes that of local law enforcement. You know that."

"Mebbe I can't force you to leave town, but I can sure as the devil make your lives miserable if you stay," Franklin retorted. "Don't worry about your friend. Me and my men can handle any trouble. He'll be safe until the inquest on Monday."

"Johnny, what do you want us to do?" Dan asked.

"You'd better listen to the sheriff," Johnny advised. "Like he says, don't worry about me. Anyone he can't handle I sure can. I'll be fine. You're the ones who'll be missin' out on the rest of a good time."

"All right," Charlie reluctantly agreed. "Sheriff, I'd bet a hat you'll see either Lieutenant Huggins or my father here tomorrow morning, soon as we tell them what happened."

"I've got no problem with that," Franklin assured him.

"That's settled," Charlie said. "Johnny, you be careful. We'll see you Monday mornin'."

As they headed for their horses, Ty observed, "I certainly ain't in any hurry to face Lieutenant Blawcyzk. I reckon we sure didn't keep our promise. We got ourselves into a whole heap of trouble."

CHAPTER NINETEEN

Jim Blawcyzk was in a foul mood when he rode into San Angelo early the next afternoon, the day after the brawl in the Lady Victoria. The usually easy-going Ranger's amiable nature had been sorely tried by the news four of his men had gotten involved in a saloon fight, a fight that had led to the death of one of the sons of the area's most prosperous rancher. Jim himself had never thought much about Negroes one way or the other, indeed he had met and worked with quite a few, like Bill Dundee, whom he admired for their courage and considered his friends. He was pretty certain that most of his men hadn't thought much about Negroes either, or else had kept their feelings well hidden, but he was well aware that quite a few white folks, in fact the vast majority of them in Texas, including many of his fellow Rangers, either didn't like or downright hated coloreds. A wagon-train load of Negroes heading for west Texas to establish a new town was a powder keg ready to go off, and that fight in the Lady Victoria might just be the match needed to ignite the explosion. Even his son Charlie couldn't escape the lieutenant's blistering tongue-lashing. When Jim's tirade had

295

finally subsided, it was only to have his anger rekindled when he was then informed the Rouse family intended to run Adrian Chatman's people off their land. Now it was apparent the fight he'd hoped to avoid was inevitable, unless he could somehow convince the Rouses to realize starting that battle would only lead to plenty of bloodshed, with no winners. Jim would bet his hat that was one argument he couldn't win. So, despite the entreaties of Charlie, Dan, and Ty, to ride back to San Angelo with him, Jim ordered them to remain in Freedom, and not to leave the new settlement under any circumstances. He headed for San Angelo alone, and by the time he reached town his temper was still near the boiling point. He decided he'd meet with Sheriff Franklin before talking with Johnny Dexter. Jim wasn't sure if the old saw about redheads being quick-tempered was true, but right now, the way Jim felt, Johnny would have no chance against him, fiery temper or not. Perhaps he'd calm down a bit after meeting with the sheriff, and not follow his current desire to kick Dexter's backside all the way from San Angelo to San Antone . . . and back.

Jim had placed his badge in his shirt pocket before starting out. No sense in advertising who he was and attracting unwanted attention. Now that he'd reached San Angelo, the distinctive silver star on silver circle remained hidden.

Instead of leaving Sizzle in front of the sheriff's office, where the gelding would be exposed to the hot rays of the sun, Jim reined him in across the street, where the hitchrail was still partially shaded, and where the shadows would lengthen as the sun continued its daily descent toward the western horizon. When he pulled his horse to a stop in front of the Take Your Chances Saloon, one of the two cowboys standing in front of it drained the last of the whiskey from the bottle he held, then tossed the empty directly at Sizzle's front feet. The bottle bounced off Sizzle's left front hoof, shattering and causing the even-tempered horse to shy, snorting a protest. Both cowboys laughed.

Without a word, Jim dismounted, led his horse a few feet away from the shards of glass, which could cripple the animal if he stepped on a sharp piece and pierced his heel or the frog of his hoof, looped Sizzle's reins over the rail, patted his shoulder, and gave him a peppermint. That done, he climbed the stairs to where the two men stood, smirking.

"I reckon you think that was pretty funny, don't you?" he asked them, his blue eyes blazing.

"As a matter of fact, yeah, we do, Mister," the man who'd thrown the bottle replied.

"Well, as a matter of fact, it wasn't."

Jim drove his left fist deep into the man's belly, doubling him up and dropping him to the boardwalk. Before his partner could react, Jim spun and sank his right into that man's gut. He jackknifed and fell to his knees alongside his downed partner. Jim planted his boot into the man's backside and kicked him into the dusty street, then did the same to his partner. He pulled his Colt and leveled it at the pair.

"You're gonna stay down there on your hands and knees and pick every last piece of glass out of that dirt," he ordered. "Don't, and I'll plant a couple of slugs in your sorry butts."

The man who'd tossed the bottle started to object, then, seeing Jim's eyes, now cold as chips of blue ice, choked back his words. Silently, he and his partner began sifting the dirt for pieces of glass.

Once the pair had picked up the remains of the bottle, Jim ordered them to their feet.

"Now, get outta here, the two of you, and if I see you anywhere around we'll pick this up where we left off. Consider yourselves lucky that glass didn't cut my horse, because if it had I'd've used that same piece to slice open your throats from ear to ear. Get movin'."

Jim waggled his Colt for emphasis.

"We're goin', but you ain't heard the last of this, cowboy," the bottle thrower grumbled. "In case you don't know who we are, the names are Jody and Mark Rouse."

"Well, just to make certain you know who I am,

the name's Jim Blawcyzk." Jim dug in his shirt pocket, removed his badge, and pinned it to his vest. "That's Lieutenant Jim Blawcyzk of the Texas Rangers. You run right home to your daddy and tell him I've got some business with him that needs to be settled, *pronto. Comprende?*"

"We *comprende*, all right," Jody sneered. "It'll be a real pleasure doin' business with you, Ranger. A real pleasure."

He spat in Jim's direction before he and his brother stalked off, retrieved their horses, and galloped out of town.

Jim sighed. Now there was even less chance of avoiding real trouble with the Rouses. Well, there was no helping it. Disgusted, he crossed the street and entered the sheriff's office. Cecil Franklin was at his desk. He came to his feet when he spotted the big Ranger.

"Lieutenant Blawcyzk, howdy. Reckon I don't have to ask why you're here."

"No, I reckon not, Sheriff," Jim agreed. "I've already gotten my men's story of what happened last night, but I'd like to hear what you've got to say."

"Sure. Take a chair and settle into it. You want some coffee?"

"I wouldn't mind some."

"Fine." Franklin poured two full mugs, and passed one to Jim. He took out the makings.

"Smoke?" he offered.

"No, thanks. Never got in the habit," Jim explained.

"All right." Franklin rolled a quirly, lit it, and sat back down.

"You talked with your man Dexter yet, Lieutenant?" he asked.

"No, I wanted to see you first, and get your version of last night's events," Jim answered.

"I appreciate that," Franklin replied. "Far as what happened last night, from all appearances your man's in the clear. Plenty of witnesses say Pete Rouse started that trouble by pawin' at one of Victoria Norman's dancers. Dexter pulled him off her, then Pete took a swing at him. Big mistake on Pete's part. However, he made an even bigger one when he challenged Dexter to draw, then when Dexter didn't rise to the bait tried to plug him in the back. Folks who saw it claim they'd never seen anyone pull and fire a gun as quick as that red-headed Ranger. Accurate, too. Drilled Pete plumb center."

"Then why're you holdin' Johnny?" Jim questioned.

"I'm not exactly holdin' him," Franklin answered. "Just need him to stay in town until we have an inquiry. Even though Dexter's a Ranger, the county'll insist on it."

"Kind of unusual," Jim rejoined. "Sheriff, I have the feelin' you're not bein' completely honest with me. What're you holdin' back?"

Franklin shrugged his shoulders, took a long puff on his cigarette, then blew a smoke ring toward the ceiling.

"Reckon there's no point in keepin' this from you, since I'd imagine your men already told you. Pete Rouse, the man Dexter killed, was the son of Lucas Rouse, the biggest landowner and cattleman in these parts. Around here, whatever Lucas says pretty much goes. He's not gonna take the killin' of his boy lyin' down, Lieutenant."

"Mebbe I can talk some sense into him," Jim said.

Franklin shook his head.

"Not likely. He's had his way for too long now. Besides, Pete was his youngest, and spoiled rotten. Anything Pete wanted daddy would give him."

"What about Rouse's wife? Mebbe I can talk to her," Jim suggested.

"I'm afraid that's impossible. Shelby Rouse died quite a few years back, a couple of years after Pete was born. Before you ask, there's no daughters, either. Only boys."

"That's too bad. Lotta times a woman can talk sense to a man, and convince him not to do something foolish. I've still gotta try and meet Rouse, however. How many sons does he have? Mebbe I can convince him it ain't worth losin' any more."

"Countin' Pete, there were seven of 'em. Matthew's the oldest, then Luke, followed by John and Mark."

"The four Evangelists," Jim said.

"Huh?" Franklin answered.

"The four men who wrote the Gospels. Matthew, Luke, John, and Mark."

"Never thought about that, but I reckon you're right, Lieutenant. Makes sense. Mrs. Rouse was a church-goin' woman. Can't say the same for Lucas, or his sons. Anyway, the others are Jody and Eugene. Tough customers all. Of course, you have to be to run a big spread out here. You'll find that out when you meet them."

"I've already met Jody and Mark," Jim said.

"You have? Where?" Franklin asked.

"Right across the street, although I didn't know who they were at the time. Jody threw a whiskey bottle at my horse. It hit his hoof and broke. Jody and his brother thought it was funny. I didn't. No one messes with my horse. I punched both Jody and Mark in the gut, then when they folded kicked 'em into the street and made 'em pick up the pieces of glass, and told 'em to ride outta town."

Franklin again shook his head and took a long drag on his cigarette.

"Then, Lieutenant, you just made enemies of the entire Rouse family. You'd've been better off killin' those boys rather than humiliatin' 'em.

That's what got Pete so riled last night. No one makes a fool of a Rouse."

Franklin started to say more, but was interrupted by a man bursting through the office door, a man dressed in the clothes of a bartender, his outfit clean and neatly pressed.

"Sheriff, come quick! There's big trouble at Miss Hattie's," he shouted.

CHAPTER TWENTY

Even though it had only been the remainder of the night and a good chunk of daylight the next day, Johnny Dexter chafed at his enforced confinement in the San Angelo House. Not wanting to give Sheriff Franklin an excuse to toss him in a cell, he remained in his room, except for short respites in the dining room for breakfast and dinner, plus a couple of needed trips to the outhouse behind the hotel. He'd spent most of his time restlessly pacing around his room. Johnny considered himself a man of action, the reason he'd joined the Rangers. He loved the challenge of a Ranger's job, the long days on the trail, the tracking down of outlaws, and most of all the excitement of the gunfights. Johnny was a fast draw and a dead shot with a six-gun, and knew it. He wasn't shy about letting folks know about it or showing off his skills, either. What some others called cockiness on the young red-headed Ranger's part he just considered confidence, knowing he could back up any brag he made with a quick jerk of his Colt and an accurate shot. Being stuck in a stuffy hotel room gnawed at his guts.

He'd just stretched out on his bed to attempt a

nap when a knock came at the door. Johnny stood up, lifted his Colt from its holster, and leveled it at the entryway.

"Who is it?" he called.

"Jason, the front desk clerk. I have a message for you, Ranger Dexter."

"The door's open. C'mon in."

Johnny kept his gun aimed just above the doorknob, until the door opened, and Jason stood there, alone. He held a note in his hand.

"Lady left this for you, Ranger," he said, handing Johnny the paper.

"Much obliged." Johnny gave the clerk a nickel. "Close the door behind you."

"Thanks."

Once Jason had departed, Johnny unfolded the note. It was written in a delicate, feminine hand.

Ranger Dexter, *it read,* I wish to show my gratitude for your coming to my rescue last night. In appreciation, I have arranged for an afternoon of pleasure for you at Miss Hattie's Parlor House. Upon your arrival, ask for Dinah. She will be available exclusively for your entertainment for the entire afternoon.

Sincerely, Amanda Cruz.

Johnny folded the note and slid it in his jeans pocket.

The sheriff can go to blazes, he thought, *I'm not missin' a chance to spend some time with one of Miss Hattie's gals, and even havin' it paid for. 'Sides, the odds are he won't spot me. Once I reach Hattie's place, I'll be out of sight for the rest of the day. I can sneak back here after dark.*

Johnny stripped out of his shirt, gave himself a rudimentary washing at the basin, then dug in his saddlebags, removing his spare shirt and bandanna. He shrugged into the fresh shirt and tied the clean bandanna around his neck. That done, he beat the dust from his jeans and Stetson as best he could, then wiped off his boots and pulled them on. Using the back door, he slipped out of the hotel and made his way through the side streets and alleyways until he reached Miss Hattie's Parlor House, a two story brick building with a long staircase leading to the front door. He took the stairs two at a time and headed inside. A buxom woman behind a huge carved oak desk greeted him as he entered. She had thick black hair piled high in an elaborate pompadour, which was topped by an enormous feathered hat. Her dress was green silk, her dark eyes inviting. In a room off to the side of the foyer, several women lounged. They stirred at the sight of the handsome young lawman.

"Welcome to Miss Hattie's, sir. I'm Hattie. What is your pleasure?"

Johnny dug in his pocket, removed the note, and handed it to her.

"I'm Johnny Dexter. I was told to ask for Dinah."

"Ah, yes. Ranger Dexter. We have been expecting you." Hattie handed the note back to Johnny and beckoned to one of the waiting women. "Dinah."

"Yes, Miss Hattie?" a long-legged brunette replied, walking over to join them.

"This is Ranger Dexter."

"Pleased to meet you, Ranger," Dinah said, boldly looking him up and down. "I hope you like what you see. I sure do."

Johnny ran his gaze over the attractive woman. She was of average height, but with a well-formed figure. Her red dress was cut low at the bosom and high at the hem, revealing full breasts and shapely legs. Her brown eyes held a promise this would indeed be an afternoon he'd long remember.

"I certainly do, ma'am," he replied.

"Ma'am?" Dinah laughed. "My name's Dinah."

"And mine's Johnny."

"Are you ready to head upstairs, Johnny?"

"I reckon that's why I'm here, Dinah. Lead the way."

"Miss Hattie?"

"There's no point in keeping the gentleman waiting, dear," Hattie said. "The afternoon is his . . . and yours. You needn't worry about any other clients today."

"Thanks, Miss Hattie," Johnny said.

"No thanks necessary. We're here to provide gentlemen pleasure, and we do that very well," Hattie answered. "Enjoy yourself, Ranger."

Dinah led Johnny up a long, wide stairway, thickly carpeted and with ornately carved banisters. At the top, they turned left, and then entered a room five doors down. Dinah gently closed the door behind them.

"This is my room, Johnny. How do you like it?" she asked.

"It's beautiful, just like you," Johnny replied. The chamber, while small, was unlike any other rooms Johnny had seen in "sporting houses" he'd patronized. The wallpaper was red and gold velvet, the furnishings all expensive, reflecting quality. A bird's eye maple dresser was topped by a large, gilt-framed mirror. The lamps were cut crystal and amber glass. The bed was brass, with thick, soft coverings piled high on the mattress. Everything was also spotlessly clean.

"I don't imagine you'd care to spend much time looking at my furnishings," Dinah said.

"No, I don't imagine I would," Johnny laughed, pulling off his hat and tossing it on a chair in the corner. He removed his gunbelt and hung it from the same chair, then started to untie his bandanna.

"Let me do that for you, Ranger," Dinah purred,

running a fingertip down his throat, then untying the neckerchief and dropping it to the floor, at the same time kissing him, hard. Her hand continued downward, unbuttoning Johnny's shirt. When she reached his beltline, she slid her hands inside his jeans. Johnny groaned slightly.

Dinah continued undressing the Ranger, sliding the shirt off his shoulders, then unbuttoning his jeans and letting them fall to his ankles. Laughing, she shoved him onto his back on the bed, jumped on top of him, then crushed her lips to his. Johnny wrapped his arms around her.

"Not quite yet, Ranger," Dinah protested. "Your boots have to come off, and I need to get rid of this dress."

Swiftly, Dinah pulled off Johnny's boots, socks, and underwear.

"What I'm seeing's even better than what I'd expected, Johnny," she huskily said, looking over his broad chest, flat belly, and slim hips, then dropping her gaze to his groin. "Let's see if you feel the same."

Johnny lay in anticipation, pulse pounding and blood racing as Dinah disrobed, her dress, petticoat, and stockings soon lying in a heap on the floor. His breathing became heavy, chest heaving when she stood at the bottom of the bed, her lithe, womanly form on full display.

"Well?" Dinah demanded.

"I'd say I've never seen a more beautiful

woman," Johnny replied. "Now let's find out if you know exactly how to treat a man."

He pulled her to the mattress and drew her close.

Johnny and Dinah lay side by side in the damp, tangled sheets after their session of lovemaking.

"Was I everything you wanted, Ranger?" Dinah asked.

"All that and more," Johnny assured her, kissing her yet again and running his fingers through her hair. "I've never made love to a woman quite like you."

"There's more where that came from, and you have the rest of the afternoon to find out," Dinah promised him. She ran her right hand down his belly and over his groin, fondling him. "But how about a drink or two first? Miss Hattie has some mighty fine brandy at the bar, and it's on the house for you. How about a cigar to go with it?"

"That sure sounds good," Johnny agreed.

"Then I'll go fetch some." Dinah rubbed her hands between his legs again, then rose from the bed.

"Don't go anywhere, Johnny," she ordered. She slipped into a silk wrap and slid her feet into velvet slippers.

"Don't plan on it," Johnny grinned. "But don't take too long, hear?"

"I'll only be a few minutes," Dinah promised.

Johnny lay on his back for a few moments after Dinah left, his body still damp with sweat, then got out of the bed, to stand in front of the dresser mirror.

"You always do manage to please the ladies," he murmured in self-satisfaction, smiling. "Looks like you'll be ready for Dinah soon as she comes back, too."

His body's readiness to resume their love-making was still evident in the mirror's reflection.

Johnny turned away from the dresser at the sound of the doorknob turning.

"Honey, that sure didn't take long," he began, then his voice was drowned out by the roar of a six-gun. A bullet slammed low into the red-headed Ranger's belly. He half-folded, then fell back toward the bed, his right hand braced against the mattress, holding him half-upright, the left pressed against the oozing bullet hole two inches below his bellybutton. The gun roared again, and a second bullet tore into Johnny's gut. He collapsed onto his back across the bed.

CHAPTER TWENTY-ONE

"What's wrong, Zack?" Franklin asked.

"There's been a shootin'. Looks like a man's dead," the bartender answered.

Franklin pushed up from his chair, grabbed his hat and shoved it on his head.

"You comin', Lieutenant?" he needlessly asked Jim as he headed for the door. Blawcyzk was already halfway across the office.

Franklin's horse was always kept saddled and tied to the rail out front of his office, so he and Jim retrieved their mounts and swung into their saddles, then followed the bartender, who was sweating profusely and breathing hard. He had made the seven block trek from Miss Hattie's to the sheriff's office on foot, running as best he could for a middle-aged man, whose only exercise was lifting bottles of liquor and polishing a bar. Now, his pace had slowed to a fast walk.

"Zack, any idea who got shot?" Franklin questioned him.

"Dunno for certain," the bartender replied. "One of the clients. Not sure who he is, but he's not one of the regulars."

He stopped, hunched over and gasping for air.

"Sheriff, you'd better go on ahead. I'm plumb out of breath. I'll be along quick as I can."

"All right." Franklin kicked his bay into a lope, Jim on Sizzle matching his pace. A few moments later they slid their horses to a halt in front of Miss Hattie's, tossed their reins over the rail, dismounted and hurried up the stairs into the foyer. Hattie was standing next to her desk, awaiting the sheriff's arrival. Her girls were huddled in the parlor, several crying, the others appearing stunned.

"Hattie, Zack tells me you had a shootin'. Where'd it happen?" Franklin asked.

"Upstairs, in Dinah's room," Hattie answered, seemingly unperturbed. "You know which."

"Reckon I do. This is Lieutenant Blawcyzk of the Rangers. Mind if he takes a look with me?"

Hattie locked eyes with Jim before replying.

"I believe the lieutenant should assist you, yes," she agreed.

"Thanks, Hattie."

Jim followed Franklin up the stairs and down the corridor. They drew their guns before the sheriff pushed the door open.

"Lieutenant, that's your Ranger, Dexter!" Franklin exclaimed. Jim felt as if he'd been kicked in the gut when he recognized Johnny Dexter, now lying lifeless in a prostitute's bed. The sick feeling was quickly replaced by one of anger, as Jim took in the entire scene, the clothing piled on the floor, the tangled sheets, and Johnny's bloodied, naked body. The stench of sweat, cheap perfume, and vomit permeated the air.

"Looks as if Matt Rouse made good on his promise," Franklin said, putting up his gun. "We'll have a devil of a time provin' it, though."

"Sheriff, I'll find Matt Rouse, or whoever did this," Jim vowed. "When I do, they'll hang, or die with my bullets in 'em. Bet a hat on it."

"Reckon I'd better cover Dexter," Franklin said. "It's not decent leavin' him lyin' there like that."

"Gimme a couple minutes first, Sheriff," Jim requested. "Close the door." He crossed the room to study Johnny's remains. The red-headed Ranger lay on his back, left hand still pressed to his lower gut, his eyes wide open and staring at the ceiling, unseeing, the expression locked on his face one of shock at his sudden demise.

Jim lifted Johnny's hand to reveal the bullet hole underneath, then rolled the dead Ranger's still-warm corpse onto its belly.

"No exit wounds," Jim noted. "Bullets are still in him." He rolled the corpse onto its back once again, to study the location of the wounds. "Shooter had to be in the doorway, with his gun already out. Plugged Johnny soon as he came through the door. Must've surprised him, 'cause from what I've seen, few men could handle a gun like Johnny. I'd wager whoever killed him knew that, too. Made sure he didn't give him a chance."

"I've got to agree with you, Lieutenant," Franklin said. "They made certain he was caught with his pants down . . . literally. My guess is Dexter was waitin' for Dinah, or whichever of Hattie's gals he was with, to come back. Instead, he got ambushed, which leads me to believe he was set up. I warned him to be careful. Sure wish he'd listened to me and stayed in his room until after the hearing."

"He sure must've been, and we're gonna find out by whom," Jim answered. "Let's see if there's anything we can find here."

Jim picked up Dinah's clothes and went through them, finding nothing of interest. Then, he examined Johnny's, again finding nothing he could use, until he reached into Johhny's left hip pocket and pulled out the note purportedly from Amanda Cruz. He scanned its contents, then passed it to the sheriff.

"You know this Amanda Cruz?"

"Sure. She's one of the dancers at the Lady Victoria. Can't believe she'd be involved in Dexter's murder, though. She's the one he pulled Pete Rouse off of. You gonna talk to her?"

"I certainly am, but I have a few questions for this Dinah woman first, as well as Miss Hattie," Jim replied. "Reckon we're finished here. Let's go talk to those ladies."

Johnny's body was covered, then Jim and the sheriff headed back downstairs. Hattie was still next to her desk. Zack, the bartender, was now with her.

"Hattie," Jim snapped. "You knew that was one of my men who got himself killed in your place, didn't you?"

"Yes," she replied. "I didn't say anything because I realized you'd find out soon enough."

"Who killed him?" Jim demanded.

"Why, how would I know that, Ranger?"

"First, from this note I found in Johnny's pocket. You knew Johnny would be here. Don't pull your innocent act with me. I've dealt with your kind before, and I'm pretty hard to fool."

"That note doesn't mean a thing," Hattie protested. "Of course I knew he would be here, but that doesn't mean I arranged a murder, or even had an inkling someone would gun down a Texas Ranger here in my establishment. Perhaps you should speak to Miss Cruz. She's the one who made the arrangements."

"Don't try playin' games with me, lady," Jim snapped, his eyes blazing with fury. "Sheriff Franklin's already told me Amanda Cruz is the gal Johnny saved from Pete Rouse, so she'd hardly be the one to want him dead. I'd bet my hat she didn't write that note. You're aware of everyone who comes in or out of this place, I'm certain of that. So, even if, as you claim, you had nothing to do with Johnny's killin', you sure in blue blazes must've known who was here at the time he was shot. Either tell me everything you know, or I'll shut this place down so fast your head'll spin."

"You can't do that," Hattie retorted. "You don't have the authority."

"You don't want to bet your fancied feathered hat on that," Jim snapped back. "I can have your business closed, locked, and shuttered inside of an hour, and it'll stay that way, permanently.[5] Your choice, lady. Either cooperate, or be arrested for obstructin' justice, at the very least."

"Cecil," Hattie pleaded.

"I can't help you," the sheriff replied, shrugging his shoulders. "The Rangers' authority supercedes mine."

"All right. Lieutenant, as much as I would like to help you, I'm afraid I can't provide any information which would be of use," Hattie said. "The first I was aware of trouble was when I heard the shots, two of them. I sent Zachary up to see what had happened. He's the one who discovered Ranger Dexter's body."

---

5 Miss Hattie's Parlor House was an actual institution in San Angelo, thriving until 1946, when it was finally shut down by, ironically, the Texas Rangers. Today, Miss Hattie's continues on as "Miss Hattie's Bordello Museum" and "Miss Hattie's Café," which recreate the original atmosphere of a west Texas house of prostitution.

"That's right, Ranger," the bartender con-firmed. "By the time I got upstairs, there was no one around. I was so sickened by the sight I had to throw up."

"How'd you know which room to head for?" Jim demanded.

"I told him," Hattie answered. "It was an unusually slow afternoon. Ranger Dexter was my only client at the time. I knew the shots had to have come from Dinah's room."

"Or did you arrange it so no one else would be here this afternoon?" Jim challenged.

"I most certainly did not," Hattie replied. "I couldn't afford to do that."

"Not even if the Rouses paid you to do so?" Jim asked.

"No. My reputation depends on being available to provide the services my customers demand whenever they are desired," Hattie said. "Closing would send them elsewhere, and jeopardize my business. They might not come back if they found similar services elsewhere, and believe me, there are plenty of other houses in San Angelo. I pride myself on providing a classier level of service, which is why I do so well."

"Then if, as you claim, Johnny was your only client, how did someone get past all of you, shoot him, then get away unseen?"

"Lieutenant, much of the success of my busi-ness depends on my discretion," Hattie explained.

"Quite a few of the prominent men in San Angelo avail themselves of my services. I'm speaking about judges, lawyers, businessmen, politicians, even some of the clergymen. Most of them are also married. You can certainly understand what would happen if the identities of these men were discovered and made public. To help prevent that, there are several tunnels which run from this building to others in the area. That allows my clients to reach here without their presence being known. There's even one which runs from here to the county courthouse. In fact, the sheriff here uses that tunnel quite often. Isn't that right, Cecil?"

Frankln flushed before answering.

"Yeah, that's so. Lieutenant, don't ever mention that. My wife would kill me if she ever found out."

"I'm not worried about what happens to anyone in this town," Jim answered. "All I'm interested in is findin' Johnny's killer."

"As are we," Hattie said. "A killing in one of my girls' rooms is hardly good for business. Anyway, to get back to what I was saying, whoever killed Ranger Dexter must have used one of the tunnels to get in and out without being discovered. It would have been easy enough for him to wait until I was away from my desk and the foyer was empty to sneak upstairs. Clearly, since he was aware of the tunnels, he must be one of my clients, but I have no way of determining which one."

"All right, but even allowing for that, it still doesn't explain how the killer knew exactly when Johnny would be here, or which room he would be in," Jim answered. "That still points to someone here working with him. If it's not you, Hattie, then who? Zachary, mebbe?"

"It wasn't me, Ranger. I've been here all day," the bartender protested.

"How about last night?"

"I worked until midnight, then went straight home. Miss Hattie and my wife can testify to that."

"You must have a very understanding wife, letting you work in a place like this," Jim answered.

"The money's real good, and I met Marcy here. She was one of the workin' gals," Zachary said. "She doesn't mind."

"Then that brings us to the gal Johnny was with, a woman named Dinah, accordin' to the note," Jim said. "I want to talk with her."

"I'm afraid you can't, Lieutenant," Hattie said. "She was so upset over what happened she became violently ill. I had the doctor give her something to help her sleep. She's upstairs in my suite."

"We'll just have to try'n get some black coffee into her and wake her up," Jim answered.

"Can't your questions wait?" Hattie demanded. "After all, Dinah is a victim also. She may never recover completely from the shock."

"I'm sorry, but I have a feelin' Dinah is not as ill as she's pretending," Jim replied. "It's kind of peculiar that the invitation Johnny received specified a certain gal, Dinah, and that she just happened to be out of the room when he was gunned down. No, I don't think Dinah is sick at all. I think she was in on this right from the start. Let's just head upstairs and see if I'm right."

"I must protest. You're being very cruel, Lieutenant," Hattie said.

"Lady, one of my men was shot down in cold blood. Until I find his killer, someone's hurt feelin's just don't figure into things."

"Lieutenant, I have a suggestion," Franklin said. "If Dinah is medicated, her answers probably won't make any sense, if she's even in any condition to answer you at all. Why not question Amanda Cruz first, then you can return and talk to Dinah."

"That seems logical to me, Lieutenant," Hattie agreed.

"Logical enough that it'll give you sufficient time to spirit Dinah away from here and get her outta town while I'm gone?" Jim asked. "I'm not that naïve."

"If it'll ease your mind, I'll remain here until you return," Franklin offered. "That way you can be certain no one will leave this building. I can also take care of having Ranger Dexter's body removed to the undertaker's. It's a hot day, so unless you're planning on having him embalmed and shipped elsewhere for burial, the arrangements will need to be made fairly soon. He'll need to be in the ground by tonight, or tomorrow mornin' at the latest."

"All right," Jim reluctantly conceded. "Johnny had no kin, so it doesn't matter where he's buried. San Angelo's as good a place as any. But Dinah better be here and ready to talk to me once I get back, or you'll be facin' charges, too, Sheriff."

"I've never betrayed the trust of my office yet, Ranger," Franklin protested.

"Mebbe not, but Hattie sure has something to hold over your head if she ever decides to blackmail you," Jim replied. "Threatening to go to your wife might make you think twice, if Hattie wanted your help with something, like say gettin' Dinah out of San Angelo."

"I would never do that," Hattie said. "Without complete confidentiality, my business would be ruined. My clients know their identities will never be revealed."

"I wouldn't submit to blackmail in any event, Lieutenant," Franklin objected. "I value my job, and my reputation, too highly."

"Okay, I reckon I have no choice but to trust you," Jim answered. "I'll take up your offer to make the arrangements for Johnny's funeral, too. He wasn't a religious man, so tell the undertaker to keep it simple. Have him arrange for a decent plot, and tell him to set the burial for around six this evenin'. The state will pay for everything."

"What about a preacher?"

"I don't think Johnny would want one. I'll say a few words. I'd appreciate it if you'd be there also."

"I will," Franklin assured him.

"What about me?" Hattie asked. "I'd like the privilege of attending. I only met Ranger Dexter briefly, but he did seem like a nice young man."

"I reckon that'll be all right, dependin' on what I turn up," Jim answered. "Long as I'm convinced you had nothing to do with Johnny's killing before the burial, I'd imagine he'd be pleased knowin' you were there."

"Thank you, Lieutenant," Hattie said.

"Sheriff, I'm gonna head for the Lady Victoria now," Jim told Franklin. "Dunno how long I'll be."

"I'll wait here as long as necessary," the sheriff assured him. "By the time you return, Ranger Dexter's body will be removed."

"*Bueno*, and thanks."

Like most cowboys, Jim hated walking unless absolutely necessary, so even though it was only two blocks from Miss Hattie's to the Lady

Victoria, he rode Sizzle the short distance. He tied his horse in front of the place, patting his shoulder, giving him a peppermint and a promise of a comfortable stall and full bait of oats as soon as possible.

Even though it was still a bit early for the saloon to be open for business, the front door was unlocked, so Jim was able to enter without any trouble. No one was at the front desk or in the main room.

"Anyone here?" Jim called out.

"We're not open yet," a feminine voice answered. "If you have a delivery, please go around the back."

"It's not a delivery, but I am here on official business," Jim replied.

"All right." A moment later, Victoria Norman appeared. She looked the Ranger up and down, her gaze settling on the badge pinned to his vest.

"Another Ranger," she said. "Sure are enough of you in town recently. What brings you by?"

"I'm Lieutenant Jim Blawcyzk. Are you Victoria?"

"That would be correct, Victoria Norman. Are you here for any particular reason? If it's to see the show, I'll arrange a good seat for you."

"I'm afraid I'm not here for pleasure," Jim explained. "I need to speak with one of your dancers, Amanda Cruz."

"Amanda? Why?"

"Dunno if you've heard, but there was a killin' at Miss Hattie's."

"I did hear something about a shooting there, yes. Word travels fast in this town. What's that have to do with Amanda, though?"

"Johnny Dexter is the man who was killed. He's the Ranger who pulled Pete Rouse off Amanda."

Tears glistened in Victoria's eyes.

"Ranger Dexter? That's tragic. I guess Matt Rouse made good on his promise to kill him. Amanda will be devastated at the news. Come, I'll take you to her."

"Before you do, I have to inform you Amanda may be involved."

"Amanda? That's ridiculous, absurd. She was very grateful for what Johnny did. Why would you suspect Amanda of being involved?"

"I'll know more once I speak with her," Jim answered. "Sooner I talk with her, the sooner I can get this cleared up."

"Of course. Follow me."

Victoria led Jim down a long corridor, to the area behind the stage.

"This is the dressing room," she explained, knocking on a closed door.

"Ladies, we have company," she called. "Are you all decent?"

"Sure, bring 'em in," came the response.

"Go right in, Lieutenant," Victoria said, opening the door.

Jim blushed when he entered the cramped room. Several women were seated at vanities, all dressed only in corsets, some brushing their hair, others applying makeup as they readied for the evening performance.

"I'm, I'm sorry, ladies," he stammered. "Thought you were dressed."

"We are," one giggled. "Didn't realize you were so shy. There's no need to be embarrassed. We have male visitors here all the time."

"Amanda, I'm afraid this is serious," Victoria said. "This is Liutenant Blaw . . . Blaw."

"BLUH-zhick," Jim offered. "Just use Jim. Easier."

"Thank you. Amanda, the lieutenant needs to speak with you for a few moments."

"Me? Why?" Amanda asked.

"Miss Cruz, is there somewhere we can talk privately?"

"Not really. Besides, there's no reason we can't talk right here. There's no secrets among us at the Lady Victoria. And please call me Amanda."

"All right," Jim conceded. "Amanda, there was a shooting at Miss Hattie's. Johnny Dexter was killed."

"Johnny Dexter, the man who saved me from Pete Rouse?" Amanda answered, in disbelief. Her voice broke slightly.

"I'm afraid so," Jim replied. "This is going to be difficult, but I need to ask you some questions."

"Of course."

"Fine. Would you take a look at this note?"

Jim reached inside his shirt and removed the note he'd retrieved from Johnny's pants pocket. He passed it to Amanda.

"Did you write that note?" he questioned.

"Me? Why would you think that, really?"

"It's signed by you."

"That's not my signature, or my writing. And I would never have anything to do with those women at Miss Hattie's. They're nothing but a bunch of cheap whores!"

"Um, actually, Amanda, they're very expensive whores, from what I hear, anyway. I'm just sayin'," Krishia Rivera spoke up.

"All right, so they're expensive whores, Krishia," Amanda retorted. "They're still whores."

"So you had nothing to do with that note?" Jim repeated.

"Not a thing," Amanda insisted.

"You wouldn't mind giving me a sample of your handwriting for comparison?"

"Of course not. There's a paper and pencil around here somewhere."

Amanda rummaged through several drawers before coming up with a scrap of paper and a pencil. She hastily scrawled a few words, then her signature. She passed the paper and the note from Hattie's back to Jim.

"See? They're not even close," she remarked.

"They certainly aren't," Jim agreed. "Looks like whoever wanted Johnny killed used your name to lure him to Miss Hattie's."

"Which had to be Matt Rouse or one of his brothers," Krishia said. "They threatened to kill Ranger Dexter after he shot their brother, not that Pete Rouse didn't need killin'. All them Rouses do. I'm just sayin'."

"That's right," Amanda agreed.

"Well, I'm sorry to have bothered you, but this will help clear things up, at least a bit," Jim answered. "I'd also advise all of you ladies to be careful, since Johnny's killer is still on the loose."

"That's good advice. Thank you, Jim," Victoria answered. She turned at a knock at the door. A man entered, carrying a huge flower arrangement.

"Victoria? I have another delivery for Miss Amanda."

"Not again." Amanda sighed. "Just put them on my dresser."

"Of course." The clerk placed the flowers as requested.

"There you are, Miss Amanda."

"Thank you, George. Please come see the show tonight, with my compliments."

"I'll certainly do that. Thank you."

"Are those from Mason Tibbals again?" Krishia asked, once the clerk had left.

"They are," Amanda confirmed. "He won't

give up. I don't know how to convince him to take no for an answer."

"Pardon me, Amanda, but just who is Mason Tibbals?" Jim asked.

"He's the banker's son," Amanda answered. "He's always hanging around and pestering me. Thinks just because he has lots of money I should marry him. Truthfully, he scares me a bit."

"You don't strike me as the type who scares easily," Jim answered.

"I'm not, but there's just something about Mason," Amanda said. "He thinks he can have whatever or whoever he wants, and can control whatever or whoever he has. He's even followed me home several times. I don't trust him at all."

"Tell me something. Was Mason Tibbals here when Pete Rouse accosted you?"

"Of course. He always is."

"So he saw Johnny help you?"

"That's right. Why?"

"Because if Tibbals is as controlling and jealous as you say, he might be the one who killed Johnny Dexter."

"Jim, now that you mention it, you could be right!" Amanda exclaimed. "Although I have to say, my money would still be on Matt Rouse or one of his brothers."

"I wouldn't bet my hat against that," Jim agreed. "Still, knowing about Tibbals does bring up another possibility. Amanda, Victoria, all of you, thank you for your help. If I have any more questions I'll be in touch."

"We'll all be happy to cooperate, Jim," Victoria assured him.

"I appreciate that," Jim answered.

"If you're finished, I'll show you to the door," Victoria said.

"I am for now," Jim replied. "Again, thank you."

Once Jim returned to Miss Hattie's, he was told he had to wait another hour before Dinah was lucid enough to be questioned. However, he demanded to see her immediately.

"All right, if you insist," Hattie conceded. "Dinah's in my room. Follow me, please."

"Not quite so fast, Hattie. Amanda Cruz never wrote that note, and it's signed by you. Care to explain that?"

"I didn't sign it either. I never saw it until you showed it to me," Hattie answered.

Accompanied by Sheriff Franklin, Jim followed the madam upstairs, then down a long hallway to a sumptuous suite. Miss Hattie's chambers were decorated with rich furnishings, the accessories ostentatious even by the standards of the times.

"In here, Lieutenant."

Hattie led Jim into a large bedroom. Dinah was sitting up in a huge brass feather bed, clad only in a thin robe. She was sipping at a cup of tea, and appeared calm and alert, not at all the picture Hattie had been painting.

"Dinah, this is Lieutenant Blawcyzk of the Rangers. I tried to tell him you were in no condition to speak with him, but he wouldn't listen."

"I suppose I'll have to talk with him sooner or later, so I might as well get it over with," Dinah answered.

"If you tell me the truth I won't be long," Jim answered. "First, mind giving me your full name?"

"Not at all. It's Dinah Delilah Davenport."

"Fine. Now, who arranged for Johnny Dexter to visit you?"

"I have no idea," Dinah said.

"You're lying," Jim snapped. "You had to know, or else Miss Hattie did . . . or both of you."

"Lieutenant, hasn't Dinah been through enough already, having a man murdered right in her bedroom?" Hattie demanded.

"If she doesn't answer my questions, she'll be going through a lot more, down at the jail. Bet a hat on it," Jim replied. He pulled the note from his pocket and handed it to Dinah.

"Did you write that note?"

"Of course not. I've never seen this."

"Do you mind giving me a sample of your handwriting, then?" Jim requested.

"Why should I?"

"Because if your writing doesn't match the

note, it will prove you didn't write it," Jim explained.

"I'm too . . . weak to write anything," Dinah protested.

"Too weak, or too afraid?" Jim demanded.

"Lieutenant, do you really have to be so harsh?" Franklin asked.

"This is a murder case, the murder of a Texas Ranger," Jim answered. "I'll do whatever needs to be done to get to the bottom of it. Miss Davenport, did you write that note or didn't you? Did Matt Rouse ask you to arrange Johnny's visit? Did he tell you he wanted Johnny set up? Or was it someone else? The truth, Miss Davenport."

"I . . . I just don't, I can't."

"Tell me the truth and I can help you if you're involved," Jim said. "Don't, and once I find who killed Johnny Dexter you'll be facing a long prison term as an accessory to murder."

"Lieutenant, stop this!" Hattie insisted. "Can't you see how upset Dinah is?"

"All right, but if I do you're out of business for good. You and Dinah will be held as suspects in Johnny's murder. So will Zachary, plus I'll have to question your other girls, and mebbe all your clients. If those names become public I don't need to tell you what will happen to this place, plus there'll be an awful lot of trouble for a lot of men in this town. Once that happens, you won't have a friend left in San Angelo, Hattie. It'll be far better for you or Dinah to tell me the truth, right now. Because I will get to the truth, bet a hat on it."

"All right, all right," Dinah cried. "Just stop, please. Just stop."

"I'll stop when you come clean, Dinah," Jim answered.

"Fine. I can't listen to any more," Dinah said. "Yes, I wrote that note."

"Who asked you to write it?" Jim questioned.

"It was Matt Rouse. He promised me five hundred dollars to get Johnny here. But I didn't know he planned on killing that Ranger," Dinah answered. "He only told me he wanted to beat him up, really badly. Matt said he wanted to hurt Dexter so bad he'd be crippled for life."

"Why wouldn't Matt just do that without getting you involved?" Jim asked.

"Because Matt was afraid of Johnny's gun, at least that's what he told me," Dinah explained. "He saw how fast Johnny was with a gun when he killed Pete. Matt knew he wouldn't have a chance against him, so he wanted to make sure Johnny wasn't wearing a gun when he confronted him. I had no idea Matt was going to shoot Johnny. You have to believe me, Lieutenant!"

"Thank you, Dinah," Jim said. "Hattie, that still doesn't leave you off the hook, though. You had to know something, because you sure weren't about to let one of your girls entertain a man without gettin' your cut."

"All I knew was I received a message, supposedly written by Amanda Cruz from the Lady Victoria, requesting the services of Dinah for the afternoon. The note said she wanted to thank Ranger Dexter for what he'd done. It also stated the writer would pay double my usual rate. Naturally, that was an offer I couldn't turn down."

"Do you still have that note?"

"Of course not. I destroyed it as soon as the arrangements were made," Hattie replied. "And yes, I will admit I did see the message Dinah wrote. Since her writing is much prettier than mine, I requested she pen the invitation. That's all, though. I had no idea the request from Miss Cruz was a forgery. I didn't admit to seeing the note sooner because I didn't believe it mattered."

"There's your answers, Lieutenant. What's your next step?" Franklin asked.

"Miss Davenport is under arrest for conspiracy to commit murder," Jim answered. "You'll have to find a place to hold her."

"There's a separate wing in the county jail for women," Franklin answered.

"Lieutenant, is that really necessary?" Hattie asked.

"Yes, at least until I find Matt Rouse," Jim replied. "Besides, Dinah will be safer in jail until Rouse is behind bars. He might decide to kill her, since she's the only witness who can connect him to Johnny's murder. When the time comes, I will let the prosecutor and judge know she did cooperate with my investigation. I'd imagine they'll go easy on her."

Dinah was quietly weeping.

"The lieutenant's right, Hattie," she sniffed. "I should have realized what Matt was up to. Oh, why did I ever get involved with him?"

"Don't worry, Dinah," Hattie attempted to reassure her. "Everything will be all right, you'll see."

"Dinah, I'll give you a few minutes to get dressed," Jim said. "We'll wait in the parlor."

"All right. I won't be long," Dinah answered.

Once they were in the parlor, Franklin built a smoke and lit it.

"What are you going to do now, Lieutenant?" he asked.

"Soon as Johnny's buried, I'm heading to the Rouse place to arrest Matt. How do I find it?"

"Take the road toward Sterling City. That's the same one you take to the new town those coloreds are building. About seven miles north of here, there's a turnoff to the right. Lucas Rouse's Bar R spread is two miles up that. You can't miss the place. But it'll be well dark long before you get there, Lieutenant. Might be smarter to wait until mornin' before headin' out there."

"Can't chance Matt Rouse decidin' to head for parts unknown," Jim answered. "I might already be too late. Besides, the moon's just about full, so there'll be plenty of light for travelin'."

"I doubt Matt'll go anywhere," Franklin objected. "His daddy's got too much influence in these parts. And do you really think the Rouses are gonna let you ride in there and arrest Matt without kickin' up a fuss? You're invitin' a bullet in the back."

"Mebbe so, but I've faced worse odds, and they won't be expectin' me," Jim answered. "I'm also pretty certain that Lucas Rouse, if he's got as much influence as you say he does, would rather chance his son facin' a jury instead of possibly havin' him killed resistin' arrest. I'd also bet a hat Rouse is smart enough to know if he or one of his boys gunned me down, that'd buy him a heap more trouble than even he could handle. No, I'm figurin' I won't have too much trouble bringin' Matt in."

"I hope you're right, Lieutenant. Good luck."

"Thanks, Sheriff. Make sure to take good care of Dinah. She's the key to this whole case."

"Will do."

CHAPTER TWENTY-TWO

Texas Ranger Johnny Dexter's funeral was a brief, graveside affair. The only attendees, besides the undertaker and Jim Blawcyzk, were Sheriff Franklin, Miss Hattie, Amanda Cruz, Krishia Rivera, and Victoria Norman. Conspicuous by her absence was the second-to-last person to see Dexter alive, Dinah Davenport. Jim Blawcyzk said a few brief words over Johnny's coffin, then the young Ranger's body was committed to the earth.

Jim's mind raced with conflicting emotions, his guts churning while he rode toward the Bar R Ranch. With the initial discovery of Johnny's body and the subsequent questioning of those who might be involved, he hadn't had time to let his feelings take over. Now, on the way to arrest Johnny's apparent killer, a touch of exhaustion was setting in, along with a deep sadness at the loss of the brash young Ranger. While Jim hadn't gotten as close to the redhead as most of the other Rangers he'd worked with over the years, there was still the affection and camaraderie all lawmen felt for a fellow officer. In addition to the sadness, there was anger, anger that Johnny's killing was senseless, brought on by a drunken, spoiled son of a rich rancher. Jim almost hoped Matt Rouse would pull a gun on him. That would give him an excuse to sink a couple of bullets into Rouse's lousy guts.

Jim let Sizzle set his own pace. The big paint, as usual, was eager to run, so once he galloped for a distance, he settled into his ground-eating lope. Under the virtually full moon, every landmark, every piece of brush on the nearly feature-less landscape was clearly highlighted. As always, Jim rode alert in the saddle, ready for the possibility of ambush. That was the only way a Ranger stayed alive.

Jim pulled his horse down to a walk once the Bar R came into view, the buildings plainly visible while he was still a mile off.

"Easy, pard," he told the gelding. "No use announcin' our arrival before we get there."

When Jim reached the gate to the ranch yard, he halted Sizzle, and sat studying the place for a few moments. The main house was a rambling affair, with a front porch running the entire length of the building, and a long wing off the right side. There was a bunkhouse some distance off, and beyond that stables. Scattered in between were a springhouse, smithy, and smokehouse. There was a lantern on each side of the front door of the main house, illuminating the stairs. Lights shone from two of the front windows of the house, as well as several of the bunkhouse windows. Jim checked his six-gun, then slid the heavy Peacemaker loosely back in its holster.

"No point in puttin' this off, Siz," Jim murmured. "Let's go."

He lifted the reins and put Sizzle into a slow, almost silent walk. No one challenged as they approached the house.

"Looks like no one's outside, Siz," Jim half-whispered. "That'll make things easier, reaching the house without bein' seen. According to the sheriff, Rouse thinks he's got a lot of influence around here. Well, he's about to find out otherwise."

Jim dismounted and dropped Sizzle's reins to the dirt, ground-hitching the paint. He patted the horse's shoulder, then climbed the stairs and knocked on the door. A moment later, the door swung open, to reveal a tall, broad-shouldered man, somewhere in his fifties. He had penetrating dark brown eyes, thick gray hair, and a huge, drooping moustache. His gaze immediately dropped to the silver star on silver circle pinned to Jim's vest.

"What do you want, Ranger?" he rumbled, not bothering with the pleasantries.

"Lucas Rouse?"

"I'm Lucas Rouse, yeah."

"Lieutenant Jim Blawcyzk, Texas Rangers. I'm here to talk with your son, Matthew."

"What about, Ranger?"

"Mind if I come in?"

"Truthfully, yes. One of you Rangers gunned down my youngest boy, with no cause. If I'd had my gun when I answered the door, I'd've gut-shot you where you stand."

"That's not exactly true, Rouse, the way the sheriff sees it. Several witnesses claim your boy tried to shoot Johnny Dexter in the back. Johnny had no choice but to defend himself. Now, I'm here to arrest your son Matthew for the killin' of Johnny Dexter. I can do that peaceful-like, or if I have to I'll bring your boy in belly-down over a saddle. Which way's it gonna be?"

"That's impossible," Rouse exploded. "You tryin' to tell me that Ranger who killed Pete is dead, and Matthew did it?"

"That's right," Jim replied.

"Then I reckon you'd better come in, Ranger. We've got some talkin' to do."

Rouse swung the door wide. Jim kept his left hand close to the butt of his Colt as he followed him into a cedar paneled living room. Rouse's six surviving sons were there. All bore a strong resemblance to their father, except for the gray hair. Theirs was all light brown, almost sandy in color.

"Boys, this here's a Lieutenant Blawcyzk, from the Rangers. Lieutenant, my sons, Matthew, Mark, Luke, Eugene, Jody, and John."

"I've already met Jody and Mark," Jim said, flatly. "Can't say it was a pleasure."

"You've got a lot of nerve, comin' here, Ranger," Jody snarled. "Must not like livin' very much."

"Take it easy, Jody," Rouse urged. "The Ranger's here makin' some serious accusations against Matthew. Apparently the Ranger who shot Pete is dead, and for some reason Matthew's suspected of doin' the killin'."

"What? That red-headed Ranger's dead?" Matthew exclaimed. His surprise seemed so genuine that Jim wondered, for a moment, whether Matthew was, in fact, not the person who had killed Johnny Dexter.

"That's right," Jim replied. "I've got a witness who claims you paid her to set up Johnny's murder. You're under arrest."

"Ranger, hearin' that Ranger who killed my little brother is dead is the best news I've received in a long time, but I didn't do it. That's not sayin' I wouldn't have, just that somebody beat me to it. If you find out who really killed him, let me know. I want to shake his hand."

Jim shook his head, then pulled out his gun and leveled it at the cowboy.

"Sorry, Matthew, but you were heard by a whole bunch of people, including Sheriff Franklin, threatening to kill Johnny Dexter, and there's a witness who'll swear in court you paid her to arrange the murder. You'll have to come with me, and face a judge."

"Ranger, if I may ask, who's your witness?" Rouse requested.

"A gal from Miss Hattie's. Johnny was shot in her room. She'll testify Matt paid her to get Johnny there, then leave him for Matt."

"That's your witness? One of the whores from Miss Hattie's?" Rouse asked, chuckling.

"That's right," Jim answered.

"Then you're wastin' your time, Ranger. No one'll take the word of one of Hattie's whores against the word of a Rouse."

"That's not my worry, Rouse. Right now I'm here to bring Matthew in. Like I told you outside, I can take him in peacefully, or if he resists, I'll put a couple of slugs in his middle and bring him in draped over his horse, which'd give me real pleasure. You can bet a hat on that. Which way do you want it?"

"You've got a lot of sand in your craw, I'll say that much, Ranger," Rouse answered. "We out-number you seven to one. What's stopping us from killin' you right now?"

"Because I'd get at least you and Matthew before you got me," Jim answered. "You'd both be dead. Probably a couple more of your boys, too. Then once word got back of my killin' there'd be a whole passel of Rangers at your door. You really want that?"

Rouse's shoulders slumped in defeat.

"No, I reckon not," he conceded. "Matthew, you'd better go with the Ranger. We'll get this whole thing straightened out right quick. I'll see Judge Hopper first thing Monday morning. You won't be locked up more'n a night or two."

"All right, Dad, long as you say so," Matthew agreed.

"Jody, get Matthew's horse saddled for him," Rouse ordered.

"Okay, Dad."

While Matthew's brother headed for the stable to saddle his horse, Jim produced a set of handcuffs, and proceeded to shackle Matthew's wrists.

"Reckon I have to wear these," Matthew said as the cuffs were tightened and locked. His hatred for Jim was plain in his eyes.

"You sure do," Jim confirmed. "Mr. Rouse, while we're waiting for Matthew's horse to be brought around, there's something else I need to bring up. My men tell me your son Pete was spoutin' off about running off the Negroes who are startin' up a new town, or burning them out. I'm hopin' that was just fool talk from a drunk young kid who was shootin' off his mouth. If it wasn't, then I'm warning you, don't even think about tryin' anything like that. You'll regret it, bet a hat on that."

"Ranger, let me tell you something," Rouse replied. "My family had a big plantation way over in east Texas, hard on the Louisiana line. We had lots of slaves, and lemme tell you, they were the most shiftless, thievin' bunch you'd ever come across. Only way to keep 'em in line was with shackles and the whip. I hate niggers, taught my boys to hate niggers, and we sure ain't gonna let any niggers move in on us. We didn't ask 'em to come here, and they ain't wanted in these parts. Not to mention I wanted that land those darkies settled on. I planned on buyin' that piece to expand my ranch. They're not real Americans anyway, just like Indians or Mexicans ain't."

Jim's blue eyes glittered with a cold fury as he replied.

"Rouse, lemme give you a little history lesson, part of which comes courtesy of Adrian Chatman, the man who brought those folks out here. One, the first man who died during this country's battle to break free from the King of England was an *hombre* named Crispus Attucks, a colored man, who was half-Indian and half-Negro. He was shot and killed by British soldiers during the Boston Massacre, back in 1770, even before the Revolutionary War. Two, none, or hardly any, of the Negroes who came to the Americas came on their own. They were brought over as slaves, by the white man. So if you blame anyone for colored folk moving into your back yard, blame your family and your neighbors who wanted free labor. Three, as long as you brought it up, the

Spanish were here long before us Anglos, and the Indians here well before the Spanish. Texicans are every bit as much United States citizens as the rest of us, and since the War, Negroes are also. I reckon some day the Indians will be too."

Rouse's voice was tight with anger as he responded.

"Ranger, I was a lieutenant colonel in the Confederate Army durin' the War, with the 10th Texas Cavalry, to be precise. We fought that war to keep the coloreds in their place, and to keep the dam'Yankees from tellin' us what to to. Matter of fact, your fine little speech sounds like dam'Yankee talk, and now that I think on it, your name sure doesn't sound like any good Texan's name. Sounds more like a dam'Yankee name. Is that it? Are you one of those carpetbaggin' dam'Yankees?"

"Not at all," Jim answered. "My family came here from Poland and settled in Bandera back in 1855. I'm as much Texan as you are, mebbe more so. However, I'm also one of those Texans who didn't feel we should secede from the Union, and I shouldn't have to remind you there were quite a few of us, especially in west Texas, who felt that way. Mebbe instead of hatin' Negroes so much, you should think on hirin' on some as cowboys or horse wranglers. I've known quite a few coloreds who made top hands. You might also find a good market for some of your beef by sellin' it to the colored settlements. Makin' money's far more sensible than startin' a fight you'd be certain to lose. Now, if you've still got a grudge against the Rangers for what happened to your boy, fine, but those folks up in Freedom have nothin' to do with that. Your fight's with us, not them. Leave those folks be."

"Dad, maybe you should listen to the lieutenant," Luke spoke up. "What he's sayin' makes sense. If we start a fight lots of women and kids are liable to get hurt. Those people didn't do anythin' to us."

"You just keep your mouth shut, Luke," Rouse ordered. "Dunno where you got that soft streak. Must be from your Ma, 'cause it sure didn't come from me. Ranger," he continued. "There ain't no way I'm gonna have a bunch of lazy, thievin' darkies that close to my Bar R. Best thing you could do is take your men and clear out."

"That's not gonna happen, Rouse. Bet a hat on it."

The two men fell into stony silence.

Once Matthew's horse, a white gelding, was brought around, he and Jim climbed into their saddles. The rest of the Rouse clan was gathered on the porch.

"Word of advice to all of you," Jim warned. "I wouldn't get any ideas about followin' us and puttin' a bullet in my back. That'd only get Matthew here killed."

"We'll let the judge handle this on Monday, Ranger," Rouse said. "With any luck we'll have your badge, too."

"Been tried before, by better men than you, Rouse. Hasn't happened yet, but you sure can give it a try, if you want to waste your time. Matthew, let's go."

Jim swung Sizzle away from the rail. Keeping his prisoner in front of him, he heeled the big horse into a trot.

Despite Jim's unease that the Rouses would attempt to drygulch him and take his prisoner back, the trip to San Angelo was uneventful. While Jim maintained a steady vigil, studying every shadow cast by the bright moonlight, Matthew rode in sullen silence. They were about four miles from town when Matthew gave out a sudden grunt, which was followed by the sharp crack of a rifle. Jim grabbed his Winchester and rolled from his saddle, sliding behind the scant cover of some brush. Matthew tumbled from his horse's back, the panicked gelding running off. Sizzle trotted some distance off, safely away from any more bullets.

Jim lay listening, trying to ascertain where the shot had come from, expecting another bullet to try for him at any moment.

"Had to have come from that bluff," he muttered, looking at one of the few variations in the table-flat land, a low mesa. "If I make a move, that *hombre'll* plug me plumb center. He's got me dead to rights. The moonlight's bright as day, so I'd be a clear target."

A moment later, the sound of rapidly fading hoofbeats came to Jim's ears.

"Huh. Guess he's givin' up." Cautiously, rifle still at the ready, Jim emerged from his shelter, then walked over to where Matthew lay. The cowboy had a bullet hole squarely in the center of his back. His spine shattered, Matt Rouse had been dead the moment the bullet hit.

Jim whistled shrilly. Sizzle trotted up to him, whickering softly and nuzzling his cheek.

"Yeah, I'm all right, bud. How about you?"

In answer, Sizzle nickered again, then dropped his nose to Jim's hip pocket.

"All right. I reckon you're okay," Jim laughed. He gave the horse a peppermint, then quickly looked him over.

"Let's retrieve Rouse's horse so we can load him up and get to town," Jim said. "One thing's for certain, I'm not headin' back to the Bar R. Rouse'll think for sure that I plugged his boy in the back, figurin' to claim he was tryin' to escape. He and his boys would kill me for certain, bet a hat on that. Truth to tell, I sure couldn't blame them. If I were in their boots, I'd think the same thing."

He climbed into the saddle and set Sizzle after

Matt's gelding, which had stopped to graze a few hundred yards distant. While the horse was still nervous, Jim's calm manner and soft voice soon soothed the frightened animal, so he was able to pick up the trailing reins and lead it back to Matt's body. The horse shied at the scent of blood, but again Jim was able to quiet the gelding. Jim lifted Matt's body over the horse's back and lashed it in place. Once that was done, he swung back into his own saddle and, leading Matt's gelding, resumed the trip to San Angelo.

Jim puzzled over Matt's killing while he kept Sizzle at a steady, fast walk. As was his habit, he talked to his horse while he rode along.

"Siz, you reckon that bushwhacker mistook Matt for me, figured he'd got me, so he took off once Matt was down and not movin'?"

Jim's big paint shook his head and snorted.

"I don't think so either," Jim said. "It'd be plumb hard to mistake Matt's white horse for you, especially under this moon. Plus, if it was any of the Rouses, they'd've come down to get Matt once they believed I was dead. No, I'd say whoever plugged him wanted Matt dead. Now, mebbe he wanted to kill both me and Matt, but then why didn't he try'n finish me off? Even more curious, if he'd wanted to kill both of us, it'd make more sense to drill me first, then get Matt afterwards. Matt would've figured it was one of his brothers who got me, and he was now

351

safe, so that drygulcher would have had an easy target. Could've rode right up to Matt and nailed him real easy. No, like I said, I'd bet my hat whoever did this shootin' wanted Matt dead, not me. But why?"

Sizzle snorted again.

"Sure wish I knew what you were sayin', horse," Jim said. "Reckon it was Rouse himself who shot his own son, tryin' to stir up trouble? Doesn't make any sense, but then again I've rarely seen as much virulent hatred in any man as I saw in Rouse when he was talkin' about Negroes. But could he really hate colored folk so much that he'd kill his own boy? I doubt it."

Jim sighed.

"Sure is a puzzlement. Does point to one thing, though. Matt Rouse bein' killed means mebbe he wasn't lyin' about killin' Johnny Dexter. Mebbe he really didn't shoot him. But if it wasn't Matt, who? And why? Reckon it was that banker's son Amanda Cruz mentioned? Seems like one possibility. Even if it was, what reason would he have for killin' Matt? I can understand why he'd want to kill Pete, or even Johnny, if he was jealous of 'em, but why kill Matt? Only reason'd be if Matt also was interested in Amanda, but that doesn't seem to be the case. Plus, Tibbals'd most likely have no way of knowin' I was riding out to the Rouse place tonight to bring Matt in. Him bein' the killer is kind of a long shot."

Jim eased back in his saddle, then yawned and stretched. The long day was beginning to tell on him.

"Boils it down to a couple of things. Someone killed Johnny Dexter, mebbe Matt because Johnny killed his brother, mebbe Mason Tibbals in a fit of jealousy. Mebbe even someone else entirely. I'll have to try'n talk to Dinah again, see if she sticks to her story. Then, someone had a reason to kill Matt Rouse, someone who knew I'd be bringin' him in tonight. The sheriff? Highly unlikely, unless he's holdin' cards he ain't showin'. Who else? And why? Only two reasons I can see. First'd be to get me blamed for killin' Matt in cold blood, and get the Rouses even madder'n at the Rangers than they already are. Second'd be to stir up still more trouble, for some reason I can't put my finger on. One thing's for certain, Siz, someone wants to get folks around here riled up, seems like in particular Lucas Rouse. All we've gotta do is figure out who, and why, real quick, before a lot of blood gets spilled. C'mon, move up there, big guy. Town's just ahead."

Jim kicked the big paint into a lope.

CHAPTER TWENTY-THREE

With the hour so late, well after three in the morning by the time Jim rode back into San Angelo with Matt Rouse's body in tow, even the saloons had closed down, so the streets were deserted. Except for some wall-bracketed lanterns illuminating a few doorways, and one or two lights shining behind curtained windows, the town's only illumination was the ghostly light of the moon, now dimming as it neared its setting. Shoulders slumped in weariness, Jim rode to the sheriff's office, which was locked, no lights showing. He turned the horses into the corral out back, tying them to the fence.

"I won't leave you like this for long," he promised the animals, "just until I can rouse the sheriff."

Franklin lived in a small house adjacent to his office, so Jim headed there. His insistent knocking was soon answered by a match flaring, then a lamp being lit.

"Who is it?" Franklin's sleepy voice called.

"Jim Blawcyzk, Sheriff. Open up."

"What is it, Cecil? Who's out there?" a woman questioned from inside.

"It's Lieutenant Blawcyzk from the Rangers,

Marian. Nothin' to worry about. Don't bother to get up," Franklin answered. A moment later the front door swung open. The sheriff stood there, barefoot, tucking his shirt into his pants.

"Lieutenant, somethin' wrong? You run into trouble at the Rouses' place?"

"Not at the Rouses', but afterwards. You'd better get your boots on and come take a look, Sheriff."

"Be with you in just a minute. C'mon in and sit down while you're waiting."

Jim settled onto a sofa while Franklin finished dressing. Once the sheriff was ready, he hurried him over to the corral.

"Who's that lyin' across his horse? Matt Rouse?" Franklin questioned, on spotting the body.

"That's right, Sheriff."

"You killed Matt and were able to ride away from the Bar R without bein' shot to pieces yourself? I'm surprised you weren't filled fulla lead by Lucas and his boys."

"Not exactly," Jim answered. "Lucas agreed to have Matt be arrested and face trial. He figured his boy would never be convicted."

"Lucas is probably right about that, too. So what did happen?" Franklin asked.

"Someone bushwhacked us on the way in, about four miles out of town. Shot Matt in the back."

"Shot *Matt?*" Franklin echoed. "That doesn't seem possible. If anyone should be dead with a bullet in his back, it'd be you, Lieutenant, no offense meant."

"None taken," Jim assured him.

"You think whoever shot Matt was gunnin' for you?" Franklin questioned.

"That was my first thought, but it'd be pretty hard to mistake Matt's white horse for my paint under this full moon," Jim answered.

"Lieutenant, I have to ask this. You didn't kill Matt, did you? It would'a been real easy for you to put a slug in his back, then claim he was tryin' to escape, so you had to shoot him."

"Sheriff, like you told me when I questioned you about Hattie bein' able to blackmail you, I've never betrayed my badge, and never will. Bet a hat on it. You can check my guns if you like. They ain't been fired."

"Lotta folks are gonna think you did exactly that, though," Franklin pointed out.

"I know," Jim answered.

"Which brings us back to who shot Matt, and why?" Franklin said.

"Sheriff, if you could answer that question, I'd buy you drinks for a month," Jim answered.

"If you were still alive to buy them," Franklin replied. "Meantime, we'd better get Matt down to Ed Shaughnessy's parlor. Then, someone's got to tell Lucas Rouse."

"Reckon that falls to me, Sheriff," Jim said.

"I don't think that's a good idea," Franklin answered. "Rouse'll kill you for certain. Better let me handle that chore."

"I can't back down from every *hombre* who'd like to put a bullet in me," Jim answered. "Besides, Matt was in my custody, so it's my job to tell his father what happened."

Franklin looked over the haggard Ranger before he answered. Jim hadn't eaten since breakfast in Freedom the previous morning. His face was gaunt and stubbled with whiskers, his clothing sweat-stained and dust covered. He was just about done in, and it showed.

"Lieutenant, beggin' your pardon, but you look like you've been through Hell," he said.

"Feel like I have been," Jim admitted.

"So why don't you get some rest, and let me handle Lucas Rouse and his boys?" Franklin insisted.

"Tell you what, Sheriff. Why don't we both ride out there?"

"If I agree to that, will you at least grab a couple hours of shut-eye first?"

"That's just what I'm planning on," Jim answered. "Sure could use a hot bath, but that'll have to wait. After I care for my horse, I'll get somethin' to eat, sleep a bit, then, since it's Sunday mornin', I'd like to get to church. I'll go to the first Mass, then meet you at your office right afterwards. Let's just hope word doesn't get back to Rouse before we do."

"I'll make certain Shaughnessy knows enough to keep quiet," Franklin assured him. "As far as your horse, you can leave him right here if you'd like. There's an extra stall in the barn, and I've got more'n enough feed. You can bunk in my office if that suits you."

"I appreciate the offer, Sheriff, but there's no need," Jim replied. "I've got a place to sleep, and I'll need Sizzle to ride to church anyway."

"Suit yourself," Franklin shrugged. "Now, I'd best get Matt's body to the undertaker's, and his horse outta sight before the town starts stirrin'."

"You want a hand with that?"

"No, it's not necessary. Besides, you need that sleep more."

"I won't argue with you there, Sheriff," Jim answered. "See you after church."

He untied Sizzle, pulled himself wearily into the saddle, and slipped into the darkness.

Even if the night had been pitch black, Jim would have had no trouble reaching his destination, in fact, he could have found it blindfolded. It was a place somewhat less than a quarter mile from the courthouse, which Jim had discovered during his first visit to San Angelo, as a young Ranger. In the middle of a tough assignment, he'd been discouraged, feeling all alone in the world, completely dejected, until he'd stumbled across Kathy Esposito's. The woman who ran it seemed to understand completely what Jim had needed, and during their first, all too brief encounter, he had become completely smitten. Since then, every time he returned to San Angelo, one of his first stops was always at Kathy's. There was a need deep inside the Ranger that only Kathy could fill, one that no other woman, not even his wife, Julia, could satisfy. No one else knew of their relationship, neither Smoky McCue nor Jim Huggins, not Jim's wife, nor his son. That was the reason he hadn't yet looked up Kathy this time, Charlie's presence. Now, with Charlie remaining in Freedom, it was high time he reunited with Kathy once again.

A short while later, Jim reined up in front of Kathy's. He needed no direction, nor invitation, about what to do with his horse. He led Sizzle into the small barn out back, stripped the gear off him, and turned him into a stall. He filled a bucket with water for the horse, then located the grain bin. He gave Sizzle a good measure of oats, and tossed several forkfuls of hay into the manger. There were two other horses in the barn, so he also gave those some hay. That done, he groomed Sizzle thoroughly, finally slipping him a peppermint and patting his shoulder. The paint nuzzled his cheek.

"You did some hard travelin' today, Siz, and

there's more ahead of us tomorrow, bet a hat on it," Jim told the gelding. "Soon as you're done with your supper, although I guess it's more like breakfast by now, you'd best get some sleep. I'll see you in a few hours."

Sizzle whickered, then went back to munching his hay. Jim shouldered his saddlebags and headed for Kathy's back door. He looked around to make certain he wasn't observed, then removed a key from under a large adobe flowerpot. Surreptitiously, he unlocked the door and slipped inside. Right now his need for sleep was far greater than his need for nourishment, or anything else, so he headed straight down the hallway. A Chihuahua mix emerged from the shadows, his hackles rising while a low growl rumbled deep in his throat.

"Shh. Quiet, Krispy. It's only me, Jim." Recognizing the Ranger's voice, the small dog wagged his tail, sniffed Jim's hand, and let his ears be scratched. He then wandered back out of sight. Jim continued to the first room on the left. A few moments later, he was undressed and lying in Kathy's soft feather bed.

Jim was awakened by the rays of the rising sun streaming through the bedroom's windows. He was still lying in bed, only half-awake, when the door opened. Kathy Esposito stood framed in the doorway, staring at him, her expression one of welcome mixed with indignation. Krispy, the Chihuahua mix, was at her heels.

"Jim Blawcyzk, as I live and breathe. When did you get here? What misfortune brings you to my door this time?" she exclaimed.

"Nice to see you too, Kathleen," Jim answered, with his crooked smile. Despite the fact he was shirtless, wearing only his drawers, the usually woman-shy Ranger felt no discomfiture at being bare-chested in her presence. "I got into town real early this mornin', so rather'n disturbin' you I let myself in."

"Jim, how many times have I told you not to do that?" Kathy replied. "What if my husband found you lyin' there before I did, or maybe my son? What would you say to them?"

"I'd say 'Howdy'," Jim chuckled. "Besides, I know Eric's at school back East, and knowin' Charlie, well, I'd guess right about now he's somewhere between here and El Paso. Am I right?"

"You're close," Kathy admitted. "Charlie's actually up in Abilene at the moment, calling on his clients up there."

"So we've got nothing to worry about on that account," Jim said. "I am in a bit of a hurry, though. Afraid this will have to be a short visit."

"You usually are," Kathy sighed. She looked at the Ranger more closely. "Jim, you look like something even the cat wouldn't drag in."

"That bad, huh?" Jim answered.

"That bad," Kathy repeated. "Why don't I get you some hot water so you can clean up a bit? After that we can get down to business."

"Never thought of what we've got goin' as exactly 'business'," Jim laughed. "Guess it sort of is, though. Sure, I'd purely appreciate that water."

"I'll be right back with it. Don't you go anywhere in the meantime," Kathy warned him.

"I'll be waitin'," Jim promised. He settled back on the pillows until Kathy returned. She carried a pitcher filled with steaming water, a basin, bar of soap, washcloth, and towel. She placed all these on the bureau.

"Take all the time you need," she told Jim. "I'll be ready for you whenever you're finished."

She started for the door, then turned and touched a finger mischievously to the end of his nose.

"But don't take too long," she warned.

"With you waitin' for me, you can bet your hat I won't, Kathy darlin'," Jim promised. "Soon as I clean up and feed my horse, I'll be with you."

Once Kathy left, Jim hurriedly stripped down, scrubbed himself as best he could, toweled off, then removed his razor from his saddlebags. Working up a lather from the soap Kathy had provided, he scraped the whiskers from his face. Once he'd finished, he again dug into his saddlebags, removing his spare shirt and a clean bandanna. He donned those, then beat the dust from his jeans, boots, and Stetson as best he could. That done, he resettled his gunbelt around his hips. After feeding Sizzle, Jim headed eagerly for where he knew Kathy was waiting. "That didn't take all that long now, did it?" he asked, once he reached her.

"No, I guess not," Kathy admitted, turning from the window, where she was silhouetted by the morning sun. Kathy was unusually tall, about five foot eight, and very slim. Her hair varied in color from almost pure blonde to medium brown, depending on how much time she'd spent in the sun. She wore it slightly longer than shoulder length, and straight. Her green eyes seemed to reflect her joyous outlook on life. She was dressed in a practical blue gingham dress and white apron.

"Are you ready?" she asked.

"Always am, you know that," Jim replied, as he settled onto a chair.

"If you are, then how many?"

"Let's start off with a dozen or so," Jim answered. "Haven't had a thing to eat since yesterday morning."

"All right."

Kathy removed a tray of fresh, warm, sugar-covered doughnuts, and another of dried-apple fritters, from the display case in her bakery's front window, then placed them on the red-checked covered table where Jim was seated. A steaming pot of coffee was already there, and Jim poured himself a mugful. He took a doughnut from the tray, and downed half of it in one bite, the powdery sugar leaving its traces on his upper lip. Jim leaned back in satisfaction, savoring every bit of the treat while he chewed, pure pleasure written on his face.

"Boy howdy, Kathy, your bakin's as good as ever," he praised. "Julia still can't make dough-nuts like you can. Not that I'd ever mention it to her."

Kathy took the chair opposite Jim, poured a cup of coffee for herself, took an apple fritter, and set it on her plate.

"You still haven't told your wife about me?" she questioned.

"Oh, Julia knows about you all right," Jim replied. "Just not that you make better dough-nuts and fritters than she does. Can't say more than that, since she's real proud of her cookin', and rightfully so. She'd take a broom to me, bet a hat on it. All I've told her is you've got the best bakery and candy shop in San Angelo."

"And for a hundred miles in any direction," Kathy said.

"That's so," Jim agreed, taking another bite of his doughnut. Indeed, Kathy's Fresh Baked Goods and Candy Store was well-known throughout all of west-central Texas. Cowboys would ride for miles just to sink their teeth into one of her powdered doughnuts or a huge, thick slice of dried-apple pie. Cooks, both male and female, were jealous of her seemingly magical skills in the kitchen. In addition, she had a few rooms out back which she rented to travelers, the extreme cleanliness of which was in contrast to most of the region's hotels. However, the room Jim always used was not one of those. It was in the family wing of the house, reserved as a guest bedroom. Only a privileged few knew where the spare key to the house was hidden.

"Jim, you haven't told me yet why you're here," she said. "I'd heard some Rangers passed through town awhile back, but I didn't realize you were one of them."

"I was," Jim admitted. "I didn't stop to see you on the way through because my son Charlie is now a Ranger, and is with me. Can't have him knowin' about you and me, at least until I know he won't slip up and tell his mom about us. He loves sweets almost as much as I do, and if he ever told Julia I like your doughnuts better'n hers . . ." Jim paused before continuing. "Anyway, you undoubtedly know a bunch of Negroes are startin' up a new settlement some miles northwest of San Angelo. We escorted them from Louisiana, and are stayin' awhile until they get settled, to hopefully stop any trouble before it starts."

"That will keep your hands full," Kathy observed.

"It sure will, and things have gotten even worse over the past couple of days," Jim answered, now biting into a fritter.

"How so?"

"How much have you heard about the shootings in front of the Lady Victoria, and now at Miss Hattie's?"

"I know a Ranger killed Pete Rouse, but it was self-defense," Kathy answered. "I hadn't heard about a shooting at Hattie's. Don't forget, I go to bed early, since I'm up at four in the morning to start the day's baking."

"Then you aren't aware the man killed at Hattie's was Johnny Dexter, one of my men. He's the same Ranger who killed Pete Rouse."

"One of your men? Jim, I'm so sorry," Kathy answered.

"Thanks, Kathy."

"Do you know who killed him?"

"I thought I did, but now I'm not so certain," Jim explained. "There's a witness who claims Matt Rouse arranged the killing."

"That would make sense," Kathy agreed. "Lucas Rouse and his boys think they can ride roughshod over everyone in these parts. So, are you going to arrest Matt?"

"I did just that, last night," Jim answered. "Only problem is, someone drygulched us on the way back to town. Plugged Matt in the back and killed him."

"Killed Matt? But who? And why? Are you certain it wasn't Matt's father, or one of his brothers who meant to kill you?"

"Kathy, I'd plumb give up your doughnuts for the answers to those questions," Jim said. "As far as hittin' the wrong target, I don't think so. Matt was riding a white horse, which stood out like a beacon in the moonlight. I'm almost positive whoever killed Matt Rouse intended to do just that. As far as who, I haven't a clue. And as to why, *quien sabe*? One thing I will hazard is whoever did it wants me blamed for Matt's death."

"Which will make you a target for the Rouses' guns," Kathy concluded.

"If I keep eatin' your doughnuts, a much bigger target," Jim chuckled.

"Jim, that's not funny," Kathy protested. "Your life's in real danger if the Rouses come gunning for you."

"I'm a Ranger. It usually is, anyway," Jim answered.

"Nonetheless, you need to be extra careful until the killer is found," Kathy said. "Promise me that."

"I will," Jim assured her.

"What's your next move?" Kathy asked.

"First, I'm going to Mass," Jim answered.

"Then I'm heading for the sheriff's office to talk to the woman who claimed Matt killed Johnny. Matt denied he did the killin', and him being bushwhacked makes me tend to think he didn't. I want to see if she changes her story. After that, Sheriff Franklin and I are riding out to the Bar R, to tell Lucas Rouse what's happened."

"Are you sure that's a good idea?" Kathy questioned.

"I'm pretty certain it's a terrible idea," Jim replied. "However, since Matt Rouse was in my custody when he was killed, it's my duty to let his father know what happened."

"I guess that's true," Kathy conceded. "While you finish your coffee, I assume you want some doughnuts for Sam."

"Sam's not with me today," Jim explained. "I'm ridin' Sizzle. Since Sam'll stay with Charlie, I left him back in Freedom. I will take half a dozen doughnuts for Siz, though, and a sack of peppermints for him and Sam, oh, and a sack of licorice for myself."

"I'll get them ready for you," Kathy answered.

By the time Jim had downed the last of his coffee, Kathy had his pastries and candy ready, tied in a neat package.

"I left two doughnuts out to give Sizzle now," she explained.

"He'll appreciate that. How much do I owe you?" Jim asked.

"The usual," Kathy answered. "There's no charge for a lawman, at least this lawman. And don't argue."

"I gave up that idea a long time back," Jim answered. "Kathy, been meanin' to say this for a long time. You've been a good friend, and I appreciate that. A Ranger doesn't make too many friends he can count on. You're one of 'em."

"Jim, don't talk like that," Kathy said.

"What do you mean?" Jim asked, not understanding her reasoning.

"Saying I've been a good friend. Say I am a good friend. Been implies something is going to end the friendship . . . like a death."

"I didn't want to imply that at all," Jim answered. "We'll be friends for years to come."

The pealing of church bells drifted on the still morning air.

"Guess I'd best be movin'. Don't want to be late for church," Jim said.

"I'm going to Mass also," Kathy said. "If you'd like, I'll go with you."

"We'd better not be seen together, at least not leavin' your house," Jim answered. "You and I know there's nothing more than friendship between us, but there's no need to give people a reason to talk. You know how folks like to gossip."

"I'm not worried about idle chatter," Kathy

370

said. "Charlie and Eric know about us, and they're the only ones who really matter."

"Perhaps that's so, but if enough rumors get spread it could hurt your business," Jim pointed out. "I'll get Sizzle ready, then meet you in front of the church. That way, no one will be the wiser."

"I suppose that is for the best," Kathy agreed. "I'll meet you there."

Arriving at the church, Jim tied Sizzle to the rail out front, then loosened his cinches. Unwilling to wear his gun into a house of worship, he unbuckled his gunbelt and hung it from his saddlehorn. He was certain no one would steal it from in front of the Lord's home.

"You wait here, Siz. I won't be long." he ordered the paint, giving him a peppermint. Sizzle whickered and nuzzled Jim's chest. By then, Kathy had joined him, so they entered the sanctuary together.

Before the Mass started, Jim lit several candles, one for his wife, another in the hope Lucas Rouse could somehow be dissuaded from starting the fight he seemed so determined to begin. The others were for the safety of his men, especially Charlie, and for Kathy Esposito and her family. He and Kathy took a pew halfway toward the altar.

The solemnity of the Mass always brought

consolation to the Ranger. It was one of the few constants in his life, the ancient Latin prayers bringing a peace to his soul. The church buildings themselves also gave him comfort. Despite the variations of the individual structures, there was always the ornate altar, the Stations of the Cross, the statues of saints, the soft, flickering lights of the votive candles. And always, the reassuring presence of Jesus Christ in the tabernacle, the living Body and Blood of the Saviour reserved in the bread and wine of the Eucharist.

All too soon, the Mass ended. While Kathy went back to her bakery, to open for the after Mass customers, Jim mounted Sizzle and headed for Sheriff Franklin's office.

"You still think Dinah is telling the truth, Lieutenant?" Franklin asked Jim, as they rode to the Rouse ranch. Despite intense questioning, Dinah continued to maintain it was Matt Rouse who had paid her to lure Johnny Dexter to his death.

"I dunno," Jim admitted. "Honestly, I think she's lyin' through her teeth to protect someone. Question is, who?"

"Mebbe Lucas Rouse himself," the sheriff speculated. "Seems far-fetched, but it'd be just like Lucas to let one of his kids take the blame, realizing it'd be highly unlikely for any jury in these parts to convict a Rouse, no matter how heinous the crime."

"I doubt Lucas'd kill one of his own sons, though," Jim answered. "Although anything's possible. Sheriff, I've been meaning to ask you something. Rouse has threatened to attack the settlers up in Freedom. I've got to be ready for that. Can I count on you for help if needed?"

Franklin took a long drag on his cigarette, then tossed away the butt before answering.

"Truth is, Lieutenant, I can't. Those niggers settled just over the county line, in Coke County. Since I'm sheriff of Tom Green County, my jurisdiction ends at the line."

"A Ranger can ask any citizen of Texas for assistance," Jim pointed out.

"That's true," Franklin agreed. "My answer is still no, Lieutenant. I calculate if you butt up against Lucas Rouse and his boys you'll lose. I like my job, and have no intention of stickin' my neck out for a bunch of coloreds."

"Sheriff, I appreciate your honesty, if nothing else," Jim sarcastically replied. He and Franklin continued on in silence. It occurred to Jim that, for some reason, he and Sheriff Franklin had never started using each other's first names, as was the usual case when he worked with local lawmen. Now he knew why. Franklin would probably be just as happy to see Adrian Chatman and his settlers run out of west Texas as Lucas Rouse.

Rouse and his sons, along with several cowboys, were gathered in the front yard of the Bar R when Jim and Franklin rode in. Rouse glared at the two lawmen.

"Cecil, I'd say good mornin', but bein' as you're ridin' with that Ranger, can't say as I'm willin'," he muttered. "You got any particular reason for bringin' him here?"

"Mind if we get down?" Franklin asked.

"Makes no never mind to me," the rancher shrugged. "Step down and say your piece."

"Thanks, Lucas," Franklin answered. He swung off his bay gelding, Jim following suit.

"Cecil, you didn't ride all the way out here on a Sunday morning without good reason," Rouse stated. "What is it?"

"Lucas, there's no easy way to say this," the sheriff replied. "Matt's dead. Shot in the back."

"What? Another of my boys was gunned down?" Rouse asked.

"That's right, Lucas. Ranger here says someone ambushed 'em on the way to town last night, and put a slug through Matt."

"Ranger, are you plumb loco, thinkin' you could pull the wool over my eyes with a wild yarn like that? You shot my boy, drilled him without warning . . . in the back. You killed him like you'd kill a rabid dog."

Rouse charged at Jim, and sank his fist deep into the Ranger's belly. Jim doubled over, gasping for air. Rouse pulled his gun, thumbed back the hammer, and leveled it at the helpless Ranger.

"Dad, no!" Luke screamed, knocking his father's arm aside just as he pulled the trigger. The shot Rouse intended for Jim's chest went wide.

"Let me go!" Rouse ordered, as Luke grabbed him, pinning his right arm. Sheriff Franklin also leapt at the enraged rancher, holding his left arm tight. Luke twisted the gun from his father's grasp.

"Lucas, try'n calm down," the sheriff urged. "From what I can see, the lieutenant's telling the truth. I checked his guns, and they haven't been used. On our way here, he showed me the spot where they were ambushed. Sure enough, there were hoofprints from another horse leadin' away. Several cigarette butts, too, which showed someone'd been waitin' there. You shoot down Lieutenant Blawcyzk and I'll have to arrest you for murder. Most likely, even you'd be convicted for that."

"Don't matter," Rouse growled. "He probably set up the whole scene, nice and tidy. Had a hideout gun which he tossed away. He shot Matt, and now I'm gonna put a bullet through his lousy guts for that. Just let go of me."

"Dad, listen to the sheriff," Luke urged. "Let the courts handle this."

"We don't need any court," Jody said. "Us

Rouses can handle things on our own, just fine."

Jim had regained some of his breath.

"Rouse," he gasped, "dunno if you'll believe me or not, and I don't much care. I didn't kill your son, and I won't quit until I found out who did. Bet a hat on it."

"Cecil, let me loose," Rouse insisted.

"If I do, you gonna behave?" Franklin replied.

"For now. You have my word on it," Rouse assured him.

"All right." Franklin released the rancher, but did take his gun from its holster and leveled it at Rouse's stomach.

"One false move and you'll be joinin' Pete and Matt," he warned.

"I'm not gonna do anythin' . . . yet," Rouse said. He turned to Jim.

"Ranger, I'm comin' after you, and the rest of your men. Far as I'm concerned, every last one of you is responsible for killin' my boys. Same goes for those niggers. If they hadn't come here, none of this would've happened. I'm gonna kill every last one of you Rangers, and I'm gonna kill every nigger I can. The rest I'll drive off into the badlands, where they'll die slow and hard. You can bet your last dollar on that."

"Rouse, if you want to pick a fight with the Rangers, that's fine, although I guarantee you'll lose, no matter how much you might think you have us outnumbered," Jim answered. "But leave those people in Freedom out of this. They've got nothing to do with your sons' deaths. You have no reason to go after them."

"They're niggers, and I don't want 'em in my back yard. That's reason enough for me," Rouse answered. "However, I'm a fair man. I'll give them twenty-four hours to pack up and move on. You pass that word to them. Tell 'em twenty-four hours. After that, me and my men'll run over them like a stampedin' herd of longhorns. You understand me, Ranger?"

"Your meanin's plain enough," Jim answered. "So's this. Only thing that'll happen if you attack Freedom is a lot of folks will die, needlessly, including more of your sons. Bet a hat on it. You might want to think on that."

"Don't worry about any of us Rouses, Ranger," John snapped. "We can take care of ourselves."

"That's right," Eugene agreed. His hand hovered threateningly over the handle of his six-gun.

"Suit yourself," Jim answered. "You've been warned."

"So have you, Ranger," Rouse retorted.

CHAPTER TWENTY-FOUR

Jim got back to Freedom late that evening, and, after explaining to the rest of the Rangers what had transpired down in San Angelo, arranged a hastily called meeting for the men of Freedom. It was a tense group which awaited him in the stockroom of Fletcher Harris's general store. The air was thick with tobacco smoke. Besides most of the male residents of the town, several of the women were also in attendance. Once everyone had found seats and settled down, Jim called them to order. He again summarized the events in San Angelo, this time for everyone's benefit, then told them of Lucas Rouse's threat to destroy their new town. He finished with a reassurance the Rangers would defend the settlement against Rouse and his men.

"I'm sure y'all have a lot of questions," he concluded. "Now's the time to ask 'em, because if I read Lucas Rouse correctly, he's not gonna waste any time to hit us."

"Jim, do you think there's any chance he was just bluffing?" Joe Fletcher asked.

"There's always that possibility, but I doubt it," Jim answered. "Adrian."

"Jim, you didn't mention anything about the

rest of us fighting against Rouse," Adrian said.

"That's us Rangers' job, not yours," Jim answered. "None of you are fighters, plus most of you have families. I want to see as few people hurt as possible. I can't ask you to take on Lucas Rouse."

Adrian's response was soft, but firm.

"Lieutenant," he stated. "We Negroes have been pushed around by the white man for far too long now. It's high time we stood up for our rights, and we can't do that by letting you Rangers fight our battles for us. Yes, we need you to stop Rouse, but we sure aren't going to just stand by and watch while you do that by yourselves. Sure, you said Rouse is mad as blazes at the Rangers, but you also mentioned he's bound and determined to drive us off our land. Well, let him try. We're just as bound and determined to stay. If Rouse wants a fight, he sure as heck is gonna get just that."

Applause broke out in the room.

"Do all of you feel that way?" Jim asked.

A murmur of assent and nodding of heads swept the room.

"Seems like they do, Jim," Smoky said.

"Okay, if you're willing then we sure welcome the help," Jim said. "However, it's got to be on my terms."

"You know what needs to be done, Jim. We'll listen to your orders," Adrian agreed.

"Fine. First, the women and kids will need to stay inside. I'll want the married men with them, posted at windows, with guns at the ready, as many shotguns as you have, since, as you say, most of you aren't all that proficient with firearms. Their job will be to shoot anyone tryin' to reach the women, or attemptin' to fire the buildings."

"Lieutenant, don't forget, some of us women also have pistols," Adrian's Aunt Ruthenia reminded him.

"I'm countin' on that," Jim grinned. "Also, any of you ladies who are willing can help by passing out ammunition and keeping guns loaded. That'll free up the men to keep shootin'. By rotatin' any spare weapons, the men will be able to hold a steady line of fire."

"We can certainly do that, Jim," Frances assured him.

"That's good," Jim replied. "The single men will be out in the street with us. Once Rouse and his men show up, you'll need to start shootin', but only after I give the word. We want them close enough to make good targets. Once the firin' starts, try'n make every bullet count. I don't know how many men Rouse will have, but I do know all of 'em will be much handier with their guns than y'all, bet a hat on it."

"I don't need a gun. I'll take on Rouse with my bare hands," Bull Mason declared.

"I believe you would," Jim laughed. He paused before continuing.

"I'd also prefer the older folks to stay out of harm's way. It'd just ease my mind some."

"Lieutenant, no one's going to drive me away from here," eighty-six year old Shirley Bell said. "I'll shoot the first man who comes near me."

"You're not leaving us out of this fight, Jim," Lawrence Young, Adrian's grandfather, concurred.

"The same goes for me," Sam Tatum added.

"If any of you are determined to take part, I certainly won't stop you," Jim said. "Except for you, Sam. There's gonna be people hurt, bet a hat on it. I'll need you to treat the wounded. I have a feelin' your battlefield hospital experience will come in handy before all this is over. That brings up another point. Some of you ladies will need to help Sam, by makin' bandages, keeping water boilin', and whatever else he needs."

"We can take on that chore," Sheryl answered. "It'll be better than just hiding behind walls. This way we can be useful."

"Good. Reverend Jones, your job will be to pray," Jim added.

"And to help defend my community," Jones answered, pulling an ancient Navy Colt from under his coat. "I still have powder, caps, and balls for this old gun."

"So you can blast 'em to Hell, Reverend, but

pray for their souls as you do," Bill Dundee laughed.

"That's right," Jones smiled.

"Any other questions before I tell everyone where I want them?" Jim asked.

"Just one," Bobby Decker, a young man of about twenty, asked. "Once the shootin' starts, how will we know who to aim for? After all, you white folks all look alike to us."

Jim laughed.

"Just don't plug anyone wearin' a badge," he said. "Besides, we've been with you long enough now you should recognize us. One last thing. If you get one of Rouse's men in your sights, shoot him. I don't care if you plug him in the back, just plug him. Any of Rouse's men would do the same to you. This ain't a dime novel, where the man in the right always gives the outlaw a break, and wins every time. When a man's tryin' to kill you, if you have the chance to get him first, do it, before he kills you. Is that understood?"

Silence was his answer.

"I guess it is, Jim," Adrian said.

"Then let's get ready. I fully expect to see Rouse ridin' in here just after sunup tomorrow. We'll post a guard tonight just in case, but I don't believe he'll make a move until morning."

By ten o'clock the next day, Lucas Rouse had not made good on his promise to wipe Freedom off the map. The town's residents grew more tense with each passing moment. In contrast, the Rangers waited alertly, but calmly.

"Do you think perhaps Rouse was just bluffing, Jim?" Dwain asked.

"I'd bet my hat he wasn't," Jim answered. "In fact, I know he wasn't. Here he comes now. Dwain, tell Adrian to get everyone in place."

He pointed to a smudge of dust on the horizon.

Quickly, the Rangers and townspeople took up their assigned positions. The boiling dust cloud grew rapidly, soon materializing into a large group of riders.

"How many men do you think there are, Jim?" Dan Huggins asked.

"I'd guess at least forty, mebbe a few more," Jim answered.

"Those ain't bad odds," Smoky observed.

"Perhaps not for you Rangers, but I'd prefer more of us and less of them," Bull Mason wryly answered.

"Don't shoot until I say," Jim called out. Fingers tightened on triggers as the raiders approached.

"Now!" Jim cried, when the men swept into town, guns blazing. Several were knocked from their saddles at the first volley. The rest scattered, diving from their horses or swerving them, seeking cover.

Jim shot one man, then blood sprayed crimson

from his head when a bullet from Mark Rouse struck him in the forehead. Jim half-spun, then fell on his back in the middle of the road.

"Dad!" Charlie shouted. Ignoring the bullets seeking him out, he rose from behind the rain barrel where he had taken cover, ran into the street, and shot Mark through the stomach, then again in the left breast. Before Charlie could reach his downed father, Jody Rouse, who was on the steps of Cletus Howard's saddle shop, shot him through the chest. Charlie grunted from the impact, but, staggering, kept continuing toward Jim, still shooting, blood staining his shirt. From where he had fallen, Jim rolled onto his stomach. Straining to see through the blood and sweat blurring his vision, Jim aimed and fired, putting a bullet low into Jody's belly, hitting him just above the belt buckle. Hands still clenching his six-gun, Jody jackknifed, elbows pressed to his bullet-torn gut, then pitched to his face in the dirt. Jim's gun fell from his hand, then his head dropped as he drifted into blackness, oblivious to the gun battle still raging around him.

Charlie managed to shoot another raider in the shoulder, then a bullet punched a hole through his side. The young Ranger fell, still twenty yards from his father.

In the alley alongside Fletcher Harris's store, Adrian Chatman was facing certain death. He had managed the almost impossible, for even the worst of shots. He had missed with both barrels of a loaded shotgun, and was now cornered by two of Rouse's riders.

"We've got you now, nigger!" one of them sneered. "Reckon you ain't feelin' quite so uppity, are you?" He thumbed back the hammer of his pistol.

In desperation, Adrian dove to his belly, rolled, and came up with a thick plank, as the bullet meant for his head tore through the air where it had just been. He came to his feet and swung the board at the nearest man, slamming it across his middle and breaking several ribs. The man howled with pain, doubled up, and collapsed to his face. Before his partner could react, Adrian drove the butt of the plank into his belly. The man's eyes bulged, and he spit up blood as he went to his knees. Adrian brought the plank down on his head, shattering his skull.

Ezekiel Crown, one of the few proficient marksmen among the settlers, had taken a perch behind the front window of the saddle shop. From there, his accurate shooting had accounted for at least three of Rouse's men, until Ross Lucchese, Rouse's foreman, blasted Crown out of the window with several well-placed shots of his own. Bull Mason, seeing Lucchese gun down his friend, aimed at Crown's back and pulled the trigger of his Smith and Wesson, the hammer falling on an empty chamber. Mason tossed aside the gun and dove at Lucchese, bringing him down with a hard tackle. Both men rolled, scrambling to their feet, Lucchese coming up with his Bowie knife. He lunged at Mason, but before he was able to plunge the heavy blade into Bull's guts, Mason grabbed his wrist, stopping the knife just as the point tore the fabric of his shirt and pricked his skin. Mason's other hand encircled Lucchese's throat with a powerful grip, while he forced Lucchese's hand holding his knife back, his strength far too much for the smaller and lankier man to resist. Lucchese gasped when Mason forced his knife into his own belly. Mason put more pressure on Lucchese's arm, thrusting the knife upwards and more deeply into the foreman's stomach. Lucchese gave a strangled scream, then folded over Mason's arm. Bull shoved Lucchese aside, then picked up Lucchese's gun, whirled, and shot another of Rouse's men, who was about to put a bullet in Dan Huggins's back. The cowboy managed to squeeze his trigger as he fell. Dan flinched when his would-be killer's shot went just wide, scouring his ribs. He turned, spotted Bull, grinned, and waved his thanks.

Eugene Rouse had managed to reach Sam Tatum's home, and was about to toss a kerosene-filled bottle through one of its windows. He touched a match to the rag wick, but was stopped when Ty Tremblay shot him in the back. Eugene arched in pain, then crumpled, the bottle falling from his hand to land harmlessly in the dirt. Ty was dropped by a bullet which ripped through his left thigh. He rolled under the sidewalk, out of the fight.

With casualties on both sides, the gunfire was lessening, several of Rouse's men having turned and fled. John Rouse emerged from the stable and had a clear shot at Smoky McCue's back. Before he could fire, Jim Huggins shot him through the side, slamming him into the wall of the barn. John slid down the wall, then toppled to his side.

"Lucas Rouse, give it up," Huggins shouted. "You can't win. Most of your men are dead or wounded. Most of those that aren't have turned tail and run."

"Not a chance, Ranger," Rouse answered, stepping into the middle of the street. "I'll go down shootin' first. But I'm takin' the chief nigger with me!"

He turned to where Adrian had just exited from the alley. As he thumbed back the hammer of his Colt, a barrage of lead from the Rangers, and several townspeople, tore into him. He dropped in his tracks. Seeing their boss fall, the few Bar R cowboys still in the fight tossed away their guns and raised their hands in surrender.

Silence, broken only by the moaning of wounded men, descended on Freedom. Smoke from a burning shed mingled with the powder-smoke hanging thick in the air. Adrian was halfway across the street when a shot rang out, knocking him off his feet. Bill Dundee reacted instantly, turning toward the source of the shot. He aimed his old Navy Colt and fired, striking his target directly in the center of his belly. The man stumbled into the street, dropping the Winchester he held. Adrian looked up from where he had fallen, squinting through his bent and cracked spectacles as he tried to ascertain who had shot him.

"Solomon?" he said, looking in disbelief at his land agent, the man he'd counted as a friend.

"Yes, it's me, Adrian," Solomon Burleson gasped, sagging against a hitchrail. "Guess my plans . . . didn't work out."

Jody Rouse lay where he had dropped, groaning, hands clamped to his belly. He looked around at the bodies scattered over the street. His gaze settled on his father.

"Dad, you said takin' on . . . a bunch of . . . lazy niggers . . . and a few . . . Rangers would be . . . no trouble," he choked out. "Reckon . . . you were . . . wrong."

Gun still at the ready, blood running down his right arm from a bullet slash, Smoky hurried over to where Jim lay, face-down and unmoving. He rolled the lieutenant onto his back, then looked up with tear-filled eyes. He searched out Jim

Huggins, who was kneeling alongside Charlie. Huggins gazed at McCue and shook his head. Smoky did the same.

"Jim," he called to Huggins. "It's over."

CHAPTER TWENTY-FIVE

Jim became aware of a voice, somewhere far off in the distance. It was unfamiliar, echoing and fading in and out. He wanted to concentrate on the sound, but was unable, his mind fogged and head throbbing with pain. He was able to comprehend only bits and snatches of the conversation.

"Mr. Tatum, you did a fine job treating these men, probably as fine a job as I could have done, especially considering the primitive conditions and your lack of necessary supplies," the voice said.

"Thank you, Doctor," Sam Tatum answered. "I just wish I could have done more. Do you really think there's no hope?"

"I usually believe as long as there's life, there's hope, but I can't be that optimistic here. Lieutenant Blawcyzk has a fractured skull and a severe concussion. As you can tell, he's in a deep coma. I'm certain the swelling of his brain will continue, increasing the pressure inside his skull until it kills him. Unless I am mistaken, he won't survive more than twenty-four hours, probably less."

"What about Chip?"

"The youngster? I give him no chance at all. He's lost far too much blood, and his wounds are already infected. From his high fever, I would imagine blood poisoning has already set in. It's only a matter of time until the infection overwhelms his system."

Chip? Who's Chip? Who is that doctor? Sam Tatum, do I know him? Chip? Charlie! Charlie's dyin'!

In his mind, Jim was screaming, trying to get someone's attention, but his brain and mouth would not cooperate. The men's voices faded, to be replaced by a female voice as sweet as heaven, a voice singing about coming home. The voice was joined by a chorus of others.

Angels, Jim thought. *They're callin' me and Charlie home.*

Jim's next conscious moment was of a strange face peering down at him. The face was kind, bearded and wrinkled with age, but its eyes were bright and penetrating.

"Lieutenant, how many fingers am I holding up?" the face asked.

"Fingers?" Jim repeated, his speech slurred.

"Yes, fingers? How many am I holding up?"

Jim squinted, trying to focus.

"Four."

"I'm sorry, Lieutenant. I'm only holding up two. I'm afraid the concussion you suffered from the bullet's impact affected your vision as well as your speech."

"Who in the blue blazes are you?" Jim demanded.

"I'm sorry. I'm Doctor Isaiah Towne, from San Angelo. I came here at Mr. Tatum's request."

"Here? Where's here? And who the devil is Sam Tatum?"

"Jim, you don't remember me?" Sam asked, from alongside Jim's bed. "Sam from the wagon train? You're here in Freedom."

"Never heard of Freedom."

"Sure you have," Sam encouraged. "Remember you and your Rangers escorted us halfway across Texas, to just northwest of San Angelo, where we are starting a new town, Freedom?"

"I'm afraid the damage to the lieutenant's brain includes his memory, Sam," Towne said.

"Freedom? Freedom," Jim repeated, his speech halting, as vague memories began to stir. "Oh, yeah. Rancher named, what was it, Rouse, wanted to drive you folks off your land. Last thing I remember was him and his men ridin' into town, shootin' and hollerin'."

Towne pulled back the sheets covering Jim, and ran a feather over the sole of his right foot, then the left. Jim grimaced slightly, and his feet jerked at the feather's light touch.

"Good, at least you have feeling in your lower extremities," Towne noted.

"You don't remember being shot, or shooting a man afterwards, before you passed out?" the doctor continued. "Nor your son being shot?"

"Charlie! That's right, I remember Charlie got plugged. I shot the man who nailed him. Sure hope I killed that no-good snake."

"You did," Sam assured him. "Town was saved, too. Rouse and his men were all killed or run off. We owe you a debt of gratitude, Jim."

"Charlie. Where's my boy? How's he doin'? Is he gonna be all right?" Jim demanded.

"He's in the bed right next to yours," Towne replied. "If you're able to turn your head, you can see him."

With great effort, Jim twisted until he was just able to catch a glimpse of his son. Charlie was lying, covered to his waist with a thin sheet, his body drenched with sweat and his flesh deathly white.

"Charlie," Jim softly called. "It's Dad. I'm here."

There was no response.

"I'm sorry, Lieutenant, he can't hear you," Towne said.

"He's gonna be all right, isn't he?" Jim asked.

"I'm not going to sugarcoat things for you, Lieutenant," the physician responded. "No, he's not. Your son is dying, and there's nothing I, nor any other doctor, can do to save him."

"Charlie's . . . dying?" Jim said, not believing what he was hearing. "He can't be, Doc. He can't be."

"Again, I'm sorry, but he is," Towne reiterated. "Your son suffered two severe bullet wounds, one in his chest and the other in his side, which penetrated deeply into his abdominal cavity. Either of those wounds should have killed him, in fact most ordinary men would have succumbed rather quickly to such injuries. Somehow, Chip managed to survive the wounds, at least for a short while, but now infection has set in, infection which has led to blood poisoning. Between the damage the bullets caused, and loss of blood, he's far too weak to fight off the infection. I wish I could give you better news. The only thing I can offer is your son may drift in and out of consciousness, however briefly. If he does, you'll be able to speak with him."

"I appreciate your bein' honest, Doc," Jim replied. The pounding in his head had just been replaced by a hollowness deep in his gut.

"Lieutenant, I also have to be honest and say you too may not survive your injuries," Towne added. "I'm flabbergasted you even came out of the coma which you have been in for the past several days. Your skull is fractured, and you've suffered a severe concussion, which has led to brain damage. I honestly believed you would die without ever regaining consciousness. Whether you will have a complete recovery, whether the brain damage is permanent, or whether you will slip back into a coma and die, I have no way of knowing. This may just be a temporary reprieve, in which case you may remain conscious for only a few moments, a few days, or even a week or more. Just the fact you have regained consciousness is a good sign, but nothing more. You still have a long road to recovery."

"Don't mean a thing if I pull through and my boy doesn't," Jim murmured, his voice fading. "Not a thing."

"Jim," Sam called.

"It's no use, Mr. Tatum," Towne answered. "He's slipped back into the coma."

Jim was awakened by Charlie's groaning. It was apparently sometime in the middle of the night, for the only illumination in their room was a turned-low lamp. He looked over to his son's bed. Doctor Tatum had left Charlie stripped in an effort to hold his fever down, leaving a thin sheet as his only cover. Somehow the gravely ill young Ranger had tossed off even that meager protection. His fever-wracked body was perspiration-soaked, and his hair plastered to his scalp. His pale skin seemed ghostly white in the dim light, nearly the same color as the clean white bandages covering his wounds.

"Dad," Charlie moaned. "Dad."

"I'm right here, Charlie," Jim answered.

"Dad, I'm so sick . . . and it hurts so bad."

"I know, Charlie, I know."

Struggling, Jim swung his legs over the edge of his bed, head swimming. Fighting the nausea and dizziness which threatened to overwhelm him, Jim managed to stand up, then stumble the few feet to a chair alongside Charlie's bed. He took his son's hand.

Charlie's eyes flickered open. He gazed uncomprehendingly at his father. Jim nearly had to turn away, seeing those blue eyes, so much like his own, usually bright and vibrant with life, now dull and lifeless.

"Dad?"

"I'm right here, Charlie."

"Dad, I'm gonna die, ain't I?"

"No, you ain't gonna die, Charlie. Bet a hat on it. You're gonna be just fine in a few days." Jim's voice broke.

"I wouldn't bet my hat on that," Charlie replied. "I'm all tore up inside. I can feel it. My guts . . . feel like a horse stomped on 'em. Havin' trouble breathin', too."

"That's just a bellyache from eatin' too much of my bacon and beans," Jim said. "Once we get home and you get some of your mom's good cookin' down your gullet, you'll be just fine."

"Mom. Tell Mom I love her," Charlie answered. "Mary Jane, too."

"You can tell 'em your own self," Jim replied. "I'm not goin' home without you, Charlie. Your Mom'd kill me for certain."

Charlie's eyes opened wider, and he gasped.
"Charlie?"

"I'm all right, Dad. What about you, though?" he asked, noticing the thick bandage covering Jim's head. "What's that you're wearin'? Sure ain't your hat. You get scalped or somethin'?"

"No," Jim said. "Got hit by a bullet. Takes more'n one bullet to kill a Blawcyzk, so that's how I know you're gonna be okay. It'll just take a little time, that's all."

"Dad."

"Yeah, Charlie?"

"I got hit by two slugs, not one."

"Yeah, I reckon you did at that, Charlie," Jim conceded.

"Dad!" Charlie's sat half-up, eyes searching wildly around the room. He fell back on the mattress with a long sigh, his eyelids slowly closing.

Numbly, Jim dropped Charlie's hand, and started for the door to summon the doctor. Instead, vertigo overcame him, and he fell back across his own bed. He lay there in a stupor, not quite fully conscious.

"Charlie. Doggone it, Charlie," he murmured.

"Jim, don't worry. Julia will be just fine, you'll see," his friend, Ben Beaufort, tried to assure the frantic young Ranger.

"But Doc Landry's not here, and isn't gonna

make it on time," Jim protested. "He needs to be with Julia when the time comes."

Jim was pacing worriedly outside their bedroom, waiting for his wife to give birth to their first child. Julia had had a particularly difficult pregnancy, and now it appeared she would need to have her baby without the help of a physician.

"Jim, Mary's with her, and so are Sandra Lowery and Edith Rankin. My wife's helped plenty of babies into this world. Don't forget your wife has too, for that matter."

"None of those were my baby," Jim answered. "I'm headin' in there to see what's happening."

Ben blocked the door.

"Jim, you can't. The last thing Julia needs right now is you bustin' in there all worried. Why don't we go outside for some air? Mebbe you should let me build you a smoke. It might calm you down."

"No. No cigarette," Jim answered.

"Well, then step outside with me while I have one," Ben urged.

"All right."

They headed outside, where Ben rolled and lit a quirly. He was halfway done with the smoke when a newborn's wail sounded from inside. Jim headed for his wife on the run, Ben right behind him. Ben's wife Mary met him midway through the kitchen.

"Jim, you have a fine, healthy boy," she smiled. "Congratulations."

"See, Jim. I told you things would be fine," Ben said.

"A boy," Jim repeated. "I want to see him."

"In a little while," Mary promised. "Give us a few minutes to tidy up, and for Julia to get a bit of rest."

"All right. Not too long, though."

"It won't be," Mary assured him.

After what seemed like an eternity to the anxious Ranger, the bedroom door opened.

"You can come in now, Jim," Mary said.

Jim entered the room, then stopped at the foot of the bed, staring in wonder. Julia held their new son, wrapped in a blanket.

"Well, Jim?"

"Julia," was all he could manage. He walked alongside the bed, looking down at his wife and child.

"Here's your boy," Julia said. "Charles Edward. That's what he'll be baptized, after my father and yours. He looks just like you."

The newborn had deep blue eyes and a thin frizz of blond hair.

"You mean our boy," Jim answered. "Our boy."

"Jim, I'm sorry. I must look a fright," Julia said.

"You've never looked more beautiful to me," Jim answered.

"Don't try and lie to me," Julia objected.

"I'm not," Jim answered.

"Jim, would you like to hold him?" Julia asked.

"You mean I can?" Jim said.

"Yes, silly," Julia laughed. "Just make sure to support his head."

Julia passed the baby to her husband, who took him gingerly.

"Jim, he won't break," Julia smiled.

"What if I drop him?" Jim worried.

"You won't."

"Can I look at the rest of him?" Jim requested.

"Go ahead," Julia agreed.

Jim opened the blanket, then fingered the baby's toes, resting his tiny hand in Jim's large one.

"He's so little," Jim said. "His fingers and toes, even his fingernails and toenails. And his ears and nose. I could hold him in one hand."

The baby opened his mouth and started to cry.

"He's got your lungs and mouth though, Julia. Nice and big," Jim chuckled.

"Jim . . ." Julia warned.

"I was just kidding," Jim answered.

"Jim, you should probably give him back to Julia now," Sandra suggested. "He's most likely ready to nurse."

"I guess you're right." Jim passed the baby back to Julia.

"I'm a father," he said, took one step back, then fainted dead away.

• • •

Jim became aware of that same female voice again, this time recognizing it as Christine Fletcher. She was singing *"Were You There?"*

> "Were you there when they crucified my
>   Lord?
> "Were you there when they crucified my
>   Lord?
>   "Oh! Sometimes it causes me to
>   tremble, tremble, tremble
> "Were you there when they crucified my
>   Lord?"

"Oh Lord, help Charlie," Jim pleaded, just before losing consciousness again.

"Jim, what do you think you're doing?" Julia screamed, when she returned home from a short visit with Mary Beaufort.

"I'm watchin' the baby, like you asked me to," Jim replied.

"You've got him on your horse!" Julia shouted. Indeed, Jim had their now six month old son perched in front of him on Sam's bare back, holding him while Sam trotted around the corral.

"It's never too soon for a boy to learn to ride," Jim said. *"Besides, he's enjoying it."*

"Jim, get our baby off that animal right now, or you won't be sitting on a horse for a month, I

promise you that. I'll get your rifle and shoot you right in your dupa," Julia threatened.

"All right." Jim reluctantly complied, bringing Sam to a halt and jumping from his back. He allowed the usually ornery paint to sniff and nuzzle Charlie. When Sam licked the baby's face, Charlie smiled.

"Jim!" Julia shouted, horrified. *"How could you let that filthy horse lick Charlie's face?"*

"Sam's not filthy," Jim objected. *"Besides, Charlie liked it. He likes Sam, too. And Sam likes him."*

"Do you like your dupa?" Julia asked.

"I'm rather fond of it, yeah," Jim answered.

"Then if you want to keep it, get Charlie out of that corral right now." Julia warned.

"I guess you're givin' me no choice," Jim replied, adding to Charlie, under his breath. *"Sorry I ever taught your Mom the Polish word for 'backside.' Don't worry, little pard, you'll be ridin' Sam again in a day or two at the most. Bet a hat on it."*

Christine's voice pierced the fog of Jim's mind once again.

> "Were you there when they nailed Him to
>   the tree?
> "Were you there when they nailed Him to
>   the tree?

"Oh! Sometimes it causes me to
tremble, tremble, tremble
"Were you there when they nailed Him to
the tree?"

"Don't shoot me, Charlie," Jim pleaded.

Jim was working on a rotted section of barn. He'd removed his shirt, allowing the sun to warm his bare back. Charlie was tagging along, as always when Jim was home, and copying Jim's every move, right down to pulling off his own shirt and hanging it from a nail next to his father's. He picked up a piece of wood Jim had discarded and pointed it at his dad.

"Bang! I shooted you, Dad!" Charlie giggled.

"You what, Charlie?"

"I shooted you."

"I don't think you shooted me, Charlie," Jim disagreed, chuckling. "I didn't feel a thing. I guess you missed me."

"I didn't miss. I shooted you, Dad!" Charlie insisted.

"Is that so? Well, just exactly where did you shooted me?" Jim asked.

"I shooted you right in your bellybutton," Charlie answered. "And I'm gonna do it again. Bang!"

"Ow! Ya got me that time," Jim yelped. "Like ya said, right in my bellybutton." He

grabbed his middle, spun, and fell onto his back.

"Yay! I shooted you, Dad!" Charlie laughed. He ran to his father and started bouncing up and down on his belly.

"Oof!" Jim grunted. "Charlie, your bullet might not've killed me, but you sure will. You're gettin' awful heavy, pardner."

"That means I'm gonna grow up big to be a Texas Ranger just like you, right, Dad?"

"Right, Charlie," Jim agreed, grunting when Charlie bounced on his middle yet again. "Unless you squish out all my guts first." He grabbed his son and lifted him in the air. "Can't hardly pick you up anymore."

A dead Texas Ranger, and it's my fault for lettin' him join up, flashed through Jim's mind.

> "Were you there when they laid Him in
>   the tomb?
> "Were you there when they laid Him in
>   the tomb?
>   "Oh! Sometimes it causes me to
>   tremble, tremble, tremble
> "Were you there when they laid him in
>   the tomb?"

"Ted! What will Ted do without Charlie?" Jim moaned. "Splash, too."

• • •

"Charlie, c'mon outside. I've got something to show you," Jim called to his son. "Bring your mom out, too."

"All right, Dad. Be right there."

A moment later the door burst open, and Charlie rushed across the porch. He stopped in his tracks, seeing his father standing there, holding a lead rope, at the end of which was a yearling tobiano paint gelding. The horse had a buckskin and white coat which glowed resplendently in the afternoon sunshine.

"Dad! Is that my horse?" Charlie screamed.

"It sure is. I've been promisin' you a horse of your own, ain't I? This is him."

"My own horse!" Charlie shouted with joy, rushing up to the young gelding. The yearling dropped his nose to nuzzle the boy's face.

"Mom! My own horse!" Charlie called to Julia, who was standing in the doorway.

"I can see that, Charlie," Julia smiled. She'd long since conceded this argument to Jim, who had worn down every objection she had as to why Charlie didn't need his own horse.

"You have to promise to take good care of him," Jim warned Charlie.

"I will, Dad," Charlie answered. "I'll brush him, and feed him, and give him carrots, and I'll help clean his stall, and we'll ride everywhere."

"No ridin' quite yet, little pard. He's a bit

young. You and he'll learn a lot together, until he's big enough to be ridden."

"What's his name, Dad?" Charlie asked.

"He's your horse. You name him," Jim answered.

"His name's gonna be Ted," Charlie stated. "Ted."

Jim roused briefly.

"Never figured Charlie'd die before his old horse," he whispered.

Jim's thoughts raced with memories for hours. There was the first time he took Charlie fishing, the day when he taught Charlie to swim. The riding and roping lessons, the lessons in how to use a gun. There was the day Charlie started school, his first day as an altar boy. The day Jim brought home Charlie's first pup. These and more flooded Jim's mind.

There were the unpleasant memories, too. The day Charlie broke his arm by falling out of a cottonwood. The serious illness when Charlie was ten, a severe case of grippe and high fever which had nearly taken his life. The time Jim's ranch had been raided, and Charlie shot his first man before being shot himself. And of course Jim hadn't seen his son sworn in as a Texas Ranger, since Jim had been gravely wounded at the time, by a traitorous Ranger colleague he'd counted as a friend.

"Dear Lord," Jim prayed, "please don't take my

son. Please don't take Charlie. Take me if You need to take one of us, instead of my son. My life's better'n halfway over, but Charlie's is just startin' out. He's got a lot of years ahead, long as You don't take him. I'm beggin' You, Lord, please, let Charlie pull through.

"Dear Blessed Virgin Mary, our Mother," Jim continued, "you suffered the agony and sorrow of the loss of your own Son, Jesus. You understand how devastated Julia would be if Charlie dies. Please intercede for me, and ask your Son not to take our son. I ask this in the name of the Father, Son, and Holy Ghost. Amen."

"Dad," Charlie called, weakly. "Dad, where are you?"

"I'm right here, Charlie. I'm comin'."

Jim forced himself to stand, and began to cross the room to Charlie. Blinding pain shot through his head. He clamped both hands to his temples, screamed, and collapsed to the floor.

CHAPTER TWENTY-SIX

Doctor Towne stuck his head into Jim and Charlie's room.

"How are my patients today?" he queried.

"Not too bad, Doc," Jim answered, looking up from the stack of hotcakes with bacon he was working on. "Still got a headache, and my scalp itches somethin' fierce, but all things considered, I'd say I'm feelin' fine."

"Same here," Charlie said, "except you're starvin' me half to death, Doc, bet a hat on it." He looked with distaste at his half-finished bowl of thin oatmeal, and the soggy remains of a soft-boiled egg. "I need real food like my dad's getting, meat and potatoes, not this stuff."

The physician went over to Charlie's bed.

"Chip, as I told you, a belly wound's nothing to fool with, not that the bullet you took in your chest wasn't also serious. However, you're one of the very few men I've known to survive being shot in the abdomen, so we need to take things easy until we're certain you're completely healed inside. A few more days of a light diet absolutely will not kill you."

"That's easy for you to say, Doc," Charlie responded.

"Jim, can't you get your boy to listen to reason?" Towne requested.

"Charlie, listen to Doctor Towne. He knows what's best," Jim urged.

"Oh, like you've always done whatever your doctors told you, Dad," Charlie retorted.

"He's got me there, Doc," Jim ruefully admitted. "Sorry."

"It doesn't matter. Chip, only light, bland food until I say otherwise," Towne ordered. "Now, let me check you over."

Towne lifted Charlie's wrist to check his pulse rate, then placed his stethoscope to the young Ranger's chest.

"Ow! Doc, that thing's freezin' cold," Charlie objected.

"Shush," Towne ordered. "I need to listen to your heart."

"Well?" Charlie said, when Towne removed the instrument a few minutes later.

"So far, so good," Towne said. "There's no sign of fever, and your heart seems strong. Now I've got to check on your father. After that, I'll change both your bandages."

The doctor repeated his actions with Jim. When he placed the stethoscope against the lieutenant's chest, Jim looked at Charlie and grinned.

"This thing's not a bit cold now. Thanks for warmin' it up for me, son."

"Don't mention it, Dad," Charlie sarcastically replied.

Once Towne finished his examination of Jim, he shook his head.

"Lieutenant, I don't understand it, but you're also progressing quite well," he said.

"Doc, I'm Polish. We're known for being thick, especially our skulls," Jim answered.

"Hey, can anyone get in on the fun, or is this a private affair?" Sam Tatum asked from outside the room.

"Heck no, c'mon in, Sam," Jim answered.

"All right. Brought along some company, too." With Tatum was the preacher, Devon Jones.

"Howdy, Sam, Preacher," Jim said.

"Yeah, same here," Charlie added. "Glad to see you."

"We're glad to see you, also, especially looking so well, Chip," Jones answered. "Doctor, how are our friends doing?"

"Remarkably well," Towne replied. "I truly am confounded by their recovery. A week ago, the lieutenant had apparently suffered some kind of seizure, for as you know, I found him convulsing on the floor. And, Chip was at death's door, there is no question about that. Despite everything I had done, I was convinced both of these men were dying."

"Takes more'n a couple of bullets to kill a Blawcyzk," Jim said.

411

"Jim, I guess the doctor hasn't told you yet, but while both you and Chip were near death, Devon here came in, prayed over you, and laid hands on the two of you," Sam said. "As Doctor Towne says, there was nothing more medical science could do. Your lives were in the hands of the Lord."

"Which is the best place they could be," Jones added.

"Boy howdy, don't I know that," Jim answered. "Thanks, Preacher. I'd been prayin' too, for Charlie. Didn't matter so much about me."

"Jim, every life is precious," Jones replied. "I'm certainly glad that God decided it wasn't time to take yours quite yet."

"Meaning no disrespect, Preacher, but I'd rather think it was the treatment Sam and I gave them, plus a powerful will to live, and bodies in fine physical condition, which gave these two men the necessary resources to survive," Towne said. "In fact, I'm positive of that."

"No sense in arguing about who did what," Jim said. "I'm certain, without God's help, neither Charlie nor I would have pulled through. That said, I'm just as certain that, without the skills He gave you and Sam, plus your determination to use every bit of your knowledge to save me and my son, we would have died, bet a hat on it. I'm grateful to God, and to all of you."

"You mean you don't believe in miracles, Jim?" Jones asked.

"Of course I believe in them," Jim answered. "What I'm saying is that Doctor Towne, and Sam, were given the skills to cause my recovery, and Charlie's. I also believe the power of your prayers was a key to our pulling through. I'm not sure if that qualifies as a miracle, but of one thing I am certain. Without God's help, neither Charlie or I would be here today."

"Amen, Dad," Charlie said. "Now, if y'all are through jawin', can I get some real food?"

"Sure, Chip," Towne agreed, laughing. "All you need to do is ask God for a miracle. Until then, oatmeal, dry toast, soft-boiled eggs, and weak tea."

"Lord, if it's not too late to change Your mind, please, take me now," Charlie groaned.

"Enough of this," Towne ordered. "Miracle or medicine, if these men don't get enough rest, we could still lose them."

"Hey, hold on a minute, Doc. You told me I could meet with my men, and find out for certain what happened," Jim objected. "It's been three days now, and I still haven't been allowed to talk with anyone but you and Sam, and now Devon."

"That's because I know you won't rest once your men arrive, but will insist on rehashing everything that happened that day, and probably want to write a full report," Towne replied. "I want you to rest one more night. Tomorrow, I promise, you can have that meeting."

"All right, but if you renege, I'll walk outta here. Bet a hat on it," Jim answered.

"Only if you can find that hat . . . and the rest of your clothes, Jim," Sam replied. "I've got them well hidden, so unless you're willing to walk down the street naked as a jay bird, I'd recommend you stay right where you are."

"It is a mite chilly out there," Devon noted. "Not at all conducive to strolling around in the clothes God gave you."

"All right, all right. You've convinced me," Jim conceded.

"Good," Towne said. "Sam, would you mind helping with changing their bandages?"

"Not at all," Tatum agreed.

"Good."

"I'll lend a hand also," Jones offered.

"Thank you, Preacher. Once we're done, Jim and Chip, you're both to get more sleep. Understood?"

"Understood," Jim sighed.

"Boy howdy, never thought I'd see you two alive again," Smoky McCue boomed, as, late the next morning, he and the rest of the Rangers, along with Adrian Chatman, piled into Jim and Charlie's room.

"That's for certain," Jim Huggins agreed.

"Chip, I'd have sworn you weren't breathin' when I rolled you over and saw those bullet holes in you."

"Same goes for you, Jim," Smoky added, taking a drag on his ever-present quirly. "In fact, I know for sure you must've stopped for a minute, 'cause there wasn't any air comin' from your mouth or nose, pard. Plus, with all the blood it looked like the top of your head had been blown clean off. I figured you were dead for sure. Don't ever scare me like that again."

"I'll try not to," Jim grinned.

"Chip, how are you doin'?" Ty asked his friend.

"I'm dyin' of hunger," Charlie answered. "The doc plumb refuses to feed me. Besides, what happened to you?"

Ty was using a cane to support his weight, taking pressure off his wounded leg.

"Took a bullet through my leg. It's nothin' much," he answered, shrugging.

"What about you, Adrian?" Jim asked. The bulk of a bandage around his left shoulder was apparent under Adrian's shirt, while his left arm was bound tightly with a sling.

"I was hit too," Adrian answered. "Hurts a lot, but I'll be fine."

"Bill, Dan, at least it looks like you two avoided takin' any slugs," Jim noted.

"With all the lead flyin' out there, we were lucky," Bill said.

"Boy howdy, that's the gospel truth," Dan agreed.

"That's good," Jim said. "Now, enough palaverin'. I want to know exactly what happened that day. All I recall is the shootin' startin', then gettin' plugged. And I vaguely recollect drillin' the *hombre* who got Charlie."

"Jim, you're second in command. You tell the story," Smoky said.

"All right," Huggins agreed. "I'll keep it short and sweet as possible."

"Wait. Before you start, how's my horses?" Jim said.

"And mine," Charlie added.

"They're all fine," Smoky assured them. "Sam's ornery as ever, of course, but they're all fine."

"Good. Jim, go ahead."

"Well, you know there was quite a bit of shootin'," Huggins began. "Rouse and his men got the worst of it, by far. He and all his boys are dead, except one, Luke."

"Luke? He's the only one who didn't seem to want this fight," Jim said.

"That's right. He didn't take part in it," Huggins confirmed. "Since he's the last surviving Rouse, he's now the sole owner of the Bar R. He's promised not to try'n finish what his father started."

"In fact, we're negotiating to buy some beef

416

from Luke, and also some breeding stock for the ranch I'm starting," Adrian added.

"Looks like one good thing came out of this, anyway," Jim said. "So, it appears most of the trouble around here might be finished. How many men did we lose?"

"Three," Huggins answered. "Ezekiel Crown, Cotton Smith, and Chris Copperthwaite. Could've been a lot worse."

"I reckon." Jim sighed. Even three good men were three too many.

"Once Lucas went down, the rest of his men gave up, or there would have been a lot more bloodshed," Huggins said.

"Sure would've been," Dan agreed.

"How about Matt Rouse? Did Luke admit he killed Johnny?" Jim asked. "If not, we've still got a Ranger killer on the loose."

"No, Matt didn't kill Johnny," Huggins answered. "You'll never guess who did."

"Don't keep me waitin'. Who was it?"

"Solomon Burleson."

"Solomon Burleson," Jim echoed, not quite recalling the name. "Who the devil is that?"

"Solomon Burleson, my land agent and supposed friend," Adrian answered. "You never did meet him."

"Your land agent?" Jim said, clearly puzzled. "Why would your land agent want to kill a Texas Ranger?"

"Just keep shut and I'll explain," Huggins ordered. "Burleson was behind a lot of the trouble right from the start. You see, Burleson wanted the land Adrian purchased for himself. He knew Lucas Rouse also had his eye on that land, and was aware Rouse really hated Negroes. That's why he made sure Adrian settled right here. Then, he made certain to stir up the pot, telling Rouse Adrian had plans to move thousands of Negroes down here, enough to overrun the entire county. He figured once we Rangers pulled out, Rouse would wipe out Adrian and his people, which would force the governor to either arrest Rouse or risk the federal government sending troops in again. Once that happened, Burleson figured he'd pick up both the Bar R and Adrian's land for next to nothing. He worked on the quiet, keeping so much out of sight hardly anyone was aware he was even in the area."

"But why would Burleson kill Johnny?" Jim asked.

"Because Pete Rouse played right into Burleson's hands," Huggins explained. "He was in the Lady Victoria that night, and saw everything that happened. When Johnny killed that hot-headed kid, then Matt threatened to kill Johnny, in front of plenty of witnesses, Burleson saw his opportunity. He's the one who set Johnny up, and the one who shot him. Burleson knew Matt Rouse would get the blame for Johnny's murder, which would poison the atmosphere even more. He's also the one who ambushed you on the way back from the Bar R, and killed Matt. He was well aware a lot of folks would believe you gunned down Matt in cold blood in revenge for Johnny's murder. He also was aware Matt's death would really get Lucas riled up against the Rangers."

"How'd Burleson know when I rode out to the Rouse spread?" Jim asked.

"Tom Morton, one of the sheriff's deputies, who was working with Burleson. He watched your every move, and let Burleson know what you were up to. Morton's part Apache, so he's real good at stayin' out of sight. Of course, now he's in jail," Huggins explained.

"How'd you figure all this out?" Jim asked.

"Burleson confessed to everything," Huggins answered. "He was with Rouse and his men when they raided Freedom. Once he saw Rouse was dead, he figured then his only chance to see his plans come to fruition was to kill Adrian. Burleson's the one who shot him. Luckily for Adrian, Burleson's shootin' was nowhere near as good as his schemin'. He only winged Adrian, rather'n gettin' him plumb center in the back."

"Where's Burleson now?" Jim questioned.

"He's dead," Huggins replied. "Bill plugged him."

"Yeah, Chip, Burleson couldn't handle bein'

gut-shot like you can," Smoky interrupted, punching Charlie lightly on his shoulder. "Some men just can't stomach takin' a bullet in their belly."

"Smoke," Huggins groaned.

"What? That's the kind of bad joke the lieutenant would make," Smoky protested.

"That joke was pretty below the belt, even by my standards, Smoky," Jim laughed.

"I think I'm gonna call the doc. That slug you took definitely addled your brain, Jim," Huggins said. "Now, if you'll let me finish, yes, Bill did put his bullet through Burleson's guts. Once again we were lucky. Bill was usin' a six-gun he'd taken off one of Rouse's men, instead of his old Sharps. If he'd been usin' that buffalo gun, he'd have blown Burleson clean in two. Instead, he lived long enough to admit everything. Reckon he wanted to come clean before he met his Maker. We also have Dinah's testimony it was Burleson, not Matt Rouse, who paid her to have Johnny come to her room. She finally admitted that."

"Hard to believe all this," Jim said. "At least I reckon things will be peaceful around here now."

"Seems so," Huggins answered. "Which brings us to this. You and Chip still have a long recuperation ahead of you, a few more weeks at least. With all the troubles all over the state, Captain Storm has decided the rest of us can't remain here any longer. We've been ordered back to Austin, and will be ridin' out soon as we leave you."

"Except me," Bill Dundee added. "I'm gonna settle right here in Freedom, and live out the rest of my days in peace. My assignment's done, so there's no need for me to head back to Austin. I like these folks, and besides, there's several ladies here I'd like to get to know better."

"That sounds like a fine idea," Jim agreed.

"As peaceful as the life of a town marshal can be, that is," Adrian corrected. "Bill neglected to mention we offered him the job, and he accepted."

"You couldn't have chosen a better man, Adrian," Jim said. "Bill, congratulations."

Doctor Towne came into the room.

"Men, I hate to break this up, but I've already allowed you far more time than I should have. Remember, they're not supposed to have any visitors at all. The only reason I made an exception for you Rangers is because you're leaving town. It's time for Jim and Chip to get some sleep."

"Just a few minutes while we make our good-byes, Doc," Smoky said.

"All right. Just a few minutes."

"Chip, you take care of yourself," Ty ordered his friend. "I'll tell Mary Jane you're doin' fine. In fact, I'll give her a hug and kiss for you . . . mebbe several."

"You do and you'll be the next Ranger lyin'

in a bed with a bullet or two in his guts . . . or mebbe lyin' in a coffin," Charlie warned, with a grin. "You just let me handle that chore, once I get home."

"All right," Ty agreed.

Hands were shaken all around, and more than a few eyes were moist as the other Rangers bade farewell to Jim and Charlie. Smoky McCue, in particular, was reluctant to leave Jim, his long-time riding partner, behind.

"Jim, I know we kid a lot about gettin' our-selves shot up," he said, "and we've both had some close calls before, but this was too darn close, pardner. Don't ever do this to me again."

"To you?" Jim said. "I'm the one who got shot."

"Yeah, but if you'd died, I'm the one who would have had to tell Julia . . . and somehow get your horse Sam back to your place," Smoky retorted. "That'd be far worse than takin' a slug. You and Chip just get better quick, hear?"

"We'll do our best . . . Uncle Smoky," Charlie said, reverting to the name he'd called Smoky for most of his life, until he'd joined the Rangers.

"I'll hold you to that," Smoky answered, a tear rolling down his right cheek. "*Adios*, kid."

Once the other Rangers had left, loneliness settled on the now-silent room like a dead weight.

"Doc, how much longer are you gonna keep us here?" Jim demanded, ten days later. "We're both goin' plumb loco stuck in this room. It's high time we got back to work."

"At least another two weeks, probably more," Towne answered. "You still have some dizziness and nausea, while Chip still needs to rebuild his strength. In addition, I have to be certain his internal wounds are fully healed before allowing him to make that long ride to Austin."

Towne checked both men, changing the bandages each still wore.

"Chip, I don't have to replace the dressing on your chest," he said. "That wound has closed quite nicely. Letting air reach the scab will be the best thing for it right now."

"See, Doc, like my dad says, we are gettin' better," Charlie answered.

"I do have to admit, you're both progressing quite well, well enough, in fact, that I'll be returning to San Angelo later today. Sam will be taking over your care from here on, although I will be returning every three days just to make certain there aren't any setbacks. And no," he continued, before either Jim or Charlie could object, "Sam won't be allowing you to leave without my say so. Trust me, a few extra days to be positive there are no unexpected complications will be worth it."

"If you say so, Doc," Jim conceded. "Reckon we've got no choice."

"That's right, you don't," Towne answered.

"Just keep doing what I say, get as much rest as possible, and tell Sam immediately if there are any unforeseen changes, and you'll be back on the trail before you know it. I'll see you on Friday."

"See you then, Doc."

Once the physician had left, Charlie glanced at the crusted scab, surrounded by puckered skin, on his chest, and the fresh bandage taped to his side. He then looked over at his father, studying the bullet and knife scars Jim's torso bore.

"Dad, looks like I'm startin' a nice scar collection just like yours," he chuckled.

"You just forget that idea right now, Charlie," Jim ordered. "Last thing you want is to get shot up as much as I've been. Things are changin', and pretty soon, I'd bet my hat, us Rangers won't be involved in anywhere near as many gunfights as we have in the past. You'll be usin' your brains a lot more'n your fists and guns . . . at least I sure hope so."

"I dunno, Dad," Charlie disagreed. "There's still an awful lot of unsettled territory in Texas, with plenty of renegades usin' it to try and outrun the law. I have a feelin' it'll be quite some time, if ever, before the Rangers will be able to hang up our guns. In fact, I'd bet my hat on it."

"Be that as it may, I sure hope you've learned your lesson from this. What'd I tell you about steppin' in front of bullets?" Jim replied, grinning.

"Not to do it, even though you've done that

very thing quite a few times," Charlie laughed. "Sometimes the bullets find you, though. Besides, when I saw you go down, I couldn't stop myself. I had to try and help you."

"And nearly got yourself killed," Jim said. "I'm not worth that, Charlie."

"Oh, yes, you are, Dad," Charlie replied. "Don't ever say you aren't."

Sam Tatum knocked on the door.

"If I could interrupt this discussion, you've got some company, if you're up to it."

"Sure am," Jim answered. "Send him in."

"Not him . . . her." Kathy Esposito entered the room, carrying a covered wicker basket. She set that on the bedside table, then gave Jim a kiss on the cheek.

"Kathy!" he exclaimed. "What are you doin' here? Not that I'm not glad to see you."

"I brought you something," Kathy replied. "Plus, it's high time I got to meet your boy. I would have been here a few days ago, but Sam said you weren't allowed any company until yesterday."

Charlie was staring in bemusement at Kathy and his father.

"Charlie, this is Kathy Esposito, an old friend," Jim explained. "Kathy, my son Charlie, or Chip as his friends call him."

"I'm right pleased to meet you, Miz Esposito," Charlie said.

"Not Miz Esposito. It's Kathy," she replied. "Jim," she continued, "I'm certainly glad to see you're both doing better. I was devastated when I heard what had happened, and that neither of you were expected to survive."

"Thanks, Kathy," Jim answered. "But I have a feeling we'll be feeling even better once we see the contents of that basket."

"Of course," Kathy agreed. She took the cloth off the basket, removed two plates, then a huge platter of doughnuts and cookies.

"Will these do?"

"Will they ever!" Jim exclaimed. "Charlie, let's dig in."

Kathy filled the plates, and passed one to each man. Charlie's face lit up at the prospect of fresh doughnuts. He groaned in ecstasy when he took his first bite.

"Kathy, this is wonderful," he noted. "Dad, I have to say, this doughnut is far better than the ones Mom makes."

"Don't ever tell your Mom that, if you know what's good for you, kid," Jim warned. "Unless you don't ever want one of her cakes again. You know how proud she is of her baking."

"And rightfully so," Charlie agreed. "But this doughnut . . . it's heaven."

"Yeah," Jim agreed, shoving another in his own mouth.

Jim and Charlie emptied the contents of the

basket, then visited for a while with Kathy, until Sam ordered her out.

"I'll be back tomorrow with an apple pie," she promised.

"That sounds good," Jim replied.

"It sure does," Charlie agreed. "Kathy, if you weren't already married, I'd take you courtin' just for your cookies."

"Don't let my being married stop you," Kathy smiled, running a fingertip down the youngster's chest and belly, then winking at him. Charlie flushed beet red.

"Good-bye, boys," Kathy purred.

Over Doctor Towne's and Sam Tatum's objections, Jim and Charlie left Freedom ten days later. The entire town turned out to see them off. Nathan and Isaiah McGraw insisted on one last ride on Sam before seeing him leave. True to his nature, Jim's foul-tempered paint allowed the twins he'd taken a liking to have a final trot up and down the street, but lunged at anyone else who came near him.

"Some day we're gonna be Texas Rangers just like you and Ranger Chip, Ranger Jim," Nathan said.

"So am I," Daisy Cutler declared, from where she was perched atop Ted, Charlie's old paint.

"Girls can't be Texas Rangers," Isaiah protested. "That's a job for a man, not a girl."

"You just wait and see," Daisy insisted.

"Daisy could be right," Frances Watley noted. "After all, whoever could have imagined that a group of Negroes would ever be allowed to establish their own community in Texas, yet here we are. It just goes to show you anything's possible, God willing."

"Jim, we know you and Chip want to get movin'," Adrian said. "However, before you do, we want to give you tokens of our gratitude. Before you object, we won't take no for an answer. The rest of your men received the same gifts when they left. Devon, if you would."

"Certainly," Preacher Jones said. "Jim and Chip, we can never possibly repay you for all you've done for us. However, we hope you will always remember us when you use these coats. Miriam Hansen and her daughter Chloe made them. Miriam and Chloe."

"Rangers, these are for you," Miriam said. The seamstress handed Jim a thick, sheepskin coat. Chloe gave one to Charlie.

"Miriam, Chloe, all of you, these are wonderful," Jim said. "Thank you. We'll wear them proudly."

"We sure will," Charlie agreed. "Come next January, when it gets down to ten degrees on the plains, these coats will sure come in handy. Thanks."

"Guess we've said all there is to say, except

whenever you're over this way, you be sure and stop by. You'll always be welcome in Freedom," Adrian concluded.

"We'll do that," Jim promised. "Now, we'd better get goin'. I want to cover as much ground as possible before sundown."

He pulled himself onto Sizzle's back, swaying slightly as he did so. On Splash, Charlie was hunched over in his saddle, wincing from twinges of pain still shooting through his gut.

"Jim, are you two sure you're going to be able to make the ride all the way to Austin without any problems?" Sam asked. "I still say you need to take a few more days rest. So did Doctor Towne."

"Sam, we haven't been home for over three months, which is a good stretch even for a Ranger. That means I haven't seen my wife for way too long."

"Nor tasted Mom's cookin', especially her fried chicken," Charlie added.

"So, what do you think?" Jim asked. "Will we get home all right? You can . . ."

"Don't say it," Adrian interrupted. "Everyone." "YOU CAN BET A HAT ON IT!"

EPILOGUE

The town of Freedom thrived and prospered until the Great Depression and Dust Bowl of the 1930s. With crops failing due to extreme drought, and topsoil blowing away in blinding dust storms almost daily, gradually the residents of Freedom, like those of so many other towns of the southern Plains, moved away, to seek better lives in California or the big cities of the North, Midwest, and East.

Today the only indications of Freedom's site, between present-day U.S. 87 and the North Concho River, about eighteen miles northwest of San Angelo, are a Texas Historical Commission marker, and a few scattered, weathered gravestones. One of those stones is engraved with a silver star on silver circle badge, and the inscription "Bill Dundee, Special Scout, Texas Rangers. Birth Date Unknown, Died November 18, 1901." Its erection was arranged and paid for by Jim Blawcyzk, Smoky McCue, and Jim Huggins.

In Texas presently, there is another settlement called Freedom, which has a population of approximately sixty. It is located in rural Rains County, about three hundred and fifty miles east of the Freedom in this story.

Author James J. Griffin

James J. Griffin is the author of several Texas Ranger novels, notably the Jim Blawcyzk and Cody Havlicek series. Jim is a lifelong horse man, western enthusiast, and unofficial historian of the Texas Rangers. He has contributed a large and varied collection of Texas Ranger artifacts to the **Texas Ranger Hall of Fame and Museum** in Waco, and is a member of **Western Writers of America** and **Western Fictioneers.**

When not traveling out West, Jim divides his time between Branford, Connecticut and Keene, New Hampshire.

Books are produced in the United States using U.S.-based materials

Books are printed using a revolutionary new process called THINKtech™ that lowers energy usage by 70% and increases overall quality

Books are durable and flexible because of Smyth-sewing

Paper is sourced using environmentally responsible foresting methods and the paper is acid-free

Center Point Large Print
600 Brooks Road / PO Box 1
Thorndike, ME 04986-0001 USA

(207) 568-3717

US & Canada:
1 800 929-9108
www.centerpointlargeprint.com